CAST ADRIFT

(CAST ADRIFT—BOOK I)

CHRISTOPHER G. NUTTALL

The characters and events portrayed in this book are fictitious. Any similarity to real persons, living or dead, is coincidental and not intended by the author.

Text copyright © 2021 Christopher G. Nuttall

All rights reserved.

Printed in the United States of America.

ISBN: 9798729690336
Independently published

No part of this book may be reproduced, or stored in a retrieval system, or transmitted in any form or by any means, electronic, mechanical, photocopying, recording, or other-wise, without express written permission of the publisher.

Cover By Tan Ho Sim
https://www.artstation.com/alientan

Book One: Cast Adrift

http://www.chrishanger.net
http://chrishanger.wordpress.com/
http://www.facebook.com/ChristopherGNuttall

All Comments Welcome!

CONTENTS

PROLOGUE I vii
PROLOGUE II xi

Chapter One 1
Chapter Two 10
Chapter Three 19
Chapter Four 29
Chapter Five 38
Chapter Six 47
Chapter Seven 56
Chapter Eight 65
Chapter Nine 74
Chapter Ten 83
Chapter Eleven 92
Chapter Twelve 101
Chapter Thirteen 110
Chapter Fourteen 119
Chapter Fifteen 129
Chapter Sixteen 138
Chapter Seventeen 147
Chapter Eighteen 156
Chapter Nineteen 165
Chapter Twenty 175
Chapter Twenty-One 184
Chapter Twenty-Two 194
Chapter Twenty-Three 203
Chapter Twenty-Four 212
Chapter Twenty-Five 221

Chapter Twenty-Six 230
Chapter Twenty-Seven 239
Chapter Twenty-Eight 248
Chapter Twenty-Nine 257
Chapter Thirty 266
Chapter Thirty-One 275
Chapter Thirty-Two 285
Chapter Thirty-Three 294
Chapter Thirty-Four 303
Chapter Thirty-Five 313
Chapter Thirty-Six 323
Chapter Thirty-Seven 332
Chapter Thirty-Eight 342
Chapter Thirty-Nine 352
Chapter Forty 362

EPILOGUE 369
AFTERWORD 371
HOW TO FOLLOW 377
APPENDIX: THE ALPHANS 379
APPENDIX: A BRIEF OUTLINE OF ALPHAN EARTH 383

PROLOGUE I

WASHINGTON WAS BURNING.

The President of the United States gritted his teeth in helpless humiliation as Marine One skirted the edge of the disaster zone, heading remorselessly towards what remained of Joint Base Andrews. Giant pillars of eerie yellowish smoke rose from the ruined city, casting a sinister light over the countryside. The haze was so thick he couldn't see the heart of the city, although he knew it was nothing more than a blackened ruin. The White House was gone. The Pentagon was gone. Congress and the Senate and everything else within five miles of the White House…all gone.

His stomach churned. A day ago, he'd been the most powerful man in the world. His country had been the most *powerful* country in the world. He'd looked to a future of boundless optimism, a chance to make his legacy as one of the great presidents of his century…he'd even regretted, deep inside, that he wouldn't face a crisis that would ensure his name was forever praised or damned. The world had seemed safe and predictable…

…Until the aliens arrived.

The President still couldn't believe it. He'd been lucky—or unlucky— enough to be out of the city when the aliens had announced their presence, when they'd systematically wiped out the satellite network, dropped kinetic projectiles on most of the navy and, just to make it clear the planet had new masters, nuked Washington, DC. International communications had been shattered, practically effortlessly, but intelligence reports suggested the aliens had *also* nuked London, Paris, Berlin, Moscow, Beijing and five or six other cities. Not *knowing* burned at him as much as anything else. He'd grown far too used to having information permanently at his fingertips to make it *easy* to handle the fog of war.

And the nukes are gone, he thought. It was brutally clear that the US nuclear deterrent was no more. The ground-based missiles had been hammered from orbit, the nuclear-capable aircraft had been wiped out and the submarines were out of contact, presumed sunk. What few missiles they'd been able to fire at the orbiting spacecraft had been swatted down so casually that it was clear the aliens were used to much *faster* missiles. *There's no way we can hit back.*

Marine One shuddered, again, as it started to descend. The aliens hadn't landed everywhere, if the reports were to be believed, but they'd dropped troops around Andrews JBA and set up defences. The hastily-organised counterattack, drawing on a combination of soldiers, marines and national guardsmen, had been effortlessly smashed. The President wanted to believe that armed civilians and the remnants of the military would be able to wear the aliens down, but the surviving joint chiefs had made it brutally clear that further resistance would be utterly futile. The aliens controlled the high ground. They could bombard humanity into submission, while remaining outside the range of humanity's remaining weapons. They'd shown a frightening—utterly terrifying—lack of concern for human casualties. Millions of people had already died, all over the globe. They could simply keep dropping nukes until the human race surrendered.

The President stared, feeling too numb to care as he saw the alien shapes orbiting over the airfield. Alien fighters...he'd seen the reports. The USAF had sent F-22s and F-35s against the alien craft, only to watch the jets casually blasted out of the sky. There had been no survivors. His eyes narrowed as he saw armoured shapes—armoured combat suits and small hovertanks—moving around the edge of the base. The nearby civilian housing had been turned into rubble. He thought he saw refugees heading south, trying to reach a safety that no longer existed. The country was steadily sinking into chaos. It had only been a day—a *day*, his mind screamed—and America was already damaged beyond repair. He shuddered to think how long it would take to restore some semblance of normality...

His skin crawled as he saw the figures gathered by the runway. No, things would never be *normal* again. It wasn't just a crisis, not any longer. It was the new reality. The human race had believed, truly believed, that it was alone in the universe. The President had read the reports dismissing the very *concept* of alien life, insisting that even if aliens existed they'd never be able to reach Earth. There had been no truth, he'd been told, in any of the UFO reports. Grey-skinned aliens did not abduct humans for anal probing. The witnesses were hoaxers, or drunk, or simply misunderstood what they saw. Aliens simply did not exist.

And yet, they did. The figures weren't human. They were...just *wrong*.

The helicopter touched down with a bump. The President watched the crew spin down the rotors before they opened the hatch. He wanted to draw a gun and open fire, he wanted to carry a nuke into the very heart of alien power...he knew, all too well, that it was impossible. The aliens would shoot him down in seconds and go on to make their demands to his successor. He wasn't even sure who that *was*. The Vice President and the Speaker of the House of Representatives had both died in Washington. There had been no reason to think the United States *needed* a designated survivor. The Secret Service was working frantically to discover who was *alive*, let alone where they stood in the line of succession. Too many government officials had been in Washington when the bomb fell. They were missing, presumed dead. The President had a nasty suspicion the aliens had planned it that way.

He stood, feeling his legs shake. He'd made innumerable diplomatic visits, during the course of a long career, but this was different. This was *surrender*. The President's heart wanted to fight to the last; the President's head knew a prolonged conflict would end in the destruction of the human race. He felt a wave of heat brush across his face as he clambered out of the helicopter. The aliens watched him, silently. He stared at them. All but one were concealed behind powered armour.

The unarmoured alien was...*alien*. The President shivered. The alien was slightly taller than he was, with reddish-orange skin, bulbous eyes and a mouth that was curved in something that looked like a faint sneer. He—the President assumed the alien was a *he*—had no hair, no ears. He wore a blank tunic that seemed completely unmarked. He...

"Mr. President," the alien said. His English was oddly accented. "Have you accepted our terms?"

At least they're not making me wait, the President thought, savagely. *Damn them.*

"Yes," he said. The shame of surrender washed down on him as the words hung in the air. "We do."

"Then we bid you welcome to the galactic community," the alien said. "Come. We have much work to do."

PROLOGUE II

NO HUMAN HAD EVER SET FOOT within the council chambers. No human ever would. They were reserved for the Alphans and the Alphans alone, for the very highest of their species. Even the *servants* were Alphans, a sign of wealth and power on a scale most sentient beings would have found unimaginable. No aliens—not even the few races the Alphans considered their equals, or their servants—were ever invited into the chamber. It was the very core of Alphan power.

Yasuke, Viceroy of Earth, took a deep breath as he stepped into the chamber. The invitation would normally have been the very pinnacle of his career, a promise—in so many words—that the ruling elite respected and trusted him. He had never had any doubt they cared for him—the core council cared for *everyone*—but respect and trust? *That* had been denied, until his invitation to visit the elite in the seat of his power. There was no greater honour for someone who hadn't climbed to the very top of the ladder.

There was no formal protocol for greeting the core councillors. He bowed once, in salute, then looked around the chambers as the councillors studied him thoughtfully. Massive holodisplays dominated the room, showing a mixture of views from the tower to live feeds from right across the Empire. A newscaster was babbling about something in tones of great excitement, as if the broadcast was in real time. Yasuke knew better. The news broadcasts would have been cleared through a dozen different committees before going live. Events had probably already moved on. He made a mental note to check the government network before he boarded his ship. He'd need to know if something—anything—had happened that might change the core council's policies before he could put them into practice.

He kept his face impassive as the live feed panned across a gleaming white tower. The city was *dominated* by white towers, each one housing hundreds and thousands of Alphans from birth to death. Their every need met by the government, they lived and died without ever making an impression on the universe. Even now, even after the Empire had come closer to defeat than ever before, the population seemed unmoved. They didn't realise—not yet—that they'd built their towers on sand. They didn't realise that the servile population was no longer content to be servile. None of them even understood how close they stood to total disaster.

We built our Empire on alien labour, Yasuke thought. *And now those aliens want a piece of the pie for themselves.*

He turned his attention back to the councillors as the chairman called for attention. There were nine in all, nine people who controlled the destiny of the entire Empire. They were wealthy and powerful beyond compare, yet—now—there were limits to their power. It had always been true, he admitted in the privacy of his own mind, but the vast majority of the population preferred to believe in the council's omnipotence. There were very few races that would have stood in the way, if the council decided it wanted something. But now, the Empire was tottering and the scavengers were gathering. The war had smashed forever the perception of invincibility. It had been won, but the cost had been far too high.

The chairman's voice echoed in the silence. "Viceroy. You wished to speak to us about the humans."

"Yes," Yasuke said, flatly. "The human problem is growing out of hand."

He waited for the nod, then proceeded. "Five hundred years ago, we invaded and occupied Earth. We assimilated the humans into our Empire. Humans worked for us—work for us—on almost all of our worlds. We trained them to fight for us, we taught them to use modern technology, we encouraged them to build up a sizable industrial base of their own. They are no longer a first-stage race, if indeed they ever were. There is a strong case to be made that, five hundred years ago, they were actually a second-stage race."

"Absurd," a councillor snapped. "They had barely even reached their moon!"

Yasuke frowned, inwardly. He'd spent much of his adult life on Earth, climbing until his word was law right across the Sol System, but he couldn't say he truly understood his human subjects. It baffled him that the humans, given rockets and surprisingly advanced computer technology, hadn't settled their star system by the time the first explorer vessel popped out of the crossroads and advanced on Earth. If they had, they would have qualified for a certain degree of respect. They certainly wouldn't have been summarily crushed and assimilated, whether they liked it or not. Instead, they had been too primitive to offer meaningful resistance when the invasion force arrived. Galactic Law was clear. Primitives had no rights.

And yet, they'd been strikingly advanced in other ways. Their computer technology had been second-stage, at the very least. They'd envisaged uses for GalTech long before they'd realised they weren't alone in the universe. Their political systems and philosophical background had been astonishingly advanced, in some respects. It was almost as if they'd started advancing to a post-scarcity level without truly being a post-scarcity society. And then their development had come to a screeching halt. The invasion had ensured they no longer controlled their world.

"The fact remains, honoured councillor, that the situation is getting out of hand," Yasuke said, coolly. "If you'll permit me to elaborate...

"The humans have been growing restless over the last hundred years. They increasingly see themselves as our *partners*, not our subjects. They have been offended, massively, when we have moved to put them back in their box. The rise of human political parties demanding equality, or even independence, is a direct result of our meddling. And now, without them, we would have lost the Lupine War…and they know it. Their demands for greater autonomy can no longer be denied."

"Of course they can," the councillor insisted.

"My staff believes the Humanity League will win a majority in the Sol Assembly, displacing the Empire Loyalists," Yasuke stated. "The Empire Loyalists themselves are demanding some form of reward for their loyalty. If we fail to come through, their assemblymen may defect to the Humanity League. That might well trigger an early election or a series of by-elections that will put power in the wrong hands. And if *that* happens, honoured councillor, we will have the flat choice between agreeing to concede a measure of independence and risking a war that will rip the Empire apart."

A ripple of disbelief ran around the chamber. Yasuke understood, better than he cared to admit. The councillors might never have laid eyes on a human, even one of the uncounted millions who lived and worked on Capital itself. They'd certainly never studied the human race. Why should they? There was no one on Capital who cared about human history, beyond a handful of dusty academics. But Yasuke couldn't allow himself the luxury of ignorance. Human history was astonishingly violent. The longer they managed to keep the lid on, the greater the explosion when they finally—inevitably—lost control.

"The Earth Defence Force is more powerful, I think, than you realise," he said. "The humans control most of the military installations within their system. Titan Base is the only real exception and even *that* installation has a major human presence. They might be able to liberate themselves, if they wished. That's not the real problem. There are millions of humans scattered across our worlds. What will they do when they see us move to crush their dreams of equality or independence? We will find ourselves fighting a war on our homeworlds!"

"We have them under tight control," another councillor said. His skin was blotchy, suggesting he was starting the transition from male to female. "Rig the election."

"That's no longer possible," Yasuke said. "They use exit polls to gauge the electorate's views—and votes. They've been strikingly accurate over the last two decades. They'd have good reason to think we rigged the election if there was a sizable discrepancy between their results and ours. And that might trigger off the insurrection we hoped to avoid."

"You paint a grim picture," the chairman said. "How do *you* propose we proceed?"

Yasuke took a breath. They weren't going to like what he had to say. He didn't like it himself. But there was no choice. The Empire itself was at stake. They had to make concessions now or risk an explosion that would destroy everything they'd built over the last ten thousand years. And yet…they wouldn't want to believe him. They had good reasons not to *want* to believe.

"I propose we start granting Earth, and the other human worlds, an increased level of autonomy," he said. "There will be a steady transfer of powers, and an acknowledgement of human equality on their homeworld, over the next two decades. This will, hopefully, satisfy them without risking total collapse…"

"Out of the question," the first councillor snapped. "They'll be passing judgement on us!"

Yasuke kept his face impassive, somehow. The councillor's corporation had run into trouble, forty years ago, when a human judge had ruled against them. They'd honestly never realised that—technically—a human judge *did* have authority, if only because he'd studied and qualified on Capital itself. And they'd used their immense clout to not only override the judge's decision, but insist that human judges were to have *no* authority over Alphans. And *that* had turned the most intelligent and capable human lawyers into independence and equality activists.

"On their homeworld, quite probably," Yasuke said. "But if you treat them as Alphans, you should be fine."

"And how do you know it *will* be fine?" The councillor glared at Yasuke. "What if this is just the beginning of a human takeover? Or…"

The chairman held up a hand. "I think we must consider the issue carefully," he said. "You ask us to fly in the face of all precedent."

"Yes," another councillor said. "A committee must be appointed to consider all the ramifications!"

"With all due respect," Yasuke said, "we don't have time for a committee."

"Really?" The chairman didn't sound convinced. "How long do we have?"

"The elections are due in thirteen months," Yasuke said. The humans had a superstition about the number *thirteen*. He didn't believe it himself, naturally, but he had to admit it was a disquieting omen. Thirteen months...the committee probably couldn't come to any conclusions in less than thirteen *years*. "That's our deadline. If the Humanity League wins, they will start pressuring us for immediate independence. And then we will have to decide how far we're willing to go to keep them in the fold."

"We could lose the war," the chairman said.

"Or weaken ourselves to the point one of the other third-stage races can overwhelm us," Yasuke said. "The Pashtali, for example. They've already been fishing in troubled waters, using their Vultek clients as deniable assets. It's only a matter of time before they start supporting human rebels. They could win the galaxy without firing a shot."

The chairman silently canvassed his fellows. "I believe we have no choice, but to proceed with your plan," he said. "If nothing else, it will allow us to limit the pace of change."

"Unless something unpredicted happens," Yasuke warned, tightly. He knew better than to think they *all* supported the plan. "Here, things change very slowly. On Earth, the pace of change is a great deal quicker."

But he knew, as he bowed his way to the exit, that they didn't really believe him.

CHAPTER ONE

James Bond, Gammon System

CAPTAIN THOMAS ANDERSON tried not to grimace as *James Bond* shuddered and groaned her way through the crossroads and back into realspace. The modified freighter had passed through so many refits that hardly anything, save perhaps for the hull and some of her bulkheads, could be said to be truly original. Her engineers had spliced components from a dozen different races into the ship, turning her into a patchwork mess that defied the best efforts of the certification board. It was a minor miracle, outsiders had noted, that *James Bond* was even allowed to exist. She should have been scrapped hundreds of years ago.

And we should probably work on that, Thomas thought. The display blinked, then started to fill with a handful of icons. *Sooner or later, someone's going to start wondering where we got the money to bribe the inspectors.*

"I'm picking up a dozen contacts, Dad," Lieutenant Wesley Anderson said. Thomas's son never looked up from his console. "They're heading in all directions!"

"I'm sure they are," Thomas said, dryly. There was much to be said for raising a family on the tramp freighter, rather than trusting them to the schools, but there were downsides too. The crew knew what they were doing, but none of them were particularly *professional.* "Are any of them close enough to prove a problem?"

"I don't think so," Wesley said. "None of them are within weapons range."

"Good," Thomas said. "Sarah, set course for the planet. Best possible speed."

Commander Sarah Anderson, his wife as well as his first officer, nodded curtly. "Yes, sir," she said. A low shiver ran through the tramp freighter as her drives came online. "We'll be entering orbit in roughly eight hours."

Thomas nodded. "No hurry," he said. "We'll be there when we'll be there."

He leaned back in his chair and brought up the live feed from the sensor suite. The inspectors—if there had *been* any inspectors—would have raised their eyebrows if they'd seen the military-grade sensors concealed within a civilian chassis. Anyone on the far side of the border would have been seriously concerned, assuming—correctly—that *James Bond* was a spy ship. It would be more accurate, Thomas considered privately, to class his ship as an *intelligence*-gathering ship, but it would make no difference to anyone who caught them. The ship and crew would never be seen again.

The system sat on the border between the Alphan Empire and the Vultek Hegemony, itself a semi-client state of the Pashtali Consortium. Thomas didn't pretend to understand alien politics. The Pashtali didn't *precisely* rule the Vultek Hegemony, but—if the intelligence reports were accurate—they had enough influence to steer the Vulteks in whatever direction they preferred. Thomas suspected that was bad news for the Alphans—and Earth. The Second Lupine War had been incredibly costly. The Alphans were in no state to fight another war with *two* interstellar powers.

He frowned as he watched the ships heading in and out of the system. Gammon was technically independent, if only because the system was of limited value. Too many crossroads to be easily secured, a barely-habitable planet without a single gas giant for HE3...there was little in the system to interest any of the interstellar powers. There were no intelligent inhabitants, nothing that might convince someone to take the system and keep everyone else out. It was lawless, to all intents and purposes. No one, not even the Vulteks, had bothered to stake a claim to the system.

And yet, there were more ships moving in and out of the system than he'd expected. The dregs of the galaxy might have made the system their home, but...he shook his head as more and more data flowed into the datacores. It was quite possible that the planet was seeing an influx of newcomers. Refugees from the wars, religious migrants hoping to find a homeworld well away from any of the interstellar powers, mercenaries and smugglers conducting their business...it was someone else's problem. As far as anyone outside the crew, and the EDF, were concerned, *James Bond* was a tramp freighter moving from one isolated system to another. His superiors would assess the data he brought them and decide what, if anything, should be done about it.

He unbuckled himself and stood. "Sarah, you have the bridge," he said, calmly. "I'm going to check on our supplies."

His wife nodded, tightly. "Have fun."

Thomas concealed his amusement as he turned and stepped through the hatch. *James Bond* was surprisingly large, for a tramp freighter, but most of her bulk was devoted to cargo. The family itself lived in cramped accommodation, so cramped that he was uneasily aware that any dispute could blossom out of control very quickly. It was only a matter of time before Wesley and his siblings decided they wanted to transfer to a different ship...something that might get awkward, if they joined the *wrong* crew. He reminded himself, sharply, that Wesley was a grown man. He was old enough to make his own mistakes.

And it isn't as if you haven't made your own mistakes, his thoughts mocked him. *You fucked up your life good and proper, when you were his age.*

He put the thought out of his head as he opened the hatch into the cargo hold and walked past the heavily-secured pallets. The weapons were primitive, by Galactic standards, but they were very useful. No one ever asked questions of gunrunners, in his experience; no one wanted to deter them from bringing *more* guns. And while there were people who would look askance at a gunrunner, they might not realise there was something more to Thomas than a man who profited from war and someone else's misery. Better to have them look down on you for *something*, Thomas had always thought, than have them trying to get too close to you.

The intercom bleeped. "Captain to the bridge! Captain to the bridge!"

Thomas blinked as he hurried back through the hatch, slamming it firmly shut behind him. Sarah—like the rest of the family—enjoyed command. She wouldn't call him to the bridge unless it was urgent. His mind raced, trying to determine what had happened. A distress call? A systems failure? *James Bond* was in better condition than she looked—and she looked alarmingly like a derelict from a bad horror flick—but something could easily have gone wrong. And yet...he dismissed the thought. The alarms would have sounded if something had failed spectacularly.

And if it failed so spectacularly that the alarms failed to sound, he told himself, *we'd all be dead*.

He stepped onto the bridge and retook the command chair. "Report!"

"Unknown warship on approach vector," Sarah said. Her voice was very cold. She'd never been comfortable with their work for the EDF, even though she'd grown up on a freighter herself. The risk of death might have been a constant companion, but there were limits now she was a mother herself. "She'll be within weapons range in twenty minutes."

Thomas nodded as he pulled up the sensor report. The warship was a light cruiser, origin unknown. That meant nothing, he reminded himself. *James Bond* wasn't the only ship that had passed through dozens of hands since she'd come off the slipway. The Galactics had no qualms about selling their older and outdated ships to the younger races, who would do their level best to refit them with newer technology. The ship angling towards them might have been refitted so extensively her original builders had been lost in the mists of time. Or...she could just be a pirate ship. Gammon played host to pirates and their fences too.

And if she was on a legitimate mission, she would have hailed us by now, he thought. A chill ran down his spine. *We might be in some trouble*.

"Send a standard greeting," he ordered. "If they don't respond, send a wide-band distress call."

"Aye, sir," Sarah said.

Thomas forced himself to consider their options. There weren't many. *James Bond* carried two plasma cannons…they might as well be peashooters, for all the damage they'd do to the enemy hull. She could alter course and try to evade, perhaps even double back and retreat to the crossroads… no, that wasn't going to work. The warship would have no trouble running them down before they could jump into multispace. They could prolong the chase, perhaps long enough to convince the enemy ship to go looking for easier prey, but it wouldn't last very long.

"No response," Sarah said. "And they're picking up speed."

"Transmit the distress signal," Thomas said. "And then alter course to evade."

He gritted his teeth. Pirates…they had to be pirates. And that meant… he hoped, grimly, they weren't *human* pirates. The crew might survive long enough to be ransomed if they were captured by non-humans. Humans, on the other hand…Sarah and his daughters would be brutally raped to death. Pirates were pathologically insane. They'd kill the males, then torture the females to death. Thomas thought cold thoughts about the ship's self-destruct system. It would be relatively simple to lure the pirate ship into point-blank range and deactivate the antimatter containment chambers. The resulting explosion would destroy both ships. It wasn't ideal, but what was?

"They're angling to remain on intercept course," Sarah said. "They'll be within weapons range in ten minutes."

"And no response to our distress call," Thomas said, sourly. He wasn't surprised. Gammon had no navy. The Galactics didn't bother to patrol the system. And it was unlikely the mercenaries would drop everything to come to their aid. Who *cared* about a tramp freighter in the middle of nowhere? "Divert emergency power to the drives."

"Aye, sir," Sarah said, in a tone that told him she *knew* it was futile. He knew it too. There was no way they could do more than delay matters. "I…"

She broke off as her console chimed. "They're hailing us."

"Put it through," Thomas ordered.

He tried not to show any reaction as a bird-like alien face materialised in front of him. It wasn't the first Vultek he'd seen, and he'd spent most of his life around non-humans, but the aliens always left him feeling a little uneasy. It was the way they looked at him, he thought; it was the way they always looked as if they were considering when and where to pounce.

"This is Captain Anderson," he said. "I…"

"The Vultek Hegemony has assumed control over this system," the alien said. It spoke Galactic with a faint whistling accent. "You have intruded upon our territory without permission."

Thomas blinked. The Vulteks hadn't occupied Gammon…not as far as he knew. Why would they bother? And…they were risking a confrontation with the Alphans and at least two other powerful races. And humanity, of course. There were three human-dominated worlds bare *days* from Gammon, linked by the tangled thread of safe routes through multispace. Interstellar powers that had been content to leave Gammon independent would be concerned, very concerned, if one power took control and drove everyone else out. The Vulteks were risking a major conflict…

Unless they've decided the Alphans are too weak to push the issue, Thomas thought, coldly. It was possible. Everyone knew the Alphans had lost hundreds of their prized warcruisers during the war. They could trash the Vulteks in a few days, if they massed their surviving ships, but at what cost? *They might just get away with it.*

"We were unaware of any change in power," he said, carefully. "In any case, under the Convocations…"

The Vultek cut him off. "You will power down your drives and prepare to be boarded," he said. "Resistance will result in the destruction of your vessel."

Thomas forced himself to think. The Vulteks were signatories to the standard interstellar conventions. In theory, there shouldn't be any trouble.

The ship would be searched, then returned to the crossroads or simply interned. In practice...who knew? The courts might take years to decide if *James Bond* was trespassing or not, particularly if one or more interstellar powers decided to dispute the Vultek claim to the system. He shuddered as a deeper implication struck him. If the Vulteks discovered the sensor suite, they'd realise the ship's true nature. And who knew what they'd do then?

Make us vanish, Thomas thought. *We dare not let them board us.*

He glanced at the display, already knowing they were trapped. They could neither outrun nor defeat their enemy. And triggering the self-destruct might start a war. The EDF—and the Alphans—wouldn't know what had happened, but that wouldn't stop the Vulteks from using the incident as an excuse for war. And yet...he couldn't let his ship fall into their hands either.

"In line with the Convocations, I cannot allow you to search my ship," he said. "However, as a gesture of good faith, we will return to the crossroads and..."

The display bleeped an alert. "Missile separation," Sarah said, quietly. "They're aiming to miss, but not by much."

"You will power down your drives and prepare to be boarded without further delay," the Vultek said, coldly. "Resistance will result in the destruction of your vessel."

So you said, Thomas thought. His thoughts ran in circles. Earth couldn't push the issue. It wasn't clear if the *Alphans* would push the issue. *And there's no way out.*

He keyed his console, bringing up the limited destruct program. The sensor suite could be reduced to dust with the push of a button, once he inserted his command codes. In theory, there would be no proof that *James Bond* had ever been anything other than a simple tramp freighter. In practice, he simply didn't know. The Vulteks might search the ship so thoroughly they turned up proof...if, of course, they didn't simply destroy the ship in a bid to secure their new holdings. And if they swept the datacore...

"We understand," he said. "We'll deactivate our drives as ordered."

"Good," the alien said. "And..."

Thomas glanced up as the proximity display flashed another alert. A gravimetric distortion had appeared out of nowhere, a bare three kilometres from their position. He let out a sigh of relief as the distortion became a crossroads, which opened to reveal a warcruiser. The giant warship glided into realspace, its sensors already searching for targets. The Vultek ship didn't move, but Thomas liked to think he saw it jump. Warcruisers were the most powerful warships in the known galaxy. The Alphans would have no trouble blowing the Vultek ship out of space if they so much as looked at them funny.

"They're ordering the Vulteks to leave," Sarah said. She let out a sound that was half-giggle, half-sob. "That was really too close."

Thomas nodded, watching as the Vulteks reversed course and headed straight for the nearest crossroads. They didn't have the technology to create their own, not yet. The Alphans were the only race known to possess such technology, although Thomas wouldn't have cared to bet the other Galactics didn't have it. The technology offered too many advantages to whoever held it.

"Reverse course," he ordered, firmly. "We'll pass through Gammon, then head home."

Sarah gave him a sharp look. "And you don't think we should head home now?"

"I think we have weapons to sell," Thomas said. "And we need to know what's happening on the surface."

And see who's really in control of the system, he thought, grimly. He understood his wife's point. They'd pushed their luck dangerously close to the limits. But they also needed to find out what was actually going on. *If the Vulteks landed a major ground force, digging them out might take a full-scale war.*

"Aye, sir," Sarah said. They were going to have a screaming match as soon as they were alone. Thomas was sure of it. "We'll enter orbit in five hours."

"Keep monitoring local space," Thomas ordered. He didn't relax. He wouldn't until they had completed their mission and left the system safely behind. "I want to know the moment the Vulteks show up again."

He sucked in his breath. The Vulteks weren't stupid enough to pit an outdated light cruiser against a warcruiser, but they wouldn't *like* being told to leave at gunpoint. They might assemble their fleet, if they *had* a fleet within the system, and gamble the Alphans wouldn't want to start another war. Or try something, hoping their patrons would come to their aid if things got out of hand. The crisis might have only just begun.

His eyes slipped to the display. The warcruiser was moving ahead of then, gracefully displaying her power—and her masters' resolve—to the entire system. He felt a sudden stab of envy that surprised him with its intensity. Humanity had advanced far in the last five hundred years, learning from its masters and even improving—in some respects—on their technology. But they didn't have anything to match the warcruiser. The ship was so advanced that she had been designed for aesthetics, not practicality. There was no way anyone could mistake her for a *human* ship.

Wesley had the same thought. "She's beautiful, isn't she?"

"Yes," Thomas agreed. He'd seen the recordings. And read the secret files, the ones that officially didn't exist. The fact the EDF kept a wary eye on humanity's masters, as well as its enemies, was a closely-guarded secret. "But she also took five years from her builders laying down her spine to her crew activating the ship's drives and deploying her for the first time."

And if the Alphans hadn't had us fighting by their side, he added silently, *they might just have lost the last war.*

CHAPTER TWO

EDS *Washington*, Earth Orbit

COMMANDER NAOMI YAGAMI BRACED HERSELF, then carefully removed the rank badge from her sleeve before stepping into the next compartment. A handful of crewmen stared up at her in shock, their expressions caught in a frozen rictus of alarm, guilt and anger. Naomi stared back at them evenly, keeping her face under tight control. The crewmen were already on the verge of crossing the line. A single show of weakness might encourage them to mutiny. And it would end badly. The Earth Defence Force's commanders wouldn't hesitate to fire on a mutinous ship. Naomi was all too aware the marines were already primed and ready to intervene if—when—the shit hit the fan.

She allowed her eyes to sweep the compartment as the hatch closed behind her. Twelve crewmen were hastily scrambling to their feet, snapping salutes that were distressingly sloppy. Senior Chief Nigel Thompson appeared to be in charge, although it was hard to be sure. The pre-war military structure had broken down under the stress of war, allowing a degree of social mobility that would have been unacceptable in peacetime. Thompson was tough, but was he tough enough to impose himself on his fellows? Crewmen Harris Pettigrew and Isabel Ruthven were a little more surprising, particularly the latter. Naomi happened to know she'd been earmarked for officer rank, if she was willing to become a mustang. She'd shown promise in the last two years.

"I trust," she said calmly, "that you were not *actually* discussing mutiny."

Pettigrew spoke first, quickly. "Merely airing our grievances, Commander."

"Indeed?" Naomi looked from face to face, wondering if they were willing to cross the line. "And what would those grievances be?"

Thompson shot Pettigrew a nasty look. "Commander, with all due respect, is there any point in discussing our grievances?"

"I am the executive officer of this ship," Naomi said, coolly. She squatted, resting her hands on her knees. "And crewmen, as has long been established, have the right to bring their grievances to me."

She waited, wondering if they'd see the *out* she was offering them. They *could* air their grievances to her, without fear of punishment. They didn't *have* to hold a secret meeting that might get them in *real* trouble, let alone do something that certainly *would*. But...too much had happened, during the war and afterwards, for the lower ranks to have any real faith in officialdom. *She* might be trustworthy. The Empire's bureaucracy was anything but.

Thompson leaned forward. "Commander, we were promised shore leave immediately after the war," he said. "Proper shore leave, not a couple of days in a seedy spaceport strip. It's been two *years* since the promise and we haven't had our shore leave!"

"I was told my enlistment would end with the war," Pettigrew said. "And I can't even leave this ship! My job won't wait for me much longer!"

Naomi winced, inwardly. Pettigrew—and thousands like him—had been yanked out of his pre-war job and involuntarily conscripted into the navy. The EDF had needed the manpower desperately, and it had the legal authority to draft whoever it needed, but it couldn't be denied that the impressments had caused all sorts of problems. Pettigrew's growing resentment was actually the least of them. Naomi had heard there were skilled manpower shortages all over the system. She'd even heard suggestions the human-owned and -operated industries were being deliberately starved of manpower, just to allow the alien-owned combines to compete on even terms.

"My brother says he'll have to find someone else if I don't rejoin him soon," Pettigrew said. He shot her a challenging look. "Why shouldn't I desert?"

"Because you'll be arrested and dumped on Liberty without anyone bothering to court-martial you," Naomi said, dryly. "You might have a point, crewman, but that point will be lost if you commit an offense against good order."

"And the peacocks aren't helping," Isabel said. "That prick upstairs..."

"*Don't* insult the captain in front of me," Naomi said sharply, cutting the younger woman off before she could say something dangerous. Everyone knew the bulkheads had ears. The Alphans didn't have a concept of *privacy* and didn't expect their human subjects to have one either. "If you have a valid complaint, make it."

"We're fed up," Thompson said, glaring at Isabel. "Commander, we didn't sign up for the long haul. We knew we'd be retained if war broke out, and it did, but the war is over now. We should be discharged..."

"Or given shore leave, at the very least," Isabel put in. "Commander, we're worn down as well as fed up. It's only a matter of time before someone makes a deadly mistake and blows the entire ship to atoms."

Naomi nodded, keeping her face expressionless. The hell of it was that they had a point. The crew *had* been retained, even after the war. And there had been no shore leave...there hadn't even been any hazard pay. The bureaucrats hadn't bothered to think, as always, before they ordered the navy to retain its people. They could have solved half the problems if they'd bothered to exercise their brains and realise that discontent would spread rapidly. Or simply offered extra pay to anyone willing to stay. In these times, the navy was actually a pretty good employer.

"We're orbiting *Earth*, not some godforsaken outpost along the border," Pettigrew snapped. "They could easily give us a couple of weeks off before we resume our patrol!"

"Yes, they could," Naomi said, although she wasn't so sure. The official newscasts from Earth were rosy, but she'd heard—through the grapevine—that the security system was deteriorating rapidly. Too many people had suddenly found themselves out of work, too many people had suddenly found themselves desperately short of money...too many politicians were trying to make hay while the fields burned down. "And I will suggest as much to the captain."

"That *peacock*," Isabel snapped. "Commander..."

Thompson elbowed her, hard. Naomi gritted her teeth and pretended not to notice. The captain wouldn't understand the context, if he heard a junior crewman had insulted him. He'd want Isabel flogged...Naomi wondered, grimly, if she could convince the captain that discharging the younger woman would be a suitable punishment. She'd never liked the idea of flogging a grown adult. She would do everything she could to ensure it didn't happen.

"The captain will take your words under advertisement," she said. "For the moment..."

She looked from face to face, trying to gauge how serious they were about causing real trouble. Thompson and Pettigrew wanted out. Isabel... Naomi wasn't so sure about Isabel. The younger woman had potential, but she'd come very close to saying something she couldn't take back. The others...she frowned as she noticed the Humanity League literature someone had tried to hide at the back of the compartment. That was, technically, banned onboard ship. Legally, she should confiscate it and arrest whoever had brought it onto the cruiser. Practically, there was no point. Political messages spread, whatever the captain and his superiors said. She'd just make an ass of herself if she tried to stop the message and failed.

"For the moment, I want you to remember that times are not easy for anyone," she continued. "I know, it doesn't feel that way. I know, you're thinking how unfair life has been to you over the last two weeks. But we are doing the best we can."

"Even a few days off-ship would be good," Thompson said, shortly.

"I'll do what I can," Naomi said. She hardened her voice. "And until then, it would make my life a great deal easier if you refrained from holding secretive meetings. Understand?"

"Yes, Commander," Thompson said.

Naomi concealed her relief as she stood, brushed down her uniform and strode out of the compartment without looking back. They were discontented, but they weren't mutinous. Not yet. It would take something—*an incident of some kind*, she thought—to turn them to outright mutiny. Thompson wasn't stupid. He'd been in the navy long enough to know that mutiny would lead to total disaster. Even if they took the ship, where would they go? There was no way they could get down to Earth with the EDF and the Alphan Picket Squadron bearing down on them.

She kept her back ramrod straight until she reached Officer Country and stepped into her cabin, where she allowed herself to sag and wipe the sweat from her brow. Thompson wasn't the only one to feel the crew was being worked to death. She'd had to break up a dozen fights over the last two months, then issue sharp reprimands to enterprising spacers who'd decided to supplement their wages by selling moonshine. It wouldn't have been a problem if crewmen hadn't started reporting for duty while drunk. She'd had no end of trouble trying to write creative explanations into the logbook...

I guess I'm lucky the captain doesn't bother to follow the log, she mused, as she walked into the washroom and splashed cold water on her face. *I'd be in real trouble if someone more intelligent was posted here.*

She shook her head, suddenly feeling very tired. Things had been better, before the war. The peacocks—the Alphan officers appointed to the EDF—had been intelligent, capable and very driven, quick to respect their human subordinates. They spoke English, they often studied human history and they treated humans as close to equal. But the war had drawn those officers back to the Alphan Navy, their slots filled with stodgy oxygen thieves who didn't have a gram of imagination between them. She supposed she was lucky. *Her* CO was merely lazy and disconnected. She'd heard there were others who were sadistic, cruel and generally unpleasant.

Her lips quirked as she lifted her head and stared into the mirror. Green eyes, short red hair and a pale complexion stared back. She'd had boyfriends who'd told her she was pretty, once upon a time, but now there were dark shadows around her eyes and her face was set in a permanently displeased expression. Thompson was right. *Everyone* needed shore leave. She understood, better than she cared to admit, why otherwise loyal officers and crew might be considering desertion. They were coming to the end of their rope.

She walked back into the main cabin, poured a cup of coffee and drank it slowly. Navy coffee was universally foul, she'd found in a lifetime of service, but it did keep her awake. She wasn't getting anything like enough sleep. She wasn't even getting a few hours of rest and relaxation. She finished her coffee, put the mug aside and surveyed her tiny metal box. The bulkheads looked to be looming closer. She knew it was an illusion—the bulkheads were older than her great-grandfather—but it was alarmingly persistent. She'd been in the cabin too long.

The intercom bleeped. "Commander," Captain Nobunaga said. "Report to my office at once."

"Yes, Captain," Naomi said. "I'm on my way."

She checked her appearance in the mirror—Captain Nobunaga had a habit of reprimanding officers for their uniforms, while ignoring or overlooking more serious issues—then strode from the cabin and up to the captain's office. It should have been right next to the bridge, but Captain Nobunaga had insisted on occupying the room next to his suite and converting it into his workplace. Naomi wasn't sure what the Alphan did all day. She was his XO, true, but she seemed to be doing half his duties as well as her own. He certainly wasn't socialising with the crew, even his servants. Perhaps he had a sexbot in his cabin. She smirked at the thought, then schooled her expression into calm impassivity. Captain Nobunaga had never learnt to read human faces, but there was no point in taking risks.

The marine on duty outside the office ran a scanner over her body, then opened the hatch and motioned for her to enter. Naomi nodded her thanks as she stepped into the warm chamber, feeling her skin prickle as dry air washed over her face. The Alphan homeworld was hotter and drier than Earth, although they had no trouble coping with colder temperatures. Captain Nobunaga had tried to insist the entire ship be matched to his homeworld, but someone higher up the chain—Naomi had no idea who—had had a word with him and he'd dropped the request. Naomi wished she knew who to thank. The crew would have crossed the line into open mutiny if they were sweating as well as everything else.

"Captain," she said, lowering her eyes and dropping to her knees, sinking into the posture of respect. "You summoned me?"

She felt an odd little chill run down her spine as Captain Nobunaga studied her thoughtfully. She was no xenophobe—she'd served on a dozen multiracial and multicultural starships and stations—but the Alphans had always worried her. Perhaps it was just the simple fact that their slightest wish was everyone else's sternest command. They ruled a vast swathe of the known universe and never let anyone forget it. A word from Captain Nobunaga could propel her career into orbit or send her crashing down to Earth—or Liberty.

He was unusually short for an Alphan, but still taller than she was. He wore a simple harness and pants, decorated in a style that marked him as outrageously rich and well-connected even by Galactic standards. Naomi had a private suspicion he was actually the black sheep of the family, as his connections should have been more than enough to enter the Alphan Navy at a very high level. Or so she'd been told. Family relationships among the Alphans were hideously complex. It was possible he was actually quite poor by their standards, but—as long as he was well away from Capital—he could pretend to be rich.

"Commander," Captain Nobunaga said. "You may rise."

Naomi stood, carefully staring at his leathery neck. Direct eye contact was rude amongst the Alphans, unless one was addressing a social equal. And, no matter her rank, Captain Nobunaga would never see her as an equal. He would never invite her to join his social network, he would never socialise with her...he would never do *anything* for her, unless it benefited him in some way.

"The Viceroy is returning to Earth next week," Captain Nobunaga said, as if he expected her to know the Viceroy had *left* Earth. "We will be part of his reception committee."

"Yes, sir," Naomi said.

"You will see to it that the hull is clean and shiny," Captain Nobunaga said. "And painted in my colours, of course."

"Of course," Naomi echoed. The Viceroy wouldn't notice, unless he deigned to inspect *Washington* personally, but Captain Nobunaga wouldn't thank her for pointing it out. "I'll see to it immediately."

"Very good," Captain Nobunaga said. "Dismissed."

Naomi bent into the posture of respect. "If I may, My Captain...?"

Captain Nobunaga sounded displeased. "You may."

"The crew is tired and worn," Naomi said. "And we're already earmarked for patrol duties one month from today. Please, could I arrange a shore leave period for them before we depart?"

"The ship has to be ready to depart on time," Captain Nobunaga said. "You may not."

"The ship will not be ready to depart if the *crew* isn't ready," Naomi said. She kept her face expressionless, despite her anger and despair. "Captain, with all due respect, they need shore leave."

"They can go virtual," Captain Nobunaga pointed out. "Your human desires"—he managed to load the word with a staggering amount of contempt—"will be satisfied by illusionary realities."

"They won't," Naomi said. She'd kept a wary eye on the growing number of crewmen using—and abusing—the VR facilities. So far, no one seemed to have crossed the line into addiction. She had a feeling that was going to change. "Captain, virtual realities are not *real*."

"But good enough," Captain Nobunaga said. "They can have a day on Luna, if they must."

He waved a hand towards the hatch. "Dismissed."

Naomi bowed deeper, then backed out of the cabin. She didn't rise until the hatch was firmly closed. Her former commanders would *never* have been so dismissive of her concerns. They understood their human subordinates weren't machines, that even *real* machines needed to be maintained regularly in order to keep functioning. She wondered, sourly, if she should send one of them a message. The EDF *needed* those officers if it was to continue to function properly. Thompson and his friends wouldn't be the only human crewmen considering desertion—or mutiny.

She turned and strode down the corridor, feeling the marine's eyes on her retreating behind. The rumour would be out, sooner rather than later, that the captain hadn't been generous…she was tempted to turn and tell the Marine to keep his mouth shut, but it wouldn't matter. They'd know the truth the moment the shore leave roster was posted. Or wasn't posted, as the case might be.

And all hell will break loose when the crew realises they're not going to get a break, she thought, as she reached the etching of George Washington outside the bridge. *And we might have a real mutiny on our hands.*

She studied the etching for a long moment. The Humanity League and the Renaissance Faire had pressed for warships to be named after human heroes, insisting the EDF should do honour to humanity's past. They'd been surprised, no doubt, when the Alphans had raised no objection to naming a warship *Washington*. George Washington had led a successful war of independence, after all. It was hardly the sort of thinking the Alphans wanted to encourage.

Except they destroyed Washington, DC, when they invaded Earth, she reminded herself, morbidly. *It isn't an honour. It's a subtle threat.*

CHAPTER THREE

Pournelle Shipyards, Sol Asteroid Belt

IT WAS SAID, IN ALL THE PARTY BROADCASTS and broadsheets, that Speaker Abraham Douglas travelled alone. It was not entirely true, as Abraham himself would happily testify, but he saw no need to travel with a small army of aides, assistants, gofers and servants. The Alphans might enjoy showing their wealth and power by never going anywhere alone; Abraham preferred to go the other way and make a point of not hiring people just to prove he could do it. And besides, he'd been in politics long enough to know that every new hire was a potential security risk.

He sat in his chair and watched through the starship's sensors as she made her way through the security perimeter and into the Pournelle Shipyards. The Alphans had poured scorn on the design, when they'd first seen it, and declined to invest, but the Human Assembly had seen the potential and poured a considerable sum of money into the project. And it had paid off. The dispersed shipyard might look scattered and disorganised, compared to the giant assemblies near Capital, but they were more efficient. They represented the key to the future, he'd argued. He was pleased to discover he'd been right.

His eyes tracked a handful of freighters—and a new-build cruiser—as they were put through their paces. The ships wouldn't win any design awards—they were starkly functional, compared to starcruisers and warcruisers—but they were remorselessly practical. They might lack the advanced tech of their alien counterparts, yet they were cheap, effective and—above all—easy to repair. The Pournelle Shipyards had pioneered modular design, working hard to make sure their ships and starship components were perfectly interchangeable. It took the Alphans *years* to repair a damaged warcruiser. Their human counterparts could be back in action within a month.

Perhaps, he reminded himself. *The ships are also more fragile than their warcruiser counterparts.*

He looked up as Rachel Grant, his aide, entered the compartment. Rachel was the only person he truly considered a travelling companion, the only person he trusted to put his interests—and those of the league—ahead of everything else. There were too many factions within the Humanity League for his peace of mind, ranging from groups that feared the worst if they pushed too hard to forces that wanted an immediate declaration of independence and a war if the Alphans refused to abandon Earth. Abraham was grimly aware that his position was nowhere near as solid as he would have liked. He had to maintain a balancing act between pushing for more autonomy and not demanding something that might drive both the aliens themselves and their human loyalists into mounting a crackdown.

"Sir," Rachel said. She was a tall woman in her early thirties, with long brown hair that fell to her waist. If she had any hobbies beyond serving the cause, Abraham had never found them. "We just received an update on the Steven Whitmore case."

Abraham nodded, curtly. Steven Whitmore was a known member of Direct Action, the hardline political pressure group that had—so far— managed to stay on the right side of the law. He'd expected *something* to happen ever since Direct Action broke away from the Humanity League, perhaps a ban on the group's existence and involuntary emigration for any of its members who didn't get the message. He hadn't expected Whitmore to be busted under the Empire's moral laws. Indeed, it had happened in a manner that made it impossible to tell if Whitmore was genuinely guilty or if he'd been framed.

"Our sources within the EIS confirmed that Whitmore was busted for possession of pornographic material," Rachel said. "However, none of it was *actually* illegal and...well, it represented *all* manner of legal porn. There was no rhyme or reason to the collection."

"Odd," Abraham mused. "And we have no way to know if it was a frame-up."

"Or a plan to embarrass the government," Rachel agreed. "Or...sir, for all we know Whitmore could actually be guilty."

"Of collecting porn," Abraham said. It was legal, but distasteful. "Has there been anything from Direct Action?"

"Not yet," Rachel said. "It sounds as if they were caught by surprise."

"Yeah." Abraham considered it for a long moment. "The peacocks wouldn't be able to tell the difference between different kinds of porn, would they?"

Rachel shrugged. Abraham understood. The Alphans didn't really have a *concept* of pornography. They'd been bemused when they'd discovered that humans *did*. The whole concept sounded absurd to them, just as some of their quirks baffled their human subjects. If it was a frame-up, planned by someone on the Viceroy's staff, they might have provided Whitmore with all manner of porn without realising they were scattering their fingerprints on the plot. Or Whitmore could just be a colossal pervert. Abraham had been in politics long enough to know that *some* politicians had no qualms about abusing their positions.

"Keep me informed," he said, finally. A low quiver ran through the ship as she docked with the shipyard. "We'll pick up the affair when we get home."

He wondered, sometimes, what his famous ancestor—and namesake—would have thought of Earth's alien masters. The Alphans weren't cruel and sadistic, by and large, but they were very definitely the people in charge. Abraham was honest enough to admit the Alphans had done a lot of good for humanity, yet they'd also done a great deal of harm. He'd once had dreams of rising to the top. Cold experience had taught him that, as long as humans remained subordinate to alien masters, that would never happen. He didn't want total independence, not really. He just wanted to be able to stand face to face with an Alphan and look him in the eye.

The gravity shifted, slightly, as they disembarked from the starship and passed through a brief security scan. The shipyards hadn't been targeted during the war, but it was only a matter of time. Direct Action was already talking about open war—foolish, given the existence of literally *millions* of loyalists—and there were alien races beyond the border who'd be happy to go fishing in troubled waters. Abraham had heard all sorts of rumours, from humans being hired as mercenaries to alien operatives disguising themselves as humans and landing on human-dominated worlds. He was fairly sure most of the rumours were nonsense, but it was hard to be sure. The universe was a very strange place. Even the *Alphans* conceded there were mysteries beyond their ken.

And anyone who wanted to cause trouble could just hire humans to do it, he mused, as they were shown into a large conference chamber. *There's no shortage of people willing to sell their grandmothers for enough cash to survive the next few months.*

"Speaker," Martin Solomon said. The Director and CEO of the Pournelle Shipyards Corporation nodded politely, rather than dropping into the posture of respect. "Thank you for coming."

Abraham nodded. They were old friends, although they'd gone in different directions after graduating from university. Abraham had set out to become a lawyer, then a politician; Solomon had set out to build a corporation that could compete with the interstellar combines and largely succeeded. Abraham had tried hard to convince him to join the Humanity League, although Solomon preferred to keep his distance. The Alphans could crush his corporation if they chose to boycott it.

"You look older," Solomon said. "The wig does nothing for you."

"And the lack of hair does nothing for you," Abraham countered. He wasn't a paid-up member of the Renaissance Faire, but he styled himself in a manner he thought his ancestor would appreciate. "Why did you shave yourself?"

"Hair isn't always an advantage out here, as you know," Solomon said. He gestured to the seats. "Please, sit. I'll have coffee served in a moment."

"No hurry," Abraham said. "How are matters out here?"

Solomon looked pained. "They would be better without political interference, I'll tell you that for free," he said. "This place—and the others like it—could transform the galaxy, if they let it happen."

Abraham nodded. There was no need to ask who *they* were. "How bad is it?"

"Pretty bad," Solomon commented. "I don't know if it's deliberate, Fred, but it's pretty damn bad."

A servant entered, carrying a tray of coffee and biscuits. He placed it on the table, nodded politely to Solomon and retreated as silently as he'd come. Abraham glanced at the hatch as it closed, then rested his hands on the table. Solomon poured the coffee, placed a biscuit beside each cup and saucer and then handed it round. Abraham kept his mouth shut. He knew his friend was gathering his thoughts.

"There are two problems," Solomon said, when he'd sat back down. "First, we're short of skilled manpower. We lost thousands of trained and experienced workers to the draft, pretty much all of which was done with a great deal of panic and an absolutely complete lack of common sense. We didn't just lose the workers. We lost the experienced trainers who could train *new* workers too. We really need those workers back, as quickly as possible."

"I understand," Abraham said.

Solomon snorted. "If that's true, you're the first politico to understand since...ever."

"I'll take that as your endorsement," Abraham teased. "And the other problem?"

"Export licences," Solomon said. "The vast majority of our produce, Fred, is not on the restricted list. There shouldn't be any barrier between us and eager customers. It isn't as if we're selling antimatter blazers or heavy-duty planetcracker bombs. But the assembly is delaying our licences, apparently because of pressure from the Viceroy's office. I understand they'd be reluctant to have us sell warships to potential enemies, but freighters and spare parts? Give me a break!"

"I'll raise both issues with the assembly," Abraham said. "But as long as the Empire Loyalists remain in power..."

"They won't," Solomon predicted. "The economic downturn following the war is starting to bite. People want change, not empty promises."

"I know," Abraham said. "But we'll run into problems if we win *too* big."

He sighed. It would be ironic indeed if he became First Speaker, displacing the Empire Loyalists from their decades of majority, only to discover he couldn't give his supporters what they wanted. No matter what he did, he couldn't satisfy everyone. It was an open question if he could satisfy *anyone*. And who knew what would happen if his supporters turned to Direct Action instead?

"If the barriers are removed, we should experience a major economic *boom*," Solomon said. "Our freighters are cheaper than most alien designs, our systems are simpler yet easier to repair...we don't even sell them with crappy propriety software to limit their use. Given time, even a first-stage race can learn to use and repair our hardware. And yet, the peacocks are determined to stop us. Hell, Fred, we could keep the EDF running if they let us!"

Abraham's eyes narrowed. "Are you sure?"

"Pretty much." Solomon grinned. "Have you ever studied the Type-V medium freighter design?"

"You do realise I don't know the bridge from the bulkhead?" Abraham grinned back at him. "And I do know you *love* telling me all about your ships."

Solomon laughed, then keyed a switch. A holographic image of a mid-sized freighter appeared, hovering over the table. It looked as crude and inelegant as anything else from the human-designed and operated shipyards. He could understand why the Galactics looked at the design and laughed. There wasn't so much as a *hint* of elegance, let alone humanity, around it.

"You'll notice the drive structure is considerably larger than strictly necessary," Solomon said, seriously. "In fact, economically speaking, the holds are smaller than they should be for a ship of that size. However, with the advantage of modular design, it would only take a few weeks to replace the civilian-grade systems with their mil-grade counterparts. The hull's armour can be enhanced, weapons fitted to the internal network and a few other modifications that would turn the freighters into warships. And we could churn them out very quickly."

Abraham looked up. "And how would they compete with a warship? Or a warcruiser?"

"It depends," Solomon said. "A purpose-built warship would have the edge, assuming equal levels of technology and suchlike. However, the modular design and standardisation would ensure the modified freighters could be converted into warships—and then repaired, if they took damage—relatively quickly. We could churn out a thousand such freighters in the time it takes the peacocks to construct a single warcruiser. If nothing else"—his eyes met Abraham's—"we could take a page from the Lupine handbook and bury the warcruisers in expendable ships."

"Which was immensely costly for the Lupines," Abraham said. He had no military experience, but he'd attended enough briefings to understand the basics of tactics and strategy. "They lost a hundred starships for each warcruiser."

"But they could afford to take the losses and press on," Solomon said. "If we hadn't been involved, Abraham, the peacocks might have lost the war. Yes, the warcruisers are formidable ships. I don't think anyone can doubt it. But the peacocks simply didn't have enough of them to win the war easily. Now…their fleet has been grossly weakened. I'd be surprised if some of the bigger powers aren't wondering what they can do while the peacocks try to rebuild their fleet."

Abraham nodded, shortly. He had no illusions about interstellar power politics. The strong—those lucky enough to develop spacefaring technology and figure out how to access multispace before they were discovered by someone else—did whatever they liked; the weak, everyone else, suffered what they must. The Alphans had had no qualms about invading and occupying Earth when they'd stumbled across the human race. Now the Alphans looked weak, a dozen other races would be plotting to take advantage of the chaos. Who knew which of them would be the first to try?

And who knows what concessions they'll make to us, he mused, *in order to keep us from revolting?*

He studied the image for a long moment. "Could you build a warcruiser? I mean, could you build something that'd match a warcruiser?"

Solomon looked doubtful. "Yes and no," he said. "I could duplicate some of their systems...not easily, perhaps, but I could do it. Their armour is really little more than enhanced ablative armour. Expensive as fuck and difficult to repair, but yes...we could duplicate it. The weapons, sensors and drives? Maybe not. We still don't understand how they manage to navigate multispace so well. The black boxes have remained resistant to all tampering."

Abraham nodded. "And if you had a crash program into studying their technology?"

Solomon shrugged. "We *have* a research program," he said. "We've learnt a great deal about how multispace and realspace interact, but little else. So far, we haven't cracked the problem. Between you and me—and Rachel, of course—I have a theory the Alphans themselves don't understand how the tech works. It's been a long time since they were on the cutting edge of research and development. They haven't made any significant technological breakthroughs in centuries."

"I see." Abraham considered it. "Do you think they stole the technology off someone else?"

"It's possible," Solomon said. He shrugged. "And it would be consistent with their arrogance to pretend they invented it for themselves. It wouldn't be the first time someone found something interesting on an abandoned world or drifting alien wreck and claimed to invent it, rather than admit what they'd found."

His face darkened. "Did you hear about the Erehwon Affair?"

"Just rumours," Abraham said. "What happened?"

Solomon scowled. "Long-range multispace pinging station picked up an artefact, not too far from explored space. You know the drill—they ping the folds of multispace and sometimes they pick up something interesting. We were putting together a mission to explore the...well whatever it was...when the Viceroy's office takes it away from us. I think they sent a starcruiser to have a look at it."

"Ouch," Abraham said. "What did they find?"

"We don't know," Solomon said. "It could have been anything."

"I can make a few enquiries," Abraham said. "But if it was something truly old..."

"Or even something they didn't want us to find," Solomon said. "I'd say the odds are even, myself."

He stood. "Anyway, I promised you a tour of the shipyards. I think you'll enjoy what you see."

"I hope so," Abraham said. "Your shipyards could be the hope of humanity."

"Until everyone starts duplicating our idea." Solomon shrugged. "It isn't as if we can copyright the concept..."

Rachel's datapad bleeped. "Excuse me."

Abraham frowned. The starship's datacore would have held any messages that weren't priority-one. Protocol was clear. Meetings were not to be interrupted unless it was a full-scale emergency. A chill ran down his spine. It could be anything, from terrorism to a legal crackdown or...anything. The world might be about to turn upside down.

"You're being recalled to Earth," Rachel said. "The Viceroy has called an urgent meeting of the assembly."

"Crap," Abraham said. The Viceroy had been away for two months. His return had been surprisingly devoid of ceremony. Abraham had suspected that portended trouble of *some* kind. A high-ranking peacock would normally be livid if he wasn't given the proper respect. "How long do we have?"

"It's scheduled for tomorrow morning," Rachel said. She checked her datapad, calculating travel times. "You'll have time for the tour."

"Perhaps not," Abraham said, reluctantly. "I don't want to give them an excuse to expel me if all hell is about to break loose."

CHAPTER FOUR

Star City, Earth

LIEUTENANT TOMAS DRACHE GRITTED HIS TEETH as the protestors marched down the streets. The protest march wasn't authorised—the protestors hadn't bothered to so much as *ask* for permission before they'd boiled onto the streets—but there had been no orders from higher up the chain of command. Tomas had been in the corps long enough to know *that* meant the higher-ups were running around in circles, trying desperately to pass the buck to someone who might have the nerve to take strong action and the willingness to take the blame if the shit hit the fan. Sweat trickled down his back, the heavy riot gear digging into his skin as the squad took up their positions. The sound of chanting—"jobs, jobs, jobs"—grew louder, until it felt as if the entire city had taken up the cry. It chilled him to the bone.

He glanced at his HUD, hoping and praying that *someone* had taken command. Star City was normally the most extensively-policed city on Earth. The Alphans wanted to make damn sure that crime and social deviation was kept as far from their capital as possible. There was almost no privacy in Star City, even in the bathroom! And yet, the mob had formed and swept down the streets without anyone having the slightest indication it was coming. Tomas checked his rifle, hoping desperately the protest wouldn't turn violent. He didn't want to kill people protesting their sudden unemployment.

His heart twisted as he saw a young girl, barely older than himself, amidst the protesters. A university student, suddenly aware her studies might be for naught? A former employee who'd been let go as businesses tightened their belts and cut down on surplus workers? Or a troublemaker who'd helped shape and lead the protest? It didn't matter. Tomas didn't want to hurt anyone. But he was starting to fear it was inevitable.

The city's authorities had been slow to react, when the unemployed and homeless had started to drift into their city. Star City had always had an excellent social safety net, with free food and drink handed out to all registered residents. But now, the influx of newcomers had strained the system to breaking point. They wanted to be fed, they wanted to be housed...they wanted the jobs and dignity the economic slowdown had stolen from them. Tomas cursed under his breath, knowing it was only a matter of time before despair turned to violence. The massive white skyscrapers, the giant towers that reached for the skies, were a slap in the face to someone forced to grub in the dirt. He'd heard the rumours. People were talking about open violence, if the government didn't give them what they wanted.

But the government can't give them what they want, he thought, numbly. *And all hell will break loose if they even try.*

He glanced back at his squad, trying to determine how they were bearing up. Sergeant Ross looked as firm and determined as ever, but the younger men seemed nervous. Tomas felt old, compared to them. They hadn't seen enough action during the war. And yet...Tomas *had* seen action and yet *he* was worried by the crowd. A mob of angry people could be more dangerous, in many ways, than enemy soldiers. The soldiers, at least, might follow the laws of war.

A squad of police flyers roared overhead. The crowd jeered and threw bottles. Tomas doubted the police gave a damn. They were safely out of range of anything less than an HVM or a smaller MANPAD. The cowards hadn't been seen on the streets since the assembly had—reluctantly—directed the marines to reinforce the police. Tomas hadn't been surprised to discover the police kept remembering urgent appointments elsewhere. They weren't trained to deal with a full-scale riot. Everyone had believed Star City was *safe*.

He led his men forward, breathing a sigh of relief when they reached the security barriers and marched into the Viceregal Complex. The Alphans had never bothered to give it a better name, something that nagged at his mind when he wasn't thinking about something more practical. The Viceroy's office sat within one of the giant towers, the Assembly—right next to it—trapped within the tower's shadow. Tomas wondered if that had been deliberate. He hadn't met many Alphans, but—as far as he could tell—*subtle* wasn't a word in their vocabulary. They were often refreshingly direct. They didn't delight in mindscrews for the sake of mindscrews.

"Lieutenant," Captain Hicks said. The sound of chanting grew louder. "Turn your squad over to your sergeant and report to Briefing Room A."

"Sir," Tomas said. Hicks was a stranger—Tomas's unit had been hastily redeployed when martial law had been declared—but he had a good combat record. "Is there any good news?"

Hicks snorted. "Optimism? You've not been in the corps for long, have you?"

Tomas laughed, saluted, and nodded to Sergeant Ross before heading for the briefing room. Ross practically ran the squad, when he wasn't running the company. He could handle the men long enough for Tomas to attend the briefing and return. Hopefully, it wouldn't be a waste of time. The briefing officers seemed to think they were the be-all and end-all of life, with whatever they considered important *actually* important. Tomas had been in the corps long enough to know they were often wrong. An officer who'd never seen the elephant was prone to making stupid mistakes.

Briefing Room A was surprisingly crowded. A dozen officers, some accompanied by sergeants, sat around a small podium. A holographic map of the city rotated in front of them, red icons marking homeless encampments, protest marches and other threats to law and order. Tomas had heard, through the whisper network, that the residents of Star City had been complaining non-stop since the unemployed and unemployable had started to crowd their streets. He'd seen the police datanet, the endless list of crimes against public order that would never be investigated, let alone solved. Homeless people sleeping on the streets, spitting in the streets, defecating in the streets...the residents seemed to have forgotten their common humanity. Law and order were gradually breaking down, no matter what the mayor and his councillors said. It was only a matter of time before something exploded.

He stood, with the rest of the officers, as General Willis strode into the room, followed by a tired-looking aide. The general was a short, aggressive sparkplug who'd made his name in several campaigns and holding actions during the war. Tomas wasn't sure Willis was the sort of man *he'd* want in command during a delicate peacekeeping operation, particularly one that could lead to severe violence right across known space, but no one had bothered to ask *his* opinion. Perhaps someone higher-up the chain had thought Willis's reputation would be enough to deter the protestors from starting a fight they could only lose. Or, now the war was over, perhaps Willis was the designated scapegoat if the matter couldn't be settled with a little compensation and fawning media coverage.

"Relax," Willis growled. He stood beside the podium, glaring at the map. "Smoke them if you've got them."

He waited a moment, then pressed on. "I'll keep this short and sour. We have specific orders from the assembly. We are to protect the Viceregal Complex, Spacetown and Human Heights. And, to be clear on this point, we are authorised to use whatever force we deem necessary, up to and including the use of lethal force. If any of the priority sectors are threatened, the gloves are to come off."

There was a long chilling pause. Tomas shivered. The sectors made sense—protesters attacking *any* of them would unleash one hell of a can of worms—but lethal force? It was a licence to kill. Or worse. And yet, what could they do? If Spacetown was stormed, with its alien population put to the sword, it would be a diplomatic disaster. The Alphans would be embarrassed—at best—in front of their fellow Galactics. And, at worst, it could lead to a whole new war.

"Intelligence reports that terrorist groups and sympathizers have been moving agitators into the city," Willis continued, coldly. "Our reports suggest their deployments include a sizable number of illicit weapons. We have been cautioned that these individuals intend to spark a riot, perhaps immediately after the Viceroy's speech to the Assembly tomorrow morning. Our operatives have located some of the agitators and we will be taking firm and vigorous steps to remove them before they can become a threat. Some of you will be deployed on missions to arrest them. Others, unfortunately, remain unidentified."

And if they're unidentified here, Tomas thought, *they might pass unnoticed until it is too late.*

"I understand that many of you have doubts about your role here," Willis concluded. "I appreciate you didn't sign up to play cops and robbers. But it is vitally important that we keep the city under control. The last thing we need, right now, is a diplomatic disaster."

Tomas nodded, shortly, as Willis stepped back to allow the ops officer to start handing out assignments. His squad was being assigned to a snatch-and-grab mission, something that bothered him. Marines *weren't* policemen. He'd practiced snatch-and-grab missions in the past, but always against terrorists or alien commanders. They'd never had to carry out such an operation in the middle of a friendly population. God knew the police should be able to handle it. They had the training and experience to do it without causing too big a scene.

If that's even possible today, he thought, as they were dismissed. *Too many people are spoiling for a fight.*

"Lieutenant," Captain Hicks said, when Tomas returned to the makeshift barracks. "You'll have a tagalong on your deployment."

"Sir," Tomas said, automatically. His mind caught up with him a second later. "A tagalong?"

"Yes," Captain Hicks said. He bent into the posture of mild respect. "Colonel?"

Tomas blinked in surprise as the Alphan emerged from the office. The Alphan...he bent into the posture of respect himself, cursing his delay under his breath. They were both hugely outranked by the Alphan. A single word from him would be enough to destroy their careers and put them out amongst the mob.

"I am Colonel Tallinn," the Alphan said. "You may rise."

Tomas straightened, trying desperately to look as if he'd heard of Colonel Tallinn. He hadn't. The whisper network shared all sorts of details on alien officers, from the brave who shared the hardships with their human subordinates to the cowardly and incompetent who stayed at the rear and issued orders from a safe distance. But he'd never heard of Colonel Tallinn. His uniform harness marked him as a liaison officer, but...he shook his head. It didn't matter *what* formal position the alien held. He was superior by virtue of being an Alphan.

"I've taken the liberty of ordering your squad to assemble at the landing pads," Hicks informed him. "Colonel Tallinn will ride along with you."

"Yes, sir," Tomas said. He kept his real opinion to himself. A tagalong wouldn't be helpful at the best of times. If something happened to Colonel Tallinn while he was under Tomas's care...Tomas might as well jump out of the shuttle and save everyone the trouble of a court-martial. "If you'll come with me, sir."

He surreptitiously studied the alien as they walked to the landing pad, where an assault shuttle was waiting. The Alphan looked calm and composed, but that was meaningless. He didn't have any combat pips on his harness, no hint he'd actually seen action...no hint of where and when he'd served, if indeed he'd served at all. The elite Alphan special forces were the equal of any human formation—Tomas conceded the point without rancour—but Colonel Tallinn simply didn't *feel* like an experienced officer. And Tomas couldn't even remind him that *Tomas* was in charge, during the operation. It was going to end badly. He knew it.

Sergeant Ross greeted them as they reached the shuttle. "Sir. We've had a mission download. The lads have been studying it."

"Good," Tomas said.

Colonel Tallinn paused. "You allow them to read their orders?"

"They have to know what they're doing, sir," Tomas said, trying to keep the dismay out of his voice. Colonel Tallinn was *definitely* not a special forces officer. "If something happens to me, sir, they'll have to complete the operation themselves."

He took a datapad as they stepped into the shuttle and took their places. The orders were relatively simple, although—in his experience—that generally meant trouble. He would have preferred to spend hours going over the mission, determining how best to carry it out and planning for as many contingencies as possible. And General Willis had signed off on the mission...it wasn't a good sign. The government had to be panicking.

And maybe we should be panicking too, he thought. The shuttle whined to life, the gravity field flickering and fading as the craft glided into the sky. *We'll be right on top of our target within seconds.*

"ETA, two minutes," the pilot called. "Ready to drop?"

Tomas glanced at Ross, who nodded. The squad was ready, taking hold of the ropes and preparing themselves to abseil to the rooftop below. Tomas wondered, grimly, if their target realised the shuttle was coming for him. There'd been hundreds of shuttles flying over the city in the last few weeks, but *their* shuttle had been flying dangerously low. It was the sort of thing that would get a pilot in real trouble in a warzone, if an enterprising enemy officer hadn't shot an HVM up his tailpipe first. But here...

"Ready," he said. He checked on Colonel Tallinn, who looked ready. "Open the hatches."

The hatches opened. Tomas didn't hesitate. He jumped through the hatch, rappelling to the rooftop as fast as he dared. Someone shouted, outside, as he hit the rooftop and slammed open the hatch. Four of his men threw stun grenades down the hole, then jumped into the room below as the blue light flickered and faded. Tomas barely had a second to realise that Colonel Tallinn hadn't followed him before he jumped himself. The alien hadn't left the shuttle.

Fuck, Tomas thought. *Why the...?*

He put the thought aside as they rampaged through the house. Two men grabbed for guns, only to be knocked to the ground and zip-tied before they could take aim and open fire. A trio of women sat in the next room, screaming loudly. Tomas shoved them to one side and hurried downstairs. If he was any judge, their target would already be heading for the door. It was his only hope. But, when he reached the ground floor, it was empty. There was no hint their target had ever been there.

"Shit." Tomas keyed his mouthpiece. The shouting outside was growing louder. It was only a matter of time until the mob started to break down the door. "Does anyone have eyes on our target?"

"No, sir," Ross said. "We have nine captives, including two children, but our target isn't here."

An intelligence fuck-up? Tomas cursed savagely as the squad searched the house thoroughly, checking for secret passages and compartments that hadn't been on the plans filed with the city administration. *Or did the bastard have time to get off his ass and run before we smashed our way into the home?*

He put the thought aside. There was no time for recriminations. "Get the prisoners to the shuttle," he ordered. There *had* been illegal weapons in the house, if nothing else. "And then scatter some bugs around as we pull out."

"Yes, sir," Ross said. The sergeant would have made his disagreement known, if he had disagreed. "You'd better get back to the shuttle."

Tomas nodded, looking around as he made his way back to the rooftop. The prisoners were making one hell of a fuss as they were hoisted through the hatch and into the shuttle. Their home was surprisingly nice, although smaller than he would have expected. Housing was expensive in Star City, he reminded himself. He couldn't have bought an apartment within the city limits on *his* salary. Even the rent would be enough to break him.

He kept his expression under tight control as he clambered back into the shuttle. Colonel Tallinn was sitting by the hatch, his face unreadable. Tomas hesitated, unsure what to say. The alien should have followed him out...

"I thought I shouldn't get in the way," Colonel Tallinn said. "I thought I..."

You mean you panicked, Tomas thought, coldly. He would have understood if the officer had stayed back, if he'd made it clear he *intended* to stay back. Hell, a smart officer *would* have stayed back. But Colonel Tallinn had gone right to the hatch before turning back. *And you expect me to cover for you.*

He sighed, inwardly, as the shuttle headed back home. The mission had been a tactical success, but—practically speaking—a failure. They'd missed their target. They'd shown they were willing to harass activists... worst of all, they'd learnt Colonel Tallinn was a coward who didn't even have the sense to hang back. Tomas wasn't given to reflection, but he had the feeling it boded ill for the future.

I'll have to discuss it with Hicks, he thought, wishing he knew the senior officer better. Was he an officer who could be relied upon? Or was he someone who would throw a subordinate under the shuttlecraft? The corps was normally good about learning from mistakes, rather than looking for scapegoats, but times were far from normal. *And hope this piece of bad luck doesn't get any worse.*

CHAPTER FIVE

Star City, Earth

IT WAS CLEAR TO ANYONE WHO LOOKED with an unbiased eye, Viceroy Yasuke had often thought, that it was a *human* who had designed the Assembly Chamber. The building seemed designed to strip the honour and dignity from those who entered her doors, even from the elected representatives and their appointed lords and masters. There was no elegance to the seating arrangements, merely a combination of comfortable benches and seats organised to showcase which of the major political parties controlled which seats. Yasuke had never worked out why they bothered. It was almost pitifully easy to calculate which party held the majority, which party was in the minority and which—if there was a third party—held the balance of power.

And they might have to redesign the entire building if there's a viceroy after me, Yasuke thought, as he strode through the chamber. The humans struck and held the posture of respect, but he knew many of them didn't mean it. *That worthy might insist on a building and social formalities that truly matched his status.*

He kept the amusement off his face as he reached his chair and sat, allowing his eyes to sweep the room. First Speaker Nancy Middleton,

Empire Loyalists, sat on the other side of the chamber, facing him. He'd never found it easy to read human facial expressions, but he rather thought she was nervous. Rumours had been spreading everywhere since his return to Earth. In the middle, he had no trouble picking Speaker Abraham Douglas out of the crowd. The man might rail against the Alphans and their sense of formality, even of social theatre, but he wore clothes that would have been outdated years before Earth had been dragged into the Alphan Empire. In his own way, the man was just as impressed by formality as his alien masters. He just chose to focus on a different kind of protocol.

And he's already looking for ways to turn the crisis to his advantage, Yasuke reminded himself. The human was ambitious—and there were limits to how far he could go, under normal circumstances. It was a kind of ambition that was thoroughly alien to Yasuke's people. *They* saw no need to upend centuries of established protocol for their own personal power. *He's been working hard to convert the independents and undecided factions to his cause.*

Yasuke sighed inwardly as the First Speaker stood and launched into a complicated speech of welcome. The Empire Loyalists were loyal—their positions depended on loyalty—but they knew as well as everyone else that they had to get *some* concessions from their alien masters or risk alienating their voters. Too many promises had been made, when the border was crumbling and enemy hordes were pressing into star systems that had never known an invader, for everyone to pretend it was business as usual. Yasuke knew Nancy Middleton had made a number of attempts to seek a private audience, well before he addressed the assemblymen as a group. He had a nasty feeling he knew what she wanted to say. And, by declining, he'd probably weakened her position.

He nodded in acknowledgement when the speech finally came to an end, ruefully admitting that his detractors back home had a point. He'd become *too* human. A speech that lasted a *mere* thirty minutes felt as if it were dragging on forever. No purely *human* government would tolerate a speaker who waffled on for hours, he was sure. Their limited attention span would make sure of it. The humans would look at anyone who bored them and decide he wasn't worthy of their time. Yasuke admired it, in a way. They had a directness about them that his own people had left behind long ago.

"And we take pride in inviting you to speak before us," Nancy said. "We are honoured by your presence."

And that may not be remotely true, Yasuke thought, as he stood. He wasn't blind to the Viceroyalty's flaws. *While I was away, you got to play.*

He composed himself as the chamber quietened down. His mouth felt oddly dry. He'd spent weeks arguing with his superiors, and their bureaucratic servants, in a desperate bid to convince them to grant concessions before it was too late. They hadn't understood, not really. Even after the war, even after a seemingly-endless chain of disasters, they hadn't understood. Time was no longer on their side. Earth had to be placated or abandoned. And they weren't *quite* ready to let the planet go.

"Over the past centuries, we have brought you into the mainstream of galactic society," he said. "We have uplifted your technology to mainstream standards. We have tutored you in behaviour conventions that mark you as civilised beings. And we have integrated you into a galaxy-spanning trading network that reaches well beyond the limits of our Empire. We have raised you up and you have made us proud. The sacrifices you made for us, during the war, have proved that you are worthy, that you are ready to move to the next stage."

He paused, feeling hundreds of eyes watching him. The humans were probably live-streaming the speech, even though it was technically forbidden. The days when a speech could be modified before being uploaded to the datanet were long gone. It made him feel oddly vulnerable. Mistakes could no longer be fixed before they went around the planet at the speed of light. And something that proved harmful could no longer be simply erased and denied.

"We have promised you much, in return for your services," he continued. "Today, we will start the process of granting you limited—local—autonomy.

Over the next twenty years, we will transfer more and more powers to the assembly until you have the status of one of *our* planetary assemblies. Certain matters will remain reserved to Capital, of course, but the remainder will be yours. We have faith, now, that you can handle it.

"We appreciate that some of you would like us to move quicker. We realise that some of you expected an immediate transfer of powers. But it is our belief that a rapid transfer would cause violent instability, would unleash forces that neither you nor we would be able to control. Your planet was divided, hopelessly divided, when we arrived. You seemed almost to be *regressing* from a path towards planetary unity. Do you really wish those days to return?"

He let the words hang in the air as he tried to gauge their reactions. There wasn't a single living human who recalled the days when they'd thought they were alone in the universe. There wasn't a soul who remembered what the planet had been like, hundreds of years ago. They'd grown up, for better or worse, on an alien-dominated world. They would see the advantages of independence without the downsides. Humans had been killing themselves over everything from resource allocation to religious ideology. They'd *needed* a paternalistic race to teach them a lesson before they blew themselves back to the Stone Age.

But it is in their nature to rebel against their parents, he thought, grimly. Human children became rebellious, difficult to control, as they grew up. *Sooner or later, they will rebel against us.*

He felt a twinge of sympathy for the first Viceroy. He'd known that humanity *needed* a firm hand, to guide and punish a race that simply couldn't look to the future. But the humans had rebelled against his guidance, even when they admitted it was for their own good. Humans saw paternalism as condescension. And they argued their alien masters exploited the human race as much as they taught it. Yasuke had to admit they had a point. The Alphan Empire had benefited hugely from human servitude. There wouldn't be millions of humans scattered across hundreds of densely-populated worlds if humans hadn't proven themselves so useful.

"We will be detailing how the process is to begin over the next few days," he concluded, keeping his voice calm. "We will be working with you to outline the process for transferring powers, then steadily withdrawing ourselves until you can stand on your own two feet. We ask for your patience, as we dismantle a structure that has been in existence for hundreds of years. And we ask you to remember that we have brought many great things to your homeworld. Do not be so quick to throw them away."

...

Speaker Abraham Douglas kept his face under tight control as the alien Viceroy brought his speech to an end. He'd hoped for more. He'd hoped... he hadn't been fool enough to think the Alphans would simply grant humanity independence and withdraw at once, but he'd hoped they'd realise that Earth was steadily turning into a pressure cooker. It was only a matter of time until something exploded and all hell broke loose.

He ignored the muttering from his fellows as the First Speaker rose to thank the Viceroy in a manner that would have embarrassed any merely *human* despot. The Alphans seemed to *like* being praised, even if they *had* to know little came from the heart. And yet...Abraham schooled his face into immobility as Nancy yammered on and on. The Empire Loyalist leadership might remain loyal, after the speech was uploaded to the datanet, but Abraham wouldn't bet on the rank-and-file going the same way. They expected some kind of reward for their service. A slow transfer of power? Twenty years to wait for local autonomy? It wasn't good enough.

And they can tie matters up in committee until we forget what we're arguing about, he thought, tartly. The pre-invasion humans had complained about government bureaucracy, according to the files. They hadn't known how lucky they'd been. *They might stall long enough to take back everything they promised when things quieten down a bit.*

He gritted his teeth, knowing he had to take a stand. There were rumours upon rumours of Direct Action—and a hundred other factions he wasn't sure even *existed*—readying themselves to cause real trouble.

He'd seen security reports cautioning assemblymen to remain inside the complex, rather than go on the streets...frightening, given that Star City was supposed to be the safest place on Earth. There were troops patrolling the streets, heavily-armed flyers orbiting the complex...he shook his head. It was hard to tell if the threats were real, but it didn't matter. What mattered was ensuring he made a stand before someone pushed him aside.

And keeping Direct Action from doing something that will spark a massive crackdown, he thought, as he pressed the buzzer for attention. *We cannot afford an uprising now.*

"The Assembly recognises the Minority Leader," Nancy said.

Abraham stood, adjusting his wig and brushing down his suit. "Honoured Viceroy, I thank you for your statement," he said, calmly. It was as much flattery as he could bring himself to offer. "We appreciate that your proposal is, by the standards of your people, remarkable and even revolutionary. We realise that it must have cost your government a great deal to concede it was even necessary. But we feel it does not go far enough.

"Earth is no longer the deeply divided world you discovered, hundreds of years ago. Humanity itself is no longer the scattered, warring race you encountered, tamed and brought into your Empire. We have grown and developed, embracing both your technology and your social concepts. You have given us much and we thank you for it. But we believe the debt has been paid in full. We have worked for you. We have *fought* for you.

"Without us, even your military concedes you would have lost the war. Without us, your Empire would have been broken by a foe who outnumbered you fifty to one. Without us, your entire system would have shattered even if your core worlds escaped occupation or isolation. Without us—yes, without us—you would have lost. Your history, the history you claim stretches back millions of years, would have come to a sudden and very final end.

"We do not hate you. We appreciate what you have done for us. But it is time for us to be free. Let us go now, as your friends and allies and trading partners, and stand upon the galactic stage as equals. Let us carve our own destiny amongst the stars. Let us be your friends, not your servants or your slaves."

He tried to keep the pleading out of his voice, but he feared he'd failed. "You made us promises, when you thought you were losing the war," he said. "All we ask is that you keep those promises."

Before all hell breaks loose, he added, silently. He knew he should be pointing out the risks of trying to suppress the human race, but he couldn't say that publicly. The Alphans couldn't be seen to bend to pressure or threats. Better to discuss the downsides of broken promises later, in private. *They have to know they're sitting on a powder keg.*

He bowed to the Viceroy, hoping the inscrutable alien would listen to him, then sat as a dozen other assemblymen buzzed for attention. Nancy, looking thoroughly displeased, was careful to make sure the Empire Loyalists spoke first. Abraham would have been amused, if they'd been debating something of little import. It didn't seem to have occurred to her that showing partiality would be used against her, during the next election cycle. Abraham made a note of it on his datapad, ensuring the recordings were collected and saved before someone a little smarter than the First Speaker made them disappear. They'd play well to the gallery. Nancy would have to explain herself to her own constituents, as well as the rest of the world.

Assuming there is a next election cycle, he thought, morbidly. *There might be a crackdown well before then.*

He kept his face impassive as assemblyman after assemblyman denounced his politics, his career and—for all he knew—his face. He stopped listening after it became clear the Empire Loyalists were caterwauling off the same song sheet. Nancy had probably gleaned *some* hint of what the Viceroy had intended to say, perhaps from the Viceroy himself. The aliens had had centuries of experience in political manipulation. They'd probably done everything in their power to smooth the speech as much as possible.

We'll have to register a protest now, then go swinging into the election cycle, he told himself, as his supporters were finally allowed to speak. The

Empire Loyalists held the majority, barely. If he could change that, if he could displace Nancy before all hell broke loose, he could make a formal demand for independence. Or at least autonomy. *We cannot look like collaborators, not now.*

He sighed, inwardly. It would have been easier, in many ways, if the Empire Loyalists had been *true* collaborators. It would have been easy to paint them as the blackest of villains, to wage a merciless war against all who served Earth's alien masters...it would have been easy, but it wouldn't have been true. The Alphans had been part of the system for so long that they were just...*normal*. One might as well wage war against males or females or people who wore alien-derived fashions. It would have been stupid.

"I will not mince words," Speaker Philip Mayberry said. "Earth deserves independence. Earth deserves—Earth *demands*—to be free."

Abraham groaned as the chamber dissolved into shouting. It was going to be a long day.

...

Yasuke wondered, not for the first time, if he'd made a mistake. It was never easy to follow the ebb and flow of human politics, not when a strong and determined individual could shape the debate and lead the remainder of humanity in a dangerous—or simply unwise—direction. There were times when he thought the debates should be conducted by text, stripping primitive emotion out of the equation and allowing pure logic and reason to flourish. But he knew the humans would never go for it. They'd suspect that whoever controlled the datanet would control the debate.

He said nothing, watching as the human loyalists and loyal opposition—a term the humans had gifted his people—argued savagely. The First Speaker was doing her best, but it was clear her party was deeply divided. Yasuke cursed his superiors angrily for not allowing him to move faster. They'd managed to worry their allies while angering their enemies. And... he conceded, privately, that they hadn't satisfied anyone. The humans who didn't want things to change were going to be disappointed, as were the humans who wanted immediate independence. He stared down at his datapad as a new set of reports blipped up in front of him. The crowds on the streets were getting larger. And angrier.

And they're far too close to Spacetown, he thought, grimly. Spacetown was hardly the only alien settlement on Earth, but it played host to ambassadors, counsels, reporters and influencers. He'd wanted to close the embassies, just to keep outsiders from fishing in troubled waters, but his superiors had overruled him. *Whatever happens here will be broadcast across the galaxy before we can put a lid on it.*

He forced himself to relax. Alphans understood patience. If nothing else, they could wait for the shouting to die down and then start negotiations with the grown-ups. Hopefully, they could get the transfer of power agreements sorted out before everyone involved—himself included—died of old age. If they lasted so long…he'd have to make it clear, to the bureaucrats, that there was no time for delay. Their stalling tactics couldn't be tolerated. The humans would see them for what they were.

Yasuke shivered. He had a nasty feeling time was no longer on his side.

CHAPTER SIX

Earth Defence Force One, Earth Orbit

IT SEEMED TO BE AN INEVITABLE CONSEQUENCE of the end of hostilities, Captain Thomas Anderson had often thought, that the bureaucrats and pen-pushers and other oxygen thieves came back into power as soon as the actual *fighting* came to an end. He wasn't fool enough to believe everything would be rosy if all the bureaucrats were put against the bulkhead and shot—after being allowed to spend their last moments writing memos deploring the waste of bullets when there was a perfectly good airlock only a few short metres away—but there were limits. Each successive layer of bureaucracy not only made it harder for officers to get things done in time, but also increased contempt and hatred for bureaucrats among the rank and file. And that weakened the military.

He breathed a sigh of relief as he was *finally* shown into Admiral Adam Glass's office. His original orders had made it clear that he was expected to report to the admiral as soon as he returned to Sol, but the bureaucrats hadn't got the memo. They'd made him cool his heels in orbit for two days before they'd allowed him to complete his mission. He'd filed a formal complaint, but he doubted anyone would care. Earth, if the newscasts were accurate, had too many other problems. Privately, Thomas was tempted to just reverse course and head into unexplored space.

"Captain," Admiral Glass said. "Welcome home."

Thomas nodded, studying the older man grimly. Admiral Glass had always been short, but he seemed to have aged a decade in the months since their last meeting. His face was lined, his hair had steadily lightened until it was white; Thomas rather suspected the old man had lost weight. It couldn't be easy, directing the EDF as it grew from a system patrol force into a regular—and formidable—navy. Thomas saluted, then took the proffered chair as Commander Evensong stepped into the office. *She* hadn't changed. Her tinted skin, almond eyes and treacle-coloured hair turned heads wherever she went.

"Commander," he said. "Good to see you again."

"And you," Evensong said. If she had another name, she'd never shared it. "I hear you had an adventure."

"Adventure is someone else in deep shit far away," Thomas said. He was no coward, and he was happy to accept risk in the line of duty, but there were limits. His kids didn't deserve to be blown away because their father was an intelligence officer. "I take it you read my download?"

Admiral Glass cleared his throat. "We're interested in your impressions," he said. "If you please..."

"Yes, sir." Thomas took a moment to gather his thoughts. "We passed through Riker-23 on our way to Gammon. There was no suggestion that *anything* had changed within the system. We didn't even have a *hint* of trouble until we entered Gammon itself, whereupon the Vulteks tried to run us down. Thankfully, a warcruiser showed up before it was too late."

"Thankfully," Glass agreed. "The Alphans have resumed patrols of the neutral zone between their Empire and the other interstellar powers."

"The warcruiser was able to determine that the Vulteks hadn't laid political claim to the system," Thomas explained. "However, they *did* land a sizable force of colonists...heavily-armed colonists. Given the lack of a planetary government, it's quite likely they'll take control of the surface—directly or indirectly—within the next few years. I think it's just a matter of time before they take formal control of the system itself."

Evensong raised her eyebrows. "With a warcruiser on patrol?"

"The warcruiser is only a threat if her master chooses to intervene," Thomas pointed out, coolly. "And if she has orders *not* to start a shooting match that could easily become a war, she'll leave plenty of room for enemy misbehaviour. The Vulteks might win the planet and system by default."

"Which is worrying for us," Glass mused. "Do you think they intend to test our defences?"

"Yes, sir," Thomas said, flatly. "We passed through Delaine and a couple of other systems on the way home. There's nothing on the open datanets, naturally, but the covert grapevine warned of alien ships being seen probing the border. I think—no one was able to confirm it—that the reports were the only reason the warcruiser was there. A couple of sightings of what *could* be unfriendly ships in our systems…"

"It would be worrying," Glass agreed.

"Yes, sir," Thomas said. "There were also reports of more traders passing through the system, traders who seemed more interested in looking around than actually *trading*. I think they're considering something a little more severe than merely *testing* our defences."

"They'd be going to war with the Alphan Empire," Evensong pointed out. "And we're not exactly *weak* either."

Glass narrowed his eyes. "Captain?"

"Admiral, over the last five years, I've only seen *one* warcruiser patrolling the borders," Thomas said. "And that was the ship that saved our asses three weeks ago. There aren't many other ships on duty, beyond a handful of converted freighters and a lone—heavily outdated—warship. The planetary defences are weak, unable to keep an enemy fleet from securing the high orbitals and bombarding the colonies into submission. If I was in charge of the enemy fleet, sir, I'd be thinking about a smash and grab operation too."

"Except you'd start a war with the Alphans," Evensong reminded him.

"The Alphans took a beating in the *last* war," Thomas countered. "They've lost, once and for all, the aura of invincibility that kept their Empire together. They still have a powerful fleet, Commander, but everyone knows how to beat it. Frankly, given how many interstellar powers resent their predominance, I'd be surprised if some of them weren't getting together and plotting how to make sure the Alphans stay down."

"It's easy to come up with plans," Evensong said. "Carrying them out…"

"The Vulteks are an aggressive race with powerful patrons," Thomas said, flatly. "If they bite off the border worlds, there's a better than even chance the Alphans will allow it to slide."

"They wouldn't," Evensong said.

Thomas cocked his head. "How much are those worlds worth, economically?"

He went on before she could answer. "I did the math, during the voyage home. The entire sector isn't worth *that* much, not now. Delaine is the most important world in the sector, at least to us, but…she isn't worth a war. The Alphans might decide there's no point in expending countless lives and starships recovering a sector they consider to be valueless. And it is, to them. I think we have to prepare for trouble."

"But they'd look weak, if they let it slide," Evensong insisted.

"Their population doesn't want another war," Glass said, quietly. "They might resist any suggestion they fought for the border stars. Their homeworlds won't be threatened."

"But Earth will be," Thomas said. "If they take Delaine, they'll be within two weeks of Earth. And there are enough threadlines through multispace to make it very difficult to stop them short of Earth itself. We'd never be able to mine the entire region extensively enough to keep them from breaking through."

"We might be able to stop them at Santa Maria," Glass said. "The crossroads is quite small, relatively speaking. It was earmarked for a fallback position, but we didn't have the budget to turn it into a fortified system."

"We might need to find the money, somewhere," Thomas said. "Sir..."

Glass laughed, humourlessly. "Have you seen the reports from Earth?"

"Yes, sir," Thomas said.

"Right now, the Assembly is struggling to find the money to do anything," Glass said. "The Alphans have the same problem, so we can't look to them. I have a nasty feeling they'll be demanding cuts, not budget increases, in the next few months."

Thomas rubbed his eyes. "Sir, with all due respect, that will not go down well along the border."

"I know." Glass looked tired. "But, right now, we have too many other problems."

He leaned back in his chair. "I'll want you back out there as soon as possible," he continued, after a moment. "Take a few days to visit Luna, if you like, then head off again. I'll see to it you get priority for everything you need."

"I may need to offload my children," Thomas said. "Or transfer them to other ships."

"I can't guarantee their safety anywhere," Glass said. "The asteroids should be safe enough, unless the shit really *does* hit the fan."

"My parents might take them," Thomas said. "I know my oldest son is an adult, but I don't believe it."

"No one ever does," Glass said. "Our kids are our kids, even if they have kids of their own."

"Yes, sir." Thomas stood. "I'll discuss it with my wife, then let you know when we'll be ready to depart."

"I'll forward you an intelligence briefing," Evensong said. "But it might be a little out of date."

Thomas nodded. The intelligence briefing would be days or weeks out of date. There was no solid communications network along the border, forcing starships to serve as couriers or try to ping messages through multispace. The shipping guilds had been begging for a dedicated relay network for decades, but nothing had ever been done. Evensong, thankfully, was smart enough to realise that she couldn't steer events from hundreds of light years away. The Alphans had run into problems, during the early stages of the war, because they'd thought they *could*.

He saluted the admiral, then turned and walked out of the office. A pair of mid-ranking officers glanced at him in surprise, no doubt wondering why a mere captain—a civilian captain—had been prioritised over them. Thomas wanted to sneer. Their uniforms were a little too neat—and lacking in campaign pips. REMFs, basically. The EDF tried hard to rotate officers between combat assignments and desk posts, but there were limits. He hoped Admiral Glass would ensure they didn't reach the very *highest* levels. A man who didn't know what he was doing—and was too ignorant to know it—would be very dangerous if he climbed into the wrong post.

And Sarah isn't going to be happy, he thought. His wife was going to explode like a damaged antimatter containment chamber. *She'll say I'm putting the family at risk.*

His thoughts darkened as he headed down to the shuttlebay. *And she'll be right.*

• • •

Admiral Adam Glass knew, without false modesty, that he'd climbed to the top through a combination of sheer tactical brilliance, an instinctive understanding of how to manipulate the bureaucracy for his own advantage and a certain awareness of where some of the bodies were buried. He'd been ambitious as a young man, joining the EDF as soon as he reached the age of majority and scrambling up the ladder with a haste some of his alien superiors found unseemly. He liked to think he'd mellowed, as he commanded starships and task forces and even an entire *fleet* before he'd finally been shunted to a desk job. His ambitions were no longer *personal*. He wanted—he needed—to see the EDF become the front-line fleet it could be.

It wasn't an easy job. The Alphans had never envisaged the EDF as anything more than a minor system-defence formation. They'd been surprised when the EDF had mushroomed into something more, purchasing outdated starships and turning them into everything from training vessels to first-grade warships. Adam had feared a crackdown, before the war had exploded into open violence. The EDF had continued to expand, but at a cost. His plans for steady expansion had been thrown out the airlock. Instead, the fleet was effectively tottering under its own weight.

He was no fool. He'd served in junior posts before climbing to command and flag rank. He *knew* the EDF was running hot. He'd read the reports from Internal Security. The officers were grumbling, the crewmen were discontented and the messes were in open rebellion. And the embedded alien officers were making matters worse. The pre-war embeds had known what they were doing—or, at least, they'd been willing to learn. The post-war embeds could have given the rest of their species lessons in arrogance, bloody-mindedness and general idiocy.

And that would be funny, under other circumstances, Adam thought. He felt his bones ache as he keyed his terminal, bringing up the latest reports. Something was going to break, sooner or later. The news from Earth hadn't helped. Internal Security hadn't managed to track down whoever was distributing humanist literature all over the fleet. *Right now, those idiots are just pouring fuel on the fire.*

He leaned back and brought up the planetary display. Earth was surrounded by starships, orbital battlestations and asteroids that had been mined for raw materials, then converted into industrial nodes or orbiting habitats. It was an impressive sight, although he'd seen bigger and better orbital halos deeper within the Empire. Capital itself was so heavily surrounded by orbital stations that it was a wonder the sunlight ever reached the planetary surface. The Alphans had even talked about building a Dyson Sphere, but—as far as he knew—the plan had never gotten off the ground. They simply hadn't been able to dismantle an entire star system for raw materials.

His gaze sharpened as he focused the display on a cluster of green icons. Seven warcruisers, holding position in high orbit. Officially, they were protecting the planet; unofficially, they were a reminder that Earth was still part of the Alphan Empire. Adam had heard rumours that the Alphans had drawn up contingency plans to put down a human mutiny, although it would cost them dearly. The EDF could take the warcruisers, if they opened fire at random. It would be a costly victory, but...

Adam shook his head. *We might win the battle, but never the war.*

He clicked off the display in a moment of irritation. He didn't *hate* the Alphans. He'd outgrown the lingering resentment years ago. The Alphans were a fact of life. One might as well hate one's own parents. There was nothing to be gained by agonising over an invasion that had taken place so long ago it was ancient history. But it was infuriating to be reminded, constantly, that humanity was a *young* race, to be seen—at best—as children who could be smacked and sent to bed without supper. That had been true, once. Now, humanity was catching up fast. Adam wasn't blind to the steady advancement of human understanding. The EDF's researchers believed it was just a matter of time before they matched and superseded their masters.

And what do we do, he asked himself, *if they try to stop us?*

He stood, pacing the compartment. He was loyal. He'd taken the oath, seventy-two years ago, and he'd meant every word of it. And yet, where did his loyalties lie if things flew right out of control? Or if the Alphans chose to abandon human settlers to their fate? Captain Anderson might be right. The Vulteks might be planning to test the waters. And Adam had met enough bullies to know the only thing that would stop them was a punch in the nose.

The news from Earth wasn't good. Adam welcomed the promise of a slow transfer of powers, if only because he knew enough history—human history—to accept that an immediate transfer would be disastrous. But twenty *years*? Adam suspected he wasn't going to live long enough to see it. The genetic modifications spliced into his genes might keep him going another ten, if he was lucky, but twenty? He shook his head. He didn't blame the crowds on the street for being angry. Twenty years was absurdly long, by human standards. The Alphans should have realised they'd only make matters worse…

His intercom bleeped. "Admiral," Ensign Corey said. "Speaker Douglas has sent a message, requesting a meeting. He's citing assembly privilege."

"Brilliant," Adam muttered. He didn't *like* Speaker Douglas. The man flirted with radicalism. Either he was playing a double game or he simply couldn't keep his own people under control. "Did he say why?"

"No, sir," Corey said. The ensign sounded worried, as if he expected his head bitten off at any moment. "The message merely requests a meeting at your earliest convenience."

And I can't stall for long, Adam thought, coldly. Douglas had citied assembly privilege. He couldn't be denied unless there was a real emergency. *And I think I know what he wants to discuss.*

"Tell him that I should be free to speak to him tomorrow morning, barring accidents," he ordered, finally. A few hours…he couldn't stall more than a few hours. It would be long enough to consider the problem carefully. "Give him one of the reserved spots on my calendar. And clear him for travel to the station."

"Aye, sir," Corey said. "Do you want me to send him a shuttle?"

"We had better," Adam said, after a moment. He was tempted to refuse, to insist that the Speaker found his own shuttle, but it would be petty and stupid. Besides, it would be safer to use a military shuttle. Who knew who might try to compromise a civilian craft? "Yes, see to it."

"Yes, sir," Corey said.

Adam returned to his chair and sat. He had a feeling he knew what Douglas wanted to talk about and…he didn't want to talk about it. Where did his loyalties lie? Where did the *EDF's* loyalties lie? And what would they do if—when—the shit hit the fan?

Shatter, his thoughts mocked him. Too many factions, pulling in too many different directions…the entire edifice could come crumbling down. *And that will be the end.*

CHAPTER SEVEN

Star City, Earth

"YOU KNOW," SOMEONE MUTTERED from the rear, "I was always told the streets of Star City were paved with gold."

Marine Lieutenant Tomas Drache did his best to ignore the speaker as the marines marched down the road. A year ago, the district had been charming—in a distinctly urban sort of way—and reserved solely for government workers and their families. They'd had gardens, schools, a park and even a private swimming pool. Now, the families were gone, their gardens and the park had been turned into tent cities, the swimming pool had been drained dry and the school had become an emergency aid centre. Thousands of sullen eyes watched the marines as they kept moving, never stopping in one place. There were enough reports of squads being harassed—or openly attacked—for Tomas to insist they kept moving.

Sweat trickled down his back as he glanced at Colonel Tallinn. The Alphan had insisted on staying with the squad, even after the Viceroy had thrown oil on the fire by promising humanity autonomy in twenty years. Tomas had tried to complain to his superiors, to ask them to suggest the Alphan went elsewhere, but he'd been told to shut up and soldier. The Alphan was sticking with the squad and that was that. He gritted his teeth as the alien looked back at him, holding his rifle in a dangerous pose. Tomas couldn't decide if the Alphan was trying to look good or if he was just an idiot. *Real* soldiers knew to keep their fingers off their triggers unless they intended to open fire.

God help us, he thought, as they rounded the corner and marched past a soup kitchen. The householders had been screaming blue murder about the homeless—they'd called it an invasion—and demanding that someone do something about the poor bastards. *What the fuck can we do?*

The sense of unease grew stronger the longer they walked The squad had raided three more houses—and he'd heard, through the grapevine, that over thirty *other* houses had also been hit—but they'd found nothing. The agitators seemed to have managed to cover their tracks perfectly, somehow. It shouldn't have been possible. Tomas had heard rumours that Internal Security had been losing control of the surveillance systems, or that they'd been destroyed, or even simply compromised. It sounded quite plausible. There was no way someone could remain undetected for a week, not without tripping a sensor *somewhere*. But if the system had been compromised, or the agency itself, they might be able to remain off the grid indefinitely.

A series of angry shouts echoed through the air. Tomas braced himself, but the shouter vanished back into the crowd without further ado. The street closed ranks around him. Tomas was tempted to give chase, to give the idiot a proper thrashing, but he knew it would only make matters worse. The crowd was already angry. It could turn on the marines in a second, if it felt provoked beyond reason. And yet, doing nothing would only make things worse too.

"We should go after him," Colonel Tallinn said, sharply. "Lieutenant..."

"The Viceroy ordered us not to make matters worse," Tomas said. It was a...*creative*...interpretation of the Viceroy's orders, passed down through the chain of command, but a fairly safe one. The colonel might argue with *him*, a mere lieutenant; he wouldn't risk getting into a pissing contest with his ultimate boss. "We'll catch him later."

He did his best to ignore the alien's angry muttering as they picked up speed, heading out of the estate and back towards the government complex. The feeder roads in and out of the city had been cleared, thankfully, but the side-streets were crammed with angry people, some carrying makeshift weapons. Tomas eyed a large man carrying a baseball bat, wondering if he'd try to crack it against a marine's helmet. A baseball bat was a serious threat in the wrong hands. The government might have ordered a full ban on weapons, but there was no way they could round up all the baseball bats. Or a lot of *other* things that could be used as makeshift weapons. Tomas hoped no former marines had joined the crowd. *They'd* know how to make weapons from all sorts of common household junk.

And they might, he thought. Rumour insisted the emergency recall of military personnel hadn't been heeded by *everyone*. There were hundreds of names missing from the rolls. Or so he'd been told. Marines generally retired to colony worlds, where their skills were in high demand. *It would just take one or two former bootnecks to make the homeless a lot more dangerous.*

His earpiece bleeped. "Discontinue your patrol route and report to the Street of the Endless," Hicks ordered. "I say again, abandon your patrol route and report to the Street of the Endless."

"Yes, sir," Tomas said, automatically. "We're on our way."

He nodded to Sergeant Ross, then checked his HUD. The live feed from the orbiting drones showed a huge crowd gathering near the Street of the Endless, despite strict orders to remain indoors and a growing military presence. He hastily plotted a route, then marched down the street. His men followed. The route was a little longer than it should be, but it would keep them out of the jam-packed streets. He could hear the crowd shouting, baying for blood, as they reached the CP. Hundreds of marines were already setting up barriers to keep the crowd from getting too close to Spacetown.

"There are hundreds of ambassadors in there," Colonel Tallinn said, as they reported to Hicks. "The crowd will kill them."

Tomas blinked in surprise. It was, as far as he knew, the first piece of tactical acumen Colonel Tallinn had shown. But then, Spacetown *was* obviously not a human settlement. He hoped the aliens were smart enough to remain indoors, if they hadn't already been evacuated. Xenophobia was rare on Earth, after hundreds of years of interaction with alien races, but it wasn't gone. The crisis had brought out the worst in people.

"The crowd is to be steered down the freeway, away from the alien residences," Hicks said, quietly. "They are *not* to be allowed past the barriers."

"Yes, sir." Tomas felt a lump in his chest. The alien ambassadors *had* to be protected, or Earth would find itself in the centre of a galactic storm. "We need tangle fields as well as barriers."

"They're on the way," Hicks said. "Take your place and wait."

"Aye, sir."

Tomas cast an eye down the Street of the Endless as the shouting grew louder. It was a outsized road, lined with towering statues of humans and aliens who'd served the Empire in some fashion. The Humanity League had insisted on including a statue of Captain Khan, the lone submarine commander who'd launched a successful nuclear strike during the invasion and taken out an alien base. Tomas had often wondered if the statue had been included in hopes of keeping the League under control or a droll reminder that Khan hadn't actually stopped the invasion. In hindsight, it had been clear Khan hadn't even known there *was* an invasion. He'd thought his country was fighting a conventional war against its historic foe.

"They don't get past us," Colonel Tallinn said. The Alphan sounded nervous. It was hard to be sure, but…he definitely sounded nervous. His finger rested on his trigger. "They don't get past us."

"You could go back to HQ," Tomas said, quietly. "Sir…"

"I have to be here," Colonel Tallinn snapped. "Stand your ground!"

Tomas swore under his breath as the protestors came into view. They looked angry, waving signs that had probably come off some underground printer…printing shops were banned within the city, but there was no shortage of them outside the border. A number were openly carrying makeshift weapons, including a sizable number of baseball bats. Tomas wondered, suddenly, if someone had purchased every bat in the city. It wouldn't be hard to order hundreds of bats. Hell, even Internal Security's famously paranoid filters wouldn't normally flag them up as articles of concern.

The shouting grew louder as the crowd approached. Tomas checked his rifle, then glanced back to see if they had an escape route. It would be difficult...he feared they'd crash into each other if they tried to fall back. A handful of flyers roared overhead, the crowd hooting and howling curses at them. Tomas was tempted to curse them too. The flyboys weren't the ones on the front lines, bracing themselves to stand off an angry crowd. They were just agitating the crowd for no good reason.

Hicks took the loudspeaker. "TURN DOWN THE FREEWAY," he bellowed. His amplified voice was so loud Tomas thought he was going to crack windows and shatter the riot barriers. "TURN DOWN THE FREEWAY AND WALK AWAY!"

The crowd kept coming. Tomas shuddered, catching sight of a handful of protesters who'd suddenly realised they were being pushed forward by the thousands of people behind them. They might be smart, but the mob itself was dumb. It was nothing more than a wild animal, a collective mindset unable to understand that it was stumbling into the abyss. He saw a young boy—he looked barely old enough to shave—fall to the ground. The protestors trampled him before he could regain his footing, crushing him below their weight. Tomas checked his rifle again, readying himself to fire a warning shot. If the protestors started to push through the barriers...

Where the fuck are the tangle fields? The thought echoed through his mind, time and time again. *Where the fuck are they?*

The roar grew louder, the deafening sound vibrating deep in his bones. He glanced at his squad, reading fear and nervousness in their stances. They were holding their weapons at the ready, but the shouting and screaming was burning through their training...sweat glistened on their faces as they held the line. He wished, suddenly, that he'd pushed for different duties, that he'd put his name forward for starship service at the end of the war. Here...he had the awful feeling that something else was going to go wrong.

A rock flew through the air and clattered against the barrier. And Colonel Tallinn broke.

"Fire," he ordered, as he opened fire himself. "Fire!"

Tomas barely caught himself, an instant before he could squeeze the trigger and open fire into the crowd. Others weren't so quick. A dozen marines opened fire, sweeping the crowd with bullets. Tomas watched in horror as the front lines disintegrated, the bullets cutting through their bodies with horrific ease and going on to burn through the next few rows. The crowd recoiled, the wounded and dead stumbling even as the rear lines kept pushing forward. And the marines were still firing!

"CEASE FIRE," he shouted, as loudly as he could. The mouthpiece picked up his words and relayed them. "CEASE FIRE!"

The squad stopped shooting, but Colonel Tallinn was still firing. Tomas grabbed his rifle and shoved the muzzle up, then yanked it away as soon as the alien took his finger off the trigger. Colonel Tallinn stared at him, too shocked to even protest at being manhandled by a mere human. Tomas shoved him to the ground, knowing it would end his career. Colonel Tallinn had just started a civil war!

He swallowed, hard, as gas canisters began to burst. Sleepy gas was dangerous in open areas. It was never easy to tell who might breathe too much of the gas and never wake up—even if they weren't allergic to the mixture—but someone higher up thought there was no choice. The crowd broke, hundreds of people running in all directions or stumbling to the ground. The dead lay still, blood staining the cobblestones. The wounded screamed desperately for help, for something that might never come. Tomas stared at them, wondering if he'd be put in front of a court-martial or simply shot. He could have stopped Colonel Tallinn...

Laying hands on an Alphan and *being an accessory to mass murder,* he thought, numbly. *I'll never get a job with a record like that.*

Hicks ran up to him. "What happened?"

Tomas waved a hand at Colonel Tallinn. "The fool panicked," he said, stiffly. "We're fucked."

"Focus," Hicks snapped. "We'll worry about the peacocks later."

"Yes, sir," Tomas said.

He wanted to believe it was a nightmare, as the medics arrived and started doing what they could, but his body resolutely refused to wake up. He was no stranger to horror—he'd seen men badly wounded or killed outright, during the war—but this was too much. No inhuman race had carried out the slaughter, no gang of pirates intent on looting and raping their way across the universe…*he'd* done it. His *men* had done it. He jumped as he heard gunshots in the distance, saw a flyer racing across the sky. They'd committed the single greatest act of human-on-human slaughter since the Islamist Uprising and…

Tomas couldn't look away as the dead were loaded onto hovertrucks for transport…somewhere. A young boy, perhaps the one who'd been trampled to death, wounded so badly it was a mercy he'd died. A slightly older girl, with two bullet wounds just below her neckline, her face untouched even as she'd died in agony. A headless body, so badly mutilated that he couldn't tell if the victim had been male or female. A man who'd been carrying a baseball bat…the cynical side of his mind wondered if Colonel Tallinn would try to claim the crowd had been armed. God! There'd been no threat! A handful of men with automatic rifles had slaughtered the crowd.

Disgust welled up within him, disgust and a bitter sense of guilt. He hadn't fired, but he hadn't stopped anyone *else* from firing, had he? Not until it was too late. He raised his eyes, trying to determine how many people had been killed, but drew a blank. Some bodies looked as if they'd been reduced to bloody chunks. Others were surprisingly intact, save for bullet wounds. And still others looked to have been trampled into the cobblestones.

"They took the peacock," Ross said. Tomas was so far out of it that it took him several seconds to recognise the sergeant. "Internal Security. They marched him away."

"Fuck," Tomas said. It would have meant certain death if he'd shoved his pistol in Colonel Tallinn's face and pulled the trigger, but...right now, it was a price he would have gladly paid if it had kept the slaughter from ever happening. "Just...*fuck*."

He wondered, idly, if there was a chance he could find the alien and kill him before Internal Security managed to get him off-world. No one would want to admit what had really happened, not now. They'd blame it on the crowd, or him, or...he shook his head as he gazed at the towering skyscrapers. There would have been eyes up there, people watching and recording as the protest march turned into a slaughter. The newscasts might be heavily censored—he was sure of it—but news would get out. The protestors who'd escaped would tell their friends, then go online. The entire datanet would have to be shut down...

And even that won't keep word from spreading, he thought. He wanted to draw his pistol, put the weapon to his head and pull the trigger. *There's no way to keep a lid on it.*

A uniformed officer—a major, one he didn't recognise—strode over to him. "Drache?"

"Yes, sir," Tomas said.

"You and your men are to report to Barracks Seven and go into immediate lockdown," the officer said, crisply. "I am obliged to inform you that failing to carry out these orders will be regarded as desertion and treated accordingly."

Internal Security, Tomas thought. The major *had* to be Internal Security. He'd never met a *real* marine who'd talked like that. Even the redcaps—the Military Police—tended to be less formal when they were being unpleasant. *It's only been a few hours and they're already trying to get the fix in.*

"Yes, sir," Tomas said. "Sergeant, round up the squad and escort them to the barracks."

Ross nodded. "Yes, sir."

Tomas watched him go, then looked at the major. "Sir? What's going to happen to Colonel Tallinn?"

The major's face remained blank. "That's none of your concern, corporal," he said. His voice grew louder, as if he wasn't used to having his orders questioned. "Report to the barracks at once."

Corporal, Tomas thought. *Have I been demoted or are you too ignorant to read my rank pips?*

"Yes, sir," he said. There was nothing to be gained by arguing, not now. "I'm on my way."

He resisted the urge to glare at the major's back as he hurried away. Instead, he looked around. The medics were working desperately to transport the last of the wounded to the nearest hospitals, if they had room. Tomas didn't know. There were supposed to be dozens of medical facilities in the city, but they might not have enough beds—and doctors—for the wounded. He wanted to scream, or hunt down Colonel Tallinn and kill him. What the hell had he been thinking? What the hell had he *done*?

He wasn't thinking, Tomas thought. The Alphan had been a coward and a fool. One was quite bad enough. A combination of the two was disastrous. *And that was the problem.*

CHAPTER EIGHT

Star City, Earth

"WOULD IT BE TOO MUCH TO ASK," Yasuke demanded, as he stepped into the holding cell, "that you have a good explanation?"

He felt a surge of anger—very *human* anger—as he glared at Colonel Tallinn. The colonel hastily bent himself into the posture of respect, far too late to do any good. He wasn't precisely under arrest, but...Yasuke wondered, suddenly, if anyone would complain if he strangled the idiot with his bare hands. A viceroy had vast powers, with very vague limits on just how far those powers could go. For a long moment, Yasuke allowed himself to enjoy the vision of Colonel Tallinn being brutally strangled, then put it aside. He didn't have time to enjoy himself. All of his plans had just crumbled to dust.

"They shot at me," Colonel Tallinn said, sullenly. "I returned fire."

"I read the preliminary reports very carefully," Yasuke snapped. "It was a rock. It was a rock that posed no threat to either you or the men who were not, technically speaking, under your command. And you ordered the marines to open fire."

"It was my duty," Colonel Tallinn insisted. "My Lord Viceroy, I must..."

"Be quiet," Yasuke said. "Do you know how many people you killed?"

Colonel Tallinn said nothing. He probably hadn't bothered to think about it. Yasuke had. It had been seven hours since the slaughter and the death toll kept rising as more people were reported dead or wounded or simply missing. There was no way to be sure, not yet, but over four *hundred* people—all human—had been confirmed dead. He was all too aware that number would rise over the next few days. And it had happened right in front of every alien ambassador on the planet.

"You gave the order to fire," Yasuke snapped. "You killed hundreds of people."

"It was my duty," Colonel Tallinn repeated. "My Lord Viceroy, I did what needed to be done."

"Did you?" Yasuke let the words hang in the air for a long, chilling moment. "You *needed* to kill hundreds of people? You *needed* to destroy humanity's faith in us? You *needed* to give the independence activists a bloody shirt they'll use to unite humanity against us? You needed to practically murder the *entire* Empire?"

He clenched his fists. "What were you *thinking*?"

"My Lord Viceroy, I…I don't answer to you," Colonel Tallinn said. "I…"

"Wrong." Yasuke controlled himself with an effort. "You're in *my* Viceroyalty. A state of emergency has been declared. I can have you *shot* and no one will do more than file a *pro forma* complaint. Your connections"—he was sure Colonel Tallinn had connections—"are already scrambling to disown you. *That's* how badly you fucked up!"

"My Lord…"

"Be quiet," Yasuke said. "This is what you are going to do. You are going to remain here. You are going to write a full report covering *everything* that happened from the moment you were assigned to the human Marines until you wound up in this cell. If there is the *slightest* disagreement between your report and the facts, as they emerge, your career will be at an end and you will be tried for mass murder, perhaps even *treason*. There's enough precedent to put you in a cell for the rest of your very long life. Do you understand me?"

"My Lord," Colonel Tallinn said. "I...my family..."

"Is already struggling to disown you," Yasuke snapped. It wasn't true, but he was sure it *would* be true. The word was already out and spreading. "You are alone. Get used to it."

He turned and stalked to the door. "And the humans might demand you be handed over to *them* for trial," he added, as the guard opened the door. "If that happens, you *will* be shot."

There was a faint sound of shock behind him. Yasuke ignored the sound as he walked through the door, allowing the guard to slam it closed. Colonel Tallinn would be kept in isolation until the facts were fully understood, ensuring he couldn't rally his family and political connections to his side. Yasuke was fairly sure the colonel's family would disown him, but...he wanted to grind his teeth in frustration. Who'd thought that assigning Colonel Tallinn to a marine squad was a good idea? And why hadn't they thought better of it when the streets had started to fill with protestors?

His aide met him as he returned to his office. "My Lord, you have over two hundred messages from human politicians, military officers and newscasters," he said. "And the Humanity League has demanded the assemblymen be recalled for an emergency debate."

"Naturally," Yasuke snarled. They hadn't wasted any time, had they? He sat at his desk and stared at the reports waiting for him. He'd thought things were going well. He'd thought the negotiations were proceeding perfectly. And then Colonel Tallinn had thrown everything into the crapper. "I suppose we have no choice but to honour their request."

"Under emergency protocols, you could delay the recall," his aide said. "You'd have some support in the chamber..."

"No." Yasuke knew it wasn't going to work. Any human politician who collaborated with him now, with blood still staining the streets, would pay a savage price during the next election cycle. The election was too close for the electorate to forget. The Humanity League would make sure they *didn't* forget. "Do we have an updated report from the streets?"

"Yes, My Lord," the aide said. "People are staying indoors, mostly. We've thrown open sports centres and schools to house the homeless. But we've had some patrols harassed and a couple of lone soldiers have been mobbed and killed. There's also rumblings in a dozen other cities. The media lockdown isn't working."

"No," Yasuke agreed. There was no way to shut down communications completely, not without taking down the entire datanet. Human hackers were expert at hijacking the system to send uncensored messages. It was illegal, but when had that ever stopped them? "There's no way to keep word from spreading."

He closed his eyes for a long moment. The original timetable had been smashed beyond repair. Any hope of a gradual transfer of power had been lost with it. And that meant…he eyed the updates from the military command network wearily. If there was an uprising, or even a steady descent into chaos, could he count on the military? The inexperienced embeds hadn't realised there was a problem—idiots, the lot of them—but the more experienced officers were sounding the alarm. The human troops might turn their weapons on their former masters.

And that would mean a civil war, he thought, grimly. In theory, he could call for enough reinforcements to overwhelm any humans foolish enough to resist. In practice, the government might just wash its hands of the whole affair. Or it might discover it had problems back home. *The entire Empire could be destroyed.*

"My Lord?"

Yasuke looked up. "Inform the communications office that I want a direct line to Capital in an hour," he said. "I need to speak to the core councillors themselves."

His aide started in shock. "My Lord, the councillors won't speak directly to anyone."

"They'll speak to me," Yasuke said, flatly. "This is a priority call."

And we have to hope they learnt something from the war, he thought, as his aide hurried off. *Matters wouldn't have gotten so far out of hand if they'd been alerted to the invasion before it was too late.*

But, for once, he was utterly unsure what to do next.

• • •

"You are not—precisely—under arrest," Captain Grogs said. He'd introduced himself as a Military Police lawyer, the moment he'd stepped into Tomas's holding cell. "But you would be wise to remember that anything you say will be recorded and may wind up being used as evidence against you during court-martial proceedings."

"Yes, sir," Tomas said. He felt numb, too numb to care about anything. "I understand."

He stared down at his hands. They were clean, but it was easy to imagine them soaked with blood. *Human* blood. He'd never killed a human before...cold logic told him he still hadn't, that he'd done everything in his power to stop the slaughter, but raw emotion told him otherwise. He was almost glad he'd lost the capability to *feel*. The numbness was a relief, after the guilt. He wished he'd thought to shoot Colonel Tallinn himself before it was too late.

"Good," Grogs said. "Now, starting from the beginning, tell me what happened."

Tomas said nothing for a long moment, trying to marshal his thoughts. What *was* the beginning? When had it all started? He took a breath, then carefully outlined everything that had happened since the company had been pulled away from training duties and assigned to patrol the city. The marches, the raids, the protest...and the bloody slaughter. He wondered, numbly, how his men were coping. He'd had to leave them in the barracks, knowing it was only a matter of time before the redcaps descended like wolves on sheep. This wasn't a harmless little prank like getting blind drunk and getting into bar fights or seducing the commanding officer's daughter. This was...his mind wanted to believe it had never happened. He couldn't allow himself the luxury.

"I see," Grogs said. "Do you think the protest was on the verge of turning violent?"

Tomas swallowed. "I don't know, sir."

"But you must have an opinion," Grogs said. "Do you not?"

"I don't know, sir," Tomas repeated. "Protesters can turn into a mob at the drop of a hat. It could have turned violent very quickly, leaving us with nowhere to run. I don't know if it would have done…"

"But someone threw a rock," Grogs said. "Didn't they?"

"A rock?" Tomas tried not to giggle like an idiot. "A rock. We had body armour! It wasn't as if they were firing automatic weapons at us!"

Grogs nodded, curtly. "And what do *you* think caused the…incident?"

"The bloody slaughter, you mean," Tomas corrected. "Colonel Tallinn panicked. He ordered the men to shoot. And they did."

"Panicked," Grogs repeated.

"Yes." Tomas felt a hot flash of anger. "He was a coward and a fool who should never have been given a weapon and put on the streets. His mere presence screwed the chain of command into a pretzel. He shouldn't have been anywhere near us. Instead, he issued the order to open fire. How many thousands of people are dead because of him?"

"We've been told not to speculate," Grogs said.

"Of course not," Tomas said. "What now? Do I get blamed for the slaughter? Does he get a free ticket to Capital and I get one to Liberty? Or do I get put in front of a wall and shot?"

"I have no idea," Grogs said. "What do *you* think should happen?"

"Colonel Tallinn should be shot," Tomas said, flatly. "And the chain of command needs to be smoothed out before we have another"—he allowed his tone to turn mocking—"*incident*."

Grogs didn't rise to the bait. "You and the other witnesses are currently being held in isolation for your own protection," he said. "You will be given a datapad. You are to write down everything you can recall, from start to finish. I am obliged to remind you that this will be considered legal testimony and any discrepancies between your recollections, other people's recollections, and hard evidence will result in an investigation and may result in criminal charges."

"I can tell you were trained as a lawyer," Tomas said, sharply. "Tell me...when they put me in court, will you be allowed to defend me? Or will the judge order you out on the grounds you're human?"

"On the record, we're not allowed to speculate about future proceedings," Grogs said, sharply. "Off the record, I will tell you that everyone above us"—he jabbed a finger at the ceiling—"is running around like a bunch of headless chickens. I can't swear to what will happen in the next few hours, let alone the days and weeks to come. All I can do is advise you to tell the truth, as you see it, and let the future take care of itself."

Tomas laughed. "And when they start looking for scapegoats...?"

"Right now, I think they have other problems." Grogs stood. "And so do you."

"Hah," Tomas said.

He watched the lawyer bang on the door, the guard opening it and shooting Tomas a nasty look before closing it again. REMF. Tomas didn't know anyone, even the redcaps themselves, who actually *respected* the Military Police. They could be tough, in roving bands, but none of them had ever seen *real* combat. Even the units that served as occupation troops were rarely blooded. The *real* fighters normally killed anyone who even looked at them funny before the follow-up units arrived.

Fuck, he thought. He forced himself to stand. *They're going to kill me.*

He stared at the dark metal walls. They were solid, too solid to do more than bruise his skin and crack his knuckles if he punched them. He'd grown used to small quarters in the barracks, but...there was something about the holding cell that just felt oppressive. He wondered sourly if they'd move him to a proper cell within the next few hours or simply take him outside, put him against the wall and shoot him. There were all sorts of rumours, each one wilder than the last, about just how far the Alphans would go to maintain their power. Tomas hadn't believed any of them until now.

I guess I'll just have to wait, he thought, as he started an exercise routine. It would take his mind off his plight, at least until the guard shoved the promised datapad into the cell. *And see what happens next.*

• • •

"Good God," Rachel said, quietly.

Abraham nodded, curtly, as the horror unfolded in front of him. The datanet had been placed on semi-lockdown, which was all the proof he needed that *something* bad had happened, but the League had plenty of experience in moving data from one place to another without being shut down. The recordings had been taken by a sympathiser in the city, transferred to a datachip and hand-carried to the League's headquarters. And they were ghastly.

He felt sick, his stomach churning with horror and fear. *True* fear. The death toll had to be in the hundreds, perhaps even the thousands. He'd heard rumours of hundreds of thousands, even *millions*, of dead. Cold logic told him that was absurd—even now, there couldn't be more than a million people in the city—but the rumour mill was out of control. Asteroids blown apart, entire planets scorched clean of life...he'd even heard a story the aliens had nuked Star City again. He only had to look out the window to disprove *that* story.

The recording came to an end. He forced himself to look up. "Has there been any response to our demand for a recall?"

"No, sir," Rachel said. "But I happen to know the Empire Loyalists have echoed our demand."

Abraham nodded, unsurprised. The Empire Loyalists were fucked. It would have been good news, if the streets weren't stained with blood and the very real prospect of armed intervention looming over the entire planet. Abraham had no illusions. The human race could put up a fight, if the warcruisers arrived to teach the planet a lesson, but it would end with everything they'd built over the last century blasted into atoms. And that would be the end of everything.

Rachel glanced down as her datapad bleeped an alert. "Sir, William Grey is requesting a private meeting."

"Of course he is," Abraham snarled. "The whole crisis is practically tailor-made for him."

He forced himself to calm down. Direct Action could not be allowed to take *any* sort of action. Not now. He'd heard enough to know their planned campaign of slow-downs, strikes, sabotage and outright terrorism would only plunge the planet into civil war. The loyalists wouldn't be the only ones calling for their heads. A terrorist campaign would rapidly cost Direct Action—and the Humanity League—all the sympathy it had earned.

And then everyone would be demanding our immediate extermination, he thought. *And the Alphans will be happy to oblige.*

"Inform Grey that I'll see him in an hour," he ordered, finally. "By then, I should have a plan ready to take the lead—to take control. And hopefully keep him from doing anything stupid."

"Yes, sir." Rachel didn't sound optimistic. "I'll let him know."

Abraham tended to agree. Word was out and spreading. So were rumours, each one more exaggerated than the last. The Empire Loyalists might be fucked, but so was *he* if he wasn't careful. He had to lead the protest, while—somehow—keeping it from getting out of hand. There were enough hotheads out there to ensure that *something* would happen... something *else*, he supposed. They had to avoid giving the Alphans a ready-made excuse for a crackdown. And yet, many of those hotheads regarded him as a borderline collaborator himself.

"And then see if you can arrange a meeting with the First Speaker," he said. "We may as well see if we can put forward a joint resolution."

"Yes, sir," Rachel said. "Might I say that seems unlikely?"

Abraham laughed. "In the words of my ancestor, we must all hang together or hang separately," he said. "The Empire Loyalists may no longer be *quite* so loyal."

Rachel looked doubtful, but merely nodded.

CHAPTER NINE

EDS *Washington*/Earth Defence Force One, Earth Orbit

COMMANDER NAOMI YAGAMI STARED DOWN at the two sets of updates, wondering—numbly—if all hell was about to break loose. One update came directly from Earth Defence Force One, so vague she was sure it had been written by a committee of politically-minded officers; the other came from the whisper network, so blunt and crude she suspected that whoever had originally written the message intended to cause trouble. The truth...she sucked in her breath. The truth might lie somewhere between the two extremes.

She let out a long, bitter sigh. The first message referred to an *incident* in Star City, something that might cause unrest and even outright violence. Captains and senior officers were ordered to put their crews under lockdown and to do everything in their power to keep rumours from spreading. The *second* message claimed the Alphans had slaughtered hundreds of thousands of people in Star City, perhaps as a precursor to re-establishing direct rule over the Solar System. Naomi refused to believe so many people had been killed, but...she could easily believe that *something* had happened. And where did that leave her?

Her hand touched the pistol at her belt. She'd taken the weapon from the safe, the moment she'd read the update, and checked it carefully. She'd never fired a pistol in anger, but she'd made sure to spend at least an hour on the firing range every week. A spacer could never be too careful, particularly when crewmen were being run ragged by commodores and admirals who'd never stood on a command deck. And yet now...she forced herself to think. What would she do, if *Washington* was ordered to provide direct support? What side was she meant to be on?

She tossed the question around and around, trying to come up with an answer. She'd sworn an oath to the Empire. She hated the thought of breaking it. But the Empire hadn't been very good to her. She knew, without false modesty, that she should have reached command rank herself years ago. *She* should have been in command of *Washington*. And yet, the alien-dominated command structure had placed a well-connected idiot in command. It hurt, more than she wanted to admit to anyone. She'd worked hard to earn her place. She knew she deserved it. And yet, it had been stolen from her by someone who'd been lucky enough to be born to the *right* species.

And that species just carried out a brutal slaughter, she thought. The precise death toll might not be known for days, if at all, but she knew hundreds of people had been killed. *What do I do if I get told to carry out one myself?*

The thought chilled her. She had no qualms about killing enemy starships intent on killing her. She had no hesitation in blowing away pirate ships, crewed by monsters intent on looting, raping and killing their way across the universe; she had no doubts about escorting captured pirates to the nearest airlock and throwing them out, once they'd been drained of everything they knew. But firing on innocent civilians? She was no shrinking violet, no virgin who'd yet to see hostile action. She *knew* there were times when civilians were in the wrong place at the wrong time, where they were injured or killed...she knew there was no way to *guarantee* there would be no civilian causalities. Only a particularly idiotic politician could be so fatuous. But deliberately slaughtering civilians?

She shuddered. She'd never been ordered to drop KEWs on civilian targets, let alone get up close and personal with the people she'd been ordered to kill. It was easy to forget, sometimes, that destroying ships meant killing people, that bombarding planetary targets meant killing people...they were just icons on the display. Operators whooped and hollered and slapped their palms as icons blinked out of existence, unwilling or unable to acknowledge they'd killed people. And yet...she knew, all too well, that bombarding a city meant killing thousands of innocents. She liked to think she'd refuse if someone told her to commit such a ghastly atrocity.

And yet, it would be perfectly legal. The Alphans had no qualms about carrying out nuclear strikes on inhabited planets if they felt them necessary. They'd nuked a dozen cities on Earth, hundreds of years ago, just to make it clear that *they* were the masters now. She'd read the warbook extensively during long and boring deployments. She knew an order to put down a riot by bombarding the city would be perfectly legal. But it would be morally wrong.

And what will I do, she asked herself shortly, *if I get told to do it?*

She closed her eyes, thinking hard. It wouldn't be *difficult* to commit mutiny. Or barratry. There was only one non-human onboard and she'd have no trouble taking him out. She could just walk to his cabin, open the hatch and shoot him. And yet...which way would the crew jump? Would they support her? Or their legal captain? They might detest the peacock, but he *was* their rightful commanding officer. And his orders would be defensible, both legally and practically. Hell, there were even protocols written into the legal framework that insisted anything an Alphan did was legal by definition.

I take the ship, she thought. She knew she could rely on the command staff. She'd been the one to meld them into a team. And she knew discontent was spreading below decks. *But what do I do then?*

She turned her attention to the display. The warcruisers were still in position, holding station near Earth. They were out of range, but that would change quickly. Naomi was sure the EDF could take them, if all hell broke loose, yet...there was no way to plot and carry out a mutiny on such a scale without being detected well before it was too late. Internal Security would realise *something* was up. Naomi was pretty sure they monitored the whisper network closely. She was mildly surprised they'd never tried to shut it down. And even if the EDF *did* take out the warcruisers, what next? The Alphans would send a fleet to exact revenge and put the human race back in its place.

And that will be the end, she told herself.

Her heart twisted. Was she condemned to do *nothing*? Or was she... she looked up, sharply, as the buzzer rang. There weren't *many* people who'd call on her, in her office, without calling ahead. Trouble? Her hand dropped to her pistol, ready to draw the weapon. She told herself not to be silly. She'd never drawn on a member of her crew before, not ever. She was damned if she was starting now.

"Come," she ordered.

Her eyes narrowed as Senior Chief Nigel Thompson stepped into the compartment. He was alone, thankfully, but his visit could *not* be a coincidence. Petty Officers like him had whisper networks of their own, if rumour were to be believed. They knew too much about what was going on, at any given time, for Naomi to doubt it. And that meant...what?

"Commander," Thompson said. He sounded more urgent than their last meeting. "Have you heard the news?"

"Yes," Naomi said. "And, right now, we can do nothing."

"That isn't going to sit well with the crew," Thompson said, flatly. "Hundreds of people are dead."

"I know," Naomi said. "Did you get a more accurate count?"

"The message stated nine hundred people were killed," Thompson said. "But the figure could be a great deal higher."

"It could also be a great deal lower," Naomi pointed out. "The first reports are always wrong, Mr. Thompson. And it's only been seven hours since the...incident."

"Since hundreds of people were killed," Thompson corrected. "Commander, the crew is not happy."

"Neither am I," Naomi said. "And what do you propose we do about it?"

She waited, wondering if Thompson actually had a *good* answer. It was easy, in her experience, to say that *something* must be done. It was a great deal harder to come up with *'something.'* She'd forgive Thompson stepping outside all bounds of naval protocol if he actually came up with a workable idea. So far, she'd come up with nothing.

"We take the ship," Thompson said. "And stop them."

"And then what?" Naomi waved a hand at the display. "Those war-cruisers will blow us away!"

She met his eyes before he could muster another suggestion. "Right now, we have no option but to wait and see," she said. "If things get worse, we can...reassess the situation."

"And let them get away with it?" Thompson stared back at her. "They murdered countless innocents!"

"I know," Naomi snapped. "But we don't even know what really happened. Do we? We just have vague reports! Give them a chance to work out what happened and what they're going to do about it. If they decide to do nothing, we can do something ourselves."

She winced, inwardly. Thompson wasn't *stupid*. He knew—he had to know—that he was coming very close to advocating mutiny. He had to know she should—technically—arrest him for sedition. And yet...was he a spy? A plant? Internal Security might be trying to trick her into saying something that could be held against her. If she arrested him, she might trigger a mutiny; if she didn't arrest him, she might be arrested herself...

"We must not act rashly," she said, pushing her doubts aside. "Give them a chance. And if they fail to handle the situation properly, we can rethink our stance."

Thompson looked displeased. "Yes, Commander."

"And make sure everyone gets the message," Naomi said. "We cannot afford rash action."

She watched him go, grimly aware it was only a matter of time until something exploded. Thompson was smart and tough, but he'd find it hard to ride herd on the hotheads within the crew. Someone would do something stupid, or start walking down a path that would lead to outright mutiny and eventual execution...she cursed under her breath. The hell of it was that she wanted to do something too. She was just all too aware that there was *nothing* she could do.

Not yet, she thought. She started to mentally draw up contingency plans. She didn't dare write any of them down. *But we have to think of something and fast.*

. . .

"The reports are clear, Admiral," Commodore Yang stated. "Incidents of sedition have increased by several hundred percent in the last nine hours."

Admiral Adam Glass gave him a sharp look. "Are you surprised?"

Yang blinked. "Admiral?"

"The reports are clear," Adam said, deliberately echoing the commodore's words. "Upwards of five hundred people—the death toll keeps changing—were killed. The rumours started spreading—and growing—before the last of the bodies had even hit the ground. Right now, there are people convinced the entire *city* was depopulated and then burned to the ground. And they're getting angry."

"Sir," Yang said. "Sedition must be suppressed."

Adam met his eyes, evenly. "Is it sedition or just grumbling?"

He shook his head before Yang could try to answer. Internal Security officers had no sense of proportion. They couldn't tell the difference between spacers letting off steam by grumbling and outright sedition. Spacers grumbled, it was a law of nature. There was no way anyone could crack down on it without sending morale into a black hole. Hasty repression might easily lead to a *genuine* mutiny.

"You will continue to monitor the situation, but you will do nothing unless there is a clear and present threat to system security," he ordered.

"And you will inform me *ahead* of time before you take any corrective measures. Do you understand me?"

Yang frowned. "Admiral, with all due respect..."

"Do you understand me?" Adam held his eyes. "Or do I have to assign someone else to your role?"

"No, sir." Yang bent into the posture of respect. "I understand perfectly."

"Good," Adam said. "Dismissed."

He turned his attention to the display, not bothering to watch as Yang backed out of the compartment. *That* was an insult, a slap across the face by Alphan etiquette. The nasty part of Adam's mind wondered if Yang would care. He'd notice, of course, but would he care? Or would he just be glad he'd escaped without being replaced? Adam would have to burn a great deal of his political capital to have Yang removed and replaced by someone a little more sensible, but he could do it.

Or maybe I can't, he thought, with a flash of dark humour. *Internal Security doesn't have anyone with any common sense.*

He snorted at the thought as he pulled up the latest set of reports and scanned them quickly, feeling his heart sink. The death toll now stood at four hundred and thirty people—a note, at the bottom, stated that the remaining wounded had been stabilised and nearly all of the missing had been accounted for. Four hundred and thirty people...he shuddered, trying to comprehend what had just happened. The war had killed *millions*, but they'd all lived on worlds on the other side of the Empire. *This* incident had taken place on Earth. The entire planet was outraged.

The reports were clear. There were angry protests in over twenty cities, with wildcat strikes taking place all over the system. The interstellar relay network had been shut down, save for emergency messages, but it was only a matter of time before word spread right across the Empire. God knew there were enough alien powers with an interest in making life hard for the Alphans. They'd ensure the exaggerated reports were spread well ahead of the truth.

Although the truth is pretty bad, he reminded himself. *Pretty bad*...it was a disaster and everyone knew it. The slaughter had smashed all hope of a peaceful transfer of power. Yang might be an ass, but he was right. Sedition was spreading. Adam knew enough about spacers to know *some* of them would be plotting trouble. *And if we don't manage to get ahead of the crisis, we're going to be smashed flat.*

He turned his attention to the communications log. The Viceroy hadn't returned his call. He couldn't talk to any other politicians without speaking to the Viceroy first, although the log stated that over a hundred politicians had tried to speak to *him*. And dozens of officers had sent him private messages, expressing their concerns. He was standing on a powder keg that might explode at any moment. He honestly didn't know what to do. If he spoke to his subordinates, it might be held against him; if he didn't take the lead, someone else would push him aside and do it instead.

The intercom bleeped. "Admiral," Ensign Corey said. "His Lordship the Viceroy is calling on a priority line."

Adam frowned. The disdain in the ensign's voice would have been all too clear to a human. He hoped she hadn't sounded like *that* to the Viceroy's aide—or whatever lower-ranking staffer had been assigned to arrange the call. The Viceroy himself knew humans very well, perhaps well enough to read human emotions. It wasn't easy—it was *never* easy to read alien expressions—but the Viceroy had spent more time on Earth than Capital. He might be able to do it.

"Put him through," he said, calmly. He'd speak to her about her tone later. "And hold my other calls."

The Viceroy holographic image materialised in front of him. "My Lord Viceroy," Adam said. "Thank you for returning my call."

"You are most welcome," the Viceroy said. It was hard to be sure, but the alien looked harassed. Worrying, in someone who had the power of life and death over the entire system and everyone living within it. "Is the EDF reliable?"

Adam felt a chill run down his spine. The warcruisers weren't *that* far from the orbital station. If they opened fire without warning, they could cripple the EDF before anyone could fire a volley in return. And…

"I believe the vast majority of my officers and crew will remain loyal," he said, carefully. "But there is considerable anger over the slaughter. It will have to be handled, somehow."

The Viceroy looked thoroughly displeased. "My government is currently trying to decide how to handle the situation," he said. "But they may not come to a decision before matters get out of hand."

They're already out of hand, Adam thought. *And if you're getting desperate, My Lord, what are you going to do next?*

"The Assembly will meet tomorrow," the Viceroy said. "Keep your people under control, Admiral. I believe things will change, but I don't know how."

"I'll do my best to buy you time," Adam said. "Do you intend to charge Colonel Tallinn?"

The Viceroy gave him a sharp look. "If I can, I will," he said. "But that won't be easy."

"No," Adam agreed. "It won't."

He glanced at one of the reports someone had hastily thrown together for him. Colonel Tallinn could be charged with a dozen different offences, but making them stick would be a political nightmare. The Alphan Government wouldn't be happy if Colonel Tallinn was tried in a human court. They'd want to try him themselves, but Colonel Tallinn could claim Alphan privilege if he wasn't quietly discharged and dispatched to a colony world on the other side of known space. It would be a horrible mess.

"Do what you can," the Viceroy ordered. "And tell your people a final decision will be coming soon."

"Yes, sir," Adam said. "Good luck."

The Viceroy made a very human snort. "Good luck to you too, Admiral," he said. "We're both going to need it."

CHAPTER TEN

Star City, Earth

IT WASN'T EASY TO KEEP HIS EXPRESSION under tight control, Abraham discovered, as he strode into the chamber for the emergency session. He'd been surprised that neither the Empire Loyalists nor the Viceroy himself had made any attempt to bar the session, although he supposed that both parties knew they were in deep shit. Rumour had it the Empire Loyalists were on the verge of shattering into a handful of smaller parties. He would have been pleased if he wasn't ruefully aware the Humanity League was in trouble too.

If we take the lead, we become targets, he thought. *And if we step back, others will take our place.*

He took his chair and waited, watching as the room steadily filled to capacity. The viewing gallery was heaving with newscasters, pointing portable recorders and sensors at the assemblymen below. Abraham nodded to a particularly intelligent reporter, then returned his attention to the assemblymen himself. The First Speaker looked as if she didn't quite know where she was. Abraham supposed he couldn't blame her. Two days ago, she'd looked to be on the verge of true power; now, the only reason she hadn't already been replaced was the simple fact that no one *else* wanted the job. The most powerful position any human could hold had suddenly become a poisoned chalice. And it hadn't even been her fault. It would have been funny, if it hadn't been a foretaste of what the future might hold for him. He was all too aware his supporters might turn on him too, if he failed to lead them where they wanted to go.

The Viceroy entered the chamber, looking tired and worn. He didn't make any sign for the assemblymen to rise as he took his chair. Abraham wondered if that was a sign of guilt or simple exhaustion. The Viceroy hadn't been directly guilty, if the reports from reliable sources were accurate. He hadn't given the command to open fire. But he was part of a system that kept the human race under strict control. He might not be personally guilty—Abraham conceded the point without rancour—but the system he upheld was as guilty as hell.

And his superiors have to be mad at the poor bastard too, Abraham thought, with a flicker of sympathy. *No wonder he didn't get any sleep.*

The First Speaker's expression didn't sharpen as she keyed her console. "Speaker Douglas has requested the floor," she said, without the usual preamble. "Please remember that this is an emergency session"—her eyes swept the chamber—"and interruptions are not tolerated."

Abraham nodded politely as he rose. By custom, having asked for an emergency session, he had the right to make his speech without interference. The First Speaker could make her response, also without interference. And then the knives would come out. The assemblymen could tear him to shreds, if they wished. Very few emergency sessions had ever been called, outside wartime. The political costs were sometimes too high.

"I will not mince words," he said. "I will forgo propriety and etiquette and speak to you bluntly. The matter is too important for such distractions. It is no exaggeration to say that the future of both the human race itself, and the greater Empire, may rest upon what happens today."

He took a breath. His career was about to go into orbit or be buried so deeply no one would ever mention his name. He'd done everything in his power to keep the speech from leaking out, but he was all too aware that his political enemies could guess what he was about to say. They'd understand his problems as surely as he understood theirs. Even the Viceroy—and his staff—would understand him. They knew what he was about to say.

"Yesterday, a marine squad was ordered to open fire on a protest march," he said. "By the time the squad was ordered to cease fire, four hundred and thirty people lay dead on the streets. A further two hundred and seventy were wounded, some seriously enough to require immediate transport to the hospital. And, even as word started to get out, the government chose to shut down the datanet in a bid to prevent the news from spreading far and wide. All they managed to do was give credence to the wildest of rumours.

"But it is no rumour that four hundred and thirty people are dead. It is no rumour that four hundred and thirty people were *murdered*.

"I have it on good authority that the officer commanding the marines was a coward and a fool. I have it on good authority that his family connections, utterly beyond reproach, were allowed to override common sense. I have it on good authority that the marines were told to follow his orders, whenever he chose to issue them. And we know, because four hundred and thirty people died in the streets, that he chose to order his men to open fire. And we know that commander's family are already doing what they can to get him off the hook.

"That man is a murderer. And yet they're trying to save him from the consequences of his own stupidity."

He allowed the words to hang in the air. "I believe I speak for the majority of the human race when I say I have lost all faith in the Empire's goodwill. I believe I speak for us *all* when I say *enough*. Public opinion demands I take a stand, that I make it clear we have reached the point of no return. The changes wrought by the war were weakening us well before the murderer took a squad of men and set out to commit an atrocity. And he has, in a single bloody second, killed the Empire itself.

"In the name of humanity itself, I demand two things. First, that Colonel Tallinn be handed over to us for judgement. He will be given a fair trial, following procedures laid down when the last of the pre-invasion governments were dissolved, but his family and his political connections will have no opportunity to put their finger on the scales. He may speak for himself, or hire a lawyer; he will not be allowed to claim privilege and skate punishment for his crimes.

"And second, I demand that the Empire grants us immediate independence."

A rustle ran through the air. Abraham smiled to himself. They'd known it was coming, they *had* to have known, but it was still a shock. The words threatened to upend everything they knew about how the world worked. He glanced at the Viceroy, noting the alien showed no visible reaction. Had *he* been caught by surprise? Abraham doubted it.

"Two days ago, it was possible to have faith in the ultimate goodness of the Empire," Abraham said. "It was possible to believe that a steady path towards autonomy would satisfy both sides. But that is no longer the case. Our faith was murdered by Colonel Tallinn and his family. Let us part now, without further ado, and meet as friends and equals on the galactic stage. Let us put this whole sorry affair behind us and look to a better—and brighter—future for us all."

He sat down, smiling inwardly at the numb shock on some faces. The Empire Loyalists had known what was coming, yet they hadn't been able to do anything about it. Today, Imperial unity was a losing cause. The First Speaker had to know it. And yet, what else *could* they do? What was the point of a loyalist party if there was nothing to be loyal to?

The First Speaker stood. "No one can deny that the events of yesterday were a ghastly tragedy," she said. "No one can deny there is a need to come to terms with the incident, that there is a need to clearly establish what happened and make sure the guilty parties are punished. No one can deny it. But no one can *also* deny that this is no time to score cheap political points, to advance an agenda..."

There was a roar of anger from the benches. Abraham kept his amusement under tight control as the assemblymen, Empire Loyalists as well as

Humanity League, started shouting Nancy down. The First Speaker gavelled for silence, but it never came. She might have a point, he conceded, yet it didn't matter. Right now, people were angry. They wanted blood. They didn't want someone calling for calm, promising an investigation that would be carefully planned to avoid pointing the finger at the wrong people...

He smirked as the shouting grew louder. It was going to be a *very* bad day for his rivals.

And if it looks like I'm doing something, he told himself, *the hotheads won't do anything stupid either.*

• • •

Yasuke would have gladly thrown Colonel Tallinn to the humans without a moment's hesitation, if he'd thought it would put a lid on the brewing disaster. The colonel's report hadn't been the greatest piece of military fiction he'd ever read, but it was certainly the most outrageous. His story kept changing, sometimes within the same wretched paragraph. He'd felt he needed to send a message, he'd felt afraid for his life, he'd simply not thought about what he was doing...Yasuke had found himself seriously considering just having the idiot shot or thrown to the mob. It could hardly have made matters worse.

He watched, grimly, as the human politicians shouted at each other. He'd expected the session would be bad, with politicians lining up to take shots at the government and the wretched colonel, but it was worse than he'd feared. The loyalists were no longer loyal. He could see a dozen Empire Loyalists attacking the First Speaker—and, by extension, the government—with a savagery that awed and terrified him. It was a far cry from the genteel discussions from home. He found it hard to believe *his* race had ever been so...riotous.

But they know they can lose everything, he thought. *And that forces them to fight to the finish.*

He glanced at his aide. The arguing looked as if it was on the verge of turning into a *real* fight. Yasuke was tempted to call the troops to separate them, but it would only make matters worse. Instead, he rose and stepped through the concealed rear door. It felt as if he were running away, but it was the only thing he could do. His superiors were already annoyed. They'd be a great deal angrier if they thought a viceroy had been manhandled.

"There was an update from Edinburgh," his aide said, as they slipped into the tunnel leading back to the Viceregal Complex. "The strikes have got out of hand. Half the policemen sat on their hands when fighting broke out."

Yasuke nodded. "I see."

"Colonel Talc has requested permission to send in the marines," the aide continued. "He insists that, without them..."

"No." Yasuke cut him off. "We don't want another...*incident.*"

He kept walking, thinking dire thoughts about the mess Colonel Tallinn had inadvertently created. Earth was rapidly becoming ungovernable. The industrial nodes, asteroid mining facilities and even HE3 cloudscoops were experiencing slowdowns, where the crew weren't openly striking. There was trouble on the ships, even on some of the *warcruisers*. His more experienced officers and crew had a great respect for humanity. They weren't going to take kindly to orders to slap the human race down.

And word is already spreading, he thought, grimly. *We couldn't cut the ambassadors off forever.*

The thought mocked him. His career was probably deader than the ancients themselves. The alien ambassadors had sent messages home, as soon as they'd been granted access to the interstellar communications network. Right now, their governments would be *helpfully* relaying the messages to the human-dominated worlds...perhaps even aiming them into the Empire itself. They wouldn't even have to *lie*. The truth was quite bad enough.

He let out a long breath as they reached his office. He'd let himself believe he could control the pace of change. For all the time he'd spent on Earth, he hadn't quite understood just how quickly things could move. And now...the damage was beyond repair. There was only one choice left.

"Get me a priority link," he ordered, curtly. "I need to talk to the councillors."

He took his chair, poured himself a mug of water and waited. The councillors would keep him waiting, just to make it clear *they* were the ones in charge. Normally, it wouldn't matter. They wouldn't keep him waiting for long, not when he'd opened a priority channel. But now…any delay felt disastrous. Time was running out. They were staring down the barrels of a full-fledged insurrection, perhaps even civil war.

The terminal bleeped. Holographic images started to materialise around him. He bent into the posture of respect, held it for ten seconds, then straightened. It was the only way to convey urgency. They *had* to understand the growing crisis. They had to…

"Viceroy," the chairman said. "You wish to speak to us about the humans? Again?"

"Yes," Yasuke said. "They are demanding Colonel Tallinn's head—and independence."

"It would be easier to give them independence," the chairman said. It sounded like a joke. Yasuke knew it wasn't. "The colonel's family has not—yet—disowned him."

And they'll have trouble disowning him when they'll be throwing him to the human courts, Yasuke thought. *Their enemies will paint them as betrayers.*

"The situation is getting out of hand," he said, shortly. "The humans are angry at us—with reason. There have been a string of nasty incidents over the past five hours alone. There are rumours of mutinies, even uprisings. Even if none of them materialise, the economic damage is going to be considerable. The slowdowns alone are going to have nasty knock-on effects. My most optimistic projection suggests the crisis could send the entire Empire into recession."

"Impossible," another councillor insisted. "The humans are not *that* important!"

"They supply us with cheap goods," Yasuke reminded him. He'd had his staff work out the details, shortly after the war. "And many of those goods fill important holes in our supply chain. And...they also serve in our armies, and work on our streets, and do all sorts of tasks our people are unwilling or unable to do for themselves. There is no way we can put them back in their box without doing immense harm to ourselves."

He leaned forward, willing them to believe. "And the longer the crisis continues, councillors, the greater the chance someone else will start to meddle."

The councillors said nothing for a long moment. "You paint a grim picture," the chairman said, finally. "What do you propose we do?"

"I think we need to implement the withdrawal plan," Yasuke said. "And abandon the human sector completely."

"Are you mad?" A councillor glared at him. "Do you know how much that'll cost?"

"Less than a war," Yasuke said. "We could lose."

"No," another councillor insisted. "We outgun the humans ten to one. Fifty to one!"

Yasuke took a breath. "The humans have enough firepower, at least in theory, to take out the picket squadron," he said. "They might well have contingency plans to secure the EDF and do just that. They'll certainly fear that *we* intend to strike first, which will encourage *them* to strike first...

"We'll retaliate, of course. But the humans are capable warriors, *innovative* warriors. Putting the rebellion down will be costly, even if our victory is assured. And, lest you forget, we have a massive human population scattered across the homeworlds. There will be trouble, from terrorism to outright uprisings, that will cost us *more* to put down. And...*that* will bring in outside powers. We could win the war, councillors, but lose everything."

"So you have said," the chairman reminded him. "We have not forgotten."

No, Yasuke thought. *But you've been safe in your towers for so long, you can't really comprehend you might be threatened.*

"We are short of time," he said, instead. "I believe we must concede now, to keep from losing more. We are *still* their major trading partners.

We are *still* their employers, in many ways. Losing direct control of Earth will hurt, councillors, but we will recover. It will certainly be cheaper than the alternative."

The chairman nodded. "And Colonel Tallinn?"

Yasuke took a breath. "I would suggest handing him over for judgement," he said. "We could strike a deal, giving him to the humans if they rule out the death penalty. Or simply put him on trial ourselves, find him guilty and remand him to a penal colony."

"We will discuss the issue," the chairman said. "We will contact you shortly."

"Time is not on our side," Yasuke said. They didn't understand. He'd told them, time and time again, but they didn't understand. Things moved *fast* on Earth. "I need a decision within a standard day."

"We understand," the chairman said. "You will be contacted."

The holographic images vanished. Yasuke leaned back in his chair, feeling cold despite the warm room. The humans were on the verge of revolt, none of the loyalists could be trusted any longer and his leaders were…what was the human expression? Playing string instruments while the city burnt to the ground? His entire *race* had done the same, before the war. It had been so long since they'd faced a truly dangerous opponent that they'd forgotten it could happen. And they'd been lucky to survive their misjudgement.

He keyed his terminal. "Send a signal to the warcruisers," he ordered. He had to put his people on alert, if the council did the wise thing. Or if they ordered him to put the revolt down as savagely as possible. "Code Theta. I say again, Code Theta."

"Yes, My Lord," his aide said.

CHAPTER ELEVEN

Star City, Earth

"I'M STARTING TO THINK," ABRAHAM SAID as the aircar headed towards the Assembly, "that emergency sessions and recalls are growing disturbingly common."

Rachel made a show of considering it. "Prior to the war, there were only two emergency sessions and there were over a hundred years between them," she said. "Now, there have been three within seven years, but only two in quick succession."

"This one and my one," Abraham said. "How many would we need to call before it became a trend?"

"It depends," Rachel said. "How many disasters do you want to face?"

Abraham nodded, curtly. The first emergency session within his lifetime had been called when the Second Lupine War had broken out. The second had been the one he'd called himself. And now, a third... called by the Viceroy. He felt a cold hand clench his heart and squeeze. There had been no reply to his demands, no acquiescence or casual dismissal. He felt as if the walls were closing in on him, even though nothing had happened. He felt like a criminal who feared his guilt was written all over his face.

Which is stupid, he told himself, sharply. *You've done nothing wrong.*

His heart started to pound as the aircar landed neatly on the pad. The Viceroy had vast powers. If he wanted, he could arrest Abraham and the entire Humanity League and sentence them to exile—or death—without hope of appeal. He could charge them with treason and deny them the right to a trial—or put them in front of an emergency court, with the conviction and sentence planned well in advance. He could...Abraham forced himself to remain calm as he passed through the security checkpoint and walked down to the hall. The Viceroy knew the planet was on the verge of chaos, perhaps even open rebellion. He wouldn't turn off the antimatter containment chamber without good cause.

He schooled his face into immobility as he passed the guards and took his seat in the hall itself. The government had never been so weak. The Empire Loyalists were fracturing, on the brink of splitting into two separate parties. Abraham himself stood to gain hugely, if he survived the next few days. And yet, there were rumours of everything from a lockdown to outright military intervention. Troopships were supposed to be on their way, bringing a small army to keep the planet under control. The EDF would be disarmed and...who knew? The planet hadn't been so unstable since the invasion itself.

The hall filled slowly. A number of loyalist assemblymen seemed to have decided to stay away, he noted; they'd probably passed proxy voting powers to their fellows. They were feeling the heat from their voters, he thought; they knew they couldn't be seen to be taking a stand without paying a severe price when the election rolled around. His lips curved into a cruel smile. Whatever those assemblymen did, they'd piss off at least half the voters. It was unlikely their careers would survive. Cowards they might be, but he had to admit they were also quite practical. They probably told themselves they could take a stand when it became clear which side was going to win.

He stood, with the other assemblymen, as the Viceroy entered the chamber and made his way to his seat. The alien looked tired and worn, although it wasn't easy to be sure. Abraham had spent years studying Earth's alien masters, only to discover there were aspects of their psychology that were seemingly beyond human understanding. Their behaviour wasn't easy to predict. They could move from being extremely generous and compassionate to oppressive and spiteful at the drop of a hat. And it was hard to say who was calling the shots. The Viceroy had spent long enough on Earth to adapt, in some ways, to humanity. His superiors might never have left their homeworld. They might not even have *met* a human.

The Viceroy reached his chair and turned to face the assemblymen. Abraham tensed, inwardly. It was something important, then. Normally, the Viceroy sat and watched his human servants—and the loyal opposition—do their business. It was rare for the Viceroy to take the lead…he reminded himself, again, that the current situation was unprecedented. Anything could happen, and he was at Ground Zero. The Alphans would have no trouble seizing him and the others if they wished…

He braced himself as the Viceroy started to speak. This was it. Whatever was going to happen, it was about to happen. And whatever happened, he promised himself, he was going to be ready.

...

Yasuke took a moment to run through his speech, then contemplate the latest report on human political developments, before he opened his mouth. The Empire Loyalists were on the brink of coming apart at the seams, even formerly loyal assemblymen demanding accountability and the murderer's head—they never referred to Colonel Tallinn by name—on a platter. It was possible, as some of his superiors had argued, that the humans would forget Colonel Tallinn…in time. Yasuke didn't believe it. There was no way to stop word from spreading. The mere fact they'd *tried* had given credence to the claim Colonel Tallinn had killed *millions* with his bare hands.

Anyone who bothers to think rationally would know that couldn't possibly be true, he told himself, as the chamber quieted. *But no one is thinking very rationally at the moment.*

He felt an odd little pang as he prepared to speak. It felt as if he were admitting defeat, as if he were betraying humans—and aliens—who'd placed their trust in his government. Things were going to change, things were going to careen out of control...he wanted to sit, to hold back the speech, to wait and see in the desperate hope things would get better. But he knew, all too well, that they wouldn't. Chaos would come, despite his best efforts. And the whole edifice would crumble into ruin. The Empire itself might be doomed.

Be blunt, he thought. His speechwriters had worked for *hours*, trying to put together a speech that would satisfy everyone. They'd failed. *Let them know, for once, that you think of them as equals.*

"Hundreds of years ago, my people found a divided world, a world and a people warring against themselves," he said, quietly. "We took the world, as was our right as a superior species; we took the people and uplifted them into civilisation. It was, perhaps, inevitable that those people would eventually demand their rights as citizens of the galactic community. It was, perhaps, inevitable that they would clash with their teachers...and that, eventually, something would happen that would tear the relationship apart.

"My government deeply regrets Colonel Tallinn's actions. My superiors have condemned him in the strongest possible terms. They have made it clear that the current situation is unsustainable, that things will have to change. We have spent the last three days deciding how we should proceed, then sorting out the details. We thank you for your patience."

He kept his face impassive with an effort. By human standards, they'd moved slowly; by theirs, they'd moved at breakneck pace. There hadn't been any *real* contingency plans for anything beyond a minor uprising—and they hadn't been updated since the war. The government had buried its collective head in the sand and pretended they wouldn't be necessary. Yasuke cursed the idiots under his breath. If they'd spent even a few days considering other possibilities, they might have been better prepared for this day.

"It has been decided, at the very highest levels, that the Empire will grant you and your worlds the independence you crave," he said. "An election will be held within two weeks, so a caretaker government can take office and handle the independence negotiations. Martial law will be declared, to ensure the election can be held safety and no one—of whatever faction—has a chance to put their thumb on the scale. After that, the majority of our forces will withdraw within a month. My role will switch, at that point, from viceroy to ambassador. We will continue to provide a certain degree of border security until you are ready to stand on your own two feet, but I must caution you that will not last.

"My staff has already devised a list of issues that will have to be discussed, once the caretaker government takes power. A number are relatively simple and can be dismissed within the day. Others, such as the legal status of non-humans on Earth, may take longer. My government has agreed to repatriate non-humans who wish to leave, but—as time goes on—that offer may be closed. We ask you to be careful, when you decide what you want to do with your non-human population. You will no longer have our protection if you decide to mistreat them."

Yasuke paused, studying their faces. They seemed shocked, too shocked to hide it. The Empire Loyalists were astonished, no doubt considering he'd shoved them out of the shuttlecraft, but the Humanity League looked equally surprised. They were getting everything they wanted on a silver platter...Yasuke concealed his amusement with an effort. Perhaps they should have followed their ancestors' warning about being careful what they wished for. Earth would stand alone, against a hostile universe. And the rest of the galaxy would know how dangerous the humans could be.

"This isn't what any of us expected," he concluded. "My office hoped there would be a steady transfer of powers, not an immediate withdrawal from your territory. We ask you—I ask you—to look to the future, to put the past in the past and think about the future of your people. You have—you have always had—remarkable potential. It is up to you, now, to decide if you will live up to it or not."

He took one last look around the chamber, then turned and walked out. The silence was deafening. They were stunned beyond words, suddenly finding themselves standing at the brink of apotheosis or nemesis. Yasuke felt a hot flash of anger, cursing Colonel Tallinn—again—for his sheer stupidity. His superiors had refused to let him surrender the colonel to human justice, pointing out it would set a terrible precedent. They'd refused to listen to his argument that *not* handing him over would *also* set a terrible precedent. He was mildly surprised he hadn't been ordered to put Colonel Tallinn on a ship and send him home. Perhaps his superiors wanted to keep their options open.

His datapad bleeped as he made his slow way back to his office. The media had broadcast the speech to the entire world. Reactions were already flooding in, some of them curiously muted. The world had just changed, turned upside down in the blink of an eye. Even the most xenophobic humans, the ones who lived in places devoid of non-human life, would have problems coming to terms with what had just happened. The planet hadn't been changed so badly since the invasion itself, hundreds of years ago.

Yasuke felt another pang, of guilt and grief and sheer frustration. He'd grown to love the planet, and the human race, over the last few decades. The viceroyalty had been the culmination of his professional career. He wasn't fool enough to think he could keep climbing the ladder, not when his enemies were already gathering. And even if he did…it would take years, years he didn't have, to reach a level where he could wield raw power again. On Earth, he was a big fish in a small pond. Back home…

Not that it matters, he thought, coldly. *The humans will already be looking to the future.*

He sat, checking his datapad as yet more reports flooded in. His staff were still working on the list of matters that had to be discussed, drawing up working papers on everything from military collaboration to the distribution of economic assets. The big combines were already demanding huge payments or…or what? He wanted to laugh. It wasn't as if they could dismantle an asteroid mining station and ship it back home. Half the industrial nodes were owned by humans and nearly all of them were *operated* by humans. Who knew which way their operators would jump, if push came to shove? Who knew?

They'll side with their fellow humans, he told himself. He was morbidly sure of it. Why would the operators accept being subordinate when they could be equals? *And that will mean bad news for the combines.*

He smiled, humourlessly. Right now, that was someone else's problem.

• • •

"On your feet, Lieutenant."

Tomas stood, feeling old. He'd been in the holding cell for days, but it felt like years. He'd always had a pretty good time sense—he'd grown up on a series of military bases—yet he'd started to lose his grip as time plodded onwards. It didn't help that no one had so much as *hinted* he might be released, or charged with failing to prevent an atrocity or *something*. He'd had the nasty feeling, as hours turned into days and days turned into... *more* days, that no one really knew what they were doing. They were just marking time, waiting for something to happen.

He scowled at the intelligence officer. They were all the same, weedy men who asked the same questions time and time again. Tomas was entirely sure that everything he'd said, time and time again, had been recorded and dissected by an entire *team* of intelligence officers, intent on finding something they could use to toss his career into the crapper. The psych tests hadn't helped. He was morbidly certain they intended to blame him for everything. First, for failing to stop the atrocity; then for stopping it. Consistency had never been a priority when the shit was hitting the fan.

"What now?" His throat felt uncomfortably dry. "Have you reached the limits of what anal probing can teach you?"

The intelligence officer gave him a sharp look. "What are you talking about?"

Tomas snorted. "You've kept me here for days," he said. He wasn't going to admit he wasn't sure *just* how long he'd been in the cell. "Aren't you supposed to charge me with something? Or…"

"There are no charges," the intelligence officer said. "You're being returned to barracks."

"Oh." Tomas felt his head swim. After everything…they were just returning him to barracks? They were just…letting him go? It made no sense. "And Colonel Tallinn?"

"Is no longer your concern," the intelligence officer said, forbiddingly. "His fate won't be decided here."

"Oh," Tomas repeated. A nasty thought occurred to him. "And what about my men?"

The intelligence officer turned and headed for the door, beckoning Tomas to follow him. "I believe the matter was discussed at the very highest levels," he said. "A failure to follow orders would have been counted as mutiny, which—in a state of unrest—could have led to the death penalty. The government has decided to class them all as being personally blameless—you included. The whole affair is being swept under the rug."

"Fuck," Tomas said. He felt a surge of anger. He'd watched the slaughter time and time again, every time he closed his eyes. His dreams had been so bad he'd been tempted to beg for sleeping pills. "How many people died?"

"Around five hundred," the intelligence officer said. He stopped and turned to face the younger man. "Did you watch the broadcast?"

Tomas laughed. "Where the fuck do you think I've been for the last few days?"

"The peacocks are pulling out," the intelligence officer said. His voice was so flat there was no way to believe he was joking. "They're picking up their crap and going back home. Right now, martial law has been declared and we need every last soldier on the streets. I suggest"—his voice hardened—"that you go back to the barracks, report for duty and try to forget what happened over the last few days. And be grateful the public doesn't know your name. There's a *lot* of anger out there."

"And it will be worse, when it becomes clear that Colonel Tallinn's gotten away with it," Tomas said. He felt a chill settle in his heart. "And he has gotten away with it, hasn't he?"

"I don't know," the intelligence officer said. "But you know what? It's above your pay grade. Above mine too, for that matter. I dare say the provisional government will raise the issue soon enough, once the election cycle is completed and we start rushing towards independence. That's their problem."

Tomas said nothing as they reached the door and headed into the open air. He could see a plume of smoke rising from the other side of the city, suggesting...suggesting what? A terrorist bomb? Or a bonfire? Or... or what? He knew he should be relieved he hadn't been blamed for the massacre, that he hadn't been shoved in front of a court-martial or secret court and condemned to death to save Colonel Tallinn. And yet...too many people knew the truth, too many to bribe or intimidate into silence. The secret couldn't be kept. And trying would only make it worse.

"Thanks," he said, sourly. The system was fucked. Independence couldn't come soon enough. "And what do we do after independence?"

"Fucked if I know," the intelligence officer said. He sounded a little more human, now they'd moved to a less politically unsafe topic. "Right now, everyone else is wondering the same thing. And *some* of them will make their move."

CHAPTER TWELVE

Star City, Earth/Earth Defence Force One, Earth Orbit

"I DON'T UNDERSTAND IT," Abraham admitted. "Why did they just...*give up*?"

He stared at his hands as the conference room slowly filled with politicians, their aides and a handful of reporters who could be trusted to put a good spin on affairs. It had been two days since the Viceroy's speech, two days since the world—the entire universe—had been knocked off its axis. The Alphans had been a part of the world for hundreds of years, long enough to be...normal. It was hard to grasp the idea of a world without them, even though he'd been working towards it for years. He didn't want to admit it, even to himself, but he'd never really believed it could happen. Now...he'd read the books, the accounts of life immediately after the invasion. He thought he understood—now—why so many of them had sounded as if they'd been smacked on the head with a baseball bat.

"They're not human," Rachel said, simply. "I think we forget that, sometimes."

Abraham gave her a sharp look. "What do you mean?"

"They're not human," she repeated, dryly. "We instinctively think of them as being like *us*. We project ourselves onto them, as a man might project himself onto a woman or vice versa. But they're not human. A human might fight to the last, despite the ever-increasing cost of fighting and the certainty that even *victory* would be meaningless. I mean, look at it from *their* point of view."

She ticked off points on her fingers as she spoke. "They don't have many options. They can fight to keep us under control, but that would cost them heavily even if they won. They'd be so badly weakened their other enemies would jump them. They can do nothing, but that would ensure a revolt that could trigger off a war. Again, even if they win, they lose. They can give up the murdering bastard and make concessions, but that would only whet our appetite for more. And"—she shrugged—"they can cut their losses, evacuate the planet and concede independence. It's their best option."

Abraham frowned. "They'd still be giving up one hell of a lot."

"Yes," Rachel agreed. "But they'd be losing it anyway, wouldn't they? This way, they come out looking good. They may even be able to capitalise on our regard for them."

"We'll see," Abraham said. He leaned back in his chair as the doors were firmly closed, then tapped the table for attention. "As you know, there will be an election in two weeks. I intend to win that election."

He allowed his eyes to wander the room. The Humanity League had always been a pretty big church, although he and his predecessors had worked hard to keep rebels and outright terrorists out of the inner party. There were people who wanted economic freedom sharing a table with people who wanted *religious* freedom. Abraham himself was very much an atheist, with as little regard for religion as the Alphans themselves, but he understood the desire to worship—or not—as one chose. It wasn't something that should be dictated by the government. It was just a shame, he felt, that Admiral Glass had declined his invitation. They wanted—they needed—the EDF onside.

"Right now, the Empire Loyalists are in a state," he continued smoothly. "What's the point of being loyal to an Empire that's just abandoned you? Given time, they will no doubt come up with *some* kind of platform, but

I don't think they can come up with something in less than two weeks. I imagine they will push for close relations with the Empire even after it abandoned us. I think we can do better than that."

He smiled, coldly. "We have a week to put together our message, then present it to the public. The people are shocked, fearful of what the future will bring. The economy is wobbling, hundreds of thousands of people are unemployed...we need to speak to those people, to convince them they can put the future in our hands. And that means we need to promise them something they can grasp, something *practical*. We—right here, right now—are going to put that campaign together.

"The polls—both physical and electronic—cannot be trusted right now. Everyone is holding their breath, waiting for something to happen. The slightest mishap will send them running in all directions, screaming for everything from a return to the Empire to further independence, to a revival of the curse of nationalism that destroyed our hopes of becoming a second-stage race before we were brought into the Empire. We must be calm, yet promise a future—a future that speaks to the people, a future that can be ours. We must convince them to have faith, once again. Faith in us. Faith in humanity. Faith in a common—and glorious—destiny."

His words hung in the air for a long chilling moment. "My staff have compiled a list of issues that will have to be addressed, sooner rather than later. I've taken the liberty of outlining prospective stances on each of the issues, from points we can let slide to concerns we *cannot* let go unaddressed. Many of them will bore people"—he grinned, openly—"and others will confuse them. However, we have to appear on top of them. It is only a matter of time before we face political opposition."

He tapped the datapad. "I've forwarded you the list," he said. "And now...let us be about it."

• • •

Admiral Adam Glass had suspected, through a handful of sources in the viceroy's office, that *something* big was about to happen. The clues hadn't been too clear, but he'd been fairly sure the Viceroy wasn't about to declare martial law, purge opposition politicians and gamble it wouldn't trigger a more general revolt. He hadn't thought to put troops on alert, let alone start moving them to jump-off positions. The Viceroy was experienced enough to understand that launching a coup—to all intents and purposes—required a considerable degree of planning and preparation. And yet...

He sipped his coffee, feeling stunned. He'd served the Empire loyally for his entire adult life, yet...he was being tossed aside, like something that had outlived its usefulness? He found it hard to wrap his head around the sheer *scale* of the betrayal. There were hundreds of thousands of humans—millions, really—who served their masters loyally. It was impossible to believe they'd just been abandoned. And yet, the Alphans had decided to simply withdraw from Earth and the surrounding sector. They were just...letting go.

Adam felt old, old and tired, as he contemplated the news. He'd studied human history well before it became popular amongst the young. He knew pre-invasion Earth had been a mess, with endless wars over everything from raw materials to religion. He knew the Galactics looked down on Earth for not growing up, for not reaching for the stars and leaving childish superstitions behind them. He knew...he shook his head. It didn't matter. There was nothing he could do to change things. The Empire was pulling out, abandoning humanity to its fate. And the EDF would go to the new government. And then...who knew?

He looked up as the intercom bleeped. "Admiral, Commodore Tyne and Captain Henderson are here."

"Send them in," Adam ordered tartly. The staff officers were running around like headless chickens. In hindsight, perhaps it had been a mistake to place strict limits on the number of officers flying a desk at any given moment. Right now, he could do with a few more pen-pushers and beancounters. "And then bring more coffee."

He turned and took his seat as the hatch opened. Commodore Tyne and Captain Henderson both looked tired, as if they hadn't slept for the last two days. Adam didn't blame the younger officers. The EDF had been designed as an auxiliary formation, not an independent fleet in its own right. Divorcing the human units from the Alphan Navy would be... interesting. There were formations that were effectively independent and units that were so closely entangled with their alien counterparts that it could take years to separate the two. And they didn't *have* years. They had a month, perhaps less.

They're slow to make up their minds, he recalled. *And yet, when they do, they move fast.*

"Be seated," he said. "Commodore?"

"In some ways, we're fortunate," Tyne said. "The war actually removed most of the embeds from the fleet, allowing us to replace them with human officers. There were plans to have the embeds return, but...one thing led to another and none of those plans ever actually came to anything. The remaining alien officers, by and large, are not regarded as particularly competent. That said"—his eyes narrowed as he looked at his datapad— "I'd like to try to convince some of them to stay with us."

"If they will," Adam said. "And if their government agrees."

"Yes, sir," Tyne said. "Logistically speaking, we can meet roughly ninety percent of the fleet's operational requirements from human-owned and operated industrial nodes. The handful of exceptions are going to be a problem, at least until we can either convince them to licence the components to us or develop ways to produce them for ourselves without violating the copyrights. We can presumably purchase them, but... frankly, I don't know how long that'll last. The Alphans have to rebuild their own navy first."

"Better than I feared," Adam commented. "And crew?"

Tyne glanced at Henderson. "Captain?"

"There are two aspects of concern," Henderson said. "First, we will have to move officers up to replace the embeds, when they depart. That may or may not be a problem, depending on how long we have to smooth things out. It won't be possible to tell how many of those officers are really competent until they get thrown into combat. We may have to replace some of them—again—as they lose our confidence."

Adam nodded, curtly. "And the second?"

"We drafted vast numbers of trained and experienced crew, mainly from the merchant marine," Henderson said. "Many of those crewmen were kept in service, even after the war. We were simply too short of manpower to do anything else. But they aren't happy about it and many of them are—frankly—mutinous. We also extended enlistments, which *really* didn't help. We could—and did—get away with that while the war was on. Now..."

There might be another war, sooner rather than later, Adam thought. *What will the Vulteks do when they realise the Alphans are pulling out?*

He turned his attention back to Henderson. "How do you propose we proceed?"

"I suggest, very strongly, that we release the vast majority of drafted crewmen," Henderson said. "Some *do* want to stay in the navy, but...most of them want to leave. We should probably also release crewmen who had their enlistments extended, with higher pay and more shore leave for those who choose to remain. I think we could solve many of our remaining problems, Admiral, by treating the enlisted with some respect."

"True," Adam agreed, dryly.

Henderson frowned. "And we might also want to look at expanding the mustang program," he added. "The lack of promotion, beyond a certain point, rankles."

"It isn't as if we don't have mustangs," Adam pointed out.

"Yes, but they're relatively rare," Henderson countered. "And really... we don't want our navy to be contaminated by favouritism and political appointees. That's what cost the peacocks so badly during the war."

"I wouldn't put it that way," Adam said. "But I take your point."

"Yes, sir," Henderson said. "The Alphan warcruisers are scheduled to leave in just over a month. I propose we start replacing the embeds now, then trust the new commanders to handle the demobilisation process. That should give us time to work the kinks out before we have to stand on our own two feet."

"Very good," Adam said. He looked from one to the other, then back again. "Commodore, start the process at once. And be polite, when you're telling the embeds to leave."

"Aye, sir," Tyne said. "We don't want any diplomatic incidents."

"No," Adam agreed. "It would make the negotiations a little harder."

He dismissed them both, turning his attention to the latest series of reports as they left the compartment. There were too many things that had been allowed to slide, during the war and its immediate aftermath. If only he'd known what was coming…he sighed, inwardly, at a rumour Colonel Tallinn had been put on a warcruiser bound for Capital. The murderer was likely to escape justice. His superiors might be horrified at what he'd done, but it wasn't technically illegal. He could make a pretty good case if he ever stood in front of a court-martial.

Bastard, Adam thought.

He keyed his terminal. "Get me a secure link to *James Bond*."

"Aye, Admiral," Ensign Corey said. "Priority one?"

"Yes," Adam confirmed. "Priority one."

He leaned back in his chair, wishing he could just go to bed. There was no way to know what would happen to him personally, once the new government took power. The polls were all over the place, predicting everything from a sham independence to outright war. He rather suspected no one really knew what was about to happen, not even the humans who'd agitated for independence over the last few decades. And…whoever took power might not want *him*. He was a loyalist. He'd been a loyalist longer than most people had been alive. They might not want to keep him…

They can't penalise us for being loyalists, he thought, glumly. *The entire planet is crammed with loyalists…*

He put the thought aside as Captain Anderson's face appeared in the terminal. "Admiral," he said. "This is a surprise."

"I'm sorry for disturbing you," Adam said. "I take it you've heard the news?"

"Yes, sir," Anderson said. "How does this change things for us?"

"The election hasn't taken place yet, so nothing can be said for certain," Adam said. "However, it looks as if we'll inherit all the human-majority worlds as well as a cluster of other settlements and crossroads within the sector. I don't know how long we'll be able to keep them."

"The Vulteks," Anderson said, flatly.

"And others, perhaps," Adam said. "Previously, the Alphans handled our border security. The EDF didn't develop major naval bases outside Sol itself. We're looking into ways to project power, but"—he shrugged—"it may take some time. I need you back out there, quickly."

Anderson grimaced. "Yes, sir."

"I know it won't be easy," Anderson said. "But any immediate threat is likely to come from that direction. I want you to survey the border systems as you trade within the sector, watching for potential threats. If you find anything, return to Delaine at once. I'll clear you to use the FTL transmitter."

"Understood." Anderson looked pensive. "My kids are refusing to leave the ship."

Adam had to smile. "Do you want a marine squad assigned to remove them?"

"No, sir," Anderson said. He laughed, humourlessly. "I just need permission to tell them the truth."

"Which they might repeat to the wrong person," Adam said. He let out a breath. "I understand your concerns, but...if they say the wrong thing at the wrong time, you will be in some trouble."

"Yes, sir," Anderson said. "I'd still like to tell them the truth."

Adam considered it for a long moment. Anderson's family *should* be good at keeping secrets. Most spacer families were surprisingly insular. And yet, if they said the wrong thing...they might be caught, sentenced to death and shoved out the nearest airlock. The Vulteks would be entirely within their right to execute them on the spot. It wasn't as if Earth could do anything about it.

"Use your own best judgement," he said, finally. "But I strongly advise against it."

He shook his head slowly. "The border might get very dangerous, very quickly," he added. "If you want to offload them, do it now. We can arrange a transfer to Mars or Luna..."

"I'll let them choose," Anderson said. "They're old enough to make the call for themselves, if they wish."

"I'll take your word for it," Adam said. "And watch your back out there."

"I have eyes in the back of my head, just to watch my back," Anderson said. He grinned, then sobered. "We won't let you down."

"Good." Adam lifted a hand in salute. "I'll see you when you get home."

He watched Anderson's face vanish, then keyed the terminal to bring up the starchart. The Vulteks would know, now, that things were going to change. They'd already been pressing the border hard. Would they have the patience, he asked himself, to wait for the Alphans to leave? Or would they push harder, convinced the Alphans wouldn't put up more than token resistance? There was no way to know.

And there are millions of humans along the border, he mused. *What'll happen to them if their colonies are invaded?*

The starchart altered at his command. There were few outposts and no major naval bases between Delaine and Sol itself. If the enemy mounted a major raid—or a full-scale invasion—humanity was going to take one hell of a beating. There was little hope of stopping them short of Sol, unless...he tapped his terminal. The staff were going to be working overtime, drawing up contingency plans. Everything they'd taken for granted had suddenly changed...

And if our enemies take advantage of the chaos, he warned himself, *we could lose the war before it is fairly begun.*

CHAPTER THIRTEEN

EDS *Washington*, Earth Orbit/*James Bond*, Earth Orbit

"IT ISN'T FAIR," Captain Nobunaga said. "Why should *I* have to be recalled?"

Commander—Captain, now—Naomi Yagami tried and failed to hide her smirk. Thankfully, Nobunaga couldn't read her face. The Alphan embed had never bothered to study his subjects, even when he'd realised his life depended on his subordinates doing their jobs…hell, she wasn't sure he'd ever realised he was dependent upon his people. His orders to turn command over to her and return to Earth, to wait for repatriation back to Capital, had not come a moment too soon.

And *she* was the new captain. She wanted to dance and sing and throw military order to the wolves. She wanted…she calmed, reminding herself that she was about to become responsible for the entire cruiser, for all three hundred lives aboard. She could afford to be generous, now she'd won her chance to show what she could do. She tightened her face, then bent into the posture of respect as Nobunaga headed for the hatch. His staff had already taken his bags to the shuttle. Naomi suspected they were rather more eager to head home than their master.

"Why?" Nobunaga stopped and gazed at her. "Why?"

"We must not question the will of the council," Naomi said. "They must have a role for you back home."

Nobunaga straightened up. "Perhaps a warcruiser command," he said. "Or even a deep-space starcruiser."

"Perhaps," Naomi said. She'd bet her entire paycheck that Nobunaga was going to vanish into obscurity. The Alphans had learnt hard lessons during the war. They knew better than to let well-connected, but incompetent officers into positions of power. Nobunaga was unlikely to get a desk job, if he was allowed to stay in the navy at all. "I'm sure they'll make the right decision."

She walked beside him as he strode down to the shuttle hatch. Technically, he should have been seen off by the entire senior crew, but half of the officers had been reassigned and the other half were too busy trying to get the ship back into fighting trim now a quarter of the crew had been sent home for discharge. Naomi had known it would happen, sooner or later, but she was still astonished by the sheer *scale* of the chaos. Two of her prospective XOs had already been reassigned to other ships. She had no idea who—if anyone—would take her former place. She might wind up serving as her own XO.

I guess I'll have to shout at myself later, she thought, with a flicker of humour. *Just to keep myself from taking my feelings out on the crew.*

"Good luck," she said, as Nobunaga stepped through the hatch. "I'm sure we'll see each other again."

The Alphan said nothing as the hatch slammed closed. Naomi wasn't too surprised. Nobunaga had never seen her as anything other than a particularly talkative pet. It would have hurt his pride to say goodbye, let alone treat her as an equal…she shook her head as the light switched from green to red. Nobunaga was on his way home, the ship was hers and…she wanted to jump in the air and cheer. It was *her* ship now.

She nodded to the hatch, paying what little respect Nobunaga might be due, then turned and walked back to the bridge. The crew—her crew—gave her a wide berth, unsure how to treat her now that their commander had been promoted to captain. It was rare for a commander not to transfer to a different ship when they were promoted. She'd expected as much, but...she shook her head. She knew *Washington* like the back of her hand. The cruiser might not be the most advanced ship in the known universe, but she was *hers*. And Naomi knew how to use her ship to best advantage.

The bridge hatch hissed open as she approached. The marines, who should have been on duty, were absent, called back to the planet to enforce martial law. Naomi let out a breath as she stepped into the compartment, her eyes wandering over the consoles—some manned, some on standby—as she drifted to the command chair. It had been designed for the vessel's original commander, back in the mists of time, but there was no need to have it replaced. The Alphans were humanoid. She paced across the bridge and took her seat...*her* seat. A thrill ran through her as she rested her hand against the captain's console, the computer network unlocking at her touch. It was *hers*. *Hers*, and hers alone.

She took a moment to enjoy herself, then looked at Lieutenant Roger's back. "Status report?"

"The engineering team report we will be at full readiness within four days, assuming we don't lose any more crewmen," Roger said. "And then we'll be ready to depart."

Assuming we manage to get some orders, Naomi mused. There was no shortage of rumours running around the fleet's whisper network, but they were so contradictory it was hard to tell which of them—if any—should be taken seriously. They were going to war. No, the entire EDF was going to be disbanded. No, they were going to remain tied to the Alphans...there were so many stories, none confirmed. *And, perhaps, some shore leave.*

She rubbed her cheek as she brought up the readiness reports. The crew really *did* need shore leave, something beyond a couple of days on Luna or Earth. She doubted anyone was going to get any shore leave, not after the draftees had been discharged and allowed to go home. There was too much work to do...she frowned as she scanned the more detailed reports.

It was easy to see that errors were on the rise. It was only a matter of time before one of them proved disastrous.

And that's my problem now, she told herself. *What the fuck do I do about it?*

She stood. "Lieutenant Roger, you have the conn," she said. "Alert me if *anything* happens."

"Aye, Captain," Roger said.

Naomi stepped into her ready room, shaking her head in dismay as the hatch closed behind her. She'd wanted command, yet…she had too much to do, with a crew that was tired beyond all endurance. She poured herself a mug of coffee and sat at her desk…her desk in name as well as fact, now Nobunaga was gone. He should have kicked her out of the ready room years ago. That he hadn't…she put the thought aside as she pulled up the latest set of messages. The EDF command network wanted a personalised update.

Which makes perfect sense, she mused. *In all the chaos, it would be hard for them to tell who's really doing what.*

Naomi keyed her terminal and started to speak. "EDS *Washington* will be at full combat readiness within four days, barring incidents. However, there are certain matters I must bring to your attention. In particular, the crew is both exhausted and severely depleted. I have been unable to hold drills, even before assuming formal command of the vessel, which will have dangerous effects on crew efficiency. *Washington* requires at least another thirty billets filled as soon as possible. Therefore, I propose…"

She took a sip of her coffee and continued, marshalling her thoughts and arguments as best she could. Admiral Glass would have hundreds of problems, scattered over dozens of warships, freighters and orbital defence installations. It was unlikely he or any of his immediate subordinates would even hear her message, let alone pull out all the stops to resupply her ship. And shore leave…she shook her head in irritation as she finished talking and replayed the message to make sure she'd covered all the bases. Earth was in a state of chaos, even under martial law. The crew would be safer onboard ship.

We need to invest in a luxury liner to accompany the fleet, she thought. The Alphans had done that, she'd heard. They couldn't send the crew to shore leave, so they'd brought shore leave to the crew. But the EDF couldn't afford it. *Or even just turn a freighter into an entertainment complex.*

Her eyes narrowed as an icon popped up in front of her. A cluster of political speeches had been uploaded onto the datanet, speeches from politicians intent on retaining or gaining office after the withdrawal was complete. Naomi hesitated, reminding herself she was supposed to be on duty, then keyed the icon. The speeches unfolded in front of her, ready to play. She told herself, firmly, that it was her duty to consider the issues carefully, then vote as she saw fit. This time, her vote actually mattered.

Unless someone finds a way to rig the election, she reminded herself. She'd been assured, in civics class, that it was impossible, but she'd been a naval officer long enough to know that any computer network could be hacked. *Even with paper ballots and exit polls, it would be hard to be sure.*

"It is easy to forget," Abraham Douglas's image said, "that humanity had a long history well before the outside universe crashed into our system and turned everything we thought we knew upside down. It is easy to forget that there was a time when humanity stood alone, when we built a civilisation that was truly ours. We made mistakes, as any student of history will tell you, but they were *our* mistakes. They were not inflicted upon us by alien masters.

"And so I believe we should grasp independence with both hands. The human race has vast potential. There is no reason to fear independence, as if we're children who would starve without our parents. There is no reason to think that independence would become total disaster. Instead, let us look to the future. The time has come to cast away our shackles and make our mark on the universe, for better or worse. Whatever happens, whatever our fate, it will be *ours*.

"The Humanity League intends to seize this opportunity and make the most of it. We will cut red tape and remove bureaucratic edicts standing in our path. We will devote massive resources to developing our colonies, expanding our economy and fuelling a human renaissance that will take us—and our allies—to heights even the greatest of galactic civilisations never grasped. We will grow and develop and become something new. And it will be *ours*.

"Let us not fear the future. Let us, instead, stride purposefully towards a glorious destiny."

Naomi frowned as the speech came to an end, a textual note stating that a more detailed manifesto was open for inspection if she wished. She promised herself she'd read it carefully, when she had a moment. She wanted to believe in Douglas's words, but the cynic in her knew it wouldn't be so easy. The galaxy was filled with alien races, some more powerful and threatening than humanity. If the Alphans pulled back, someone would seek to fill the power vacuum. She was all too aware the EDF was nowhere near powerful enough to hold the line, if one of the major races came calling. They might be battered all the way back to Earth if they were forced to fight a full-scale war.

She frowned, then played the second speech. Nancy Middleton looked stunned, as if she'd been slapped across the face and never quite recovered. Naomi found it difficult to blame the older woman, even if she *was* a politician. She'd dedicated her life to serving her alien masters, and now her masters had abandoned her. She might not look like a villain, but she sure looked like a fool. Naomi felt a twinge of pity. The First Speaker deserved better than to be cast aside on the rubbish heap of history.

And yet, she can't make a case for being loyal now, Naomi mused. *What's the point?*

She paused the message as her intercom bleeped, calling her to engineering. Technically, it was the XO's job...but she was the XO, at least until someone was transferred or promoted into the slot. She stood and headed for the hatch. She'd wanted to command a ship. And that meant she had to take command.

And prove I can handle it before we get orders, she thought. *We're not going to spend the rest of my career hanging around in orbit, are we?*

There was no such thing as a conference room on *James Bond*. The very idea was laughable on a ship where space was at a premium. Captain Thomas Anderson gathered his crew on the bridge, looking from face to face as they studied the ship's planned flight to Delaine. They were all family, from the youngest to the oldest. He knew better than to trust anyone who wasn't linked to him by blood.

"We're going to be heading back to Delaine, then along the border," he said, curtly. The crew had had a few days in port, visiting asteroid facilities that rivalled anything Earth had to offer, but it wasn't really enough. "And we're going to be heading into danger."

He took a breath. Sarah knew, but everyone else…they might have *guessed*, he told himself sharply. They hadn't raised any fools. They knew he'd made a trip to Earth, something that was far from easy in the current climate. The government had shut down the spaceport strips, as well as the red-light districts and everywhere else that might appeal to bored and lonely sailors who wanted to spend their cash before going back out again. Thomas honestly couldn't think of anything more likely to spark riots. Bloody bureaucrats knew nothing about the hardships of interstellar space.

"We have a secondary mission, beyond trading what we can," he said, curtly. "We have to…collect intelligence on the local situation and send it home."

Wesley looked unsurprised, he noted. The two younger girls blinked in astonishment. He tried not to think about them being blasted out the airlock, or simply being sold into slavery if they were captured by a pirate crew. Or worse. He would have preferred to put them off the ship, regardless of their feelings on the matter. Only the certainty they'd resent him for the rest of his life—and the awareness they were old enough, by interstellar standards, to make up their own minds—kept him from doing it. And yet…

"Spacers have always gathered intelligence, but we'll be doing it in the middle of a…disputed zone," he added. "There is a very real prospect of being shot, or worse, if we are captured. They'll treat us as spies, because we will be spies. And there will be little hope of being rescued."

He kept his face under tight control, trying not to show his dismay. He was a spacer. He knew, better than any groundhog, the realities of interstellar war. Earth was puny, compared to any of the Galactics. The Vulteks could march in and take the border worlds any time they liked, once the Alphans had pulled out. They might even try to menace Earth itself. He hated to admit it, but Admiral Glass was right. They needed intelligence, they needed to know what was going on...he had the nasty feeling they'd just be watching the inevitable unfold in real time. The Vulteks might not be stopped until they ran into something strong enough to make them.

"You know the risks," he said. He ignored the glare his wife directed at him. "If any of you want to leave, no hard feelings. I'll write you a proper referral letter"—he tried not to think about the fact he'd half-expected his son and oldest daughter to leave anyway—"and no one will hold it against you. But if not..."

A dozen words ran through his head. He dismissed them all. "We leave tomorrow," he said, instead. Admiral Glass had made sure the ship was given priority in the repair and maintenance queue. "I need your answer by the end of the day."

"I'll stay," Wesley said, at once. "I don't want to leave you now."

"We *might* meet some good-looking young men along the border," Sally Anderson said, grinning at her mother. "Someone charming, someone handsome..."

"With a beak and feathers who expects you to make him a nest," Wesley put in. "Just put your feather boa on and you'll be laughing."

"Shut the fuck up, Wesley," Sally snapped. "Mom!"

Sarah rested her hands on her hips. "You heard your father," she said. "If you want to stay, then stay."

"I'll stay," Ginny said. "But if Sally wants a boyfriend..."

"Listen, you little brat," Sally snapped. "I want..."

"*Quiet!*" Anderson looked at his three children. He loved them dearly, but there were limits to his patience. "This is not a game. We may—we will—be flying into danger. And if we get caught, we will die. If any of you want to leave, let me know. And if you don't...we leave tomorrow."

Wesley smiled. "Does this mean we don't get to vote?"

"I think it means that the election won't matter," Anderson said. He wanted to believe otherwise, but he didn't. The most powerful man on Earth couldn't dictate terms to the Galactics. The more he thought about it, the more he feared the worst. Independence might prove to be nothing more than a sham. "If war breaks out along the border, which it might, whoever's in charge won't be able to do anything about it. If war comes..."

"Register a proxy vote," Sarah said. "And hope to hell it gets counted."

"Yes, Mom," Wesley said.

CHAPTER FOURTEEN

Star City, Earth

"THE HUMANITY LEAGUE IS RISING IN THE POLLS," Nancy Middleton said. "Is there nothing you can do about it?"

Yasuke winced, inwardly. It hadn't taken long—barely a day, by his count—for accusations of betrayal to start circulating. The Empire Loyalists had been feeling the pinch long before the poll results *really* started to bite. Their opponents hadn't *needed* to play dirty to make them look like fools, collaborators and generally outdated. What was the point, they asked time and time again, of being loyal when there was nothing to be loyal *to*?

"I don't believe so," he said, quietly. "The blunt truth is that we are granting Earth independence…"

"Abandoning us," Nancy said, bitterly.

"We don't have a choice," Yasuke said. "We cannot fight to keep Earth when much of the population wants us gone."

"We don't," Nancy said. "A headlong rush towards independence is a mistake."

Yasuke didn't disagree, but his people knew better than to waste time on pointless recriminations. What was done was done. He wondered if she recognised the irony. A month ago, she would never have dared speak to him like that. She would have assumed the posture of supreme respect before inching towards the topic, ready to cut and deny everything if he reacted badly. He supposed he couldn't really blame her. Whatever happened, whoever won the election, Nancy was going to lose her post. Her successor would have the task of turning the Empire Loyalists into a post-independence party.

"The point remains, we don't have a choice," he repeated, patiently. "And if we try to...influence...the election results, we risk alienating the next government. We simply cannot afford to appear anything other than impartial."

He sighed, inwardly. His superiors kept bombarding him with suggestions, ranging from openly supporting the loyalist factions to simply rigging the election. It was certainly possible, in theory. His word carried weight. His people controlled the datanet. But in practice, there was little hope of getting away with it. The truth would come out and then...there would be war. And if they tried and *failed* to rig the election, they'd be laughingstocks.

"I appreciate your position," he added. "And my government repeats its offer to you."

"To leave?" Nancy laughed, humourlessly. "Earth is my home."

"I know," Yasuke said. "And yet, I don't know what will happen to you."

His staff had dug deep into humanity's history, trying to determine what would happen to the loyalists when the withdrawal was completed. The answers hadn't been particularly encouraging, although they'd admitted there were few human precedents for such a long gap between the invasion and the withdrawal. It wasn't as if the invasion had only taken place a few short decades ago. There were no living humans who remembered the days before the invasion. The Alphans had been part of their existence for as far as any human could recall. And the loyalists had seen them as the source of power...

They weren't collaborators, he told himself. *And they won't be purged after we go.*

He remembered the reports and scowled. The humans *couldn't* purge the loyalists, not unless they wanted to trigger a civil war. There were simply too many humans who'd served alien masters, simply too many humans who hadn't seen themselves—and hadn't been seen—as collaborators. The Humanity League had to understand that, didn't they? It wasn't as if the occupation had been truly oppressive. And their grand plans would come to nothing if they allowed themselves to be consumed by a desire for revenge.

"We'll have to come to terms with the League," Nancy said, flatly. "And that will mean cutting our ties to you."

"You might want to consider a more…open approach to the universe," Yasuke countered, thoughtfully. "There is much you could learn from the Galactics."

"Perhaps," Nancy said. "Your people brought great good as well as evil. And now you're betraying your supporters."

"We will do what we can," Yasuke said. The Humanity League wasn't *stupid*. They'd understand the importance of drawing a line under the past. And if they didn't…the viceregal government might be coming to an end, but he still had some cards to play. "We won't let you down."

"You already have," Nancy said, flatly. She stood. "With your permission, *My Lord*, I will see to my people."

Yasuke rose, too. "I understand your position," he said. "And the offer of safe passage out of the Solar System remains on the table."

"Yes," Nancy said. "But for how long?"

She turned and walked out of the room, an expression of disrespect that would have driven Yasuke's superiors into paroxysms of rage. She *dared* turn her back on her social superior? She dared? His lips curved into a grim humourless smile. The Empire Loyalists were dying and *he*, their acknowledged master, had dealt the final blow. He couldn't really blame Nancy Middleton for being angry. She couldn't hope to win the coming election. She'd have to leave politics forever, at the very least. She might even have to leave her homeworld. And Yasuke knew she wouldn't be entirely welcome on Capital. There were already too many humans on the homeworld for anyone's peace of mind.

Which is something we're going to have to sort out, he mused, as his secretary entered with a datapad. *Their precise legal status is in doubt.*

"My Lord," the secretary said. "I have the latest reports from the assessment teams…"

"And?" Yasuke allowed himself a moment of very human impatience. "What do they have to say?"

"They've narrowed down the list to ten issues we need to discuss with the post-election government," the secretary said. "They range from relatively simple—the precise status of embedded officers—to the fiendishly complex. Precisely who owes who money will be tricky to determine…"

"And it depends on who exactly is doing the counting," Yasuke finished. He'd spent enough time climbing the ladder to know that facts could be massaged, even if outright lying was flatly banned. He wondered, sometimes, if anyone knew the difference. One could go a long way by making claims that were *technically* true, without ever being indicted for lying. "Are there any matters of immediate concern?"

"The single greatest issue remains outside investment," the secretary said. "My Lord, the most optimistic scenario is…not encouraging."

"They don't want to pay us and we don't want to pay them," Yasuke said. He took the datapad and glanced at it. "And we don't want to drag out the negotiations any longer than strictly necessary."

"No, My Lord," the secretary said. "They should recognise our supremacy."

"But they won't," Yasuke predicted. "And really, why should they?"

His secretary looked shocked. Yasuke ignored him. The Humanity League might be willing to negotiate—they'd practically *have* to negotiate, if they wanted some kind of post-independence relationship with their former masters—but there were limits. They wouldn't accept anything that would leave the Alphans with a controlling interest in the human-dominated sector. They certainly wouldn't accept a veto on human foreign policy, interstellar trading or anything else that might impinge upon their independence. Yasuke suspected the combines were in for a shock. Earth had been a captive market, despite its growing industrial base. They'd be competing with the other interstellar powers—and the local industrialists—soon enough. Who knew *what* they'd make of it?

And negotiating the trade treaties may prove problematic, he mused, as he dismissed the secretary with a wave. *They're not going to want us dictating terms.*

He tapped his terminal, bringing up the reports. Election Day was tomorrow—and, if the polls were to be believed, the Humanity League was going to win. Yasuke believed them, if only because the League's own polling agreed with the official figures. Perhaps things would have been different if independence hadn't already been conceded. Perhaps... he snorted. He was thinking like a human. What was done was done... and, now, they had to look to the future. The past could take care of itself.

...

Abraham breathed a sigh of relief as he staggered into his private office and slumped into a comfortable chair. The last week had been *crammed* with activity. He'd given so many speeches the memories were starting to blur together, then held private meetings with industrialists, civil servants, military officers and everyone else who had an interest in influencing the post-independence government. He hadn't realised, he admitted, just how intense a full-fledged election campaign could be. It was the first election in living memory that actually *mattered*. People *believed* it mattered. He'd shook hands and kissed babies and made vague promises he *knew* would come back to haunt him...

Rachel stepped into the room. "Sir, the First Speaker has arrived," she said. His aide sounded vastly amused, although he wasn't sure what the joke was...if indeed there *was* a joke. "She requests the pleasure of your company."

Abraham sat up. "She's here?"

His mind raced. Had something slipped his mind? Had he forgotten a meeting? He'd been through so *many*, in the last few days, that he had to admit it was possible, even with Rachel monitoring his schedule with steely-eyed efficiency. And yet...Nancy Middleton was hardly the kind of person he'd forget. She was First Speaker. She would *remain* First Speaker until Election Day was over and the results were counted. He could hardly refuse to speak to her.

He rubbed his forehead. "Did I forget something?"

"No." Rachel smiled, humourlessly. "She just arrived."

"I see." Abraham forced himself to think. It had to be important. And...perhaps something that couldn't be trusted to the datanet. There was no other reason for demanding a meeting on the spur of the moment. Normally, the arrangements would be made well in advance. "Show her in, if you would, and pour us both some coffee."

He sat upright, brushing down his trousers. What did she want? What was so important she was prepared to break protocol to demand an immediate meeting? The Empire Loyalists prided themselves on being more Alphan than the Alphans. They wouldn't break protocol unless it was urgent...he stood as Rachel showed Nancy Middleton into the room. The First Speaker looked grim. A chill ran down Abraham's spine. Something was very wrong.

"Madam Speaker." Abraham stood and bowed. "Welcome to my humble abode."

Nancy bowed in return. "And I thank you for your welcome," she said, as she took the proffered seat. "I'm afraid time is not on my side."

"No," Abraham agreed. "I imagined you'd be out pressing the flesh too."

"Right now, my party finds me something of a liability," Nancy said. The bitterness in her voice was almost palpable. "My successor will be the one to reshape the loyalists into something new."

"I know." Abraham glanced up as Rachel brought two steaming mugs of coffee. "For what it's worth, you have my sympathy."

"Thanks." Nancy took her mug and sipped thoughtfully. "Tell me...

what will you do when you discover you *cannot* wave a magic wand and make everything better? What will you do when your promises come back to haunt you? What will you do when you find yourself torn between two competing sets of demands, where granting one faction's desire will alienate the other faction and drive them into the arms of your enemies?"

"I will do as I see fit," Abraham said. He eyed her for a long moment. "Tell *me*...why did you come here?"

"My family has been loyal for generations," Nancy said. She smiled, coldly. "So was yours, I believe. Or is the official biography little more than a tissue of lies?"

"Everything within my biography is true," Abraham said.

"From a certain point of view?" Nancy's smile widened, just for a second. "Or did you dare write the *complete* truth?"

Abraham allowed his irritation to show on his face. "Is there a point to this, Madam Speaker?"

"Just this," Nancy said. "I think we both know you're going to win the election. What are you going to do with the loyalists?"

Abraham blinked. He could read the polls as well as anyone—and they *did* say he had a huge edge over the divided opposition—but he knew better than to take them at face value. People *lied* to pollsters, either because they were afraid of telling the truth—and being punished for it—or simply because they disliked being harassed by political operatives. His private calculation suggested he'd take around seventy to eighty percent of the vote, but there was no way to be sure. Nancy had every reason to cast his victory into doubt.

"I don't understand the question," he said, smoothly. "What do you mean?"

Nancy spoke curtly, as if she found the mere act of speaking distasteful. "There are literally millions of humans who served the Alphans faithfully," she said. "What do you intend to do with them?"

"I don't bear a grudge," Abraham said. It would have been different, he supposed, if humanity had fought a long and bloody war of independence.

"People did…what they thought they could do, legally. My family certainly did."

"I'm sure your enemies have made capital out of that," Nancy said. "It must be embarrassing for you."

Abraham shrugged. "Madam Speaker, the blunt truth is that the Alphans represented legitimate authority for centuries. Countless humans worked for them—served them—because they were the only game in town. That was true, right up until the end of the war. Right up until *now*, really. How can they be blamed for serving the government? It was *the* government."

He allowed himself a slight smile. "If the definition of *legitimacy* is being in charge long enough for your predecessors to be effectively forgotten, the Alphans won handily."

"True." Nancy met his eyes. "You won't seek to penalise loyalists?"

"No." Abraham looked back at her, willing her to believe. "You said it yourself. There are millions of them. We cannot afford to do *without* them. We *certainly* cannot afford a full-fledged civil war between loyalists and Leaguers. I have no intention of penalising anyone."

"Direct Action says otherwise," Nancy said, bluntly.

"Direct Action is still irked I stole their thunder," Abraham said. "And that the government conceded independence without a fight. They're growing more radical because they're afraid of becoming irrelevant."

Like you, his thoughts added, silently. What was the point of preparing to fight an insurgency—or a terrorist campaign, depending on who wrote the history books—if you got what you wanted without having to fight for it? *Direct Action will fall into the trashcan of history soon enough.*

"I hope you're right," Nancy said. "I've come to offer you a bargain."

"A bargain," Abraham repeated. "Do you have anything to bargain with?"

Two spots of colour appeared on Nancy's cheek. "I can challenge the election results," she said. "Even now, as a lame duck, I can still make a fuss. I have nothing to lose."

"If your own people don't put a knife in your back first," Abraham pointed out.

"They'll wait until after the election," Nancy said. "Right now...they'll let me lead the party to crashing defeat, then blame me for everything and elect a new leader."

"Probably," Abraham said.

"But it also gives me some room to make life difficult for you," Nancy said. "If you agree to make it clear, during your final speech, that there will be no reprisals against loyalists, I'll agree not to challenge the results. Whatever they should happen to be..."

"I see," Abraham said. He thought, fast. "And you think the election results will be in doubt?"

Nancy looked back at him, evenly. "Are you sure they *won't* be?"

"The only way you'll win is through treachery," Abraham said. "And believe me, we'll catch you in the act."

"There's a lot of scared people out there," Nancy countered. "And some of them will cling to the *status quo*."

"Perhaps." Abraham took a breath. It wouldn't damage his standing within the party, not unless the election went very badly. And it would reassure loyalists who might otherwise cast their vote for the loyalist party. "Very well. I'll make the speech tomorrow night. I trust I can rely on you to keep your word...?"

"Yes." Nancy put her mug on the table. "I have good reason to keep my word."

"Yes," Abraham echoed. "What do you intend to do? Afterwards?"

"I have no idea." Nancy shrugged. "Retire, perhaps. Or play the elder statesman. Or write the traditional volume of fictitious nonsense about how I was kicked out because of party infighting...which would be more or less true, in my case. Or...the Viceroy offered me a seat on one of the departing warcruisers. I've always wanted to see the universe."

"You could always find a berth on a trading ship," Abraham said. He wouldn't blame Nancy for leaving. Her party would turn her into the scapegoat, once the dust had settled. They'd blame her for everything, while they restructured the party for a post-independence universe. "Or stick around long enough to make your successor look a bloody fool."

"I don't think any of them need the help," Nancy said. She stood. "Keep your side of the bargain and I'll keep mine."

Abraham stood and held out a hand. "It's been an honour."

"I wouldn't have minded if you'd won fairly," Nancy said, bitterly. She didn't shake his hand. "If you'd won enough seats to challenge the government, if you'd demanded and won an independence referendum or…or something *fair*. But you know what? The Viceroy himself pulled the rug out from under my feet!"

"I'm sorry," Abraham said.

"No, you're not," Nancy corrected. "And you'll discover, in the next few weeks, that it's easy to make promises and very hard to keep them."

CHAPTER FIFTEEN

Star City, Earth

"THEY SAY HISTORY IS IN THE MAKING," Corporal Willis said. "So why are we out here, freezing our butts off?"

"Because someone might try to cause trouble," Corporal Perkins replied. "And so we can cast our votes, at the end of the day."

Lieutenant Tomas Drache did his best to ignore the chatter as the squad secured their positions outside the school. It was a building that looked more like a prison than a *real* prison, although they *did* tend to be in short supply on Earth. He felt a frisson of distaste as he stared up at the blocky mass, looming over the marines like an avalanche just waiting to happen. He'd left school as soon as he legally could, enlisting in the marines and doing his level best to put his childhood behind. It was hard to believe the ugly building produced healthy, well-adjusted children. It was far more likely, in his view, that the kids would start walking the road to prison, exile or death. They wouldn't have to go very far.

He scowled as a cold wind blew over the city. He'd barely had any time to watch the speeches, read the manifestos and decide which way he was going to vote. His superiors had kept him busy, ever since he'd been released from the holding cell. He'd marched the streets, he'd broken up gatherings and he'd steered the homeless towards temporary accommodations that would keep them off the streets long enough for the election to take place. He simply hadn't had time...not, he admitted privately, that he'd hesitated before choosing which way to vote. There was no way he could vote for the Empire Loyalists.

A shape moved through the sky, humming faintly as it passed over the school and headed north. A drone...he tensed, before deciding it was probably a reporter's personal camera unit. It wouldn't have been permitted to fly over the city if someone higher up the chain hadn't reviewed the application and granted permission well ahead of time. He wondered, idly, who'd made the call as his HUD blinked up an alert. The curfew had been lifted. Election Day was about to begin.

"I think they're trying to discourage voters," Willis said. "Who do you know who *wants* to come back to school?"

Perkins snorted. "You think that'll discourage them?"

Probably, Tomas thought. It was easy to believe that *someone* higher-up thought no one would want to go back to school. The higher-ups had a poor grip on reality at the best of times. Who knew? They might expect the voters to stay well away or...he shook his head in amusement. *This is the most important election in living memory. Who's going to stay away?*

He frowned as a handful of people—older men and women, mainly—emerged from their homes and headed towards the guardpost. They looked harmless, but he knew from bitter experience that they could be carrying bombs or hiding guns under their coats...he told himself not to be paranoid. The patrols *had* kept the dissidents out of sight. A number of anarchists had been rounded up and arrested, held in protective custody until after the election was over. And Direct Action's most extreme factions wouldn't be insane enough to start something when they were on the verge of getting what they wanted...he hoped. Their ranting, what little he'd heard, had grown increasingly unhinged over the last few years.

An aircar swooped overhead and landed just outside the checkpoint, the passengers scrambling out and hastily handing out political leaflets to the civilians as they headed to the school. Behind them, Tomas watched others set up a booth and start projecting holographic speeches promising a new heaven and a new earth. The politicians looked as if they hadn't done a day's honest work in their lives. The cynic in him was grimly sure they were going to get egg on their faces, sooner or later. And then they'd expect the military to pull their fat out of the fire.

He put the thought aside as the first voter passed through the checkpoint, his ID confirmed before he was steered into the school. Tomas wondered what the old man—he looked old enough to be a grandfather—was thinking. He would have grown up in a world where all the real decisions were made hundreds of light years away. The prospect of humanity standing on its own against the universe *had* to be a little scary. Tomas had studied mob psychology, back in OCS. People sometimes voted against their own best interests because they didn't understand where their interests truly lay—or, more dangerously, because they wanted to feel *safe*. There was a certain safety in surrendering control to someone else, he'd been told. The fool who did it couldn't be blamed…

Of course he can, Tomas thought, darkly. *He can be blamed for letting someone else make the decisions for him.*

He felt his head start to pound as the morning wore on. More political activists arrived, setting up booths, waving banners and shouting slogans at each other that threatened to drown out everything else. The voters seemed outnumbered by the activists who were trying to get their votes; Tomas watched, readying himself to intervene if the activists tried to bribe or threaten the voters. There were perfectly legal ways to do that, he'd been told. The political leaflets promised that *their* party would deliver everything the voters wanted, while warning that the opposition would do the exact opposite. The cynic in him was *sure* the leaflets were a mixture of bribes and threats.

Sergeant Ross passed him a cup of coffee. "The lads are getting bored, sir."

"Me too," Tomas said. The mil-grade coffee was as black as night, strong enough to keep him awake for hours. "I suppose it would be wrong to wish for a terrorist attack."

"Yes, sir," Sergeant Ross said, deadpan. "It would be wrong."

Tomas nodded, then checked his HUD. Election Day was surprisingly peaceful, so far. There were a handful of riots in a dozen cities—voting had been suspended as the military cleared the streets, the rioters transported to detention camps for the duration—but no terrorist bombings or shootings. He supposed he should be grateful. A peaceful election meant the new government, whoever formed it, would be legitimate from the start. It might keep others from resorting to less than legal ways to make their opinions heard.

He drained the mug and returned it. "I'll put in a request for relief," he said, knowing it would be unlikely to be granted. "We might be allowed to go on patrol instead."

"We'll probably be reassigned, shortly afterwards," Sergeant Ross said. "I don't think they'll want us on Earth."

Tomas nodded, cursing Colonel Tallinn and his people under his breath. The media hadn't picked up his *name*, or that of the men under his command, but that hadn't stopped the reporters from baying for blood. They wanted someone to pay for the massacre and, as Colonel Tallinn was unavailable, they'd turned to demanding the heads of the men who'd pulled the triggers. They didn't seem to care that the marines had been only following orders, a perfect legal defence when the marines had been commanded by an Alphan…he felt a pang of guilt. He would have been sentenced to death if he'd shot Colonel Tallinn himself, but at least hundreds of civilians would have survived. They wouldn't even have known how close they'd come to death.

"Probably not," he said. It was only a matter of time until *someone* leaked their names to the media. "Who knows? Perhaps we'll see real action."

He heard shouting and looked up. A pair of activists were trading blows, screaming slogans as they punched and kicked at each other. Three marines separated them, dragging the fighters away to calm down. Tomas let out a breath, silently praying it didn't get any worse as the day wore on and tempers grew frayed. There were too many civilians around. If the fighting got out of hand, the civilians would be drawn into the morass or simply find themselves unable to vote. And then...

"Watch out, sir," Sergeant Ross said. "Here come the reporters."

"Joy," Tomas said. The lead reporter was an attractive young woman, but he knew better than to think she was harmless. His orders were clear. Reporters were to be referred to the media liaison officers, without exception. "Warn the lads to keep their mouths tightly shut."

"Yes, sir," Sergeant Ross said.

...

"The early voting tallies have given the Humanity League a major lead," an official said, calmly. "But that may change as morning becomes afternoon."

Yasuke barely heard him as he stood at the window, gazing over the city. His people had *built* the city...in hindsight, perhaps it had been a mistake to build the complex on top of a city they'd destroyed during the invasion. The humans had surrounded the original city, ringing the cluster of alien buildings with everything from office blocks to apartments, houses and slums. Now...it was quiet, according to the reports, but that wouldn't last. Election Day would be over in five hours. And then he'd *know*.

You already know, Yasuke reminded himself. *There's no reason to doubt the polls. Not now.*

"Continue to monitor the situation," he ordered. "And let me know if there are any major changes."

He glanced at the big display as the official backed out of the room. His career was about to take a major blow, no matter what he did. *Ambassador* was a vital role, but it was hardly a viceregal position. And he'd always be remembered as the Viceroy who'd given up territory...even if it hadn't been his decision. His career was going to stall...he told himself, firmly, that it didn't matter. His career would have been utterly destroyed if the crisis on Earth had turned into a full-scale war.

Minor alerts flashed up on the display—riots, protests, a shooting—but he barely paid any attention. He'd expected worse, much worse. He'd done everything in his power to keep a lid on violence, to ensure the new government had a clear mandate from the people...he felt like a traitor, even though cold logic told him he had no choice. They couldn't rig the election, they couldn't put their people in power. Not any longer. The humans had learnt their lessons well, he admitted privately. They would make powerful allies, if they managed to establish themselves. And dangerous foes, if they felt their former masters were working against them.

He felt the hours tick by, slowly, as the datanet continued to calculate the results. The Humanity League had already won a dozen seats, unless something went spectacularly wrong. The remainder were still up for grabs, but the League had a definite advantage. Yasuke allowed himself a moment of relief that they hadn't tried to rig the election. The results were so lopsided the treachery would have been obvious. And who knew what would have happened then?

War, he told himself. *It would be the end.*

He turned and walked back to his desk. His people didn't cope well with change, even though it was a universal constant. They'd ignored hundreds of warnings, before the war, because they hadn't been able to convince themselves that things were going to change...no, that they *had* changed. And now...things were going to change again. He wondered, bitterly, if the winds of change would blow across his homeworld, convincing his government that the time had come to accept that things would never be the same again. Or if they'd keep their eyes closed to the truth until alien soldiers were marching through the homeworld's cities, the debris of the once-invincible warcruisers burning up in the planetary atmosphere as the old order collapsed into rubble. If...

"They won't forget," he promised himself. "I'll make sure of it."

But he knew, as the results ticked towards a foregone conclusion, that it was a promise he might not be able to keep.

Abraham hadn't allowed himself to relax, even as the day slowly turned into night. He'd voted himself, alongside the entire party leadership, then made more speeches over the course of the day. The voters seemed to lap it up, although he refused to take their support for granted. Nancy had been right, he conceded sourly. It was easy to carp and criticize when one wasn't in charge and therefore didn't actually have to *do something*. And, as victory came nearer and nearer with every vote cast in his favour, it became clearer that *he* would be the one who had to do something.

"Sir," Rachel said. "We have an update from Election HQ. They've confirmed that we've won seventy seats outright, with nine more still in dispute."

"We won," Abraham said. He felt elated—and fearful. "Didn't we?"

"Sir?"

"Never mind." Abraham dismissed the thought with a wave of his hand. "Has Nancy Middleton conceded yet?"

"I believe she's conceding now." Rachel paused, checking her datapad. "She's informed the media that she and her party do not intend to contest the results."

"Good." Abraham allowed himself a tight smile. The margin of victory was just too great for anyone to question. It looked as if the Empire Loyalists had secured only twenty seats—twenty-nine, if all the disputed seats went to them. They wouldn't be able to do more than harass the new government, when it took shape and form. "She kept *her* seat."

"Yes, sir," Rachel said. "That's going to be embarrassing for her party."

Abraham nodded. The Empire Loyalists were going to be in some trouble, when they tried to sort out the mess. Their leader *had* to win election...and while *Nancy* had won election, some of her challengers had not. They'd been eliminated from the leadership struggle before it had fairly begun. He wondered, idly, how they intended to square the circle. They *might* pressure one of the elected representatives to give up his seat, but that would trigger a by-election they might lose. And *that* would cause no end of trouble.

"I'm sure they'll come up with something," he said. "Maybe they'll convince her to stand down and surrender her seat."

He shrugged. "I take it that everything is in readiness downstairs?"

"The hordes have already arrived," Rachel said. "Are you ready to meet the press?"

Abraham nodded, feeling cold as they walked down the stairs to the auditorium. He would be moving into the residence tomorrow—technically, at midnight—and then forming a government…he shivered, realising just how many things he had to do in a tearing hurry. The new government would face all sorts of challenges, internal and external. If nothing else, he had to complete the withdrawal negotiations before time ran out. He had a nasty feeling they'd be patching things up for years.

He put the thought out of his head as he stepped into the auditorium. Rachel hadn't lied. There were nearly a thousand reporters, some from alien worlds, waiting. Flashes of light nearly blinded him as he walked to the podium, something that never failed to annoy him. It wasn't as if they *needed* the flashes. It was just a sneaky trick to make him look a fool in front of the watching millions…

A chill ran down his spine as he took his place and stared into the unseen cameras. He'd spoken to millions of people over the last two weeks, but now…he was speaking to billions upon billions of humans and aliens. The Galactics had paid a surprising amount of attention to the elections. It bothered him, although he wasn't sure why. Ego told him the elections had galaxy-wide significance. Common sense told him they didn't.

"The election is over," he said, calmly. "The results are not in doubt. A handful of seats remain undecided, but my party has an absolute majority and will form a government. I have already taken steps to ensure that my new cabinet will take shape and form by the end of the week, providing a degree of continuity between the old and new administrations. And yet, things are going to change.

"This is not, as a very wise man once noted, the beginning of the end. Say, rather, it is the end of the *beginning*. There remains much to be done as we take our place as an independent power. We must secure ourselves, we must work to better ourselves, we must work to take advantage of everything we have learnt over our long apprenticeship. From today, humanity stands alone. It is the beginning of a future we will make for ourselves.

"It has been an odd time for us. This was no brief occupation, lasting only a few years before the invaders were driven out. The Viceroyalty has been part of our lives for over three hundred years. It was neither wholly good nor evil. It simply *was*. And now it is gone and we must stand alone.

"We will leave the past in the past. Many people chose to serve the Viceroyalty. We will not blame them for their service, nor will we penalise them. They served loyally and well, laying the groundwork for our independence. If they wish to retire or leave, they may do so; if they wish to serve us instead, they will be welcome."

He paused, letting his words hang in the air. "There is much to be done," he concluded. "I cannot promise you perfection. But I can promise you that I—and my government—will do everything in our power to ensure that things will get better. I ask you for patience and understanding.

"And thank you for trusting us. We will prove to you that your trust was not misplaced."

CHAPTER SIXTEEN

Star City, Earth

ADMIRAL ADAM GLASS HAD NEVER really *liked* Earth. He'd grown up on an asteroid habitat and he honestly didn't understand why so many people preferred to live on a planetary surface. The environment was hard to control, the population rapidly grew out of control and the government lost touch with what was truly *important*. Asteroid dwellers, in his view, tended to be ruthlessly practical. They had to be. Their environment would kill them if they made the slightest mistake.

He felt a twinge of disquiet as the First Speaker's aide led him down the corridor and into the First Speaker's office. The Humanity League had pledged to respect the loyalists, and the spacers who'd served the military before independence, but he suspected he was going to be relieved of his post sooner rather than later. He'd been a loyalist longer than the First Speaker had been alive, long enough to have his loyalties questioned by a government that had reason to be concerned about the future. And yet... Adam wasn't sure how he felt about the withdrawal. It felt like a betrayal of everything he'd done.

"First Speaker, Admiral Glass," the aide said. "Should I order coffee?"

"Please," the First Speaker said. He stood. "Admiral. Thank you for coming."

Adam studied Abraham Douglas with some interest as they shook hands. He was a tall dark man who looked to be in his mid-thirties, although Adam knew him to be in his late forties. He wore a black suit and curly dark wig that had been outdated well before the invasion itself, a sign he preferred to draw fashion inspiration from the past rather than the galactic mainstream. Thankfully, the First Speaker hadn't adopted the fashion for fur loincloths and bikinis. Adam rather suspected that wearing anything like that was a bridge too far. There was a fine line between making a fashion statement and looking ridiculous.

"Please, sit," Douglas said. He indicated a comfortable sofa. "I've heard a great deal about you."

"All true, apart from the lies." Adam sat, crossing his legs. "I was surprised to get your invitation."

Douglas raised his eyebrows. "I'm surprised you're surprised," he said. He glanced up as his aide returned with a tray of coffee and biscuits. "You *are* one of the most important people in the system."

"That's...a matter of opinion," Adam said, as Douglas poured coffee. "I was appointed to my position by the Viceroy."

"I know." Douglas passed Adam a mug, then settled back in his chair. "First, I'd like you to continue in your position."

Adam blinked in surprise. "Sir?"

"I have good reason," Douglas said. "No one doubts your competence. You have an excellent record. You're a skilled administrator as well as a tactician. You were even seconded to the Alphans during the war, which probably helped encourage the Viceroy to select you for your current post. And just about everyone respects you, even if they don't *like* you."

"No accounting for taste," Adam said, dryly. He met the younger man's eyes. "I *am* a loyalist."

"You were, yes," Douglas agreed. "Can I rely on you to be loyal to Earth?"

"Yes." Adam would have balked if Douglas had asked for personal loyalty, but...he was loyal to Earth. "I will serve to the best of my ability, as long as I am permitted to do so."

"That's all I ask," Douglas said. "And I was hoping you'd serve in my cabinet too."

"An interesting choice," Adam said. "You do realise I'm not a member of your party?"

"Technically speaking, you don't have to be," Douglas said. "You wouldn't be in the line of succession. Even if you were...the rules aren't precisely *clear* on the subject. There's quite a bit of manoeuvring room, if things got dicey. There shouldn't be any real trouble confirming you as a cabinet member."

"And it will send a clear message to the loyalists that there will be a place for them in the future," Adam mused. He disliked the political game, but he knew how to play. "Right?"

"Right," Douglas agreed. "The loyalists weren't—aren't—traitors. And we cannot afford to let people start thinking otherwise."

Adam nodded in relief. He'd feared the worst. There were loyalists *everywhere*, ranging from men and women who'd worked directly for their former masters to people who'd simply voted for loyalist politicians. The entire EDF was loyalist, depending on how one defined *loyalist*. A purge would be disastrous, even if it *didn't* lead to civil war. The entire system was being held together by loyalists.

"I don't expect you to be constantly on call, as you'll be wearing two hats," Douglas assured him. "But I do expect you to help set military and defence policy."

He met Adam's eyes. "I understand there are issues you want to raise," he added. "And that's why I wanted to meet you in person."

"Yes, sir," Adam said. He took a moment to organise his thoughts. "If you don't mind, I'd like to start with a brief overview of where we stand."

Douglas nodded. "Go ahead."

Adam smiled. "The EDF is currently in a state of flux," he said. "The vast majority of embeds—alien embeds—have been removed from their posts and transferred to Earth to await transport home. We've compensated for their absence by promoting human officers into their slots, with mixed results. Some of them are very competent, others are either inexperienced or simply incompetent themselves. Frankly, given how many *other* crewmen we've had to move around the fleet, even the competent officers can be made to look bad by holes in the shipboard rosters and so on. We're keeping a close eye on the situation, but we won't be able to hold meaningful exercises for several weeks at the very least. I'm not convinced we'll have the time."

Douglas frowned. "How come?"

"There's trouble along the border," Adam said. "And our ability to respond is very limited."

He paused. "Logistically, we have problems supplying and maintaining the fleet. We've managed to convince a number of merchant crewmen to remain in uniform, for the moment, but there's a shortage of everything we can't produce for ourselves. We may need to come to terms with the Alphans, just to be assured of the supplies we need."

"We're planning to ramp up our industrial nodes," Douglas said, tightly.

"We may not have the time," Adam warned. "We have a fairly extensive infrastructure here, at Sol, but very limited bases elsewhere. The mid-sized base at Coriander is—technically—under Alphan control. They may object to us laying claim to it. And our fleet train is—again—very limited. We can fill some holes fairly quickly, sir, but others…not so much. In short, our ability to project power outside our core system is relatively limited."

Douglas scowled. "How did the Alphans do it?"

"They had *centuries* to build up a network of fleet bases throughout their space, along with an industrial base capable of satisfying their needs fairly quickly," Adam said, flatly. "We don't have the time or resources to match their work, not yet."

"Right." Douglas held up a hand. "How do we stand, numbers-wise?"

"Right now, we deploy forty-two warships of various shapes and sizes, most of which are either small or outdated by Galactic standards," Adam said. "There's a handful more, including a very old battlecruiser we use for training purposes. They cannot be refitted and put on the battleline in any meaningful sense. Our starfighter wings are our greatest asset, but we cannot replace our losses."

He let out a breath. "Put bluntly, sir, if we went to war against any of the major powers we'd lose—and lose badly."

"I see," Douglas said. "And you think there's trouble along the border?"

"Yes," Adam said, flatly. "Sir..."

"Call me Abraham," Douglas said. "Please."

"Yes...*Abraham*." Adam leaned forward, willing the younger man to understand. "The Vulteks were pressing against the border even *before* the Alphans told us they intended to withdraw. Now...I think it's just a matter of time before they start a series of incursions to test our strength."

"I thought the Vulteks were a second-rate barbaric client race," Douglas said.

"And they have patrons," Adam said. "And even without the patrons joining the war, sir, they'd be able to do a lot of damage. They have a bigger fleet than us."

"I see," Douglas said. "Can they be stopped?"

"...Perhaps," Adam said. "The xenospecialists have been studying them. They're...bullies, basically. Brave until they run into someone who can beat them, at which point they bend the knee in submission. Their entire society is based around a constant trial of strength. We expect their commanders to be aggressive because *lack* of aggression is a sign of weakness...at least as long as there's a prospect of victory. They only bent the knee to the Pashtali because the Pashtali beat hell out of them. Even now...I wouldn't bet on the Pashtali having *that* much influence. The Vulteks can't be easily controlled nor permanently supervised."

Douglas grimaced. "And we don't have the clout to stop them."

"Maybe," Adam said. "Right now, they're testing us. We have to show we won't be pushed around. And that means deploying forces to the border."

"Which might be difficult, because of the logistics," Douglas said. "What do you have in mind?"

"We intended to reinforce Delaine before the withdrawal anyway," Adam explained. "My staff suggested sending a convoy of troop and supply ships to the system, which would allow us to support a warship or two in the sector. The idea would be to create an impression of both strength and determination. If we look tough, they may decide they don't want to fight."

"And if they do?" Douglas looked down at his hands. "If they see it as a provocation instead or…?"

"Delaine *is* one of our worlds," Adam pointed out. He understood Douglas's concern, but—in his experience—half the problems that had bedevilled the Empire could have been stopped in their tracks by a rapid show of force. "Galactic opinion would not be opposed to us moving ships and troops there, particularly a force that couldn't pose a serious threat to our neighbours. The whole thing would be explained as an anti-piracy patrol. Putting troops and defences on the ground would just be an expansion of the whole idea."

"I see," Douglas said. "I wouldn't put too much faith in outside opinion, unless it comes with real and practical help. Will it?"

"It may not hurt," Adam pointed out, although he conceded the point. The Galactics might be outraged if the Vulteks attacked Earth, but would they do anything about it? "There's no way to know."

Douglas laughed, harshly. "And if it does come down to war?"

Adam made a face. "We'd pull back and make a stand at Coriander," he said. "It's not a perfect system for a crossroads defence, and they'd have a reasonable chance to outflank the minefields and punch through, but it would be our best hope short of Earth itself."

"You and Martin Solomon need to have a chat," Douglas said, more to himself than anyone else. "He had some ideas about building new warships fairly cheaply…"

Adam frowned. He'd heard of *some* interesting ideas coming out of the Pournelle Shipyards, but he knew from bitter experience that it was hard to translate an idea into workable hardware. Too many contractors had come up with war-winning weapons that had failed to materialise for him to be sanguine about the prospects. And yet, Martin Solomon had done some pretty good work. It was *just* possible he'd devised something new.

He met Douglas's eyes. "In what way?"

"I'll let him explain it to you," Douglas said. "He's agreed to be on the cabinet too."

"A good choice," Adam said. "He knows what he's doing."

"And is going to be trying to get as many people back into the workforce as possible," Douglas said. He stroked his chin. "How long do I have?"

"To make up your mind?" Adam considered it. "The sooner you give the order, the sooner we can pull the convoy together and assign a warship to cover it. I don't know how long we have before the Vulteks come over the border, if they ever do. Simple prudence would suggest waiting until the withdrawal was complete, when the Alphans gave up their obligation to protect us, but waiting may be seen as a sign of weakness. It could be tomorrow.

"I have some operatives along the border," he added, as an afterthought. "But I don't know if they'll be in a position to sound the alarm if the enemy attacks without warning."

"We'll discuss it later," Douglas said. "And I'll let you know by the end of the day."

He put his empty mug on the table. "Do we have any other security problems?"

"No *immediate* problems," Adam said. "My analysts believe there's at least *some* risk of a clash with the Pashtali, as they seek to replace the Alphans as the most important race in the sector, but they believe that clash can be delayed. The Pashtali may prefer to let their clients take the risk of pushing us, as long as the Alphans remain a local power. Or they may expect us to bloody their clients a little, teach them a lesson."

Douglas snorted. "How did such creatures ever beat us to the stars?"

Adam scowled. He'd read the classified reports suggesting that aliens—unknown aliens—had been meddling on Earth for centuries before the invasion, before humanity had realised it wasn't alone in the universe. They seemed fanciful to him, based on scraps of reports retrieved from archives that had been half-destroyed and then abandoned for centuries before they were finally reopened. And yet, it was tempting to believe that *someone* had been interfering with humanity's natural development. What sort of idiots, the Galactics asked, developed the technology to go to the stars...and turned away? No wonder the Alphans had considered humanity a first-stage race. It hadn't made the jump into second-stage *despite* having the technology to put a man on the moon and much more besides.

But it is very tempting to blame others for our failings, he thought. He'd learnt that lesson as a young man, well before he'd joined the navy. *It's easier than admitting we made the worst call in the known universe.*

"They kept battling for supremacy," he said, finally. It was a little more complex than that—the xenospecialists argued the Pashtali had saved the Vulteks from accidentally rendering their homeworld uninhabitable—but it was close enough. "And they rode the wave of endless battles to the stars."

"And we never did," Douglas said. There was a hint of bitterness in his tone, an odd sense he thought humanity should have reached the stars without help. "Thank you for your time, Adam."

"Thank you, Abraham," Adam said. "When's the first cabinet meeting?"

Douglas laughed. "I'm hoping to have the first meeting at the end of the week, once the final slots are filled," he said. He picked up a datapad and held it out. "This is the list of talking points I'll have to discuss with the Viceroy...pardon me, the *Ambassador*. Do you have any input?"

Adam took the datapad and glanced down the list. "We need supply lines to remain open, if they're unwilling to let us copy their designs," he said. Logistics were going to be a nightmare, at least until they started to churn out spare parts for themselves. "And we need the base at Coriander."

"Coriander will be coming to us," Douglas said. "It *is* a human-dominated world. They're not making any attempt to hold onto any of *our* worlds."

"Yes, but the fleet base may not be part of the agreement," Adam said. The Alphans might have considered the base to be something totally separate, not an installation they shared with the EDF or simply rented from its owners. Just because it was in a human-dominated system didn't mean it was human. "I think it's worth checking before they start blowing up the facilities."

"I'll see to it," Douglas said. He took back the datapad and made a note. "Anything else?"

"Not from my point of view," Adam said. He understood military matters. He couldn't claim any special expertise in anything else. "Everything else…you'll need to consult with a different set of experts."

"True," Douglas agreed. He stood, signalling the interview was over. "I'll discuss the border crisis with the rest of the cabinet and advisors and get back to you."

"I don't know how long we have," Adam said, as he clambered to his feet. He understood the politician's hesitation, but time was not on their side. The longer they waited, the harder it would be to deter a predator race. "They may not wait until the withdrawal."

"I know," Douglas said. "Ambassador Yasuke was at pains to point out that we'd be responsible for our own security. The warcruisers have orders to defend themselves only. They may intervene if we are attacked in the next few months…or they may not. I have the feeling they've already given up on us."

"Me too," Adam said. He knew the Alphans. He understood them, as far as any human could understand an alien race. Their fires had died a long time ago. They didn't have the nerve to fight, even when victory seemed certain. And the war had taught them a harsh lesson. They'd shy away from combat unless there was no other choice. "We'll just have to show them there's life in us yet."

"And the EDF will take the lead, I'm sure," Douglas said. "Good luck, Admiral."

Adam tipped a salute. "And to you, Mr. Speaker."

CHAPTER SEVENTEEN

EDS *Washington*, Earth Orbit

"CAPTAIN," ADMIRAL GLASS SAID. "Is your ship ready for deployment?"

Naomi had barely more than a few hours of sleep over the last two days, in between desperately trying to recruit more crewmen and training the ones she had. She was all too aware that her ship would fail a competent command inspection, if there was anyone to carry it out. Right now, the EDF had too many other problems to worry about. She prayed nightly she'd have her ship in working order before the EDF ran out of other things to do.

"Yes and no, sir," she said. The admiral had called her personally? The EDF was painfully informal, at least partly in response to their patron's endless formalities and polite rituals, but there were limits. "The ship herself is ready to go. However, we are short of crew. I have at least thirty billets that still need filled…"

"They'll be filled today," Admiral Glass said. An icon blinked up on the screen, informing her that she'd received a message packet. "You have your orders, Captain. You're to escort a convoy to Delaine, leaving this evening."

Naomi frowned. "Sir?"

"I originally assigned *London* to the mission," Admiral Glass informed her. "However, she suffered a major nodal failure when she brought her drives online. You'll have to take her place at very short notice."

Good thing we didn't approve long-term shore leave, Naomi thought. *That was going to cause problems, even though she'd managed to ensure her crew got a chance to travel to Luna and enjoy the fleshpots for a few days. Right now, we're going to have problems getting even the short-termers back in time.*

She keyed her console, bringing up the orders. "We should be ready to depart on time, sir," she said, concealing her concern. The newcomers would have to be integrated at breakneck speed. Something would go wrong. Even with the best will in the world, something would go wrong. "Do you intend to attach a logistics ship to the convoy?"

"There'll be a modified freighter attached to the flotilla," Admiral Glass said. "It isn't perfect, but right now we're operating on a shoestring. That isn't going to change anytime soon."

Naomi grimaced as she scanned the orders. "And you want us to defend human space without provoking an incident," she said. The orders read as if they'd been written by a politician, not a serving officer. "It may be difficult to patrol disputed space without risking a confrontation…"

"True." Admiral Glass let out a heavy sigh. "The blunt truth is that we may not be able to keep our enemies from starting something, no matter what we do. You're there to show the flag, but…no heroics. If you're confronted with overwhelming force, I expect you to retreat and wait for reinforcements. We can't afford to lose anyone."

Naomi felt a chill running down her spine. The EDF had learnt hard lessons in the *last* war, lessons that—it seemed—were now being forgotten. War meant fighting and fighting meant killing…and, sometimes, dying. She understood just how few starships were under human command, even now, but…she knew, all too well, that it might be impossible to preserve the entire fleet. A number of starships were going to die. One of them might be called *Washington*.

"I understand, sir," she said, quietly. "I'll hold the line as best as I can."

She scowled as she glanced at the starchart. The border between Imperial space—human space now, she supposed—and enemy territory was poorly charted. There were dozens of systems that had never been properly surveyed, let alone settled; there were hundreds of crossroads into multispace that had never really been explored. She couldn't hope to prevent an enemy fleet from reaching Delaine, let alone driving further into human space. She might not even know the war had begun until she returned to the human world and ran straight into enemy fire.

"We should probably work on charting the sector," she mused. "If we're going to be settling the area..."

"That's something to worry about later," Admiral Glass said. He cleared his throat, uncomfortably. "Do you have any issues you wish to raise?"

Naomi nodded. "I've requested permission to promote Lieutenant Roger to Commander," she said. "I know it would mean jumping him two grades"—she held up a hand to stave off the inevitable objection—"but right now he's the most experienced officer under my command. He's as familiar with the ship as I am, sir, and he's practically been serving as my XO since I was promoted myself. I'd sooner not try to break in a newcomer if we're going into combat."

Admiral Glass said nothing for a long cold moment. Naomi waited, wondering what he would say. It was quite possible he'd refuse outright, pointing out that there were dozens of other officers who could take the slot without being jumped up the ladder. And even if he allowed her to go ahead, Roger's career would suffer. People would assume he hadn't earned the promotion. They might refuse to even give him a chance to prove himself. She was grimly aware she was putting the interests of the ship ahead of anything else. Cold logic told her she was right, but she knew she was doing him no favours.

"People will talk," Admiral Glass said, finally. "And you know it."

He snorted. "If you feel he's up to it, you may promote him. But it will be a brevet rank until he proves himself. Make sure he knows it. There are to be no expectations the rank will be automatically confirmed, particularly as he didn't get a field promotion. And people *will* talk."

"I know, sir," Naomi said. "I wouldn't have asked if I hadn't felt it was necessary."

"Good." Admiral Glass frowned. "There's a second matter I need to raise. It was decided—at the very highest levels, wherever those are right now—that you're going to be transporting a number of marines."

Naomi's eyes narrowed. She'd expected a company of marines to be assigned to the ship. It was standard practice. Why would it be decided at the very highest level? It wasn't as if there was a shortage. Martial law might have been declared on Earth, but one company wouldn't make any difference to the final outcome if all hell broke loose. Or…

"It has been decided that the marines who were involved in the…incident…on Earth, at Star City, will be assigned to Delaine for the foreseeable future," Admiral Glass said. "Their names were leaked to the media and widely broadcast, despite our best efforts. They—and their families—may be in some danger. It was decided"—he grimaced, suggesting it wasn't his idea—"that they should serve elsewhere."

It hardly seems fair, Naomi thought. *They cannot be blamed for following orders.*

She winced, inwardly. She'd been drilled—extensively—on the difference between legal orders and illegal orders. She knew there were points when she was expected to refuse to obey, perhaps even to place whoever had issued the orders under arrest. And yet, legality was a more flexible concept than anyone cared to admit. There were no solid rules. An order that would be illegal, if *she* gave it, might be perfectly legal if someone *else* gave it. Or if the government had made a decision to put the laws of war aside for the duration.

"I understand, sir," she said. "I'll make them feel at home."

"The inquest, which was carried out at terrifying speed, held them personally blameless," Admiral Glass said. "However, we cannot expect the civilian population to believe it. There are already accusations of a whitewash, suggestions that the inquest was rushed to make sure we were absolved of blame. The families of the victims are steadily organising themselves into a whole new pressure group. Given time, they may acquire enough influence to overturn the inquest's judgement and demand a whole new enquiry."

"Yes, sir," Naomi said. She wasn't sure that was legal, but legality really *was* a slippery slope. "And then what?"

"We're hoping the transfer will keep the marines out of the public eye," Admiral Glass said, curtly. "The negotiations are in a very difficult stage right now. We don't need more complications."

"Yes, sir," Naomi said, automatically. "Will they ever get to go home?"

"I don't know," Admiral Glass admitted. "I'm loath to make any promises I may not be able to keep."

He shook his head. "You have your orders, Captain. Good luck."

"Thank you, sir," Naomi said.

She let out a long breath as Admiral Glass's face vanished from the display. She'd wanted independent command, ever since she was old enough to know what she wanted to do with her life. She'd be alone, without anyone to give her orders...without anyone she could ask for help, if she found herself in real trouble. She scanned the messages quickly, noting just how vague some of the orders actually were. Admiral Glass had given her quite a bit of leeway, if he'd written the orders. He'd been in the military long enough, she reminded herself, to know that his orders might be outdated by the time they reached the front. The Alphans had forgotten that lesson until it had been far too late.

"Well," she told herself. "You *wanted* to be in command."

She keyed her terminal. "Lieutenant Roger, report to my ready room," she ordered. "We have a mission to plan."

• • •

Tomas brooded.

It wasn't something he cared to do, normally. There was always work to do on base, be it endless drills or training exercises or...*something*. His superiors had no qualms about finding work for idle hands. But now...he brooded, lost in his thoughts as the shuttle carried him—and the remainder of the squad—to their new posting. It felt bitterly ironic that he'd followed orders, that he'd been officially cleared of all charges...and he was being sent into exile anyway.

Don't think of it as exile, he told himself. *Think of it as a chance to restart your life.*

The colonel had been brutally clear. Tomas—and his men—had been identified. The media had broadcast their names to the entire world. And the threats had come pouring in, everything from petitions for the marines to face charges of mass murder to promises of direct action. It was safer, the colonel had said, for the squad to be elsewhere for a few months. Or years. The man hadn't been clear on when they'd be allowed to return.

We could have just stayed on base, Tomas thought, sourly. *And shot anyone who tried to attack us.*

He cursed the politicians under his breath as a low rumble ran through the shuttle. He wasn't scared of civilians or terrorists. He had no concerns about what they might do to him. Direct Action talked a lot, but what had they actually *done*? Nothing. He was sure they didn't have the nerve to attack a lone man on the streets, let alone an entire marine garrison. They sure as hell hadn't tried to kill Colonel Tallinn, had they? He would have respected them a little more if they'd challenged the defences around the viceregal complex, but they hadn't. They'd contented themselves with threats from a safe distance...

Cowards, he thought, darkly. *And my superiors are cowards too.*

A low hiss echoed through the air. The gravity field flickered, slightly. They had reached their destination. He put his datapad aside—he hadn't read more than a few lines of their orders, let alone the latest updates from the military restructuring committee—and unbuckled himself. The rest of the squad followed suit, their faces grim. *None* of them looked happy to be in the shuttle.

"Thank you for flying with us," the pilot said, over the intercom. "Don't forget to tip your pilot and leer at the stewardess."

Tomas scowled at the pilot's hatch as he headed down to the airlock. He was in no mood for jokes, particularly jokes that had lost their humour hundreds of years ago. The shuttle was crudely designed, the passenger compartment crammed with heavy-duty seats and little else. There was nothing that might have made the trip seem a little shorter...a gust of air brushed against his face as the hatch opened, allowing him to step into the cruiser. It smelt faintly of too many men in too close proximity.

A naval officer stood on the far side. "Lieutenant Drache? Welcome aboard."

"Thank you," Tomas managed. It wasn't his first time on a warship. Really, he would have been happier if he'd been assigned to the cruiser permanently. There would have been some *real* excitement. "I take it you got told to hurry up and wait too?"

"We got told to hurry up and go," the officer said. "We're leaving in two hours."

Tomas frowned as he followed the officer down to Marine Country. The ship looked as if she were in the midst of a giant refit. The passageway was crammed with engineers, opening hatches and inspecting or replacing the components inside. Officers walked from section to section, updating the records on their datapads time and time again. Tomas was no expert, but he knew the drill. The ship didn't look anything *like* ready to depart.

They must be desperate to get us out of the system, he mused, as they stepped through the hatch. Marine Country was cramped—he'd have to bed down with the men—but he was used to it. *I wonder if the ship's captain screwed the pooch too.*

He tossed his carryall onto the nearest bunk, then glanced at the computer display. The cruiser was readying herself to depart, unintelligible updates scrolling up in an endless stream...he shook his head as he inspected the rest of the compartment. Marine Country was in good shape, for a compartment that had been abandoned for months. There wasn't really enough room to train properly, but they'd just have to cope.

And hope we run into some pirates along the way, he thought. Perhaps the exile wouldn't be too bad. The settlers wouldn't know or care what had happened on Earth. *That would be very satisfying indeed.*

...

I really should have had the command chair replaced, Naomi thought dryly, as she took her seat and studied the displays. The crew had worked like demons to get the ship ready for departure, cutting too many corners for her peace of mind. They were going to be spending the next two weeks sorting out the mess, replacing components that had been overstressed or simply checking and rechecking the records to make sure everything had been logged properly. *And maybe I should start running before an inspector team arrives.*

She put the thought aside as she straightened up. The bridge crew was a mixture of old and new officers. It felt *wrong* to power up the drives and head to the crossroads without drilling the crew extensively. She didn't *know* the newcomers. She didn't know their strengths and their weaknesses, she didn't know if they could be relied upon…she promised herself, silently, that they'd be running constant exercises once they were in multispace. It was better to work the kinks out of the system *before* she tried to take the ship into combat. And the reports had made it clear there *would* be combat.

"Commander," she said. "Are we ready to depart?"

"Yes, Captain," Roger said. "All departments report ready."

And let us hope they didn't do too much creative editing, Naomi thought. She'd read the report from *London*. Everything had seemed fine until the cruiser went to full military power. *A mistake here could cost us everything.*

"Power up the drives," she ordered, calmly. "And prepare to leave orbit."

She braced herself as a dull rumble echoed through the ship. It was hard to forget, as the deck vibrated under her feet, that *Washington* was old. The cruiser had been in service longer than she'd been alive, passed from navy to navy until she ended up in human hands. If something broke... she breathed a sigh of relief as the display icons stayed green. Her ship was ready and raring to go.

"Contact the convoy," she said. "Order them to fall into formation."

"Aye, Captain," Lieutenant Walcott said. "They're on their way."

"Good." Naomi leaned back in her chair, savouring the moment. She'd wanted independent command and now she had it. And all she had to do was prove herself worthy of it. "Helm, take us out."

"Aye, Captain," Lieutenant Almont said. A low quiver ran through the ship as she started to move. "We're on the way."

"All systems remain nominal," Roger said. "We're ready to go."

Naomi nodded. "Lieutenant Walcott, inform the convoy that we're heading straight for the crossroads, as planned," she said. The convoy commanders already knew it, but it never hurt to be *sure*. "They're to remain in formation until we enter multispace."

"Aye, Captain," Lieutenant Walcott said. "They're ready to go."

"As are we," Lieutenant Almont said. "Captain?"

"Inform System Command that we're departing on schedule," Naomi ordered. She allowed herself a moment of relief. She'd never quite grasped how much had to be done to ready the ship for departure until she'd had to compress a week's work into a few hours. "And then take us to the crossroads. Best possible speed."

"Aye, Captain," Lieutenant Almont said. "We're on the way."

And now to show what we can do, Naomi thought. The entire world was watching. *And hope we don't wind up with egg on our face.*

CHAPTER EIGHTEEN

Delaine

DELAINE WAS NOT, in Captain Thomas Anderson's personal view, a particularly habitable world. It was technically suitable for human—and humanoid—life, but the planet's native biosphere had been strikingly flimsy before the early settlers had embarked upon a program to introduce plants and animals from Earth. The later settlers had followed up on the program, establishing hundreds of small towns and settlements in a pattern centred on Delaine City itself. The population remained largely human, although there were a few hundred aliens living within the capital city. He was disturbed, as he walked into a spaceport bar, to see just how many were Vulteks.

"Thomas," a voice called. He smiled as he spotted Sandra Thacker, standing behind the counter. "What can I get you?"

"Some information," Thomas said, feeling a twinge of amusement. Sandra was an attractive woman who had no qualms about exploiting it. She ran the spaceport bar, the brothel next door and a handful of other entertainment complexes for visiting spacers. And she collected information like it was going out of fashion. "What's the going rate?"

"It depends on what you want to know," Sandra said. She pulled a keycard out of her cleavage and passed it to him. "Room two. I'll be along in a moment."

Thomas nodded, then headed into the backroom and up the stairs. He'd been to Room Two before, time and time again. It looked like a normal bedroom, complete with an oversized bed and washing facilities, but Sandra used it for trading information rather than sex. He had to admit it was a neat cover. No one would question a red-blooded man—or woman, for that matter—trading money for sex. And everyone would keep their mouths firmly shut. What happened in the brothel stayed in the brothel.

"It's been a while," Sandra said, as she stepped inside and closed the door. "I trust your wife and kids are fine?"

"Well enough," Thomas said. "Wesley was bitching up a storm because I refused to let him off the ship."

"I can't say I blame you," Sandra said. "There's a hundred thousand pitfalls for an attractive young man around here."

"Tell me about it," Thomas sighed. "And he wants to jump into them too."

"He's young and foolish." Sandra sat on the bed, crossing her long legs. "Don't tell me you were never *that* young and foolish."

"I have it on good authority I was born old," Thomas said. "But that didn't stop me making a fool of myself a couple of times."

Sandra's eyes widened in mock amazement. "Only a couple of times? You *were* born old."

Thomas laughed, quietly. "I need intelligence," he said. He jerked a finger up. "What are things like up there?"

"Tricky." Sandra studied him thoughtfully. "A handful of ships have disappeared—or, at least, they haven't come back. There've been sightings of warships in a dozen systems, warships that…well, no one's got a solid ID, but everyone's betting they're Vulteks."

"Yeah, I saw the buggers outside," Thomas said. "What are they doing here?"

"God knows," Sandra said. "Officially, they're traders. Unofficially, we don't know, but it doesn't look good."

"No," Thomas agreed. "How safe is it along the border?"

"Not safe at all," Sandra said. "Like I said, a bunch of ships seem to have vanished. It doesn't bode well for the future."

"It seems so," Thomas said. "I need to head further into the borderlands."

"I wouldn't advise it," Sandra said. "There's a bunch of people downstairs who've come *out* of the borderlands. They're pretty damn sure there's a war on the way, I can tell you. No one expects the peacocks to put up a fight when the shooting finally starts."

"Not with Earth on the way to independence," Thomas agreed. "They're pulling out completely."

"Selfish bastards," Sandra said, sharply. "Thomas, what the hell are people *thinking* on Earth? Don't they know we're out here?"

"I imagine they don't care," Thomas said. "Delaine isn't *that* important..."

"Selfish bastards," Sandra repeated. "We're out here, exposed as fuck, and they're demanding independence? We *need* help and support or we're fucked when the war starts. Fuck!"

"And Earth can't provide the protection you need," Thomas said. "I did bring a bunch of guns..."

"I'm sure they'll go down a treat," Sandra growled. Her lips twisted into an ugly grimace. "The planetary defences are pretty weak, don't you know? What use is a fucking popgun if they can just sit on the high orbitals and batter us into submission? God! There are rumours Gammon is being... cleansed...of undesirables. Doesn't anyone *care* about things out here?"

Thomas winced, inwardly. He was fairly sure the Humanity League *hadn't* recognised the true scale of the problem when they'd taken power. The updates he'd picked up as he'd passed through Coriander had made it clear the league had won the election, had won decisively enough to ensure it couldn't escape blame if—when—its policies led to total disaster. They hadn't realised just how deeply they depended on their colonial masters, their *former* masters. Earth couldn't pick up the slack in a hurry, no matter what the new government said or did. And there were millions of humans—and other races—exposed, practically defenceless if war came.

And it will, Thomas thought. *It's only a matter of time.*

"I'll sell the guns, as per usual," Thomas said. "And then see what I can take further into the disputed zone."

"The Vulteks are buying crops and stuff," Sandra said. "You might want to see if you can pick up a haulage contract. They might let you in and out if you're carrying their shit."

Thomas frowned. It made no sense. "Crops and stuff?"

"Yeah," Sandra said. "They're splashing money around like a teenage Alphan. I don't know why, but…they're doing it. I can give you the details if you like."

She produced a datapad from her belt and pressed her finger against the scanner. "Here," she said. "That's the advert. Crude, but effective. Pretty good money, if you're ready to take the risk."

Thomas took the datapad and studied the listing. It was blunt, nothing more than an advertisement for a freighter to haul cargo from Delaine to an undisclosed destination on the other side of the border. The timescale suggested the destination couldn't be *that* far into enemy space. He mulled it over for a long moment, shaking his head in disbelief. Why *crops?* There was no reason the aliens couldn't grow crops for themselves. He would have expected them to purchase colonial gear, machine tools… even weapons. And yet, the listing *looked* good. They were paying well over the odds too.

He frowned. It could be a trap of some kind, but…what would be the point? They could snatch a dozen freighters plying their trade along the border, without risking exposure and public humiliation. No one would trust them again…if anyone had trusted them in the first place. They had nothing to gain and a great deal to lose by trying to lure freighter captains into their service.

"It looks tempting," he said. It wouldn't be the first time he'd taken money from someone he disliked or distrusted. "Why are they paying so much for so little?"

"They haven't had any takers," Sandra told him, curtly. "Even the tramp freighters have more sense than to get into debt with the vultures. God knows what they'll do once they have you in their claws."

But it would be a good excuse to get into their space, Thomas mused. *They wouldn't kick us out if we had their authorisation to proceed.*

"I'll see what they offer," he said. "What do I owe you?"

Sandra shrugged, dismissively. "I'll forward you an infodump packet for the usual rates," she said. "No charge for the listing. I don't think I did you any favours."

"We'll see," Thomas said.

"I'll try and say something nice at your funeral," Sandra said. "And hire a bunch of professional mourners."

Thomas laughed. "You can tell the world I was a dumbass, if you like."

"Hah," Sandra said. "Do you want exclusivity? Or don't you care?"

"Unless there's something really special in the infodump, then no," Thomas said. "And thank you."

"Thank me when you get back," Sandra said. "You can have the room for a few more minutes, if you like. I'll need you to clear out before my next customer arrives."

She stood, brushed down her shirt and headed for the door. Thomas pulled his datapad off his belt, accessed the local network and went to work. There were already a dozen messages waiting, local merchants and defence associations offering surprisingly high sums of money for his cargo. He was mildly surprised the local government or the militia hadn't put in a bid. They knew better than to get between the settlers and their guns, but they also knew—he was sure—they had to put together a defence force before the shit hit the fan. Or would they fear that it would be seen as a provocation? The vultures were already circling.

I guess it doesn't matter, he thought, as he selected the best offer. *They're going to be on the front lines anyway, sooner or later.*

His frown grew deeper as he skimmed through the listings. There should have been dozens of adverts, ranging from resupply runs to mining stations to demented treasure hunts that tended to be nothing more than expensive wastes of time. There might be no shortage of tall tales about alien ruins crammed with super-technology, but—in his experience—most of them were made up of whole cloth. If there had been *any* truth to them... he shook his head. The stories were absurd. The interstellar treasure maps were even worse. And yet, there was a sucker born every minute. The shortage of listings worried him.

And the Vultek offer is really good, if we trusted them, he told himself. *Why are they paying so much for so little?*

He worked his way through the reports, scratching his head in bemusement. It made no sense. He could understand a seller trying to jack up prices, but in this case...it was the *buyer* who was trying to raise prices. Why not offer a more reasonable price? It wasn't as if there was a bidding war underway, was there? Delaine produced more foodstuffs than she needed to feed her population. Perhaps the Vulteks were engaged in subtle bribery. It seemed a little too subtle for them. Or...

They may be trying to make us dependent on their payments, he mused. *If we get used to being overpaid, we won't want to go back to being underpaid...*

He registered his interest, then stood and headed for the door. It would be interesting to see how quickly they responded. Or if they tried to bargain, once he'd told them he was interested. Trying to haggle was technically against the rules, but who was going to tell *them* they couldn't? Maybe *that* was why there was so little interest. The Vulteks might have tried to haggle, or lower the offered price...

His datapad bleeped. They'd replied. He stopped and read the message. They hadn't tried to bargain, they hadn't tried to lower the price...they hadn't even tried to attach a string of impossible conditions to the listing. No, they were being accommodating. *Very* accommodating. It was so out of character for the Vulteks that he found himself wondering if someone else was pulling the strings.

Which is possible, he mused. *They were uplifted by a more advanced race.*

He put the thought aside as he forwarded the message to his wife and headed down the street. Delaine City had always had a faint air of insubstantiality around it, as if the settlers didn't intend to remain in the city forever, but now...his eyes narrowed as he noted just how much had changed in the last two months. The transit barracks were empty, along with half the prefabricated homes and business blocks. There were signs of trouble everywhere, from signs inviting people to join the local defence force to xenophobic messages directed at non-humans. He shivered, feeling cold as a line of armed men marched past him. It was just a matter of time before all hell broke loose.

They know they're going to be attacked, sooner or later, he thought grimly. *And who knows what they'll do in the meantime?*

He reached the spaceport, passed through a brief security check and boarded his shuttle. A handful of heavy-lift craft were already heading to *James Bond*, ready to start unloading the guns and ship them down to the planet. His wife and kids could handle that, he told himself, while he sketched out a report for Admiral Glass. He might not have a very clear picture—yet—of what was happening along the border, but he was starting to have a good idea. The Vulteks were starting to tighten the noose.

"I hope you behaved yourself," Sarah said, when he reached the ship. "Wesley is still sulking."

"It's very quiet down there," Thomas said. "Too quiet. I mean...*really* too quiet."

"So I hear," Sarah said. "The longshoremen were saying they were on the verge of being put out of work."

"I think things are going to become a lot hotter here soon," Thomas said. He passed her the terminal. "And we're going to get triple-pay for flying into enemy space."

"With their permission, I see," Sarah said. She sounded as doubtful as himself. "Just crops? Food crops?"

"So it seems," Thomas said. He supposed it was *possible* the Vulteks were smuggling *something* from Delaine to their homeworld, but...but what? There weren't many things banned on Delaine and very few of the things that *were* banned meant anything to the Vulteks. Human drugs and stimulants would be useless to them. "They're not even putting a liaison officer onboard."

"Which is a good thing, is it not?" Sarah scowled. "He'd catch you with your pants down."

And you, Thomas thought, as he headed to the bridge. His wife had given him a *lot* of flak over the past two weeks, pointing out he was a terrible father by dragging his children into danger. *We'll be in real trouble if they insist on searching the ship from top to bottom.*

He put the thought aside as he stepped onto the bridge. "Wesley. Report."

His son gave him a sulky look. "Nothing," he said. "Just...a big fat nothing."

Thomas scowled. "Remind me how old you are, again?"

"Old enough to go down to the surface," Wesley said. "It isn't fair..."

"The universe is not fair," Thomas said. A message blinked up on the display. The Vulteks were ready to begin loading on command. "And down there, young man, is not remotely safe."

He sighed, inwardly, as his son made a show of turning back to his console. Jokes aside, he remembered what it had been like to be young. He remembered what it was like to want to go to bars and get drunk, then go to brothels and pick up girls...or boys...or both. And he remembered the endless bragging from the other boys, stories of sexual conquests and wild nights of passion that bore about as much resemblance to reality as an official government manifesto. It would have been easier, he thought sourly, if he'd known they were lying. But he'd wanted to believe. He'd wanted to believe it could happen.

"You'll have your chance, when we get back to Earth," he promised. "Or you can seek a transfer to a new ship."

"I should aim for command myself," Wesley said. "Can I take my stake and go elsewhere?"

"Do the math," Thomas said. "If you sold your stake, it wouldn't buy you anything more than a stake in another ship. You'd need to put together a consortium if you wanted command—and you'd have to convince them to let you *take* command."

"It seems like too much trouble," Wesley said. "What if I owned the ship?"

"Then work hard to earn enough money to *buy* a ship outright," Thomas said. "Until then..."

His terminal bleeped. "Captain," Sarah said. "We've completed the offloading. You want to start bringing the next cargo onboard?"

"Yeah." Thomas brought up the contract and reviewed it one final time. It still didn't make sense. Sure, the cargo wouldn't bring him *much* money if he stole the crops and tried to sell them elsewhere, but...there should have been *some* penalty clauses. What on Earth were they doing? "And make sure you open the boxes and check the contents."

"Aye, sir," Sarah said. "But why would they smuggle crap back home?"

"Maybe they're trying to cheat their homeworld's authorities," Thomas said. It made as much sense as anything else. "Or maybe something from Delaine is worth a lot to them."

"True," Sarah agreed. "The Alphans love maple syrup."

Thomas nodded as he inked the contract with his thumbprint. It was possible, certainly. And yet...he supposed it made a certain kind of sense. If they'd discovered they could buy crops on Delaine for peanuts and sell them onwards for real money...they'd want to keep it as quiet as possible. And yet, that wasn't what they'd *done*. It was almost as if they were trying to be covert as overtly as possible. Thomas had been an intelligence agent long enough to feel professionally offended. What the hell were they doing?

We'll just have to keep our eyes open, he thought, as he started to update his report. *And hope we can dodge when the other shoe finally drops.*

CHAPTER NINETEEN

Star City, Earth

YASUKE FELT DRAINED, physically and mentally, as he contemplated the pair of documents—paper documents—on the desk. They looked so *innocent*, as if they'd been drawn up in a couple of hours by highly trained and overpaid lawyers. There was no sense, as he looked at them, that they were the result of nearly a month of haggling, bickering and arguing that threatened to derail the entire process. He'd never really understood just how tightly the human sector and the Empire were bound together until he'd started disentangling the knot bit by bit. There were so many facilities under some kind of joint ownership, or shared forces agreement, that there would be *pain* no matter what he did.

He sat on the chair and closed his eyes. The negotiations had been incredibly difficult, especially because his superiors had set a solid deadline. Earth would be independent, like it or not, on the stroke of midnight. The vast majority of alien settlers had already departed, the remainder choosing to remain under human law. They were going to be a problem for the human government, just as human settlers back home were going to be a nightmare for *his* government. There were already voices insisting the humans should be deported immediately, despite the risk of triggering an economic crash. Yasuke was morbidly glad *he* wouldn't have to deal with that problem. It would do his superiors good to wrestle with an intractable issue for once. They might learn there were problems that lacked perfect solutions.

And we will still have ties, he thought. *And humans serving us.*

He opened his eyes as the door opened without ceremony, a gesture of respect he wasn't sure the human truly understood. It was ironic to realise the Humanity League hadn't expected immediate independence. They'd thought there would be a steady transfer of powers that would end with equality, not independence. Yasuke rather suspected *they* were about to discover the truth, that some problems were impossible to solve without pain, over the next few years. The entire world seemed to be holding its breath. There were few celebrations, few ceremonies. The human race was waiting to see what happened next.

"First Speaker." Yasuke forced himself to rise, taking petty pleasure in noting the human looked no better than himself. "Thank you for coming."

The First Speaker nodded, curtly. "I'm surprised you didn't want to sign the papers in public."

"It would be meaningless," Yasuke said. The details were already public. There was little hope of twisting the agreement into something new. And if he tried, everyone would know. "I thought we could sign now and then put everything behind us."

"We can try," the First Speaker said. He took the seat on the other side of the table. "If I can ask, why did your people give up so quickly?"

Yasuke said nothing for a long moment. The human media, more inclined to be suspicious than his own people, had loudly suspected a trap. They'd insisted the whole affair was nothing more than a stalling tactic, something to delay matters while the Alphans rushed in troops and warcruisers to keep Earth firmly under their thumb. And they'd been perplexed to watch as the remaining troops were withdrawn, the embedded officers assigned elsewhere and the warcruisers dispatched back home. He supposed it made a certain kind of sense, if one happened to be human.

The human race had a tendency to keep fighting even when it was clear there was no *point*.

"We could not have won, not in the long term," he said, finally. "If we fought and won, we'd destroy what we wanted in the process of fighting for it. If we fought and lost, we'd destroy all hope of salvaging something from the sector. Better to give you what you wanted in hopes we would be able to maintain economic ties."

"And you have," the First Speaker noted. "We'd prefer to discuss military ties."

"My superiors were adamantly against any mutual treaties," Yasuke said, feeling a twinge of guilt. He was sure things would have been different if the Alphans had been under threat. "They don't want any military commitments while they're rebuilding their fleet."

"Nor do we," the First Speaker said. "And you *are* leaving us with a border problem."

Yasuke felt another twinge of guilt. A squadron of warcruisers could sweep through Vultek space, destroying their navy and laying waste to their sector. He had no doubt the operation could be completed before anyone could intervene. And yet...his superiors had flatly vetoed the idea. The days when an interstellar power could be ruthlessly crushed at will were long gone. The raid would trigger a full-scale war that would devastate known space, whoever came out ahead. Victory would be little worse than defeat.

"We will continue to share information with you," he said. "And we've agreed to maintain some supply and logistics links. We've even deeded the naval base at Coriander to you."

"At a price," the First Speaker said.

"Yes," Yasuke agreed. Nearly a week had been spent haggling over that issue and that issue alone. "But one you were willing to pay."

"True." The First Speaker reached for one of the documents and read it. "Future generations will say we should have spent longer drawing up the treaties."

"Future generations will have the advantage of hindsight," Yasuke said. "They'll know what went wrong, while we...must stumble blindly into the future. They'll see the problems coming, because they know what they were; we'll be smacked by issues we never even considered until they became dangerously apparent."

"That's...surprisingly profound," the First Speaker said. "You've spent too long on Earth."

"My superiors say as much," Yasuke said. "They chose me for ambassador because they felt I understood you."

"*Humans* don't understand other humans," the First Speaker said. "Why should we expect *you* to understand us?"

He smiled. "I suppose you have it easier than us," he added. "You're gender-fluid. We are not."

"We are unique," Yasuke said. "It surprised us, when we learnt that other races didn't change gender regularly. And how it impacted on their society."

He hid his amusement with an effort. It had been hard for the original Empire-builders to convince his people that aliens were not universally perverse. A race that biologically *couldn't* change gender was hardly on the same level as an Alphan who took drugs to prevent the change. They couldn't help it! And yet, the endless struggles between the sexes wasted effort that could be spent on technological development and Empire building. How much potential had been wasted, he asked himself, because seemingly intelligent races held back the so-called weaker sex, instead of allowing them to work as equals?

"We thought we were alone in the universe," the First Speaker said. "And now...the galaxy is a very old place indeed."

"A curious conceit," Yasuke said. "But we often asked ourselves why *we* seemed to be alone."

"I thought you believed races evolved into something greater and went away," the First Speaker said.

"We do," Yasuke said. "But..."

He hesitated. Normally, he would never be so friendly with a fellow Galactic, let alone a human. He was an Alphan. He wasn't supposed to share confidences with anyone outside his own species. And yet, there was something he wanted to say.

"There's a crossroads on the edge of explored space," he said. "We call it...our name translates roughly as *black hole*. Any ship that tries to make transit through the crossroads is simply never seen again. It just vanishes."

The human frowned. "Why?"

"We don't know," Yasuke said. "But there's a story that something incredibly old and powerful lives there, something old and powerful and dangerous. There's no proof as far as I know, but...the entire region is completely off-limits. And there's very little that can scare my people."

"The unknown is always fearsome," the First Speaker said. "Did you never try sending a fleet?"

"We did, if the stories are to be believed," Yasuke said. "It never came back."

His terminal bleeped. It was nearly midnight.

"It's time," he said. "Do you want to sign first?"

The human smiled. "Does it matter which of us signs first?"

• • •

Abraham Douglas wasn't sure what to make of the story. It was odd to hear an Alphan say anything even *slightly* critical of his own people, let alone admit there were mysteries and powers in the cosmos beyond their understanding. If the story was true...he had a feeling the human race would have kept picking at the scab, rather than turning their back and looking away. And yet...who knew? The crossroads might open near a *real* black hole. A ship might pop through and be swallowed before the crew had a chance to realise that something was wrong. There were no black holes for thousands of light-years, if he recalled correctly, but it was never easy to predict where a crossroads led without actually jumping through the nexus and back into realspace. It was *vaguely* possible the whole story had grown in the telling.

But it was odd.

He took the first copy of the treaty and signed it with a flourish. The document wasn't perfect—he'd hoped to have Colonel Tallinn handed over for trial, along with several other concessions that had come to nothing—but it was better than he'd feared. Trade links would stay open, humans would have access to some—if not all—GalTech and…there would be a degree of intelligence sharing and cooperation. He would have preferred a defence treaty, but…it wasn't going to happen. The Alphans seemed to have simply given up.

"This day will go down in history," he said, as he signed the second copy. "And so will all of us."

"Quite," Yasuke agreed. The alien seemed oddly withdrawn, as if he'd made a personal mistake. Abraham felt a flicker of pity. The Viceroy, with the power of life and death over the entire system, had become an Ambassador. "We have faith your people will survive the months and years to come."

Abraham felt…he wasn't sure how he felt. It would have been easier, he supposed, if the Alphans had been monsters, horrible creatures from entertainment shows that had been popular before the invasion. There would have been no doubt or uncertainty about fighting creatures that viewed humans as a tasty snack, or monsters that laid their eggs within human bodies, or…creatures that hunted humans for fun. But the Alphans… they'd meant well, he acknowledged, and they'd *done* well too. They hadn't turned humanity into a slave race.

We've grown up, he thought. *We've grown up and left the nest. And yet, we want to return to our parents…*

He shook his head, sharply. It wasn't what he'd expected. It wasn't what *anyone* had expected. But they were going to have to deal with it.

"I thank you," he said. The terminal bleeped, again. It was midnight. "And, on behalf of my people, let me thank your people."

The alien smiled. "You are very welcome."

Abraham turned and peered out the window. The city of lights seemed wrapped in darkness, the curfew still in effect even as humanity claimed its independence. Spacetown was the only place that was brightly lit, the Galactics packing up or nervously contemplating a future under human law. He'd already had notes from several other governments, all of which had had to be put on the back burner until humanity became formally independent. They promised great things...he wondered, idly, how many of the promises were true. The human race had much to offer, but most of its potential would take years to develop.

"We stand at the dawn of a new era," he said. "And everything is quiet."

"Be glad of it," Yasuke said. "It will not be long before the shock hits."

Abraham nodded. Things were going to change. He'd done everything in his power to smooth things out, but who knew what would happen when it finally sank in? The Alphans, the lords and masters of Earth, were gone. There would be no higher authority, no one standing above petty human concerns and pointing out how stupid some of them were. Who knew what was coming? All the old nightmares, the ones locked away by the aliens? Or new nightmares, horrors unleashed by a combination of alien technology and human ingenuity?

"We'll be ready," he said, quietly. "Thank you, Mr. Ambassador."

• • •

Admiral Adam Glass had never been much of a drinker. He'd drunk a few glasses of moonshine in his time, but he'd never really seen the appeal. He kept a handful of bottles of expensive alcohol in his office, for important visitors or close friends, yet he rarely indulged himself. The collection of fancy wines he'd been left by his father had been allowed to gather dust on the shelves. And yet, he'd been invited to a midnight drink...

He looked up as Abraham Douglas stepped into the meeting room. "Mr. Speaker."

"Admiral," Douglas said. He waved a hand at the bottle on the desk. "Will you join me in a toast?"

Adam poured two glasses of wine. "Imported?"

"Technically." Douglas took his glass and peered at the golden liquid. "It's from Scotland. Whiskey, they call it. My family used to drink a dram when New Year's Eve became New Year's Day."

"And human," Adam said. He was too tired for word games. "Is that why you drank it?"

"There's an old joke that they used to tell, in Scotland," Douglas said. "The price was so high because they kept sending the supply overseas. It would be so much better, the joke went, if they kept it all at home. The joker would be happy to help them drink it."

"I think it lost something in the telling," Adam said. "Are you from Scotland?"

"Me? No." Douglas shrugged. "A couple of my relatives insisted their families were from Scotland. They might even have been telling the truth. Records got pretty beat up during the invasion. Who knows?"

He lifted his glass. "To humanity."

"To humanity," Adam echoed.

"Freedom at midnight," Douglas said. "It doesn't feel quite real, does it?"

"No," Adam agreed. The First Speaker had worked towards independence. *He'd* served the Alphans loyally. Even now, even after being assured he had a place in an independent world, he still felt a little betrayed. "It won't hit us until we discover just what we're missing."

Douglas looked at him. "What do you mean?"

Adam took another sip. "The Alphans gave us a lot," he said. "And they did a lot for us, as little as we might want to admit it. Everything they did—for us and for them—was based on the assumption things would remain stable. That's how they built their Empire, I think; they achieved a degree of stability few other races could match. Their investors thought nothing would change."

"But it did," Douglas said.

"Yes," Adam agreed. "And what are we missing—now—that we don't *know* we're missing. That we *won't* know we're missing, until we need it?

How much got left out of the treaty because we were desperate to complete it before time ran out? We won't know until it hits us."

"I see your point." Douglas smiled. "You know what I thought, when I was talking to the Viceroy? I thought it might have been easier if we'd fought for our independence."

"And it would have come at a horrific cost," Adam said. He understood the feeling, but it was absurd. "Have you ever picked through a drifting hulk? Have you ever seen the aftermath of a KEW strike? Have you watched icons vanish from the display, a light blinking out, and know it meant your friends and comrades were dead? I have."

"No," Douglas said. "As you well know."

"You'll get your chance," Adam said, darkly. "If war does come..."

He shook his head. "Did you have time to read the report from Delaine?"

"The Vulteks are behaving oddly," Douglas said. He grimaced. "What did the xenospecialists make of it?"

"Too many ideas, too little hard evidence," Adam said. He was mildly surprised the politician had taken the time to read the report. "There are a hundred and one possible explanations, ranging from incompetence and ignorance to outright malice."

"And you don't know which one is true," Douglas said. "It could be any of them."

"Or something we never considered, because they're alien," Adam said. He finished his drink and put the glass on the table. "I don't fault you, Mr. Speaker. I understand why you pushed for greater autonomy. I understand you had no reason to suspect the Alphans might simply withdraw from Earth, leaving us to our own devices. But..."

He ran his hand through his hair, suddenly feeling very old. "I think it's only a matter of time until we are plunged into a border war," he said. "And, win or lose, it will cost us heavily. We may come to regret losing our former patrons."

"We've had cause to regret a lot, over the past few centuries," Douglas said. "I could give you a list of mistakes we made, if you wish. But what does it matter? What would we gain by going over them, time and time again? The past cannot be changed."

He smiled. "And I choose to be optimistic about the future," he added. "There's a bright dream out there, waiting for us."

"Yes," Adam agreed. He wasn't normally so free with his opinions. The whiskey had to be stronger than he thought. "And some of us have to be worried about what can go wrong."

CHAPTER TWENTY

EDS *Washington*, J-25

"SCAN COMPLETE, CAPTAIN," Lieutenant Hawke said. "No contacts within detection range."

"Good." Naomi let out a breath as the convoy glided away from the crossroads. "Maintain a steady sensor watch. I want to know the moment *anything* shows itself."

"Aye, Captain," Hawke said.

Naomi nodded, curtly. The convoy had taken longer than she'd expected to make the passage from Earth to J-25—energy disruptions within multispace had forced them to take a longer path through the threadlines—but it had given her more time to drill the crew. She'd feared the worst—her crew was tired and worn—yet the prospect of actually running into hostile starships had galvanised them. It helped, she supposed, that she'd turned a blind eye to overuse of the recreational facilities. They could have their fun, as long as it didn't get out of hand. It was just a shame they wouldn't have time for much—if any—shore leave on Delaine.

We can't take the risk of having the crew stranded when the shit hits the fan, she thought, even though she knew shore leave was vitally important. *Who knows when the balloon will finally go up?*

She put the thought aside and turned her attention to the display as the small convoy headed towards the next crossroads. J-25 would have been useless if it didn't host three charted crossroads that—if used properly—could cut weeks or months off the journey between Earth and Delaine. The system was empty, devoid even of comets and asteroids. There were no naval facilities within the system, save for a couple of outdated scansats. The Alphan defence planners had concluded the system was impossible to defend, at least without a massive investment. Naomi suspected they were right. There were just too many ways in and out of the system.

Particularly if the theory about uncharted crossroads holds water, she mused. *The bad guys might find themselves a back door into the system.*

She scowled, remembering her instructors explaining how crossroads came in all shapes and sizes. Some of them were so small one couldn't fly more than a single starship through at any one time, some were so large one could move an entire *planet* through the chink in reality...if, of course, one could actually move a planet in the first place. She'd read studies that suggested it was theoretically possible, but no one had been able to come up with a reason for *doing* it. Why bother? It would be cheaper and safer to build a massive fleet of starships than to try to move an entire planet.

Her lips curved into a humourless smile. She didn't expect to be attacked in J-25, but...if she were planning an ambush, there were few better places to carry it out. There were no inconvenient witnesses, no one who might come to the target's help before it was far too late. She made a mental note to recommend a regular naval patrol through the system, if there were no resources available to establish a permanent base. The Alphans had been able to largely ignore the system, counting it as nothing more than a waypoint on the flight to the border. The EDF didn't have the freedom to leave the uninhabited system alone.

A chill ran through her as she realised the final treaties had already been signed. It was unlikely something had gone wrong back home, something that would delay independence or cancel it completely. Once the Alphans had made up their minds, it was impossible to dissuade them from doing whatever they'd decided to do. The EDF was alone now, alone and isolated in a sea of stars crammed with hostile races. She glanced at the tactical display and winced. There was nothing within sensor range, but that meant nothing. An entire enemy fleet could be lurking a few million kilometres from the convoy. As long as it kept its drives and weapons stepped down, there was little chance of being detected.

She rubbed her forehead as the hours wore on. Her protesting body wanted food and bed, perhaps not in that order, but she knew she couldn't leave the bridge. Not yet, not until they were through the crossroads and back into multispace. She wondered, idly, if she'd made a mistake by not taking the longer route to Delaine. It would have added two weeks to the journey, but it would have made it harder to intercept the convoy. If the Vulteks really *were* planning something—and all the reports suggested they were—she had no doubt they'd do everything in their power to impede reinforcements. Even *they* might balk at trying to land troops on a heavily-defended planet.

Or maybe they'll just see it as a challenge, she thought. *They might just be giving us time to prepare so we can put up a proper fight.*

It wasn't a pleasant thought. She'd read the files. The Alphans had a massive superiority complex—their writings dripped with condescension—and it was difficult to know how seriously to take their observations, but...the more she read the files, the more she knew war was coming. The Vulteks were aggressive. They saw the entire universe as their hunting ground. And God help anyone who couldn't stand up to them.

An alarm sounded. "Captain," Hawke said. "A lone ship just lit up her drives. She's coming in on an intercept vector."

Naomi leaned forward. "Covert alert," she said. "I say again, covert alert."

She narrowed her eyes as the display updated. The unknown starship hadn't brought up its active sensors. There was a good chance whoever was flying the ship hadn't realised *Washington* was a warship. Naomi silently blessed her foresight on insisting the ship stayed close to the convoy, her drive signature partially masked by the freighters. There would be no fooling anyone if she brought her drives and sensors to full military power, but...if she was lucky, the enemy ship could be induced to come into point-blank range without ever realising she was trying to sneak up on a warship.

Particularly as we want the ship intact, Naomi mused. She needed to know if the enemy ship was a pirate, a privateer or an actual warship. If the latter...the war might have already begun. She had no way to know what had happened—what *was* happening—along the border. *We need to know who's flying her—and who gave her crew their orders.*

"Captain," Roger said. "The ship is at full covert alert."

"Good." Naomi allowed herself a smile. They didn't *need* active sensors to target the enemy ship. The enemy drive signature betrayed her location. "Do we have an ID?"

"No, Captain," Hawke said. "She has the rough mass and power signature of a frigate, but the design doesn't match anything in our records."

Roger frowned. "A whole new race?"

"Unlikely," Naomi said, thoughtfully. There were endless folds and crossroads within multispace that remained uncharted—and threadlines leading to systems that had never been surveyed in living memory—but it was unlikely they'd encountered a previously unknown alien race. "She might just have been refitted to the point we don't recognise her."

She glanced at the communication's officer. "Send a standard greeting, then ask them to alter course," she said. "Try and sound like a frightened little merchantman when you do it."

"Aye, Captain," Lieutenant Walcott said. He worked his console for a long moment. "No response."

"I think they're trying to intimidate us," Roger commented.

"Probably," Naomi agreed. "Let them think they're succeeding."

She ran through the vectors in her mind as the enemy ship glided closer. The ambush had been planned perfectly. The convoy had no hope of evading the pirate ship, not even if it reversed course and fled. They were already within the attacker's missile range. Her eyes narrowed as she calculated possible actions and reactions. The pirates wanted the convoy intact. If they'd been intent on destruction alone, they would have opened fire the moment the convoy entered range.

Which would have been pointless, if they wanted cargo to sell and hostages to ransom, she thought. *No one will pay anything for destroyed ships.*

"Order the convoy to come about and increase speed," she said. "And then place us between the convoy and the raider."

"Aye, Captain," Lieutenant Almont said.

"Enemy ship is increasing speed," Hawke warned. "They'll be in energy weapons range in two minutes, thirty seconds."

"Picking up a signal," Walcott reported. "They're ordering us to deactivate our drives and wait to be boarded."

Roger glanced at him. "What language did they use?"

"Galactic," Walcott said. "The message was completely atonal. Analysis says it was a recording."

They're trying to hide their identity, Naomi thought. The range was closing rapidly. The enemy ship was bringing up its targeting sensors. *They're being careful.*

"Tactical, target their drives and weapons," she ordered. "Fire on my command."

She smiled coldly. The enemy ship had planned a perfect ambush. She conceded that much, even though they were pirates. And yet, they hadn't thought about the downsides. They'd trapped the convoy, unaware that they'd also trapped themselves. They could no more escape *Washington* than the convoy could escape them! She allowed her smile to grow wider as the range narrowed. It was only a matter of time before they realised it was too late.

No need to let them get much closer, she thought, tartly. It would be easy to destroy the pirate ship. She wanted—she needed—to take it intact. *We can disable them with our first barrage.*

"Fire," she ordered.

A dull shudder ran through the cruiser as her pulse cannons opened fire. They lacked the fearsome cutting power of warcruiser beamers—she *wanted* a warcruiser—but they were more than enough to do serious damage to a starship hull. The enemy ship seemed to stagger under her fire, recoiling in shock as *Washington* pounded her drives at point-blank range. She fired a spasm of shots in all directions, spinning helplessly out of control as she lost power. A stream of atmosphere poured out of a gash in her hull. It looked as if her internal airlocks had failed.

Curious, she thought. Pirates were psychotic madmen who knew, beyond a shadow of a doubt, that they'd be executed if they fell into enemy hands, but they weren't stupid. *Didn't they know they had to keep the internal systems in good order?*

"The enemy ship has been disabled," Hawke said. "I think she's lost main power as well as her drives."

"Take out her weapons," Naomi ordered. She felt no guilt. There was no doubt the pirate ship had been hostile, even though she'd fired first. And she knew what the pirates would have done to the merchant spacers if they'd captured them. "And then order them to surrender."

"Aye, Captain," Walcott said, doubtfully. "If they've lost main power..."

"We have to try," Naomi said. The pirates might hear the message, if they'd had time to get into spacesuits before it was too late. Not, she supposed, that it mattered. They *knew* they weren't going to survive the day. "Commander Roger, order the marines to board the pirate ship."

"Aye, Captain," Roger said.

"And launch four sensor probes," Naomi added. The pirate ship might not be alone. It was quite possible the pirates had friends, lurking somewhere near the crossroads. "If there's anyone out there, watching us, I want to know about it."

"Aye, Captain," Hawke said.

Someone will probably give me hell for wasting the recon probes, Naomi thought, as she checked the live feed from the convoy. *We don't have an unlimited supply any longer.*

She shook her head. Her priority, right now, was safeguarding the convoy. Expending the probes would be cheaper than losing a dozen freighters, along with their crews and cargos. The beancounters might not understand, but Admiral Glass would. He'd tell them to go get some real experience before carping and criticising the officers who did the fighting.

And they'll try to argue we didn't need to expend the probes, she thought, coldly. *What a shame they can't prove it.*

"The marines are on their way," Roger said.

"Then hold us here," Naomi ordered. "And prepare to provide fire support if they need it."

"Aye, Captain."

• • •

Tomas braced himself as he rocketed out the airlock and into open space. It wasn't the first time he'd been shot into the darkness in a vacsuit, but the sheer immensity of space never failed to awe him. The stars looked tiny, nothing more than pinpricks of light in the darkness, yet…he knew they were huge beyond words. And he himself wasn't even a grain of sand on the cosmic beach. He took a breath, rotating the suit as he rocketed through space towards the pirate ship. His HUD updated rapidly, noting gashes in the ship's hull and possible weapons emplacements. It looked as through *Washington* had beaten the crap out of the enemy ship. She didn't have any visible weapons left to harass the marines.

Which doesn't mean she's not dangerous, he reminded himself, sharply. *The crew could be biding their time, waiting for us to come close before they turn off the antimatter containment chambers…*

He put the thought out of his head as he altered his position so he'd land feet-first on the enemy hull. It was never easy to orient one's self in zero-g, particularly if the ship's artificial gravity was still online. He doubted it—the ship's main power network appeared to have crashed—but it was hard to be sure. Not *every* race was comfortable in zero-g. The pirates might have diverted battery power to keep their feet on the deck. He smiled grimly as his feet touched the hull and locked on. It felt as if the ship was completely dead.

The remainder of the squad landed, weapons raised. Tomas made a hand signal, ordering them to form up on him, then led the way to the nearest gash in the hull. It had once been a weapons mount, he thought, but *something* had smashed the unit beyond repair and burnt a hole into the enemy ship. He glanced around, then darted into the ship. There was no gravity. The atmosphere was completely gone. He shivered as he glided down the darkened corridor. The pirates had to have been killed before they had a chance to escape.

A body drifted in the darkness. Tomas studied it from a safe distance, torn between relief and fear it wasn't human. He couldn't place the species. Two more drifted further down the corridor, one clearly human. Tomas frowned. Multi-species ships were rare. It simply wasn't easy to meet the requirements of two or more different races at the same time. Even the Alphan embeds had had problems, from time to time. It was the last thing he'd expected to see on a pirate ship.

He made a note of the bodies and their location, then picked his way further down the corridor. More bodies drifted through the hulk, a handful very clearly human. His eyes narrowed as he spotted a bird-like alien, curled into a ball. A Vultek? It was hard to be sure—the lighting was bad—but there weren't many bird-like aliens. The Vulteks were the only ones within the sector, if he recalled correctly. He sent a picture of the body back to the ship, then inched onwards. The ship was a fairly standard design. If he was right, the bridge had to be just down the corridor.

His eyes narrowed as he spotted the hatch. It was locked shut. A faint glowing light suggested the bridge compartment remained pressured. And that meant...he glanced at Sergeant Ross, making a series of hand signals. The marines slipped forward, inspecting the hatch. It could be blown open, at the risk of depressurising the inner compartment and killing everyone inside. Or...he plucked a connector from his suit and pressed it against the hatch panel. It *should* be possible to talk to the inhabitants. The bastards *knew* they didn't have anywhere to go.

And that means they won't be eager to surrender, Tomas mused as he opened the channel. He had no qualms about lying to pirates, but…he shook his head. It wouldn't do to get a reputation for deceit. Not now. *We have to offer them something if we want them to give up.*

He spoke calmly, deliberately. "You're trapped. You cannot get out. If you surrender and cooperate, we'll dump you on a penal colony. If not… we'll just walk away and leave you to die."

There was a long chilling pause. "Right," a voice—a human voice—said. "And how do we know you'll keep your word?"

"You don't," Tomas said. He was fairly sure the pirates weren't suicidal. They could have triggered the self-destruct from the bridge, blowing themselves and the marines into atoms…unless, of course, their datanet was down completely. "But the only other option is remaining where you are until your air runs out."

He waited. No one would be coming to save their lives. *Washington* might destroy what remained of the ship, before heading to the crossroads. The pirates might have allies, but would they bother to intervene? Their ship was useless now, completely beyond repair. There was no point in cannibalising her for spare parts. The pirates were doomed and they knew it. Their only hope lay in trusting him to keep his word.

"You're in no place to bargain," he said. "Surrender now or be abandoned."

There was another pause. "Fine," a different voice said, finally. A female voice. "We surrender. God! We surrender."

"Very good," Tomas said. "Open the hatch."

CHAPTER TWENTY-ONE

EDS *Washington*, J-25

NAOMI BLINKED IN SURPRISE as the pirate officer was escorted into her ready room. Pirates were hardly uncommon, outside civilised and patrolled regions of space, but it was rare to encounter a pirate *woman*. She'd honestly never *met* a female pirate before, although she'd heard stories. Women had to be at least twice as ruthless, sadistic and thoroughly unpleasant as their male counterparts if they wanted to rise in the ranks. And those who fell crashed all the way down to hell.

She found herself studying the woman with some interest. She was tall and muscular, wearing a shirt and trousers that seemed designed to show off her muscles rather than her curves. Her face was scarred, giving her a fearsome appearance. Naomi had to admit the woman looked intimidating as hell. Even with her hands cuffed behind her back, the woman looked dangerous. It was hard to escape the sense that she could turn nasty at a moment's notice.

And she was the second-in-command, if the marines are right, Naomi mused. If she'd had any doubt about the woman's ruthlessness, the fact she'd acted quickly to save her life would have dispelled it. *She'd be dead now if she hadn't shot her captain in the back.*

Naomi looked up and met the pirate's eyes. "You have been charged with piracy," she said, calmly. "There will, I'm sure, be other charges when we have finished searching your ship. I can legally have you walked out the airlock, right now, without any comebacks. Do you understand me?"

The woman showed no fear. "Your marine promised we'd be sent to a penal colony."

"If you cooperate, you will," Naomi said. "We have a number of questions for you. If you answer truthfully, we'll drop you and your crew on the nearest penal world. If you lie, or withhold information, you will be thrown out the airlock."

"Of course." The pirate smiled, humourlessly. Her teeth had been filed to points. "What do you want to know?"

Naomi had a lot of questions, but she focused on the most important one. "Why did you attack our convoy?"

"The captain took a contract," the pirate said. "His backers told him that he'd be paid for each freighter he captured and handed over to them. I think they must have been bemmies because they were happy to pay for freighters that got destroyed as well as captured, but I don't know for sure. He got wind of your convoy and moved to intercept it."

"I see," Naomi said. "And who *were* his backers?"

"I don't know," the pirate said. "The captain was always very closed-mouthed. They had a shitload of money, though. I didn't want to ask too many questions."

Because your captain might have feared you were planning to stick a knife in his back, Naomi thought. *And he was probably quite right.*

She looked at the pirate for a long moment, wondering if she could ask the questions she *really* wanted to ask. Why did they do it? Why did they loot and rape and kill their way across the sector until they ran into something they couldn't handle and got blown away? And why had they accepted money from unseen backers with unknown motives? She sighed inwardly, remembering her instructors talking about how ordinary spacers became pirates. Some were forced to incriminate themselves at gunpoint, so they had nowhere to go; some were simply sick bastards who got their kicks from hurting people. And some...felt the only hope of survival lay in being bigger and badder than everyone else. But, in the end, it didn't matter. It was easy to come up with a reason to feel sorry for someone. That didn't excuse their crimes.

"The marines will interrogate you," she said. She nodded to the armoured men. "Take her away."

The pirate was spun around and marched out. Naomi said nothing as the hatch hissed closed, then looked down at the datapad without seeing a word. It was hard to comprehend a woman willingly joining a pirate crew, let alone rising to the very highest levels. She'd seen the aftermath of too many pirate attacks to see them as anything other than monsters. The fools who spoke of a romantic pirate life had never *met* a pirate.

She snorted rudely. *There's a sucker born every second...*

The buzzer rang. "Come."

Commander Roger stepped into the compartment, a datapad under his arm. "Captain, I have the final report from the boarding party," he said. "Do you want me to summarise it?"

Naomi rubbed her eyes. "Please," she said. "Take a seat and summarise it for me."

Roger sat. "With all due respect, Captain, I would advise you to get some rest."

"I will, once we're underway," Naomi said. She'd prefer to spend longer sweeping the hulk for evidence, but she'd already wasted enough time. God alone knew what was happening along the border. "What did they find?"

"The main computer datacore was completely fried," Roger said. "The engineer thinks we accidentally set off a power surge that wiped the files, then triggered some form of limited self-destruct. However, we *were* able to recover a private datacore from the captain's cabin and the technicians are going through it now. There's contact details and suchlike we *may* be able to use ourselves."

"Maybe," Naomi said. "The really important stuff won't be written down."

"No, Captain," Roger agreed. "But it is a step forward."

Naomi laughed, humourlessly. "One less pirate ship in the universe," she said. "You're right. It *is* a step forward."

"They'll be more careful about ambushing convoys, that's for sure," Roger said. "I heard rumours about a plan to arm freighters with *real* weapons."

"It would give the pirates a fright," Naomi agreed. "And if they thought we were running armed ships through the sector, they might be a little more careful."

"Yes, Captain," Roger agreed. He glanced at his datapad. "We took seven prisoners, all senior staff, and recovered seventy-nine bodies. Twenty of them appear to have been slaves, given their condition upon discovery. There might have been a trusty or two, but…it's hard to be sure. And fifteen of the bodies weren't human."

"Curious," Naomi said. "How many of them were Vulteks?"

"Thirteen," Roger said. "I…the marines don't have any hard proof, but they think they were soldiers. I'm not sure how they came to that conclusion…"

"Instinct, perhaps," Naomi said. She wouldn't mock. She'd come to conclusions herself without quite understanding her own reasoning. "They might have been there to ensure the captain kept his word."

"Perhaps," Roger agreed. "They were heavily armed and enhanced, which suggests they weren't slaves."

Naomi nodded. "And we have no proof they're anything more than mercenaries," she said. Were there any mercenary Vulteks? She didn't know, but it seemed likely. There was certainly no shortage of humans who'd signed up to fight in someone else's war. "And no proof their government was backing them."

"Or someone else," Roger said. "How many humans fight for alien masters?"

"We used to," Naomi said, drily. It was hard to remember, sometimes, that things had changed. The universe would never be the same again. "Did we manage to get any IDs?"

"None." Roger didn't sound surprised. "I suspect most of the pirate crew came from the border zone, where records are sparse and people actively *try* to stay off the books. They have that look about them, I've been told. It's possible they might have come from Liberty, but...I'd be surprised. Most Libertarians who want a life elsewhere join the EDF or seek service with a mercenary bunch. They rarely turn into pirates."

"And they probably couldn't check for us, even if they wanted to help," Naomi said. Liberty didn't keep records, beyond a handful of very basic files. It was a persistent headache when the locals wanted to join the navy. There was no way to vet anyone before accepting or rejecting their application. "It may remain a mystery."

"Unless the pirates tell us themselves," Roger said. "The marines are interrogating them now."

"I doubt they know *that* much," Naomi said. "A year ago, it would have been a big break. We could have used the captives—and the captured data—to break open an entire network of pirates and their supporters. Now...we have too many other problems to worry about the pirates."

"And we can't afford to come across as bullies either," Roger reminded her. "There's a *lot* of resentment along the border. It'll be aimed at us if we're not careful."

Naomi nodded, glumly. The Alphans had dictated the rules and crushed anyone who refused to play by them. The other Galactics had largely gone along with them, if only because the rules weren't *that* onerous. But now...would the galactic community keep playing by the rules if the enforcer was gone? Human history suggested it was only a matter of time before the rules collapsed into dust. No treaty to limit the horrors of war had survived the horrors of war. There simply hadn't been anyone with the ability and will to enforce the treaties and punish those who misbehaved.

She looked down at her hands. It was easy to believe the pirates represented a shadow civilisation, a cluster of ships, asteroids and hidden settlements that existed completely outside of human—and alien—society. Easy...and wrong. The pirates might operate in the shadows, but they would have ties—some direct, some through fences—to isolated colony worlds and mining camps along the border. A struggling colony wouldn't ask too many questions, if the pirates sold them essential goods at cut-rate prices. And there was nothing the navy could do to stop it. Threats were meaningless if the poor bastards had to choose between life or death. They *might* be punished by the navy. They *would* suffer if they didn't take the offer.

If the punishment for being late is death, and the punishment for revolt is also death, and you're already late...why not revolt? Her tutors had asked that question, in what felt like another life. *If you win, you get to live; if you lose, you die...but you were going to die anyway.*

"We'll follow it up later, when we have time," she said. Right now, it wasn't her prime concern. "Who knows? The Vulteks might have already subverted the networks."

"Or the colony worlds themselves," Roger said. "If they're offering better governorship than the peacocks, or us, the colonists would be fools not to consider the offer."

Naomi found it hard to believe. The Vulteks were not comfortable neighbours. Everything she'd read in the files suggested they had no idea how to build a solid government, let alone ensure it lasted past the death of the founder. They'd turn on their slaves—the weak—as easily as they'd overwhelm an undefended world. And yet, if someone was desperate, they might just take the offer.

If the Vulteks think to make it in the first place, she thought. *They might not have any sense they* can *seduce us into submission.*

She took the datapad and scanned the final report. The marines had been thorough, but there were hundreds of questions they were unable to answer. Where had the pirate ship come from? How many people had owned her before she fell into pirate hands? Who had refitted her and why? The hull looked familiar, she conceded, but only because it was a fairly standard design. She guessed whoever had designed the vessel hadn't had access to modern technology. The simple lack of elegance suggested they'd been more concerned about practicality than appearance. It was a very human mindset.

But the ship was designed and built well before the invasion, she thought, with a flicker of amusement. *If she were human, she would be old enough to be my great-great-grandmother.*

She yawned, helplessly.

"Captain," Roger said. "I *would* honestly advise you to get some rest."

Naomi wanted to object, but…she knew he was right. "Take command," she said. "Have the marines do one final sweep of the enemy ship, then point her away from the sun and come home. There's no point in trying to salvage her."

"Not yet, anyway," Roger agreed. "*Someone* may want to inspect her later."

"We'll see," Naomi said. "There's no need to worry about anyone trying to salvage her."

She smiled, coldly. The pirate ship was beyond repair. A full-fledged shipyard probably *could* put her back into service, but why bother? It would be easier and cheaper to build a whole new ship from scratch. If there were any watching eyes, they might try to destroy the ship themselves in order to hide the evidence…if they thought the marines had missed something. But the marines were experienced searchers. It was hard to believe they'd overlooked something. They knew all the tricks.

And we can leave a drone behind to keep a covert eye on the hulk, she thought. *Who knows what it might see?*

"Once the marines are back onboard, resume course for the crossroads," she ordered. "And wake me if we encounter any more pirate ships."

"Aye, Captain," Roger said.

"You know," Corporal Perkins said, "I used to think the barracks were bad. But...how can anyone live like this?"

Tomas said nothing as he peered through the hatch. The pirate cabin looked like a suite in a brothel of dubious repute. There were manacles attached to the bed, designed to hold someone down and draw their legs apart. He shuddered in disgust, silently grateful the bed was empty. He liked to think he was a fairly open-minded man—one learnt to tolerate all sorts of things in the marines—but there were limits. The pirates could not have deluded themselves into thinking they had *consent*. They were rapist shitheads...

"It's astonishing what someone will do, if they think they have no choice," Sergeant Ross said. "And believe me, this is not the worst I've seen."

"I believe you," Tomas said. He remembered the massacre on Earth and shuddered again. "I just wish I didn't."

He took one last look around the cabin before heading down to the next one. The pirates, it seemed, didn't trust their fellows any further than they could throw them. The searchers had, so far, uncovered hundreds of caches of everything from money to datachips crammed with blackmail information. Some of the latter would be helpful, Tomas thought, although he wasn't sure if anyone would have the time to actually make use of it. The remainder...would have to be dropped in the crapper, once it had been carefully checked. He breathed a sigh of relief that wasn't going to be *his* problem. He still felt dirty after looking at a couple of unsecured datachips.

"They rigged their airlocks themselves," Sergeant Ross said, quietly. "They wanted to kill the entire crew."

"Fuck," Tomas said. His training had made it clear that, sometimes, a senior officer might sacrifice some of his men to save the rest. It had happened, during the war. But *no one* did it without a good cause. Here... he wondered, morbidly, what sort of mindset would casually plan an atrocity committed against his own crew? Doing horrible things to one's enemies was understandable. But the crew? "Maybe they just wanted to make sure there was no one to contradict their story."

"Or testify against them," Sergeant Ross agreed. "They…"

Tomas's earpiece bleeped. "Return to the shuttles," a voice ordered. "I say again, return to the shuttles."

"Make sure you pick up the goods," Tomas said, as the squad hastily converged on his position. "And *don't* leave anything behind."

He kept his face under tight control as they glided through the passageways up through the gash in the hull and into open space. The shuttles were waiting, their drives idling as the marines scrambled through the hatch and into their seats. Tomas counted his squad, waited for the sergeant to count the men himself, then took his seat and waited for the hatch to slam closed. The shuttle rocked as it glided away from the hulk, heading back to the ship. Tomas felt an odd sense of satisfaction. After everything that had happened on Earth, it felt good to do something unquestionably *right*.

Although we should probably have simply killed the pirates on sight, he thought. They'd recovered enough evidence to make it clear that each and every one of the pirate officers were guilty as sin. Drop them on a penal world? What did the poor inhabitants do to deserve it? *If we didn't have to keep our word…*

"I'm afraid Old George is heading away," the pirate pilot said, through the intercom. "We're going to have to boost the drives to catch up before she leaves us behind."

"Terrible," Sergeant Ross said, crossly. "And I suppose you're going to ask us to get outside and push?"

Tomas tried not to smile. He'd heard the joke before, as a raw recruit. It had alarmed him until his sergeant had pointed out, rather sarcastically, that there was no way the mothership would leave the shuttles behind, not unless she was running for her life. The shuttles *certainly* wouldn't be trying to catch up if the mothership was under heavy attack. They'd be going doggo, hoping to remain unnoticed until things quietened down. *Washington* and the convoy might be heading for the crossroads, hoping to return to multispace before they ran into something they couldn't handle, but they wouldn't leave the shuttles behind.

"Pilot humour," he said. It was funnier in hindsight, the first time. Later, it just became annoying. "It never changes."

"No, sir," Sergeant Ross agreed. "You'd think they could come up with something *new*."

CHAPTER TWENTY-TWO

Landing Field, Delaine

NAOMI COULDN'T HELP A PANG OF GUILT as she scrambled out of the shuttle and took her first breath of the planet's atmosphere. It smelt vaguely distasteful, something she'd found to be true of most planetary atmospheres, but it wasn't the sterile air she'd breathed for the last three weeks. Her crew needed a break, but she couldn't afford to let them have more than a few hours each…not when they were on the edge of a warzone. She felt worse as she spotted the governor, hurrying towards her with arm outstretched. If her crew couldn't take shore leave, she damn well shouldn't be doing it either.

"Mr. Governor," she said. She started to bend into the posture of respect, then remembered herself and shook his hand instead. Somehow, she'd expected an Alphan rather than a human. He was younger than she'd expected, his face rugged rather than classically handsome. "It's good to meet you."

Governor Aakar Singh nodded as he squeezed her hand gently, then let go. "It's good to see a warship too," he said. "Things are a little unsteady right now."

Naomi nodded. She'd feared the worst, when they'd emerged from the crossroads. Her imagination had suggested all manner of possibilities, ranging from the planet being invaded and occupied to the entire surface being scorched clean of life. Genocide—and ecocide—were against interstellar conventions, but the enforcers were gone. It was only a matter of time until the more barbaric races realised there was nothing holding them in check.

"I downloaded a briefing, but I'm interested in your impressions," she said, as she allowed him to lead her towards the control tower. "What do *you* think is happening?"

"It feels as if they're biding their time before an invasion," Governor Singh said, stiffly. "My staff have catalogued hundreds of sightings of alien starships—warships—that date back well before independence. The first confirmed sighting took place a week after the war came to an end. Since then, their ships have cruised in and out of the system seemingly at will. They know we cannot go after them."

He pushed open the door, motioning for her to enter the small dining room. "They pulled out when a warcruiser flew through the sector," he said, "but they didn't stay away."

"So I heard," Naomi said.

"It's the same story everywhere," Governor Singh said. "You know there's a dozen systems that are disputed, for want of a better word? We have colonies, some of which are independent; they have colonies, which may or may not answer to their homeworld's government. They've been increasingly aggressive, insisting on searching ships and settlements and—sometimes—*suggesting* the settlers go elsewhere. The refugees out there"—he waved a hand at the wall—"come from the disputed zone. They literally have nowhere else to go."

"Shit," Naomi said.

"I understand you brought weapons," Governor Singh said. "Enough to hold the surface?"

"Enough to deter them from dropping KEWs, I hope," Naomi confirmed. "A lot depends on just what happens, Mr. Governor."

"Please, call me Aakar," Governor Singh said. "I think we'll be working together pretty closely."

"Naomi," Naomi said. "Aakar…the blunt truth is that we won't be able to hold this system if they come after us in force. I have one cruiser. It's quite possible we'll be caught out of place when the shit hits the fan. If that happens…can *you* hold the surface?"

"The vast majority of the settlers are armed," Governor Singh said. "This isn't Earth, you know. There's a bunch of bad-tempered bandits out there. Settlers without guns tend not to last very long. I've delayed calling up the militia, for fear it might be seen as a challenge, but my people have been forming their own units without my encouragement. We could give any invader a serious headache."

"As long as they can't batter you into submission from orbit," Naomi pointed out. "How many heavy weapons do you have?"

Governor Singh grimaced. "Not as many as I would like," he said. "We don't have any tanks, we don't have any APCs…the only armoured vehicles we have are a pair of police flyers and they'll be blown out of the skies in seconds when push comes to shove. I've got people working on armouring-up farm vehicles, mounting plasma cannons on their treads and suchlike, but I've been warned they won't last long against an enemy army. Really, I don't have anything like enough firepower to keep them from charging across the landscape and going wherever they please."

"We'll be offloading weapons too," Naomi said. "The marines will provide training in handling them."

"Training we have," Governor Singh assured her. "It's a shortage of actual *weapons* that'll do us in. We never saw the need to establish stockpiles of antitank and antiaircraft weapons until it was far too late."

And the Alphans might have thought twice about letting you have them, Naomi mused, grimly. *Pistols and rifles wouldn't keep them from hammering you if your world declared independence. Antiaircraft, antitank and antiship weapons would have given you far too many options.*

"I believe there will be other convoys," Naomi said. "I'm afraid I don't know the precise details."

Governor Singh nodded. "Everything has changed," he said. "And it feels like the calm before the storm."

He held up a hand as a servant entered, pushing a tray of food. "You didn't have time to come to Government House," he said. The servant nodded and retreated silently. "So I took the liberty of bringing a dinner here instead."

"It looks better than shipboard rations," Naomi said, as she ran her eyes over the piles of cut meats, potato salads and neatly-sliced pieces of bread. "I hope you didn't go to too much trouble."

"It was no trouble," Governor Singh assured her. "We haven't had the time to develop a native cuisine…well, not *yet* anyway. The settlers prefer to keep their meals relatively simple, hence"—he gestured—"cooked chicken, ham and beef without any spices and minimal seasoning. There's a couple of people who argue it's a reaction to ceremonial dining on Earth, but really…I think we're just simple folk at heart."

"They might be right," Naomi said. "I've had to attend formal dinners. They got very tedious very quickly."

"I'm sure they did," Governor Singh said. "One advantage to being out here is that there isn't much of an upper crust. We're all in this together."

Naomi took a piece of bread and meat and began to eat. "Is it really that simple?"

"There's one big city—Landing City," Governor Singh said. "We're planning to rename the city, sooner or later, but…for the moment, it's Landing City."

"Like all the other Landing Cities across the known galaxy," Naomi said. "You'll have to rename it something unique."

"And we will, sooner or later," Governor Singh repeated. "Point is, half of the city's population is transient. Settlers get moved on, sooner or later; bureaucrats get harsh lessons in the realities of life, when they spend time on the farm. The rest of the population is spread over towns, villages and farms. Sure, some people are richer and more powerful than others, but the gap isn't *that* wide. They know each other, which helps. There's no colossal social distance between the uppers and the lowers."

Naomi frowned. "Is that good or bad?"

"Both." Governor Singh shrugged. "Good, people will help you. Your neighbours will happily loan you whatever you need. They'll assist you because you'll assist them. Bad...there's no privacy. Everyone knows everyone else's business. You get a reputation...it'll linger like cat's piss. And there's nowhere you can go to get away from it."

"Sounds like the navy," Naomi said. She felt another pang of guilt as she chewed a piece of chicken. "Do you think your people will fight?"

"I'm sure of it," Governor Singh assured her. "They're very tied to the land."

He met her eyes, evenly. "And I need to know what *you* intend to do."

"Patrol the system," Naomi said. "Hopefully, drive off any intruders. Hold the line, long enough to get reinforcements out here. Or try to, if possible. I have orders to sweep the disputed systems, but...I've only got one ship!"

"I can press for more," Governor Singh said. "But I don't know if they'll be sent."

"I suspect it won't be for a while," Naomi warned. "The EDF is in a mess. We were caught on the hop when the war ended, then again when the crisis broke out and, once again, when the Alphans decided to withdraw. Our contingency planning wasn't up to the task. I dare say we'll smooth out the problems, but it will take time."

And we don't have that many ships in the first place, she added, silently. *Any ship sent out here will be a very long way from Earth.*

"Which we don't have," Governor Singh said. "My intelligence staff—which consists of one part-time officer—believes we'll be invaded within the next two months. Personally, I think that's a little optimistic. The Vulteks are tightening the noose."

Naomi's eyes narrowed. "Pirate attacks?"

"A bunch of ships have vanished," Governor Singh said. "Pirates? Perhaps...but there haven't been any ransom demands. The families of the missing have put out feelers, hoping to get *something*...nothing. No response, no demands, no...nothing."

"Offering to pay a ransom is against the law," Naomi pointed out.

"A law that was drafted by a pointy-haired moron back on Capital," Governor Singh snapped. "I know the logic. I understand the logic. But I also know the families of the hostages aren't going to sit on their butts and do nothing. If they can pay, if they think it's the only way to get the hostage back, they'll pay. And I turn a blind eye to it because they don't have a choice!"

He shook his head. "I'm sorry for the outburst," he said. "But, as you can see, I've gone a little native."

"Just a little," Naomi said. Technically, she should report the governor to his superiors. He wasn't meant to get *that* close to his people. But, right now, it was probably a good thing. "I do understand."

She took another piece of bread and ate it slowly. "We'll do whatever we can do," she said, tightly. "And once we've unloaded the freighters, we can begin patrols."

...

"Shore leave!" Corporal Hammond sounded as if he wanted to jump for joy. "Shore leave!"

"It isn't quite shore leave," Tomas said, sternly. The squad had been assigned to train and support the local militia. "There will be time to chase local girls, *corporal*, but our duty comes first."

"Yes, sir," Hammond said. "But at least we're off the ship!"

Tomas shrugged as the shuttle dropped through the atmosphere. He'd never been particularly claustrophobic—he would have failed basic training if he hadn't been able to endure small spaces—but he had to admit the starship had been wearing on him. The crew had been running around all the time, smoothing out the rough edges and generally battering themselves into shape. He didn't find it particularly reassuring. The navy had changed so much, so quickly, that he was unsure if it could be relied upon. The Marine Corps had barely changed at all.

And things even got better, after we got rid of our embeds, he thought, sourly. Colonel Tallinn might not be put in front of a wall and shot, as he richly deserved, but at least he was on his way home. *The navy might have had a few more problems.*

He put the thought aside as the shuttle hit the ground with a crash. Someone cursed loudly behind him. Tomas carefully didn't look round to see who it was, if only because he shared the sentiment. They weren't making a combat drop, were they? The locals might not be *entirely* pleased to see them—the marines were enforcers as well as defenders—but they weren't going to greet the marines with a hail of fire. It was far more likely they'd run home and lock up their daughters.

"We have landed," the pilot's voice said. The cocky sound echoed through the compartment. "Please remember to pick up your litter and stuff it up your ass before disembarking."

Tomas scowled at the pilot's hatch, then unstrapped himself, collected his carryall and headed to the hatch. It opened, allowing him to step out of the shuttle and onto a whole new world. The scent of life, in all its glory, wafted across his nostrils as he slipped the carryall onto his back and jogged towards the terminal, followed by the rest of the squad. The spaceport was tiny, hardly big enough to handle a dozen shuttles at once. It looked as if a bunch of cargo shuttles were setting down on grassy fields, rather than tarmac. The local longshoremen ran to and fro in a manner that would get them fired on Earth. Tomas hoped to hell they knew what they were doing.

Sergeant Ross caught up with him as they reached the terminal and stepped into the welcoming room. It actually managed to look welcoming, compared to the sterile establishments on Earth. A grim-faced man in a newly-designed colonial uniform stood by the desk, studying the marines thoughtfully. His rank badge was non-standard—and unreadable. Tomas wondered, idly, what was going through the man's head. He didn't look old enough to have served in the corps, or any of the mercenary bands, before joining the militia. Did he see the marines as efficient fighters, cold-blooded killers or a distant government's police force? Or something that would never have crossed *Tomas's* mind?

The officer stepped forward. "Captain Drache?"

"Lieutenant Drache," Tomas corrected. It was tempting to say nothing, but he knew the misconception would come back to bite him sooner or later. "I'm afraid they didn't bother to give me your name?"

"Captain Yates," the officer said. "I'm your liaison officer. Welcome to Delaine."

"Thank you," Tomas said. He groaned, inwardly. Legally, any marine officer was superior to a mere colonial officer. Practically, it was going to cause all sorts of resentments—and headaches—if he threw his weight around. He cursed his superiors under his breath. They could have assigned a larger force to the mission, leaving him as one subordinate amongst many. "It looks like a nice place to live."

"And it's about to get a whole lot less nice," Yates said. He nodded towards the rear door. "We've billeted your men in the transit barracks for now. I hope they're suitable...if not, right now there's plenty of abandoned buildings in the city. We're hoping to get the antiship weapons emplaced by the end of the day, after which…"

"That sounds remarkably optimistic," Tomas warned. In his experience, nothing ever went as smoothly as promised. Unload a convoy within a day? He'd be surprised if it was less than a week. "It may take longer."

"We don't know how long we have," Yates said. "My sergeant will escort your men to the barracks. If you'll come with me…"

Tomas exchanged glances with Ross, then nodded. "I take it you have a plan?"

"Right now, our plan is to get the antiship weaponry in place," Yates said. He led Tomas into the next room. It looked like a makeshift command post, with a map on a rickety table and a pot of coffee in the corner. "What do you make of our positions?"

Tomas kept his face impassive as he studied the map. It was illegible, as if the colonial militia had invented its own system of notation rather than following the more standard system. What little he thought he could read was absurd. The colonial militia didn't have tanks, did it?

"I can't read the map," he admitted, finally. "Did you invent your own system?"

"More or less," Yates said. "There aren't many people groundside who have military experience. Those who do...they're rarely elected into power. Militiamen vote for people they know, not strangers they don't. Our system is crude, we know, and it has never really been tested."

He drew a hand across the map. "We're assuming they won't try to force-land anywhere near the city itself, not when we have the antiship weaponry emplaced. We think they'll land outside the city and march on Government House. Right now, we're pulling people out of the city and establishing an underground network to retain control when the city falls."

Tomas glanced at him. "You think the city will fall?"

"I'd be very surprised if it didn't," Yates said. "Everything I know is theoretical, but...I can't see us being able to do more than slow them down if they really put on a blitzkrieg. Or do you think I'm wrong?"

"No." Tomas was mildly surprised that *Yates* saw it. Colonial officers tended to be overoptimistic to the point of insanity. "On the other hand... once they destroy the ground-based fortifications, you're screwed. You need to be ready to hold the line or risk losing everything."

"I know," Yates said, curtly. There was a bitterness in his voice that gnawed at his next words. "But we have too few heavy weapons to put up a real fight."

"I have a few ideas," Tomas told him. "But we'll have to work hard to make them work."

"Believe me, we know all about working hard," Yates said. "You ever put up a barn in the middle of a thunderstorm?"

"No, but I have had to tell a senior officer he's wrong from time to time," Tomas said. He remembered Colonel Tallinn and shivered. "It can be instant career death if you're wrong instead. Or right."

CHAPTER TWENTY-THREE

EDS *Washington*, Delaine System

"CAPTAIN," HAWKE SAID. "We're picking up a distress signal from a mining colony!"

"Red Alert," Naomi ordered. She frowned as an icon flashed up on the display. The attack was surprisingly close to *Washington's* patrol route, but too far to let her intervene before it was too late. The pirates—or whoever they really were—would have ample time to see her coming and run before she could slip into weapons range. Or would they? "Program a sensor decoy to take our place, then activate the cloaking device."

"Aye, Captain," Hawke said. The lights dimmed. "Cloaking device engaged."

"Helm, bring us about," Naomi said, tightly. "Set course for the mining colony."

"Aye, Captain."

Naomi studied the display thoughtfully as *Washington* altered course and headed straight for the mining colony. The pirates—she assumed they were pirates, as anyone else would be more interested in the planet—were pushing their luck. They could easily have waited a few hours, just to ensure they had a chance to loot the colony and escape before she so much as picked up the distress call. Unless…her eyes narrowed. Were they trying to lure *Washington* out of position? Or into a trap? It was possible, she supposed, but unlikely. A pirate ship wouldn't pick a fight with a warship. And any regular military squadron wouldn't need to bother. They'd just set course for the planet and force her to choose between engaging them or abandoning the planet.

And I'd have to abandon the planet, she thought, grimly. Her orders allowed little room for leeway. *Washington* was more important than Delaine. *And that would mean leaving the marines on the surface, trapped.*

She glanced up as Roger stepped onto the bridge, looking tired. He'd been in his cabin—he'd been ordered to get some sleep—when the alarms had sounded. Naomi was tempted to order him back to his bunk, but she knew he wouldn't go back to sleep. *She* wouldn't, if their positions were reversed. She nodded to him instead, then turned her attention back to the display as he took his seat. The cruiser was picking up speed, steadily closing the range. She wondered, idly, if the pirates had a competent sensor crew. *Washington's* cloaking device wasn't top of the range. The pirates might pick up some leakage if they were watching carefully.

Or if their electronic servants are properly programmed, she mused. Sensor-watching was as much an art as it was a science. A flicker of energy in the darkness of space might signal anything from a random fluctuation to a cloaked ship. *How careful are they inclined to be?*

"Picking up an update from the colony, Captain," Hawke said. "The pirates are demanding their surplus of HE3 and raw materials."

"Do not reply," Naomi ordered, tersely. They were too far from the colony for tightbeam signalling. The pirates could hardly fail to miss a response. "Time to intercept?"

"Fifteen minutes, Captain," Lieutenant Almont reported. "I can increase speed, but we'll lose the cloaking field…"

"Maintain current course and speed," Naomi said. She wanted—she needed—to take out the pirate ship. Driving it away was not an option. Besides, if the pirates saw doom approaching from the rear, they might destroy the colony as they turned to flee. She pulled up the colony's file and swore under her breath. Fifty-seven souls, twelve of them children. Their lives were in immense danger. She hoped the pirates weren't trying to take hostages for ransom. "Tactical, calculate an intercept pattern."

"Aye, Captain," Lieutenant Commander Janet Ruthven said. "She reads out as a mid-sized cruiser, origin unknown."

Roger glanced at Naomi. "She's a little big for a pirate ship..."

Naomi nodded. Pirates tended to prefer smaller ships, either surplus military vessels or armed freighters. They required less maintenance, as well as being less noticeable along the border. A full-fledged warship would draw attention wherever it went. And yet, the pirates had a warship...either she was undermanned, Naomi mused, or she wasn't a pirate ship at all. The Vulteks, if the files were to be believed, had built up their fleet by buying, borrowing, begging and stealing every ship within reach. She might be about to fire the first shot in the war.

"Send a signal to the planet," she ordered, quietly. "Update the governor on our status and inform him he might need to put the planet on alert."

"Aye, Captain," Hawke said.

Naomi gritted her teeth as the range continued to close. Governor Singh had drawn up a series of contingency plans, for everything from a limited incursion to a full-scale invasion, but actually implementing any of those plans would cause massive disruption. Colonials tended to be more practical than civilians on Earth, but even so...just signalling the alarm would send them scrambling for cover. Governor Singh would hesitate to put the planet on alert until he *knew* an invasion force was inbound. She didn't really blame him. He'd pay a heavy price for a false alarm in the next election cycle.

Assuming there is a next election cycle, she thought, glumly. She'd gone through the reports and forwarded them back home. *It's only a matter of time until the shit really does hit the fan.*

She tensed, feeling more alone than ever before. The freighters were armed, but she knew with a grim certainty born of experience that they couldn't do more than irritate a *real* warship. *Washington* was the only human warship for dozens of light years, the sole deterrent to an invasion. She prayed, silently, that the EDF had managed to get its collective act together and dispatch reinforcements. A genuine squadron could give the enemy pause. Her ship might just look like a target. She'd done everything in her power to ensure they didn't follow a predictable course, but...

They could be luring us into a trap, she reminded herself. *There could be an entire fleet lurking near the colony, waiting for us to show ourselves.*

She leaned forward. The display was updating rapidly, drawing on passive sensor readings *and* the live update from the colony. Whoever was in charge was a cool customer, she acknowledged silently. Someone with less nerve might have turned off the live feed, hoping to appease the pirates. Or...she frowned as she scanned the data. It was also possible the pirates were trying to lull her into a false sense of security. The colony's sensors weren't mil-grade. They might miss a cloaked fleet bare metres from their rocky hull.

"Captain," Janet said. "We'll be within weapons range in two minutes."

Naomi nodded, considering her options. The closer they got, the greater the chance of detection. The pirates were already committed to action, although they didn't know it...or did they? If they were as cool as the asteroid miners, they might have already spotted her ship...and biding their time, allowing her to slip closer and closer before they unleashed a devastating barrage. It was what *she'd* done, during the last encounter. Pirates weren't known for their nerve, but...she shook her head. It only took one pirate with balls to give someone a very bad day.

"Target their drives and weapons, fire the moment we enter burner range," she said. "And be ready to take out any missiles they fire at the colony."

"Aye, Captain," Janet said. The display updated as two shuttles left the colony and headed towards the pirate ship. "Captain..."

"Don't engage the shuttles unless they turn hostile," Naomi ordered. It was possible—all too possible—the pirates had taken hostages. There were women and children on the colony roster. They might have been taken hostage—or worse. "They'll have nowhere to run once we take out their mothership."

The display flashed red. "Captain," Hawke snapped. "They see us!"

"Drop the cloak, open fire," Naomi ordered, sharply. "And order them to surrender!"

"They're trying to come about," Hawke reported. "They're charging weapons..."

"Targets locked," Janet said. A low shudder ran through the ship. "Firing...now!"

Naomi leaned forward as the enemy ship staggered under the weight of her fire. The ship had good armour, she noted; their drive nodes had taken a battering, but they hadn't been disabled. She managed to empty a missile pod in *Washington's* direction before the pod—and the rest of her port-side weapons—were blown out of existence. Her CO seemed torn between rotating his ship to bring the remainder of his weapons to bear and trying to run for his life. Naomi hoped he'd choose the latter. It hadn't dawned on him that he had little hope of escape. Not yet.

"Captain," Hawke said. "They're bringing their missile batteries to bear..."

"Stand by point defence," Naomi said. The pirate ship staggered, then started to leak atmosphere. It was only a matter of time. "Communications, order them to surrender. Tell them we'll take prisoners if they surrender at once."

"Aye, Captain," Walcott said. Another shudder ran through the ship. "No response."

Naomi cursed under her breath. She'd off-loaded the marines five days ago. She'd had no choice—the colony needed the marines to train the militia—but she had a feeling she was going to miss them. Her crew was already putting together a boarding party...she shook her head. Her crewmen could take the ship, if the pirates surrendered and offered no further resistance, but they weren't trained to board and secure a ship by force. She had no intention of throwing their lives away...and yet, she was all too aware that destroying the pirate ship meant killing any hostages or slaves held within its bowels. She couldn't convince herself she was merely putting them out of their misery.

"Continue firing," she ordered, grimly. If she battered the ship into a useless hulk, it wouldn't matter if the pirates surrendered or not. "Tactical, prepare to..."

"Captain," Walcott snapped. "I'm picking up an encoded signal!"

Naomi looked up, sharply. "From the pirates?"

"Negative, Captain," Walcott said. "The source appears to be empty space!"

A cloaked ship, Naomi thought. *Or a concealed relay platform...*

"Launch a probe towards the source," she ordered. "And..."

The pirate ship blinked, then vanished from the display. Naomi stared in horror at the expanding cloud of debris. The pirates were gone...had they hit something vital? Destroyed an antimatter containment chamber? Or...what? It was rare for pirates to hit the self-destruct, at least until the marines boarded their ship. They'd just blown themselves up...why?

"What happened?" Roger sounded stunned. "Did they blow themselves to hell?"

"Confirmed," Janet said. "They triggered their self-destruct."

"The signal must have triggered it," Naomi said. She'd never heard of anything like it—the EDF was all too aware that communications datanets could be hacked—but it was technically possible. The pirate ship had been doomed. Someone had made damn certain she couldn't pull anything useful—prisoners, datacores, whatever—from the wreckage. "Communications, order the enemy shuttles to return to the colony and surrender. If they refuse, we'll blow them out of space."

"Aye, Captain," Walcott said.

"Captain, the probe is picking up a starship of unknown origin," Hawke said. A new icon appeared on the display. "Correction, she's a Pashtali design. She appears to be a destroyer."

And she's the sort of ship they'd gift to their clients, Naomi thought. *She'd be completely deniable if she fell into enemy hands.*

"Helm, alter course to intercept," she ordered, sharply. "Communications, raise her."

"Aye, Captain," Walcott said.

Roger glanced at her. "Captain, what do you intend to do if we catch her?"

Naomi had a sudden odd impression of a dog chasing a car down the street with no thought whatsoever as to what he'd do if he actually managed to *catch* the vehicle. Technically, she would be perfectly within her rights to bring the intruder to a halt and demand answers by any means necessary. Galactic law was clear on that point. Delaine was a human system and she had authority. But, practically speaking, it wouldn't be so easy. The Vulteks could claim, if they wished, that it wasn't wholly a human system. Or they could simply resort to force.

"Whatever we have to do," she said. She knew it wasn't an answer. Whatever the legalities of the situation, whatever her orders said, Earth might disown her if there was a prospect of a clash turning into an interstellar war. The xenospecialists claimed that showing weakness was the worst thing they could do, when confronting a predatory race, but the politicians might not believe it. They might try to appease their enemies until it was far too late. "That ship certainly shouldn't be here."

"And she was clearly supervising the pirate ship." Roger agreed.

"We don't have any proof," Naomi countered. She was certain it *was* true—either the intruder had sent the message or there was *another* ship lurking along the same vector—but she had no solid proof. She wouldn't get it either, unless she managed to convince the intruder to surrender without destroying her datacores. It wouldn't be easy to convince people who didn't want to believe.

She frowned as the alien ship altered course, turning back towards the nearest crossroads. The last message from Earth had stated that the new government was negotiating with a dozen interstellar powers. It was hard to tell if the interstellar powers were interested in actually *allying* with Earth or merely sizing the human race up before they attacked. Naomi had studied enough galactic history to know weak races very rarely got to decide their own destinies. The cynic in her insisted it was just a matter of time before *someone* tested the defences.

Which is what they might be doing here, she thought sourly. The alien ship was picking up speed, displaying an acceleration curve considerably superior to her own. She felt a flash of bitter rage. The bastards might simply outrun her, if she didn't manage to get into weapons range before it was too late. And her reluctance to fire into the alien hull, to risk the complete destruction of the vessel, worked against her. *They're gambling they can outrun us and they might win.*

"Captain," Lieutenant Almont said. "My projections suggest we're unlikely to catch them before they hit the crossroads and vanish."

Naomi studied the projections for a long moment. Theoretically, she'd have a window of opportunity to cripple the enemy ship's drives and bring her to a halt. Practically, a long-range engagement was unlikely to do more than expend missiles for no return. The enemy would do themselves more harm by laughing than anything she'd do to them. A wave of frustration swept over her, dimmed by the grim certainty there was nothing to be gained by trying to run the alien ship down. She'd gambled and lost.

"Deploy the probe to shadow her to the crossroads," she ordered. It was probably futile, but it *might* give them some useful data. "Helm, bring us about and set course to the asteroid colony."

"Aye, Captain," Almont said.

Naomi settled back into her chair. "Mr. XO, arrange for the prisoners to be transferred onboard as soon as we're within range," she ordered. "We'll drop them on the planet and have the marines interrogate them. Hopefully, some of them know something useful."

"Aye, Captain," Roger said. His face darkened. "I thought the Vulteks never ran from a fight."

"Unless they thought they couldn't take us," Naomi said. It was possible. *Washington* had charged the alien ship like a bat out of hell. She *did* have more firepower than a lowly destroyer. The Vulteks might have decided discretion was the better part of valour. Or their patrons might have made the call for them. She found it hard to believe the Vulteks would get very far without their patrons backing them up. "Or if they weren't the ones calling the shots."

It wasn't a pleasant thought. Earth *might* be able to take the Vulteks. Or, at least, look tough enough to give them pause. But the Pashtali? The datafiles suggested the Pashtali outmassed Earth ten to one. The Alphans could have stood up to them. There weren't many other interstellar powers that could give the Pashtali a hard time. They could trash Sol in a day if they were prepared to soak up the losses. If they knew how badly the EDF had been weakened by independence, and they might, they could just decide smashing the human race into slavery was worth the cost.

And everyone knows the Pashtali want to succeed the Alphans as masters of the known universe, she reminded herself. Intelligence had speculated the Pashtali had backed the Lupines, although nothing had ever been proven. They'd certainly made a show of staying out of the fighting and that, in her experience, meant they were heavily—if covertly—involved. *They might intend to use their clients to test our mettle before they show their hand.*

It made sense, she supposed. The risk of triggering off a second major war would be too great, she thought. But a limited war, fought between a pair of client races...she wondered, grimly, if the Alphans had *really* abandoned Earth to its fate. It seemed unlikely, despite everything. The Pashtali would certainly be unwilling to take it for granted. They might poke and prod the human sector, just to see if the Alphans did anything. And if they decided the Alphans *weren't* going to do anything...

She stood. "I'll be in my ready room, composing a message to Earth," she said. Her superiors had to be informed, before things really went sour. They'd probably have new orders for her. "Alert me if anything changes."

"Aye, Captain," Roger said.

CHAPTER TWENTY-FOUR

Star City, Earth

SOMEONE, ABRAHAM DOUGLAS WAS SURE, was going to make political capital out of the fact the *first* thing his government—his new government—had done was redesign the cabinet room. It was what *he* would have done, if he'd been in opposition. No political strategist worthy of the name would pass up the chance to brand the entire exercise a waste of money, a frivolous expense when there were so many other things that needed doing. And yet, he'd had no choice. The old room had been designed for the Viceroy and his government, almost all of whom had been aliens. *He'd* needed a chamber designed for humans.

He took his seat and looked around the room as the remainder of his cabinet entered. It was relatively simple, compared to the tasteless gaudiness the Viceroy had embraced. Wood-panelled walls, a large round table, a holographic projector, a simple drinks machine positioned against the far wall and comfortable chairs. An Alphan might regard it as cheap—and a human might consider it expensive—but it would suffice. He had no intention of allowing non-humans into the chamber.

Which is something we may have to reconsider, he mused. The precise status of aliens on Earth was still being hotly debated. Earth needed their expertise, but it was unrealistic to expect them to give their all for a world that refused to accept them as citizens. *What if an alien gets elected?*

He shook his head. Right now, it wasn't a problem. He really *hadn't* understood how many problems needed to be handled, or how many people needed to be patted on the head and told not to worry, until he'd become First Speaker. He'd found himself wondering if he should rename the role—President, perhaps, or Prime Minister—because it was something he *could* do, a change he could make that wouldn't come back to bite him within seconds. Or maybe it would. The Empire Loyalists were still in disarray, but it wouldn't be long before an opposition party took shape and started asserting itself. God knew there were Leaguers who were pissed he'd failed to deliver a paradise within a day. The angry muttering would turn into a dull roar, given time. And...

The hell of it is that I have an absolute majority, he thought. *I have all the power—or so it seems—and so I get all the blame.*

The servants poured coffee, then withdrew. As the doors closed, Abraham reminded himself, once again, that he'd *wanted* to be First Speaker. The privacy fields came online a moment later. The techs swore blind they were impenetrable, that no one would be able to overhear their conversation, but Abraham wasn't convinced. The Alphans had had hundreds of ways to monitor their subjects. He'd be astonished if they hadn't come up with a way to peer though privacy fields. The simple fact they'd let them be sold openly on Earth suggested they thought the privacy fields were useless.

He put the thought to one side as he tapped the wood for attention. "I see no reason to be excessively formal," he said. He indicated Rachel, sitting at the far end of the table. "My assistant will take minutes, which will be copied to you and then placed in secure storage for later generations. The general gist of whatever we discuss will, of course, become public sooner or later, but the precise details will remain classified for the next century. I will talk openly and I expect you to do the same."

His gaze moved from face to face. Martin Solomon, Director and CEO of the Pournelle Shipyards Corporation—and now Minister for Industrial and Economic Development. Admiral Adam Glass, now Minister of War. Henry Travis, Vice Speaker; Jenny Geddes, Internal Minster, Zoe Walker, Finance Minister, Richard Hawthorne, Foreign Minister...people he trusted to speak their minds, to tell him—politely—if they thought he was being an idiot. And Rachel, who had no formal place at the table, but who would give him her impressions later. It was an impressive gathering of talented men and women, even if it wasn't complete yet. He still had some slots to fill.

And the Assembly has realised it can influence my choices, he thought. It was just a matter of time before someone worked out that they could manipulate the rules to win themselves a seat on the cabinet. *And someone who's good at getting themselves into power might not be so good at wielding it afterwards.*

"I'd hoped to discuss the current situation on Earth," he continued, "but Admiral Glass has a briefing from the border. It's not good news."

He sighed, inwardly. There were just too many problems, all of which needed his personal attention. And too many people competing for power... their departments struggling for time and resources, both of which were already in short supply. He'd wanted to take steps to lift martial law, to start freeing up men and materiel for later projects, but it was simply too dangerous. The entire planet was becoming a powder keg.

"Thank you, First Speaker." Admiral Glass keyed a switch. A holographic starchart materialised above the table. "Over the last week, the situation along the border has become immeasurably graver. A series of pirate attacks—and sightings of alien warships—culminated in a brief clash between EDS *Washington*, a pirate ship and an alien warship of uncertain origin. The alien warship apparently triggered the pirate ship's self-destruct before retreating to the crossroads and slipping into multispace. *Washington* was unable to intercept before it was too late. This may have been a blessing in disguise."

He paused, allowing his words to sink in. "My analysts believe we will be at war within the next two weeks, perhaps less," he said. "The Vulteks have been pressing us hard and, I'm afraid, we have been unable to muster a significant response. To them, this is a sign of weakness."

"A war would be immensely costly," Zoe Walker pointed out. "And they'd run the risk of dragging in other powers."

"They're not human," Glass countered. "They simply don't see things like we do. And...I think we have to be honest and admit no one is coming to help. We're on our own."

"It seems that way," Richard Hawthorne agreed. "We've received a great many polite notes and expressions of interests in talks, but nothing solid. No one wants to be our ally, no one wants to trade anything more complex than foodstuffs and basic components, no one wants to be more than polite to us. I think that will change, given time, but we may not *have* the time."

Abraham nodded. "Admiral, how do you intend to meet the challenge?"

Glass looked grim. "My staff have put together a number of possible options," he said. "The best place to make a stand, before Sol itself, is Coriander. The system is a bottleneck, with only two charted crossroads... both of which are relatively small. It isn't a *perfect* place to fight a crossroads defence, but it will suffice. It would also give us the best chance to concentrate our forces against their fleet and—hopefully—achieve local superiority. If nothing else, the crossroads is small enough to allow us to use minefields to deadly effect."

"But Coriander is also some distance from the border worlds," Hawthorne said. "We'd be writing them off, wouldn't we?"

"Yes," Glass said. He adjusted the display to show crossroads and threadlines leading through the border zone. "The blunt truth is, sir, we cannot hope to intercept an invasion fleet before it reaches its target. Not there. The entire sector is poorly charted. They may evade our forces altogether. There's little hope of keeping them from booting us out of the sector if they decide they want it."

"Which makes us look weak," Hawthorne said, tartly.

"Precisely." Glass smiled. It wasn't a nice expression. "And I believe we can take advantage of it. Our weakness will lead them to push onwards, against Coriander, without taking the time to consolidate their positions. And then they'd run straight into our fixed defences."

"If we have time to establish them," Solomon said. "Do we?"

"We do have contingency plans," Glass said. "If we stop them dead, sir, we'd have two options. Depending on the outcome, we might be able to give them a bloody nose and shove them back to their space. Or...there are other options. It depends on what happens at Coriander."

"We'll discuss that later," Abraham said. "We also need more ships. Martin?"

Martin Solomon took a breath. "As per your orders, the conversion and military production program is in full swing. The first converted warships will be ready within a day. They lack some of the advantages of *real* warships, as you know, but they will give us more mobile firepower. We've started to recall other freighters for conversion too."

"Good," Glass said. "But what about real warships?"

"We produced a handful of destroyers, frigates and cruisers during the war," Solomon said. "However, there were supply problems. We're working to overcome them right now, but it may be at least six months before the first *new* warship glides out of the slips. Less, I suspect, if we manage to obtain components from the Alphans. Having to reverse-engineer everything is a pain in the ass. We might want to look into purchasing certain items from someone else."

"Which will cost us heavily," Zoe warned.

"And may not be possible, in any case," Hawthorne warned. "The Pashtali have flatly refused to open more than very basic diplomatic channels. I think—I cannot prove it—that they're twisting arms behind the scenes, pushing the other powers to refrain from selling military-grade GalTech. They *were* one of the loudest voices pushing for restrictions on technological transfers before the Lupine Wars."

Abraham scowled. "And we can assume they gave the Vulteks everything they wanted?"

"Perhaps," Glass said. "Clients like the Vulteks are always a two-edged sword. They could wind up being just as dangerous to their patrons as to everyone else. I'd expect the Pashtali held back a few surprises, just in case."

"We know the Alphans refused to give us everything," Abraham said, darkly. "Richard, is there no hope of changing their minds?"

"I doubt it," Hawthorne admitted. "Viceroy Yasuke had a great deal of influence, formal and informal. *Ambassador* Yasuke has a great deal *less*. It's hard to be sure—the upper levels of their society are practically a closed book—but I think there's a genteel power struggle going on. They won't commit themselves to helping us, or to doing *anything*, until they've sorted out their internal affairs. And that could take years."

"I don't believe it," Zoe said. "Did they learn *nothing* from the war?"

"I think they might have learnt the wrong lessons," Glass said, quietly. "And even if they didn't…we're independent now. They will come to see us as a competitor eventually, if they don't already. We can no longer rely on them."

Abraham nodded. It was another truth that had taken weeks, if not months, to sink in. Earth was independent. Earth was *alone*. The Alphans would not step in, with a loan or military support or *anything*, if the human race ran into something it couldn't handle. It was striking how limited resources had become, in the last few weeks. He hadn't realised how difficult it would be until it was too late. In hindsight, all the optimistic projections had been totally off-base. They had to cut their coat to suit their cloth and…he shook his head. The long-term projections were still good. They just had to survive the next few years.

"We'll keep trying, but we'll plan on the assumption we're alone," he said. "Admiral, your plan does give us the best chance of survival."

"Yes," Glass said. "And that's why I need to be there myself."

Abraham raised his eyebrows. "You want to take command?"

"Yes, sir," Glass said. "We don't have many officers with large-scale fleet command experience. Most of our experienced officers and crew from the war gained their experience at the lower levels. They know how to fly and fight alone, or in small squadrons, but not how to handle an entire fleet. We don't have time to train up a fleet command staff, sir. The fleet commander has to be aware of our deficiencies and how to compensate for them."

"I see," Abraham said.

He thought fast. Admiral Glass *was* an experienced officer. Nearly everyone in the EDF respected him, even if they didn't like him. And yet... he wondered, suddenly, if Admiral Glass had seen the war as his last best chance to command a fleet in combat. He was old, easily old enough to be Abraham's father. He'd been on the verge of retirement when the Alphans had abandoned Earth. He couldn't keep his position for long, even if he won the coming battle. How could he?

"If you're confident your staff can handle matters here, you may take command in person," Abraham said. Admiral Glass's arguments were *good* arguments. And it would cost him nothing to accede to the request. There was no reason to think the admiral was senile. He'd passed his last psych test with flying colours. "However, I must insist on you having contingency plans in place for the succession."

"I've identified three commodores who can take my place, if I don't come back," Admiral Glass assured him. "They don't have my experience, but I've been having them work on their strategic as well as tactical thinking. They show definite promise."

"Put together a line of succession," Abraham ordered. "And make sure they understand they may find themselves in your shoes at any moment."

"Yes, sir," Glass said. He nodded at the starchart. "I think the fleet can depart within two days. We'll be carrying out a series of exercises in the hope of confusing any watching eyes, although I doubt we can fool them completely. Anyone who looks at a map will know Coriander is the best place to make a stand. They'll expect it."

"Unless they really are alien," Abraham said. He felt a twinge of pity for the Viceroy. It couldn't have been easy, governing an alien world. The Alphans were so formal that humanity had to seem the very embodiment of chaos to them. "They might expect us to make our stand at Delaine instead."

"And if we had enough ships, I'd advise it," Glass said, flatly. "There is a second matter that requires your attention, sir. The asteroid miners in J-57 have been harassed quite badly, in the last few days. They've requested we allow *Washington* to make a sweep through the system."

"I believe J-57 is technically unclaimed," Hawthorne said. "It isn't *our* space."

"Yes," Glass said. "But, by the same token, we have every right to send our ships there without permission."

"Which might be seen as provocative," Hawthorne pointed out. "By the Pashtali, if not their clients."

"And what do you think *they're* doing to us?" Glass jabbed a finger at the starchart. "They're bullying us, sir; they're driving our people out of the system. And the longer we let them do it, the more emboldened they'll be."

Hawthorne leaned forward. "I understand your position, Admiral," he said. "But, by your own admission, we *cannot* stop them short of Coriander. Do we want to give them a ready-made excuse for war?"

Solomon snorted. "Do you think they *need* one?"

Abraham tended to agree. The human race, throughout history, had gone to some considerable effort to *justify* invasion, conquest and ruthless exploitation. There had to be something, humans had argued, beyond a simple desire for plunder. But the Vulteks didn't seem to be so complex. The strong did whatever they wanted, in their view, and the weak suffered what they must. It was an argument he liked to think the human race had left behind hundreds of years ago.

And the galaxy doesn't care about right or wrong, he thought. The Alphans had tried to impose law and order on the universe, if one believed their propaganda, but even *they* had found it hard to enforce their will. *No one will come to help us if they attack, with or without provocation.*

"There are humans at risk," Solomon pressed. "We cannot leave them isolated and alone."

"We have no formal responsibility to them," Zoe said. "They're not part of our association, are they? They're independent miners who knew perfectly well they were heading into disputed space..."

"Yes, but they're human!" Solomon scowled around the table. "We claim to speak for humanity, do we not?"

"We speak for Earth and the human-dominated worlds," Richard said. "We have no authority over human settlements outside our sphere."

"Which is a legal headache," Abraham said. He looked at Glass. "Admiral, order *Washington* to make the sweep. But make sure her commander knows to avoid action if possible."

"With all due respect, sir, those orders may be impossible to follow," Glass said. "Do you expect her to do nothing if human settlers come under attack?"

"I expect her to let the Vulteks fire the first shot," Abraham said, stiffly. "The Galactics are watching. Let them see that we were attacked."

"Yes, sir," Glass said. It was easy to tell he didn't feel it could be done. "I'll see to it personally."

"Good." Abraham turned to his cabinet. The military situation was important, but it wasn't his only concern. If he failed to improve the lives of his people, he could expect to be kicked out of office during the next election cycle. "Now, where do we stand economically."

Solomon smiled. "In the short run, it's going to be painful," he said. "There are going to be all sorts of budget cuts, more and more as we trim the fat. But, in the long run..."

CHAPTER TWENTY-FIVE

F'Tran System, Vultek Space

IT HAD ALWAYS AMUSED FLOCKLEADER TRANS that the Galactics wasted their time coming up with endless excuses to justify what everyone with half a gram of sense knew they were going to do anyway. They spoke in flowery terms, claiming to have principles they were happy to discard whenever proven inconvenient. It was impossible to deny the Galactics knew, deep inside, that the strong ruled and the weak served. There was no point in trying to convince themselves—and everyone else—that they *had* to do something when they didn't have the power to do it. One might as well try to dictate terms to an ancient race with powers beyond imagination.

His beak dropped open in a cold smile. They mocked his people—even the Pashtali looked down on their clients—but the Vulteks understood the universe in a way even their patrons found incomprehensible. And yet, their patrons knew the cold hard truth even if they didn't want to admit it. They didn't understand how deeply their clients held them in contempt. They didn't realise it was just a matter of time until the Vulteks tested themselves against the Pashtali, until the Vulteks crushed their former masters and took everything of theirs for themselves. It was the cycle of life, a truth that all knew even if they refused to admit it. The universe had no room for those who claimed power by right. The strong had to remain strong, testing themselves endlessly against the strong, or they would become weak and vulnerable. The Pashtali swore the Alphans—and *their* clients—had become weak. It didn't seem to have occurred to them that they too were becoming weak.

The holographic starchart glowed with stars, a rich field of prizes just waiting for the plucking. The humans might have settled those stars, but it was the Alphans who had protected them, shielded them like chicks under their mother's wing. And now the Alphans were gone. Their influence was fading fast. And the Vulteks could not *wait* to test themselves against the humans. Everyone knew the humans were good at war. But were they strong?

He clacked his beak in amusement. The humans hadn't responded to gentle nudges and provocations. A *strong* race would push back, hard. But the humans had done nothing. They'd ignored the pirate attacks, they'd ignored the steady probes of their defences…their worlds lay defenceless, ripe for the plucking. He wondered, idly, why the humans didn't test themselves as openly as his own people. They were a warrior race, were they not? Why were they not in constant competition for power?

Maybe the Alphans beat it out of them, he mused. The Pashtali had certainly tried to beat the Vulteks into submission. It hadn't worked. The Vulteks were no weak race, suitable only for slavery. The blows had made them hard and strong, sharpening their desire to one day surpass their masters for themselves. *Or maybe they were never truly strong.*

He stood, allowing his beady eyes to wander around the command deck. Everywhere he looked, he saw officers readying the fleet to depart. They would challenge him, if they thought he was weakening. It was their duty to remove a weak leader, to shove him down the ladder if he couldn't handle his role. He'd already seen off four challenges in the last few weeks, none of which had come close to unseating him. It was absurd. Didn't they know he'd fought his way to the top? And yet, they wanted to start the war. They wanted to take the human worlds for themselves. They didn't understand the logistics of war.

Bah. Trans snorted in disgust. The Pashtali talked of logistics, as if logistics alone were enough to win. He knew better. Aggression was the only way to win. One could defeat a richer opponent with surprise, ruthlessness and a willingness to pay the price for victory. *The sooner we move, the better.*

An officer approached, meeting his eyes once before lowering himself to the deck in full prostration. Trans studied him, wondering if the display of submission was real or merely the prelude to a surprise attack. It would be cheating...but only if the officer lost. Victory excused everything. He felt a twinge of disgust as the officer lay still. The logistics staff were easily the worst in the flock, the very dregs of the service. It was rightly said the only reason they survived was that none of their fellows wanted to soil their claws with their blood. Trans was experienced enough to understand logistics had their place, but even *he* detested them. Who would trust such...?

"Talk," he ordered.

"My Lord, the first logistics convoy has arrived," the officer reported. He didn't move from the deck. Coward. "I..."

"Signal the fleet." Trans looked up, averting his gaze from the pathetic figure. "Order them to implement the attack plan, one hour from now."

The officer quivered. It was obvious he disagreed, but he didn't have the nerve to say it outright. Trans shuddered in disgust. There were races fit only to be servants, but he couldn't believe one of his own people would sink so far. Better to die than to live as a coward. And yet...his people had served the Pashtali. He told himself it wasn't the same. There was a universe of difference between biding their time, learning all they could and overthrowing their masters...and cowardly cowering in total defeat. The Pashtali had knocked his people down, but they hadn't *beaten* them. One day...

"Go," he ordered. "Now."

He studied the display, flexing his claws as the officer hurried away. The call to battle echoed within his blood. He wanted to spring on his enemies, to take them with his bare claws. His ancestors had tamed their violent world through blood and suffering. *He* would be leading starships into battle. It wasn't quite the same. He promised himself he'd find time to hunt humans on their worlds, once the war was done. The aliens looked funny, with no natural weaponry...it would be interesting to test himself against a human mercenary. The Pashtali said they were dangerous. Good. There was no honour to be gained from slaughtering someone who couldn't fight back.

Soon, he promised his ancestors. A rustle of anticipation ran around the command deck as the flock realised it was time to go to war. *Soon, there will be blood enough for all of us.*

...

"Dear God," Sarah breathed.

Thomas shivered as he studied the long-range sensor readings. The alien ships were masked, their emissions hidden behind decoy fields that would have concealed them from civilian-grade sensors, but he could see them clearly. Seventy warships, ranging from destroyers to a trio of heavy battlecruisers. Outdated, he thought, but still dangerous. It was impossible to be sure, yet...he was fairly sure they'd been extensively refitted. Hundreds of starfighters flocked around the fleet, practicing their manoeuvres. It looked as if they were going to war.

And I ordered everyone into their vacsuits, he thought. It was a sensible precaution, but completely useless if they wound up tangling with a single warship, let alone an entire fleet. *What was I thinking?*

"Dad...Captain...most of the ships are Pashtali," Wesley stuttered. "The remainder are of unknown origin."

"Or simply refitted so extensively they no longer match our records," Thomas said. He'd seen horrors during the war, more than he cared to remember, but he'd never seen so many hostile warships gathered in one place. They were a bare five days from Delaine at full military power. And he had no way to send a warning. The local FTL communicator was unlikely to accept any messages from him. "I..."

He glanced at Sarah. "Launch both the covert probes towards the fleet, ballistic trajectories only," he ordered. "And prepare to take us out of here."

Sarah nodded as she worked her console. "Do you intend to make the delivery?"

Thomas hesitated. In *theory*, the Vulteks would let them make the delivery and leave...without ever realising they'd seen anything. A standard merchantman wouldn't have spotted a single ship, let alone the entire fleet. In practice...the aliens would be foolish to let them leave. They might intern the crew—or simply kill them—just to be sure. Docking with the alien base might get them all killed.

"That's why they wanted the food," Wesley said. "They needed us to supply their ships."

"Perhaps," Thomas said, absently. His mind was elsewhere. "Sarah, how quickly can we reach the crossroads?"

"If we reverse course now, we can get to the crossroads in thirty minutes," Sarah said. "But they'll send starfighters after us."

"We may not have a choice but to try," Thomas said. He calculated the vectors quickly. If the aliens launched their starfighters at once... they'd still need fifteen to twenty minutes to catch the freighter. They might be surprised by the freighter's acceleration curve. She was no match for a warship, and very little hope of outrunning one, but she was still faster than the vast majority of mid-sized freighters. "Prepare to reverse course."

He sucked in his breath as the probes started to report back. It looked very much as if the enemy fleet was about to move. And *that* meant it was about to attack. He didn't think anyone, even the Vulteks, would move such a large fleet to the border without plans to cross and attack the nearest human world. The exercise would cost them an arm and a leg. Perhaps literally, if some of the files were accurate. He found it hard to believe that any intelligent race could handle promotions through ritual combat, but...aliens were aliens. It might make sense for them.

We have to get back in time, he thought, numbly. *And if they overtake us in multispace...*

"Reverse course," he ordered. "And run for the crossroads."

"Aye, Captain," Sarah said. Her voice was very even. "You know, if we don't get out of this alive, I'm never going to forgive you."

Thomas laughed. "If we don't get out of this alive, I'll never forgive myself," he said. A low shudder ran through the ship as the drives powered up. "And..."

He stopped himself before he could suggest they might not manage to escape. "Wesley, prepare the guns," he ordered. Thankfully, he'd made his son run endless drills over the past few weeks. His gunnery average was better than his father's. "Get ready to engage if they come too close."

"Aye, Captain," Wesley said. "What if they shoot the guns off our hull?"

"Then we hope for the best while fearing the worst," Thomas said, flatly. Did the aliens have an antishipping squadron on standby, ready to launch at a moment's notice? *He* would have, if he'd been preparing to start a war. There'd been so much chaos along the border that a lone merchantman or mercenary raider might stumble across the fleet and alert the human defenders. There'd certainly been rumours of border worlds in the disputed zone trying to hire mercenaries...nothing confirmed, of course. "And we keep running."

And die, probably, he thought, as more and more data flowed into the terminal. The enemy fleet didn't seem to have noticed their departure yet, but it wouldn't take long. He didn't have time to be stealthy. It would be easy to turn the ship into a black hole in space, a hulking piece of debris no different from the rocks drifting closer to the primary star...as long as someone didn't look at them with the naked eye...but he didn't have time. No one had time. *We have to get home before it's too late.*

"They're signalling us," Ginny said. "They're telling us to stand down our drives and prepared to be boarded."

"Send a bunch of gibberish back," Thomas ordered. He'd hoped they'd have more time before the aliens noticed they were leaving, but...there was no helping it now. "See if it delays them a moment or two longer."

Red icons flashed into existence on the display. "It didn't," Sarah said. "They've launched a starfighter squadron after us."

"Jump us into multispace as soon as we reach the crossroads," Thomas said. He kept his voice calm. His children would panic if they saw him getting alarmed. "Wesley, hold your fire until I give the command."

"Aye, Captain," Wesley said. He sounded like every other young officer facing his first taste of combat." "I'm ready."

"But keep tracking them carefully," Thomas said. "And see if you can calculate when they'll be able to hit us."

He brought up the warbook and studied the files, such as they were. No one had seen Vultek starfighters in action, even during the handful of skirmishes along the border before the Alphans and the Pashtali had come to terms and established a neutral zone. There was nothing to suggest what the starfighters might be carrying, from plasma cannons to pulses and antishipping missiles. They might even have Alphan-grade beamers or fission rays. Cold logic told him it was unlikely—no other race had demonstrated such firepower—but he couldn't convince himself they'd be little better armed than their human counterparts. The Galactics were probably doing everything in their power to match Alphan firepower. It was what *he* would have done.

But they might not share it with their clients, Thomas thought, as the enemy starfighters picked up speed. *They'd want to keep a few tricks up their sleeves.*

He watched the enemy craft grimly, running through the calculations again and again. They were brutally simple. The Vulteks would have a brief window of opportunity to cripple or destroy *James Bond* before she reached the crossroads and jumped to multispace. It looked as if they were dispatching destroyers and frigates after them too, but they were too late. Unless they had some entirely new drive system, superior to anything the

Alphans possessed, the encounter would be decided, one way or the other, before they could reach the crossroads. He frowned as he brought the active sensors online, throwing caution to the winds. If there was a cloaked ship lurking near the crossroads, they might be flying straight into a trap.

"The screens are clear." Sarah had evidently had the same thought. "They must have been very confident we wouldn't see anything."

Thomas shook his head, without answering. *James Bond's* sensors were good, but there were limits. A cloaked ship would have no trouble spotting them now and targeting weapons without ever bringing their own sensors online. They'd just have to hope they could slip past any guardship before it was too late. And besides...there was no time to try to reach another crossroads. They were committed.

"Captain," Wesley said. "The starfighters are charging weapons."

"Sarah, start evasive rotations," Thomas said. The freighter's armour was top of the line, for a civilian ship, but he had no illusions about how much protection it would offer when the aliens opened fire. "Wesley, let them fire the first shot."

"I don't think that's going to be a problem." Wesley's voice shook. "They're about to fire..."

Thomas sucked in his breath as plasma bolts shot towards his drive section. They were trying to disable his ship, rather than destroy it outright. Good or bad? He didn't know. Dull rumbles echoed through the hull as the bolts slammed home, pushing his armour to the limit. He wished, suddenly, he'd brought a warship. Even a small destroyer would have laughed at the plasma bolts. They would barely damage her hull.

"Return fire," he ordered, calmly. "Try to disable, if possible."

"I can try." Wesley's hands danced over his console. "They won't stay still!"

"Of course not," Thomas said, dryly. "What do you expect?"

Another shudder ran through the ship as an alien starfighter strafed her hull. Alerts flashed up, but he ignored them. Either they made it through the next few minutes, in which case they could patch up the hull during the flight to Delaine, or they died. If that happened...he put the thought out of his mind as Wesley kept shooting. The alien pilots were *good*. They managed to avoid *everything* Wesley threw at them while pounding shot after shot into *James Bond's* hull.

"Crossroads in thirty seconds," Sarah said. "We'll be going through at speed. Brace yourself."

"Try not to be sick in your suits," Thomas ordered. "Ten seconds..."

His chest contracted, as if someone had punched him in the stomach, as the freighter hit the crossroads and jumped to multispace. Wesley nearly fell off his seat, the sound of retching echoing through the communications net. Thomas pretended not to hear. Throwing up was never pleasant, but doing it inside a spacesuit was the absolute worst. The poor kid would have his sisters making fun of him, even though they'd thrown up too.

"We made it," Sarah said.

"Barely," Thomas said. It was difficult to track and intercept someone in multispace, but not impossible. "Set course for Delaine. And don't look back."

"Aye, sir," Sarah said.

...

"The human ship escaped," the tactical officer said. His feathers fluttered against his chest as he started to prostrate himself. "I...I offer my life..."

"Be quiet," Flockleader Trans snarled. The human ship had seen *something*. But what? The entire fleet...? Its active sensors had been mil-grade. If it had carried mil-grade *passive* sensors too...it might have seen everything. The plan to make the humans supply the fleet had been too clever by half. "Contact the fleet, then alert the homeworld."

His beak snapped closed in a snarl. "It's time to attack," he ordered. His crew squawked their agreement. They'd been waiting for too long. "The human worlds will be ours!"

CHAPTER TWENTY-SIX

EDS *Washington*, J-57

IT WAS EASY TO SEE, NAOMI CONSIDERED, why neither the Alphans, the Pashtali or even the Vulteks had made a bid for J-57. The system lacked both habitable planets and gas giants capable of supporting a major civilisation, even though there were over thirty charted crossroads in close proximity to the primary star. The handful of asteroids, comets and drifting pieces of space debris were of little interest to the interstellar powers, all which had more interesting and immediately useful systems to develop. In their place, dozens of minor colonies—human and alien—had been established within the system. The settlers wanted to make their mark somewhere well clear of the major interstellar powers.

Which didn't stop them screaming for help when the Vulteks started pushing their claim to the system, she mused. A Vultek colony had forwarded the claim—it read more like a list of charges—as soon as she'd entered the system and announced herself. *And we're out on a limb just by coming here.*

She sighed, inwardly. In theory, her ship had a perfect right to enter the system without seeking anyone's permission. In practice, she knew her ability to practice her rights was limited. The galaxy was watching, if anyone cared enough. It was galling to think that humanity—and the

Vulteks—were too insignificant for any of the major powers to watch, but it was largely true. Earth's newly independent status was little more than a minor blip in galactic history. It remained to be seen if humanity was anything more than a flash in the pan.

And no one talks about Earth's ancient history any longer, she reminded herself, dryly. Her instructors had made that clear, years ago. *While Alexander the Great was forging an Empire and Julius Caesar was battling for power, the Alphan Empire covered thousands of light-years and was already starting to decline.*

She put the thought out of her head as she studied the asteroid colony. The settlers hadn't bothered to either spin the asteroid to produce gravity or modify their bodies to ensure they could move smoothly between zero-g and a standard gravity field. They looked rather odd to her eyes, as if they were humans playing at being spiders, but...she supposed they had the right to live as they pleased. She just wished they'd done it within space that was unquestionably human. Their exact status within J-57 would be determined by force, not legal right. Her lips twitched sourly at the absurdity of that thought. What mattered *right* and *wrong* when one couldn't enforce one's rights?

"The away team has returned, Captain," Roger said. "They're reporting the settlers don't have much to offer."

Naomi wasn't surprised. It was possible to build and maintain an asteroid colony with a surprisingly low-tech level, once one managed to get out of the gravity well. The settlers seemed inclined to stick with what they knew and understood, rather than risk becoming dependent on outside sources. They couldn't risk a shortage of whatever they needed to keep their people alive. She understood the logic, but it meant the colony was effectively useless as far as the new government was concerned. No one was going to go out on a limb for the settlers when they couldn't offer anything in return. If the Vulteks wanted the system, they could simply take it.

"Have them make a full report," she ordered. "And..."

The sensor console bleeped an alarm. "Captain," Hawke snapped. "We have three starships on attack vector! They'll be within missile range in seven minutes."

"Red alert," Naomi ordered, curtly. "Do we have an ID?"

"No, Captain," Hawke said. "No IFF, no nothing. Warbook says the lead ship is a heavy cruiser. The other two remain unknown."

Naomi swore under her breath. *Washington* couldn't hope to meet a heavy cruiser in open combat and survive. The attackers were throwing down a gauntlet, challenging her to either fight or run. She suspected it was partly psychological—they could have sneaked closer if they'd wanted to merely engage her ship—but it didn't matter. She was going to have to run, if she didn't want to be blown to atoms. And that meant abandoning the colony to its fate.

"Helm, bring us about," she ordered, stiffly. "Communications, order them to break off and stand down."

Roger gave her a look that said, quite clearly, *do you really think they're going to listen?* Naomi shrugged. She had to try, even if she was *sure* the war had just begun. The alien ships might *just* be playing a demented version of chicken, trying to make her panic and fire first before they returned fire themselves. She found it hard to wrap her head around the concept of anyone playing chicken with a heavy cruiser, but she supposed the Vulteks had ships to burn. They could trade a heavy cruiser for a light cruiser and still come out ahead. Probably. *She* rather suspected *her* superiors would break any officer who suggested anything of the sort.

"Aye, Captain," Walcott said. There was a long pause. "No response."

"All stations report ready," Roger said. "Your ship is clear for action."

"Good." Naomi knew she had few options. The Vulteks—it had to be the Vulteks—had backed her into a corner. "Helm, prepare to strafe the enemy ships."

"Aye, Captain," Almont said.

Naomi gritted her teeth. The tactical picture was both simple and complicated. If she turned and fled, or left at an angle to the incoming ships, there was a good chance they could run her down before she could build up speed and escape. *Washington* had a higher acceleration curve than any heavy cruiser ever built, than anything big enough to blow the cruiser to atoms if they *caught* her, but she wouldn't have *time* to make use of her speed. The two smaller enemy ships—the warbook was tentatively calling them frigates—would slow her down long enough for their big brother to catch up. No, her only real option was trying to blow *past* the enemy ships—firing on them in passing—and then running for deep space.

And we'll be leaving the asteroid to its fate, she thought, grimly. *What'll they do to the settlers?*

She winced at the thought. There was no reason to believe the Vulteks would honour interstellar conventions. Humanity wasn't powerful enough to force the bird-like aliens to behave themselves. They might deport the settlers and take the asteroid for themselves...or simply open the airlocks and exterminate the entire population. She tried to tell herself the Vulteks wouldn't start the war with a major atrocity, but she didn't believe it. Everything she'd read, everything she'd seen in the files, suggested the Vulteks were barbarians at heart. She found it hard to believe they could maintain their ships without assistance.

And they probably have that assistance, she thought. *Their patrons give them everything they want.*

"Captain," Hawke said. "They're sweeping us with tactical sensors."

"Bring up our own," Naomi ordered. She didn't *need* her active sensors to track the enemy ships, not now, but it would make it clear they'd been seen. Not, she supposed, that they could be in any doubt about it. They'd redlined their drives just to make damn sure they were seen. "Communications, broadcast a warning message across the system. If there are any human freighters, or friendly aliens within the system, order them to take a warning to Delaine."

"Aye, Captain," Walcott said.

"Enemy ships entering missile range," Lieutenant Commander Ruthven reported. "They're locking weapons on our hull."

They're trying to scare us, Naomi thought. *And they're overdoing it.*

She watched as the range steadily closed. The alien ships hadn't opened fire. Not yet. She saw their logic—there was little point in firing missiles at extreme range—but...she shook her head. Were they trying to lure her into firing the first shot? It didn't seem likely. If someone swept one's ship with tactical sensors, interstellar conventions agreed it was a hostile act and one would be perfectly justified in returning fire. The Vulteks might not give much of a damn, she supposed, but their patrons might have a different idea. She wondered, grimly, who was calling the shots. The Vulteks must be pondering the same question. Did they really believe Earth had been abandoned by its former masters?

"Missile separation," Janet snapped. "I say again, missile separation! Multiple missile separation!"

"Stand by point defence," Naomi ordered. "Engage when they enter range."

"Aye, Captain."

Naomi counted down the last few seconds, cursing under her breath. The bastards had timed it well. Their missiles would still have enough power for manoeuvring when they entered terminal attack range. And yet...she wanted to swear again as the missile clusters diverged. Half of them headed towards her ship, the other half were aimed directly at the asteroid colony. The *defenceless* asteroid colony. She stared in horror. It didn't matter if the missiles were nukes or crammed to the gunwales with antimatter. They'd fired enough missiles to turn the asteroid colony into a rapidly-expanding cloud of debris.

"Tactical, see if you can cover the colony," Naomi snapped. She had a nasty feeling it was futile. Or, worse, that it would lead her ship into a trap. Breaking off the engagement would be a great deal harder if she came within point-blank range...and she would, if she wanted to take out the missiles before it was too late. "Communications..."

She broke off. She'd wanted to warn the colony, but...it would be useless. They already *knew* the missiles were incoming. They were already ordering their people into shelters...into shelters that would provide no protection at all, not against the sheer weight of firepower bearing down on them. They didn't even have time to *evacuate* the colony. The entire population, from the oldest to the youngest, was about to die.

"Communications, warn the rest of the system," she ordered. "The bastards are launching genocidal attacks."

"Aye, Captain," Walcott said.

Naomi tensed as her point defence weapons opened fire. A dozen missiles died within seconds, but the remainder slipped through and out of her engagement envelope before it was too late. Her guns picked off the missiles aimed at *Washington* herself, but not the ones aimed at the asteroid. She saw a single shuttle cast off from the colony and vanishing into deep space before the missiles finally struck home, antimatter warheads detonating the moment they slammed into the rocky shell. The asteroid disintegrated in a tearing flash of light and energy. There were no survivors. She watched, numbly. Even if they'd managed to get to the escape pods—even if there *were* escape pods—they'd have been caught in the blast.

"Those murdering bastards," Roger breathed.

"Helm, take us into strafing range," Naomi snapped. She knew she couldn't do more than scratch their paint, unless she got very lucky, but at least she could make sure they knew they'd been kissed. "Tactical, target their drives and weapons."

"Aye, Captain," Janet said. She sucked in her breath as the display sparked with newer and deadlier icons. "They're launching missiles on sprint mode."

Good, Naomi thought, coldly. *The more missiles they waste on us, the fewer they'll have to expend on other colonies.*

She shuddered as the range closed sharply. The alien craft started to alter course, trying to bring themselves around and close the range still further. Good thinking on their part, she supposed. They knew they couldn't catch her if she blazed past them and vanished into interplanetary space. Better to close the range and hope their energy weapons could tear her into dust before she made her escape. But her helmsman was good. He wouldn't let them get too close.

"Weapons locked on target," Janet reported. "Firing...now!"

Naomi leaned forward as *Washington* opened fire, pounding the heavy cruiser's drive section. It returned fire, dull shudders running through *Washington's* hull as bolt after bolt of pulsar energy crashed into the armour. Naomi wished for an antimatter burner or a fission beam, something that would let her ship take on an enemy five times her size and win. Janet was doing well, but the enemy ship was just too heavily armoured for her to do more than disable a handful of drive nodes. And...

Washington shuddered. "Hull breach, deck four," Roger snapped. "Damage control teams are on their way."

"Helm, break off," Naomi ordered. She didn't dare let her ship be destroyed, not now. They *had* to get back to Delaine before it was too late. If they couldn't get a message out, the colonies closer to Earth wouldn't know they were at war until enemy ships appeared in their skies. And any reinforcements on their way would run straight into enemy fire. "Tactical, deploy mines and ballistic missiles to slow pursuit."

"Aye, Captain," Janet said.

Naomi nodded as her ship skimmed out of engagement range and fled. The irony mocked her. She'd chased an enemy ship until she'd realised it was futile...would the enemy make the same judgement? Or would they try to run her down? They might succeed, if they were prepared to commit everything to the chase. Their frigates might *just* manage to slow her down, if they got back into engagement range. But she'd have an equally good chance to take them out before their big brother intervened.

"Captain," Almont said. "If we jump through the nearest crossroads, we'll add two days to our flight to Delaine."

Naomi grimaced as she pulled up the starchart. If the enemy had launched a full-scale invasion of human space, it was quite possible their advance elements had already reached Delaine. There was nothing to be gained by giving humanity a few days warning before beginning the invasion, although...she admitted, sourly, that there was little they could do that wasn't already being done. Delaine simply didn't have the resources to protect itself indefinitely. The only thing they *hadn't* done was intern the alien settlers.

And they won't be able to do any real damage until their fleet arrives, she mused. *Or so we believe.*

She shook her head. There was no point in worrying about it, not now. There was certainly nothing she could *do* about it. Governor Singh had made the best call he could, given the limited resources at his disposal. And now...she understood, suddenly, what her instructors had been trying to tell her. There was no such thing as a perfect choice. If she flew to the nearest crossroads...each option had advantages and disadvantages. If she flew to the nearest crossroads, she'd double their chances of escape but halve their prospects of getting to Delaine before the enemy fleet. And yet, if she risked heading to a further crossroads...

"Continue on our current course," she ordered. Her orders were clear. *Washington* was more important than any colony world short of Coriander. It felt wrong to be running, to be leaving civilians to die, but she had no choice. She just hoped she could live with herself afterwards. The EDF existed to defend humanity but she'd failed. "And prepare to deploy sensor drones."

She watched the alien ships as they came about, wondering what they'd do. There were already a dozen freighters fleeing in all directions, heading to crossroads that—as far as anyone could tell—hadn't been locked down by enemy ships. In theory, the aliens *could* put the entire system under siege. In practice, they'd have to commit their entire navy to the operation. She doubted they'd take the risk, not when they'd just started a war. Sure, *technically*, the settlers they'd killed hadn't been under Earth's jurisdiction. Some asshole would probably make that argument, some REMF who'd never seen the aftermath of a pirate attack or a radioactive hole in the ground where a city had once stood. The remainder of the human race would be screaming for war.

It doesn't matter what they want or don't want, she reflected. *It takes two to make peace, but only one to make war.*

"Captain, the enemy ships are breaking off," Hawke reported. "They're heading towards the other major settlements."

"Shit," Roger muttered. "They'll have managed to evacuate, won't they?"

Naomi doubted it. If one didn't have a ship, there was literally nowhere to go. The evacuees could drift around in shuttles and escape pods until they ran out of atmosphere and suffocated, if their ships weren't mistaken for threats and simply obliterated in passing. Or simply used for target practice. Thousands of humans and aliens were about to die and there was nothing she could do about it, save promise revenge at some later date. She silently cursed the Vulteks and their patrons. What sort of morons would unleash such monsters on the galaxy? Humanity, at least, had been fairly civilised before the Alphans invaded and occupied Earth.

"Keep us on course," she ordered. They had to *try* to reach Delaine before it was too late. "Sensors, keep scanning for enemy watchdogs; tactical, prepare to engage any alien ships guarding the crossroads."

"Aye, Captain," Janet said.

"And have your staff studying the sensor records for weaknesses," Naomi ordered. "Something—anything—we can use."

"Aye, Captain," Janet repeated.

Naomi sat back in her chair. She'd done everything right. She'd done everything she could do. And yet, she was running for her life while—behind her—the Vulteks slaughtered every human within the system. It was evil on a horrific scale, the sort of atrocity the Convocations were designed to prevent. And yet...

Maybe one of the bigger powers will care enough to intervene, she thought. It didn't seem likely. *Or maybe we'll just have to do it ourselves.*

CHAPTER TWENTY-SEVEN

James Bond, Delaine System/Government House, Delaine System

"CAPTAIN TO THE BRIDGE," Wesley said. His voice echoed through the intercom. "Captain to the bridge!"

Thomas Anderson rolled out of his bunk, grabbed his helmet and glanced at the display before hurrying for the hatch. He'd overslept. Wesley had *let* him oversleep. He felt a flash of irritation, torn between the sense he should be grateful and a grim awareness his son had disobeyed orders. Thomas had needed his sleep, but...orders were orders. And they were too close to the crossroads for his peace of mind.

"I'll deal with you later," he said, as he stumbled onto the bridge. The air smelt unpleasantly rank. "And you'd better hope there *is* a later."

"Dad, you needed to sleep," Wesley said. "And nothing was going to happen until we plunged through the crossroads."

"You didn't *know* that," Thomas snarled. His son had a point, but... orders were *definitely* orders. An officer who took it upon himself to rewrite or simply ignore his orders, an officer who wasn't related to him, was an officer who would be looking for a new billet sooner rather than later. "We'll discuss this later."

He took his seat and studied the display. The ship was surrounded by the weird gravity surges and unquantifiable energies of multispace, concealed from any watching eyes by folds within the alternate dimension. There was little chance of being run down and destroyed, he told himself, although he knew better than to take that for granted. The bad guys sometimes got lucky. They might *just* manage to track the threadline and run them down. And the timer was steadily ticking down to zero. They'd reach the crossroads in ten minutes.

"Don't wake your mother and sisters," he ordered, coldly. "Let them sleep a little bit longer."

Wesley shot him a sharp look, but was wise enough not to say anything out loud. Thomas didn't really blame him. Teenagers always thought the world was unfair, particularly when it wasn't unfair in their favour. Wesley really needed some experience away from his family's ship, perhaps an apprenticeship under someone who disliked eager young space cadets who *weren't* related to him. Thomas wasn't keen on looking for a replacement either, but it would have to be done. His son wasn't going to be content to be his subordinate for the rest of his life.

Which may be alarmingly short, Thomas thought. He'd taken the quickest threadline to Delaine, but he was all too aware the enemy fleet could have simply overtaken him with neither side being any the wiser. *We might pop through the crossroads and run straight into a trap.*

"Ready the messages," he ordered. "I want them transmitted as soon as we're through the crossroads."

"Aye, Captain," Wesley said. "They're already stored within the buffer."

"Good." Thomas worked his console for a long moment. "And once we're through the crossroads, take us to the next crossroads."

Wesley blinked. "We're not going to the planet?"

"Not if we can avoid it," Thomas said, dryly. "The last thing we want is to get pinned against the planet by an enemy fleet."

He smiled, humourlessly, as the countdown neared zero. "Ready?"

"Yes, Dad." Wesley turned his attention to his console. "Crossroads in three...two...one..."

Thomas braced himself as space twisted around his ship. It was easier, somehow, to jump *out* of a crossroads at speed, although the shock of the transit had probably woken his wife and daughters. The display flared with red lights, his heart skipping a beat before the red icons turned green or yellow. Someone had emplaced sensor platforms near the crossroads, ready to track anything that came out of multispace. It would have been more impressive if the sensors had been backed up by heavy firepower. As it was, all they could do was give the planet a few hours additional warning.

"Send the signal," he ordered, curtly. "And set course for the next crossroads."

"Aye, Captain," Wesley said. His fingers danced over the console. "Signal sent."

Thomas nodded. His priority codes should get his message jumped right to the top of the queue, when it reached the FTL transmitter. But the crossroads was a good three light-hours from the planet...he hoped the enemy fleet would give the planet a little more time to prepare. Delaine wasn't *that* heavily settled, let alone defended. The aliens were likely to cause havoc if they seized the spaceport and capital city. They could worry about the rest of the planet later.

He frowned as more and more data flowed into his console. There were more freighters in the system than he would have believed possible. Delaine was important, but not *that* important. He wondered, morbidly, if they were all refugee ships. It was quite possible. The Vulteks had been throwing their weight around all over the disputed zone, if the reports were accurate. People who realised the EDF was unlikely to defend them weren't going to hang around to die, not if there were other options. They were far more likely to light out for the presumed safety of Delaine.

The hatch opened. Sarah entered, wiping tiredness from her eyes. "I sent the girls back to their bunks," she said, crossly. "I take it we've arrived."

"Yeah," Thomas said. "And our message is on the way."

Sarah nodded. "Do you think they'll listen?"

Thomas shrugged. Admiral Glass would listen. But would the governor? The priority codes *should* be enough to convince him, but...anyone worth his salt knew codes could be compromised. The Vulteks would pay through the nose for up-to-date IFF codes they could use to slip misinformation into the human datanets, or simply use to sneak up on their targets and blow them to hell. The Lupine Wars had been an endless struggle between code-makers and code-breakers, if what he'd heard through the grapevine was true. The Vulteks could hardly have failed to learn from the greatest military conflict in the last thousand years. If even the Alphans could learn something from near-disaster...

An alarm sounded. "Shit!"

"Stay calm," Thomas ordered. He didn't blame Wesley for being alarmed, but there were limits. "And report."

Wesley took a breath. "Thirty warships just followed us through the crossroads," he said, as his display updated. "Correction. Forty warships..."

"Keep us on our course," Thomas said. They'd put *just* enough distance between themselves and the crossroads to pass unnoticed. He hoped. The Vulteks were known for being vindictive. "They shouldn't pay any attention to us."

He frowned as more red icons materialised on the display. There were seventy enemy warships within the system now. Seventy...the total was still climbing, as if the bastards had decided to try to awe the system into submission. Or, more likely, ensure they had an overwhelming advantage in the early battles. The Galactics probably wouldn't get involved if it looked like the fighting would be over before they could mobilise. They wouldn't want to sully their hands if they could avoid it.

"And keep recording, save every last scrap of data," he ordered. "Someone will find a use for it."

"Aye, Captain," Wesley said.

Thomas felt his heart sink as the enemy fleet shook itself into formation.

They had enough firepower to punch their way to Earth, if they didn't waste time trying to mop up the outer colonies first. Galactic doctrine called for a steady advance, occupying or neutralising outer worlds before pushing their way to their enemy's homeworld, but...the Vulteks had enough ships in the fleet to make an all-out assault quite possible. Who knew? They might be relying on their patrons to cover their homeworlds as they concentrated their power against the human race.

We'll be back, he promised himself. *And they'll pay for what they've done.*

But he knew, all too well, that it was a promise the human race might be unable to keep.

...

The command and control centre should, by rights, have been buried under so many layers of rock and armour that nothing short of blowing the entire planet to asteroids would have smashed the bunker and killed the inhabitants. Delaine had never been rich enough to afford such facilities. The command and control centre was in Government House's basement, so flimsy—in comparison to more modern facilities—that a single direct hit would be more than enough to shatter the facility beyond repair. Governor Singh silently thanked his staff for their foresight, in scattering the governing infrastructure across the settled region. They might just ensure a degree of continuity if the command and control centre was taken out.

Which it probably will be, he reflected, sourly. The fleet descending on his world was something out of a nightmare. It wouldn't take more than a handful of ships to land troops, but the aliens had sent a small armada. *They have to have a rough idea where we're hiding.*

He took his seat and calmed himself. "Report!"

"The planetary defences are on alert," Colonel Tailor said. He was one of the very few militiamen with genuine experience, having fought in four ground campaigns during the war...during the *last* war. "Right now, we *may* be able to keep them from bombarding us into submission. We *may*. But we cannot keep them from sniping at our defences or landing troops."

"As we expected," Singh growled. The militia had been drilling extensively over the past few days, once he'd overcome his reluctance to look *provocative*. "And the troops on the ground?"

"Heading to their lodgements now," Tailor assured him. "The alert has been sounded. All radio transmitters have been ordered to go silent. People with evacuation plans have been ordered to put them into effect."

"And we'll just have to hope they stay off the roads," Singh said. He had no doubt refugees would block troop movements, even if the enemy didn't use them for target practice. Aliens might not be able to tell the difference between troops and civilians, particularly as the civilians were heavily armed. "I take it you broadcast warnings?"

"Yes, sir," Tailor said. "But I don't know how many of them will listen."

Singh nodded, stiffly. Colonials tended to resent orders from the government, regarding them more as suggestions than anything that could be enforced. They wouldn't have left Earth and travelled all the way to Delaine if they were interested in doing what they were told. He knew he was popular, as governors went, but there were strict limits to his authority. If he tried to convince them to roll over and play nice to the planet's new masters, half of them would turn on him in a heartbeat.

And they can be legally shot out of hand if they try to fight, he thought. *They're not legitimate troops.*

He cast his eye around the chamber as the enemy fleet drew closer. It was a crude room, the concrete walls cold and hard. A couple of operators sat at consoles, communing with their fellows on the other side of the colony. The last time he'd been in the chamber, it had been crammed with officers and operators. Now...there were only four people within the concrete walls. The remainder of the command and control staff had been dispersed. He hoped they were scattered enough to survive when the enemy bombardment began.

"Keep updating Earth," he said, grimly. It was only a matter of time before the invaders either destroyed or captured the orbital transmitter. "And tell them we'll do our best."

"We'll bleed them," Tailor said. "But stop them? I don't think so."

Singh nodded, curtly. His sealed orders had made it clear he was expected to continue the fight as long as reasonably possible. He had no qualms about fighting, if only because most of the population would continue the fight anyway, but he had no illusions about the cost either. The planet would take a major beating, even if the EDF returned and regained control of the high orbitals. And if they didn't...he shuddered. What would it mean, he asked himself, if Earth was forced to concede? Would he be expected to surrender? Or to evacuate the planet? Or...

"Governor." An operator looked up. "I'm picking up a message from the alien fleet. They're demanding our immediate surrender."

"No." Singh shook his head. "Order them to vacate our space immediately."

"No response, sir," the operator said. "I..."

"Alien ships have opened fire," the other operator snapped. "They're targeting the orbital network!"

"And they're hanging out of range of the ground-based weapons," Tailor observed. "I think they're taking our measure."

"I've seen the projections," Singh said. "All we can do is hold out as long as possible."

He watched, coldly, as the attack developed. The attackers were running down a checklist, systematically wiping out the orbital satellites and communications hubs. His eyes narrowed as they took out the FTL transmitter. Technically, taking out an FTL node was a slap in the face to Galactic Law. And it belonged to the Alphans...he let himself hope it meant some of the other powers would intervene, just as the invaders started hurling KEWs towards the surface. His ground-based point defence weapons returned fire, blasting the KEWs to atoms before they could strike the ground. He knew it wouldn't be enough. KEWs were little more than pieces of rock. The enemy could afford to expend hundreds of thousands—perhaps millions—in a bid to cripple his defences.

A low rumble echoed through the bunker. "They hit the city," an operator said. "I don't know how many are dead."

Tailor glanced at Singh. "I think it's time to leave."

Singh nodded. "Switch control to the remote stations," he ordered. The militia had been laying underground cables for weeks, ensuring there would be no betraying emissions to attract attention. "And then prime the bunker for destruction."

"Aye, sir," Tailor said. He raised his voice. "Let's move. Now!"

Singh said nothing as he forced himself to run up the steps and into a strangely-deserted building. Government House was sedate, compared to some of the places he'd known on Earth, but it was normally teeming with activity. Now, it was deserted. The city beyond had been deserted too, save for the militiamen readying themselves to make a stand. Their command and control networks were completely off the books, half unknown even to Singh and Tailor. If they were captured and forced to talk…it wouldn't matter. The war would go on until the aliens gave up or battered the entire planet into submission.

Or land so many new colonists that we cannot hold onto our lands, he mused, as they ran onto the streets. A streak of light blasted across the sky, striking somewhere dozens of miles to the south. He saw a flash, heard—a few seconds later—a crack of thunder. *We might be unable to survive if they drive us into the unsettled regions.*

He felt a stab of pain as they kept running, passing buildings that had been abandoned and then turned into strongpoints. His people had worked hard, damn it. They'd taken a world that had been classed as borderline and turned it into a success. They might be rough and tough and completely lacking in the social graces, to the point the Alphans had thrown up their hands in horror, but they'd worked hard. They didn't deserve to have everything taken by a greedy alien race. God knew the bastards could probably have settled and tamed the world for themselves, if they'd wanted it. No, they just wanted to let someone else do all the work. Bastards.

Another shockwave echoed through the air. He saw sparks of red light darting upwards, firing at targets only their gunners could see. The ground-based defences were tough, but dependent on active sensors. Singh had no military experience, but he'd read the briefing notes carefully. The active sensors were a two-edged sword. Every time they were activated, they told the enemy where to aim. It wouldn't take long for the bastards to wipe the defences out, if they were prepared to shower the sensor nodes with KEWs. One hit—just one—would be enough to take out a sensor head. And once they were all gone, the defenders would be firing blind.

Tailor put a hand to his earpiece. "They're launching shuttles," he said. "Tactical projections says they'll be coming down to the south."

Singh glanced at him. "Can they be stopped?"

"I don't know," Tailor said. "Right now, it's out of our hands."

. . .

"They just killed an FTL node!"

Thomas had to smile at Wesley's shock, despite the situation. Destroying FTL communicators *was* a violation of the Convocations, although he had no doubt the Vulteks would come up with an excuse the Galactics would accept. They'd probably rewrite history to make sure the humans got the blame. Perhaps they'd insist the transmitter refused to power down and surrender or…or maybe they wouldn't even *try*. Very few races had both the power and inclination to pick a fight with the Vulteks, not when it meant picking a fight with their patrons as well. The Alphans were about the only ones who *could*, and they'd withdrawn from the sector.

"You never know what you have until it's gone," he said, softly. "Hold us here. I think we'll watch for a few hours."

"Aye, sir," Wesley said. "And if they come after us?"

"We run." Thomas scowled. They weren't the *only* freighter trying to pretend to be a hole in space. It was quite possible some of them were spies too. "And get our intelligence to senior officers."

And do what we can to impede them, he mused. He didn't have any idea what, so far, but he was sure he'd think of something. *We have to buy time for Earth.*

CHAPTER TWENTY-EIGHT

Smallbridge, Delaine System

"I JUST PICKED UP A MICROBURST, SIR," Sergeant Ross said. "Long-range sensors have detected enemy craft moving towards Smallbridge."

"Probably coming down in the fields," Tomas said. He'd surveyed the area during their preliminary sweep. The fields were lying fallow for the year. The surface was rough, compared to a landing pad, but nothing that would delay an assault shuttle for more than a few seconds. "It makes sense."

He snapped orders, hastily moving the squad forward. He'd rather *liked* Smallbridge when they'd worked their way through the town, admiring its communal spirit and collective forthrightness. The settlers seemed to actually know and *like* their fellows, a far cry from the massive cities on Earth that were so densely overpopulated their governments did everything in their power to encourage emigration. He'd been tempted to ask if he could retire to Smallbridge, although he had to admit he'd probably be bored out of his mind within the week. The settlers might be armed to the teeth, but they had very few natural enemies.

And they're about to go into hiding, he thought. The women and children had already been moved, evacuated to hidden caves just outside the settled zone. Hopefully, they'd be safe there long enough for the EDF to return and drive the invaders off the planet. *The militia knows not to let itself get trapped during the early landings.*

He put the thought out of his head as he heard enemy shuttles racing towards them. The Vulteks didn't seem to want to make a HALO landing, something that suggested they were either inexperienced or extremely confident of victory. He puzzled over it for a moment—aliens that looked like birds should have no trouble making parachute drops—before dismissing the thought in irritation. They were supposed to be a numerous race. Maybe they thought they could endure the casualties to complete their mission.

"Here they come," Ross muttered. "Fast and low."

Tomas nodded. The alien shuttles were dropping with terrifying speed. Their passengers *had* to be having a rough time of it, even though they'd passed through the danger zone without being hit. Or so they thought. He glanced at his men, standing ready with HVMs. They had to give the enemy a chance to put troops on the ground before they fired on the shuttles, if only to dissuade the enemy from dropping KEWs on their heads. If the reports were accurate, the enemy had already taken out the command bunker. Tomas believed it. It was what *he* would have done.

The enemy shuttles slowed their fall and hovered above the ground, their exhausts kicking up a whirlwind of dust and soil. Tomas leaned forward, watching eagerly as the hatches opened and the first enemy soldier jumped down. The alien—the Vultek—was weird, as if someone had take a bird and given it humanoid form. His body—what little wasn't covered in armoured battledress—was covered in short blue feathers. He moved with short jerky motions that suggested he was constantly on the alert, his beady eyes darting from side to side. Tomas heard someone snigger, a sound that was cut off as they saw the weapon in the alien's claws. It didn't matter what the alien looked like, he reminded himself sharply. All that mattered was that they'd come to kill.

"At least thirty of the bastards per shuttle," Ross muttered, as more and more aliens poured out of the shuttlecraft. They moved with the squeamish determination of trained but untried troops, their weapons moving as they swept the fields for potential threats. "That means around a hundred and twenty in the first wave alone."

Tomas looked up as more shuttles dropped from the sky. "There's more on the way," he said. A number of shuttles looked larger than the others. Heavy-lift shuttles, unless he missed his guess. "I think we'd better make our move."

He glanced at the missile and mortar crews. "Choose your targets," he ordered. Lighting up active sensors would be practically *asking* the aliens to kill them, but they didn't need active sensors when the aliens were making their presence so obvious. "Fire on my command."

"Give me a moment to set up the mines," Ross said. He took the weapons from his bag and placed them between the squad and the alien landing zone. "Ready."

Tomas nodded. "Fire!"

The crews opened fire, missiles lancing towards the alien shuttlecraft as mortar shells rose and fell amongst the alien troopers. He wanted to whoop and cheer for joy as the four missiles struck their targets, blowing a cluster of shuttles out of the sky. One even managed to collide with another shuttle, bringing them both down in flames. They hit the ground with terrifying force, crashing down on top of the abandoned farmhouse and setting fire to the surrounding area. The mortar shells forced the aliens to dive for cover, but there was no cover to be found. They simply hadn't had *time* to dig trenches before it was too late. The alien troops died in droves.

But there were more. Tomas sucked in his breath as the aliens turned and charged his position, moving with astonishing speed. He knew he was in the top one percentile and yet he doubted *he* could move so fast, even if he were being chased by a Drill Instructor with a whip. The lead aliens opened fire, filling the space between the two groups with plasma bolts. Tomas ducked low, motioning for the mortar crews to pick up their weapons and run. The missile crews were already bugging out. They didn't have to worry about dismantling their weapons before they ran.

"Now," Ross said.

The mines detonated, hurling a wave of red-hot metal balls into the alien mass. It recoiled as the balls struck home, slamming them back with immense force. Tomas wondered if it would be enough to break the charge, feeling his heart sink as the rear lines jumped over the forward lines and kept moving. He lobbed a grenade into the mass, then turned and ran. Ross matched him, unhooking and throwing grenades himself. It wasn't until they slipped through a patch of trees that they broke contact and escaped. The alien CO must have regained control. Tomas wondered, sourly, just what would have happened if the bastard had waited a few minutes longer.

"They're bringing in more shuttles," Ross said. "Forty-seven, at my guess."

Tomas nodded as they ran towards the RV point. The remainder of the squad was already there, reloading their weapons. The militia liaison officer looked terrified. It was his first taste of combat, Tomas reminded himself. His training hadn't been particularly realistic. He was going to find out the hard way if he could handle the military life.

"They can be provoked," Ross noted. "And confused, if they can't figure out what happened."

"So we can lure them into a trap," Tomas agreed. He nodded to his men, then led the way towards the concealed trench. "And get them to impale themselves on our weapons."

He heard more shuttles flying overhead as the aliens brought more and more troops down to the surface. He had to admire their determination, although it seemed to him they were risking lives and shuttlecraft without good cause. There were too many shuttles within too small a patch of sky. They had to get in and out of the engagement envelope before the ground-based defences could pick them off, but still…their ATC controllers had to be working overtime just to keep them from crashing into each other. His lips curved into a cold smile. The invaders might have done better to land outside the settled zone and march to the capital once their army was on the ground and ready for deployment.

Which would have given us plenty of time to react, he reminded himself. *They want to take control as quickly as possible.*

His gaze swept the trenches as the marines linked up with the militia. They looked a little shallow for his peace of mind, but the militia hadn't had time to do more than the very basics. The machine gun and plasma cannon mounts were puny...they'd have to do. There just wasn't the time to construct proper fixed defences. They were bloody lucky they had as many weapons as they did. If the militia hadn't been so heavily armed, there would have been little hope of bleeding the aliens before it was too late.

"They'll drown the moment it rains," Ross muttered, grimly. "There's no system for getting rid of the water."

"As long as they can get out when the shit hits the fan," Tomas muttered back. He turned to peer south. Plumes of smoke dominated the skyline, and alien shuttles rose and fell at a terrifying pace, but there was no sign of ground troops. "The moment they see us, they'll start dropping rocks on our head."

Or mortar shells, he added, silently. Humanity had been the only race to invent mortars, but it wasn't as if they were difficult to duplicate. The Vulteks and their patrons had sent observers to the Lupine Wars. They'd have seen mortars in action. The Alphans might be too prideful to copy the design, but...he couldn't see anyone else being willing to put their pride ahead of efficiency. *Hell, what's to stop them simply shelling us to death?*

"Here they come, sir," Ross said. He raised his voice. "Hold your fire! Don't fire until you get orders!"

Tomas nodded stiffly as the alien tanks came into view. They hovered on beds of air, unlike comparable human vehicles; he knew, from experience, that the design had both strengths and weaknesses. They were prowling forward, dismounted infantry using their armoured hulls for cover as they followed in their wake. They probably expected to run into an ambush, sooner or later. Their tactics had more than a whiff of *advance to contact* about them. He felt a twinge of sympathy. The aliens in front of him weren't the ones who'd issued the orders to invade. They were innocent, but...he was going to kill them. He told himself, sharply, that they would kill him if they got the chance. He was sure of it.

"Plasma cannons, target the tanks," he ordered. "Fire on my command."

He counted down the seconds. He'd never seen the alien tanks in operation. How tough were they? The plasma cannons were designed to take out tanks, but...would they be as effective as the makers promised? He'd seen enough, during the last war, to know that it wasn't *that* easy to kill a tank. The armour might be able to shrug off a plasma burst while the guns returned fire. Tomas had no illusions. The trench wouldn't be able to delay the enemy for long.

"Fire," he snapped.

Streaks of blinding light flashed towards the alien tanks. The leader seemed to explode into a billowing fireball, the turret blasted upwards and crashing back to the ground. The two followers didn't seem so damaged. One came to a halt, hatches snapping open and crew fleeing in all directions; the other brought its guns to bear on the trench and opened fire. Tomas hurled himself into the mud as bullets and plasma bolts whined through the air, frantically crawling away from the plasma cannons. A wave of heat washed over his head as one of the cannons exploded. The containment chamber had been destroyed.

He reached for his whistle and blew it, hard. There was no point in trying to hold the trench any longer. The militiamen were already retreating, heading down the escape route to Smallbridge. Blasts of light followed them as the aliens pushed towards the trench, trying to clear it before they took the town itself. Tomas glanced back and saw three more alien tanks heading towards him, clearly unbothered by the prospect of running into an enemy position. He glanced at Ross, then hurried down the escape route himself. Behind him, he heard the aliens screaming in triumph as they overran what remained of the trench.

The town looked different as they pelted down the street. The militiamen were taking up positions within the houses, preparing to sell their lives dearly. Tomas wanted to shout at them as shells started landing within the town, a handful of buildings collapsing into piles of smouldering rubble. There was no *point* in trying to stop the enemy, not here. Smallbridge was nothing more than a bump in the road to the capital. The militiamen were going to get themselves killed for nothing.

"Their tanks are tougher than they look," Ross said, as they reached the end of the town and hurried on to the next RV point. The sound of shelling grew louder. He saw a flicker in the air and glanced up, just in time to see a flyer race over the town and head north. A missile swatted it out of the air a heartbeat later. "We'll need heavier weapons to make an impression on them."

"So it seems," Tomas agreed. He'd have to warn the militia, when they reached the next hardwired station. He didn't dare risk a transmission, not now. Even microburst signals could be detected at close range. "But we can keep slowing them down."

He glanced back as they reached the RV point. Smallbridge was burning, the buildings concealed by clouds of smoke. He wondered, grimly, if the smoke would provide a little cover for the defenders. Perhaps they'd manage to kill a few enemy troopers before they were wiped out. He doubted it. The town simply hadn't been designed for war. The militia hadn't had time to make up for that weakness. A handful of missiles would be enough to destroy what the shelling had left untouched.

Well, he thought. *You wanted a nice clean war.*

"We'll set up an ambush," he said, as they started to walk north. "And continue the war from the shadows."

"Yes, sir," Ross said. "And hope the navy gets back in time."

Tomas nodded, keeping his doubts to himself. The reports suggested the Vulteks had thrown everything, up to and including the kitchen sink, at Delaine. *Washington* would be completely outgunned, if she returned to the system before the ground-based defences were wiped out. She wouldn't be able to do more than die bravely if she tried to engage the enemy. And the rest of the fleet was hundreds of light-years away.

"Yeah," he said. It was hard to believe they'd be abandoned, but... it would take a long time for the EDF to liberate the world. The militia were brave—he knew that—yet they were outmatched. The invaders had more than enough firepower to smash through the defences and take the capital. "We can hope."

...

"I thought the last command bunker was bad," Governor Singh commented. "This one is worse."

Tailor laughed. "We took an outdated command vehicle and buried it below the ground," he said. "There's no record of its existence, let alone where we hid it. They'd have to dig up the communications cables to find it. We'd see them coming."

"I hope you're right," Singh said.

He let out a breath as he surveyed the vehicle's interior. It had looked big on the display, when he'd been briefed on the plan, but it was uncomfortably cramped. The engineers had crammed computer terminals, datacores and a pair of tiny metal chairs into the vehicle. The operators barely had enough room to stand up without doing their neighbour a serious injury. He didn't want to think about what it would be like if they had to run...

"We just got the reports from the landing zone," an operator said. "They've defeated the militia and appear to be readying themselves to advance towards the city."

Singh said nothing as he surveyed the map. A chunk of the planet was covered in bright red light. Cold logic told him the occupied zone represented only a tiny fraction of the colony, let alone the planetary surface, but...he shook his head in frustration. The invaders were preparing to surround the city, if they weren't planning to take it by force. And that meant thousands of people were going to die.

He looked at Tailor. "We're forwarding everything to the stealthed platform?"

"Yes, sir," Tailor said. "Unfortunately, we have no way of knowing if anyone will receive it."

Singh made a face. *Washington* had been sent to J-57...he cursed whoever had made the decision, even though he knew *Washington* couldn't have hoped to slow down the enemy fleet when it arrived. The freighters orbiting the planet had fled...they were probably still running. They probably wouldn't *stop* running until they reached Earth or Capital. Not, he supposed, that he blamed them. A freighter would be nothing more than target practice to a warship, if it was unlucky enough to be caught. Better they kept running. Who knew? Maybe one of them would get word to the next system. They might have a chance to get ready before the enemy fleet arrived.

They can mine the crossroads, now they know we're at war, he thought. He hadn't been able to take the risk, until it was too late. *It might slow them down a little.*

A chill enveloped his heart as he turned his attention back to the display. The red blot seemed to have grown. He knew reports were vague, that the fog of war had enveloped the planetary surface, but...he swallowed, hard. There was a war on. His planet was doomed, unless help arrived. And he knew, all too well, that there was no way help could arrive in time.

And they might continue the war until they reach Earth, he thought. *And if that happens, the entire human race is doomed.*

CHAPTER TWENTY-NINE

EDS *Washington*, Delaine System/*James Bond*, Delaine System

"CAPTAIN, I'M PICKING UP AN ALL-SHIPS WARNING," Lieutenant Walcott said. "The system is under attack."

Naomi nodded as the display started to fill with red icons. She'd pushed the drives to the limit, in a desperate bid to reach Delaine before the enemy fleet, but it was clear they'd lost the race. Seventy enemy ships held position near the planet, their active sensors filling space with electronic chaff. She was surprised they hadn't tried to blockade the nearer crossroads as well as the ones leading back towards Earth. They certainly had enough ships to give anyone making transit a very hard time.

They probably had no reason to expect hostiles behind enemy lines, she thought. *Even if they knew where we were, they didn't know when we'd start heading back to Delaine.*

"Tactical, activate the cloaking device," she ordered, coolly. There was no way in hell they could survive an encounter with so much firepower, if they allowed the enemy to see them. "Helm, alter course. Take us directly to the stealthed recon platform."

"Aye, Captain," Lieutenant Almont said. "We'll be within laser range in thirty-seven minutes."

Naomi nodded, watching as the enemy fleet continued to grow on the display. The Vulteks seemed to have brought their entire fleet, if the warbook was to be believed. A cluster of heavy ships held position near the planet, launching projectiles towards the planetary defences. Naomi had no illusions. Delaine didn't have a full combat grid. They'd be overwhelmed, eventually. She just hoped the settlers—and the marines she'd landed—could hold out long enough for help to arrive.

"Captain, they've taken out the FTL transmitter," Hawke reported.

"What?" Roger looked up from his console. "They've shut it down?"

"They've destroyed the platform," Hawke said. "I'm not even getting a hint of an FTL resonance from the transmitter."

Naomi winced. Galactic Law was clear. FTL transmitters and archives were *not* to be destroyed. If the Vulteks had demanded their surrender, and turned up with enough force to take the platform, the operators were legally obliged to concede. The fact they'd *destroyed* the platform…a slap in the face to the Galactics or…or what? They had to know they were going to make themselves pariahs…

Which won't matter in the slightest, if no one can be bothered to lift a finger to stop them, she thought, coldly. *And by the time the Galactics realise what's happened, the war might be over anyway.*

Ice ran down her spine as she studied the display. The enemy fleet was holding position, but it wouldn't be long before it resumed the advance. Delaine wasn't *that* important, in the grand scheme of things. The Vulteks could—and would—claim the system on the grounds they controlled the high orbitals, then bombard the planet into submission at leisure. She felt a pang of guilt—she had to abandon the marines, along with the settlers—which she ruthlessly suppressed. One day, Earth might have the numbers to be strong everywhere. One day, Earth might have a fleet that could stand in defence of a minor colony world. One day, Earth might be strong enough to do whatever the hell it liked. One day…but not today. She had her orders. She had to preserve her ship, not risk everything on one throw of the dice.

"Captain," Janet said. "We are approaching the recon platform."

Naomi nodded, silently grateful she'd had the foresight to set the platform up and tie it into the planetary defence network. It couldn't intervene—and she'd keyed it to self-destruct if any prowling alien ships stumbled across it—but it *could* record everything that had happened, including messages from the planet itself, and preserve them for posterity. It was just possible it had recorded something useful. She didn't let herself believe it had recorded something decisive, but…she wanted to believe.

"Open a laser link and download the entire contents," she ordered. "Helm, back off as soon as we complete the download."

"Aye, Captain."

Sweat prickled at the back of her neck as they drifted closer to the recon platform. The alien ships weren't sweeping the system, but they were filling space with so many active sensor pulses that they might just get lucky. Their operators would know what to expect, she thought; they *might* notice something out of place, even at extreme range. And it was equally possible they might have cloaked ships patrolling the system… she knew she was being paranoid, but she really had no choice. She didn't dare risk her ship until she'd got word back to Earth.

"Download complete, Captain," Janet said.

"Helm, take us out of here," Naomi ordered. The alien ships hadn't moved. She hoped that meant they hadn't seen her. "Tactical, I want a full analysis on the download."

"Aye, Captain," Janet said. She frowned as she peered at her console. "Captain, the freighters went to the RV point. They may still be there."

Naomi frowned. The contingency plans hadn't been *that* detailed. The freighters should have broken orbit and raced for the crossroads the moment the enemy fleet showed itself. Earth had more freighters than warships, but the planet couldn't afford to waste freighters either. And yet, they *did* need accurate intelligence of enemy movements. Admiral Glass might already be plotting his counterattack. Her eyes slid to the display, sparkling with red icons. No, that wasn't going to happen. The enemy fleet was just too powerful. It would have to be worn down before it was challenged in open battle.

"Set course for the RV point," she ordered, as she keyed her console to bring up the recordings from the planet. "We'll try to signal the freighters when we get closer."

She frowned as the recordings played in front of her. The Vultek invasion had been strikingly brutal, even by *their* standards. They'd displayed a frightening lack of concern for civilian casualties. It was perfectly legal to bombard a planetary defence installation, if the planet refused to surrender, but the Vulteks had randomly bombarded towns and villages as well as military bases. There was no rhyme or reason to their attacks, as far as she could tell; no sense they were doing anything more than trying to spread terror. Cold hatred waked in her heart. The aliens were monsters. They had to be stopped.

And resistance is continuing, she mused. The Vulteks seemed unable or unwilling to land ground troops and then redeploy their fleet. *Hopefully, they'll keep the bastards busy long enough for us to come up with a plan.*

She glanced through the rest of the records, but she already knew they'd be useless. There were no obvious weaknesses in the enemy fleet, no sense they could be beaten by clever tactics and human cunning. A handful of warcruisers would have chopped their fleet to ribbons, but... Earth didn't have a single warcruiser. She wondered, sourly, if the Alphans would get off their arses and do *something*, now Galactic Law had been openly flouted. Or would that mean merely widening the war? The Vulteks had patrons. Those patrons were unlikely to let them suffer a humiliating defeat.

"Helm, plot us a course to Coriander," she ordered. They'd have to go through one of the uncovered crossroads, unless—by sheer luck—they stumbled across an uncharted crossroads. That wasn't likely to happen. "We need to evade the enemy and get to the base before they do."

"That *is* most of their fleet back there," Roger pointed out. "We can probably evade them long enough to escape."

Naomi frowned. The long-range sensors reported enemy ships orbiting the nearer crossroads. She *might* be able to sneak past them, or blast her way through, but the risk was simply too great. It didn't sit well with her—she'd been taught to be aggressive—yet her orders were clear. She was *not* to risk her ship. And yet, if she sneaked out, there was a very real possibility of losing the *next* race. Coriander might be attacked before Earth knew the system was on the front lines.

"Let us hope so," she said, quietly. "Still..."

She leaned back in her chair as the cruiser glided towards the RV point. Long-range sensors were clear, but that was meaningless. The freighters had military crews and a considerable amount of mil-grade equipment. They knew how to pretend to be a hole in space. Her passive sensors wouldn't even get a *hint* of their presence until it was too late. Or...her lips curved into a cold smile. They might not be there at all. They might have completed their mission and withdrawn before the door slammed closed.

Once they got into multispace, they should have been able to escape, she mused. *The enemy couldn't afford to guard all the crossroads. And they're going to have problems as they tighten their grip.*

She felt a flicker of hope. Seventy warships were one hell of a lot of firepower, capable of punching out almost any human-held system...but only if they were concentrated. The Vulteks would have to choose between keeping their fleet together or tightening their grip on the occupied star systems. Either they spread out, in which case she could start picking off their smaller ships, or they left the back door open for human exploitation. She made a note of the idea, adding it to the report she'd have to forward when they reached an FTL transmitter. She wasn't sure what they could do with it—not yet—but she had an inkling.

"Captain," Almont said. "We have reached the RV point."

"Communications, trigger an energy fluctuation," Naomi ordered. It wasn't ideal, and there was a reasonable possibility the freighters might miss the signal, but there were no other options. There was no way she could use a tight-beam or a laser when she didn't know precisely where the freighters were. "See if they respond."

"Aye, Captain," Hawke said.

Naomi held her breath. The energy fluctuation could only be detected at short range...or so she'd been assured. She'd never been entirely sure that was true. The Alphan sensor technology was the best in the galaxy, but she was *certain* their rivals had spent trillions of credits on trying to duplicate and improve upon their works. The energy burst was unmistakably artificial. If there *was* a prowling enemy ship, sensors sweeping for flickers of energy that might indicate the presence of a cloaked ship, she'd just told them where to look.

"Captain," Hawke said. "We're being lased. EIS protocols, priority one."

Roger looked up. "EIS protocols?"

"Return the signal," Naomi ordered. The EIS? She hadn't known there was a spy ship operating out here. What was it *doing* at the RV point? The EIS rarely shared anything beyond raw intelligence with the EDF. "Establish a secure comlink."

"Aye, Captain," Hawke said.

A holographic image appeared on the bridge. Naomi leaned forward. She didn't recognise the man. The spy—he had to be a spy—looked like a freighter captain. She snorted at the thought. Spies didn't normally wear uniforms, even though someone captured *out* of uniform could be legally shot without trial. He would have been handsome, if his face hadn't been lined with worry. She wondered, morbidly, just how long he'd been watching the aliens from a safe distance. When had he reached the system?

"I'm Captain Anderson of *James Bond*," the man said. "And you?"

Naomi heard Roger stifle a laugh. *Aliens* might not know who James Bond had been, or why someone might name a ship after him, yet it was a dead giveaway to any human. The franchise might have been born in the days before the invasion, a time when humanity had believed itself alone in the universe, but it had adapted well to the brave new world. The last set of movies had been set within the Lupine Wars, with the latest incarnation of Bond...

She shook her head. Right now, it didn't matter.

"Captain Yagami of *Washington*," she said, curtly. There was no point in trying to conceal anything. The enemy had already got a good look at *Washington*, back at J-57. "Report."

She half-expected the spy, if he was more spy than spacer, to balk. But he didn't. "We entered enemy space and saw their fleet, too late," he said. "Our warning got here too late."

"I see." Naomi wondered, grimly, if the intelligence operative had triggered the war. It was easy to believe, but...she shook her head. The war had been brewing for months. The aliens had clearly been planning *something* well before they knew the Alphans were going to abandon the whole sector. "What happened to our freighters?"

"I took the liberty of...ah...borrowing some of their mines, then ordered them to head back to Coriander," Anderson said. "They didn't have anything that could help keep the system under observation."

Those were my freighters, Naomi thought. She understood the logic, but she resented him making the decision for her. She'd have preferred to transfer supplies to her ship before sending the freighters home. *We might have needed them.*

She shook her head in irritation. The spy had made the right call, based on what he'd known at the time. And it wasn't *that* bad. Her crew had patched up the hull breach as best as they could, without a shipyard or a mobile repair ship. And yet...

"I have to slip around the enemy fleet and take my report to Coriander," she said. "I need you to deploy mines along the threadlines leading towards Coriander."

The spy's eyes narrowed. "Is that wise, even in times of war?"

Naomi understood the unspoken question. Mining threadlines wasn't exactly illegal, under Galactic Law, but it was frowned upon. There was no way to be *entirely* sure the mines would stay on station, let alone *only* target the bad guys. The Galactics might take the incident as an excuse to sit on their hands and do nothing. And there was a reasonable possibility that the whole exercise would be useless. Worse than useless. It might accomplish nothing while weakening humanity's case.

"Yes," she said. There was no *guarantee* the Galactics would intervene. And they'd have no way to know what had happened, unless someone talked out of turn. She couldn't pass up the chance to slow the enemy fleet, even if it did come with a major price tag. Everyone involved would keep their mouths shut. She'd make sure of it. "Once the mining is complete, I need you to keep an eye on the enemy fleet."

"Which assumes you make it to Coriander," the spy pointed out. "What if you don't?"

"Then we may have a problem," Naomi said. She couldn't deny the possibility of running into a squadron she could neither outrun nor outfight. "But the freighters will have sounded the alarm even if we don't make it there."

"Understood," Anderson said. "Good luck, Captain."

"And to you," Naomi said. She hoped the spy made it out. The Vulteks were unlikely to show mercy if they realised what he'd been doing. "I'll see you on the far side."

She glanced at Hawke and drew a finger across her throat. Hawke cut the connection. The hologram vanished. Naomi sat back in her chair, thinking hard. It felt wrong to send someone else to do the dirty work, even if a freighter was less likely to draw enemy fire than a warship. And yet, what choice did she have? She *had* to take the records to Coriander and hope for the best. She had...

"Helm, set course for the nearest uncovered crossroads," she ordered. She studied the display for a long cold moment, silently calculating possible enemy vectors. "As soon as we're in multispace, take us directly to Coriander."

"Aye, Captain," Almont said. "We'll reach the crossroads in five hours, forty minutes."

Naomi gritted her teeth as her ship began to move. It was going to take upwards of ten days to reach Coriander, unless they threw caution to the winds and tried to punch their way through the enemy blockade. She was tempted, but...she knew she couldn't. And that meant she might reach the planet just in time to see the enemy fleet finish blowing the defences to atoms and landing troops on the surface. And *that* meant...

She shook her head. Earth knew what was coming. The Vulteks had destroyed the FTL transmitter, but the planet had had plenty of time to sound the alert before it was too late. People would be responding to the disaster, experienced personnel would be dusting off contingency plans and putting them into action...she shivered as she remembered that many of the contingency plans would have assumed the human race could call on support from its masters. Its *former* masters. Now, they were alone. The plans were outdated, worse than useless...

Admiral Glass is drawing up new plans, she reassured herself. She'd heard whispers through the grapevine, before she'd left Earth. *And those plans will assume we'll be fighting alone.*

She felt cold as she turned her attention back to the display. The Vulteks might be barbaric, but they were strong. Their patrons had given them enough firepower to make them a major threat to Earth. And who knew? The entire war could be nothing more than the first shot in a plan to dominate the entire galaxy.

And they won't get away with it, she thought. She tried hard to convince herself it was more than mindless bravado. The Vulteks were strong, but they weren't gods. They had weaknesses. Humanity just had to survive long enough to take advantage of them. *They didn't know what they were doing when they picked a fight with us.*

CHAPTER THIRTY

EDF *Thunderous*, Coriander System

"TRANSIT COMPLETE, ADMIRAL," Commander Emily Sanderson said. She was a tall slight girl, so young she made Adam feel every one of his years. "Welcome to Coriander."

"Thank you," Adam said, dryly. "Signal the base. Request an update."

He forced himself to sit back in his chair, reminding himself—again—that military life was a mixture of long hours of boredom combined with moments of screaming terror. The flight from Earth to Coriander had been useful, in that he and his captains had taken the time to exercise the crews until they could perform their duties in their sleep, but he'd been completely cut off from the outside universe. He'd been all too aware that *anything* could have happened, along the border or back on Earth, and he wouldn't have the slightest idea what had happened until the fleet returned to realspace. Thankfully, there was no sign that Coriander had been attacked. It was possible to believe the war had not yet started.

The display updated, showing the base and the planet beyond. Adam was mildly surprised the Alphans had abandoned the system without a fight. Coriander was a bottleneck system, with only two charted crossroads. It was the perfect place to make a stand against a superior force. And whoever controlled it could force interstellar shippers to pay their fees or take the long way to their final destinations. Given time, it would help Earth become an economic powerhouse.

Although they weren't keeping any other worlds within the sector, he reminded himself. *They'd find themselves cut off very quickly if someone hostile took the nearby stars from us.*

"Shit," Emily breathed. She cleared her throat hastily. "Admiral, we just picked up an urgent transmission from the base. Delaine was attacked four days ago."

Adam grunted. He'd expected as much—he'd been sure war was coming—but it was still a shock. The Vulteks had nailed their colours to the mast for all to see. He reached for his console and scanned the message quickly, his eyes narrowing as he took in the details. A sizable enemy fleet – seventy-plus ships—had invaded Delaine and taken out the FTL transmitter. The last report confirmed they'd fired *missiles* at the transmitter. And then…nothing. Any ships that had escaped the invasion had yet to reach Coriander.

He cursed under his breath. No one, not even the Alphans, had been able to devise an FTL transmitter that could be carried by a warship. Delaine had just become a black hole, as far as information was concerned. The only way to know what was going on was to send a recon ship, which would take at least twelve days to reach the system, perform a handful of scans and return to Coriander. Adam knew the fog of war intimately—he'd served in the military long enough to know that one *never* had perfect intelligence on anything—but he still felt crippled. He understood, now, just how the Alphans had felt during the *last* war. An entire swath of the galaxy had suddenly gone dark.

And you're wool gathering, he thought, sourly. His instincts demanded he send the fleet to Delaine. Cold logic told him it would be suicide. The fleet would be outnumbered two to one, outgunned *three* to one. *You need to react and yet you can't react.*

He made eye contact with Emily. "Forward the alert to the remainder of the fleet, then inform my captains that I will hold a conference call in"—he glanced at the chronometer—"thirty minutes."

"Aye, sir," Emily said.

"And order the fleet to assume position near Crossroads Two," Adam added. "I want to be ready if—when—the enemy attacks."

"Aye, sir," Emily said.

Adam brought up the starchart and silently calculated vectors as the heavy cruiser started to shift position. The enemy fleet *might* reach Coriander in less than a week, if they redlined their drives. *And* if they were prepared to accept the risk of funnelling their forces down a narrow threadline. They *had* to know humanity would start mining the crossroads, even if they didn't mine the threadline itself. Adam wondered, idly, if Abraham Douglas had the nerve to mine the threadline. It was a political decision, one that even a fleet admiral couldn't make.

And it might be better if I did make the decision for him, Adam thought. *He'd have a scapegoat if something went spectacularly wrong.*

He frowned as he paged through the more detailed report. The enemy fleet was overwhelmingly powerful, but it seemed to be a little light on logistics units. That was odd, very odd. And it was surprisingly light on *light* units too. He'd expected far more destroyers, frigates and light cruisers. It looked as if the enemy hadn't really bothered to balance their fleet... he wondered, sourly, if there was a way to take advantage of their oversight. Or if it was just another example of how the universe itself seemed to be tilted against the human race.

"Admiral," Emily said. "I have Commodore Orwell on the line for you."

Adam nodded. "Put him though."

"Admiral," Commodore Orwell said. He was a tall dark man, his hair cropped close to his scalp. "Welcome to Coriander."

"Thank you," Adam said. He'd meant to carry out an inspection tour, but the dates had been put back time and time again. "I wish it was under better circumstances."

"So do I." Orwell looked pensive. "We've been breaking open the stockpiles, Admiral, but we're light on mobile units. Getting the defences up and ready before they're tested is going to be a major headache."

"We have to get as much firepower in place as possible before they test our defences," Adam said. He wished, suddenly, that the Alphans had turned the bottleneck system into a strongpoint. They could have set up a dozen fortresses on the crossroads and made the system pretty much invulnerable. And if they'd manned the facilities themselves, the Vulteks might have thought twice about attacking it. "Did you put a hold on freighter movements?"

"Yes, Admiral," Orwell said. "We're holding them here. I've been bolting missile pods and weapons to their hulls. There's going to be a hefty compensation bill when all is said and done."

"If we survive, we'll pay," Adam assured him. "And if we don't, the point is moot."

He stared down at his console for a long moment. What would the Vulteks do, if they won the war? Enslave the human race? Or...or what? Would they seek to *exterminate* the human race? It was against Galactic Law, but...who would *enforce* the law? There was no way to know if anyone would step up to punish genocide. The Alphans were gone. All the old certainties were dying. Who knew what would happen when the rest of the galaxy realised the Convocations were nothing more than empty words?

"My officers and I will be discussing the matter," he said, putting his fears aside for later contemplation. "I'd like you to join the holoconference."

"Of course," Orwell said.

"And I'll have to speak to my superiors too," Adam added. "Have you heard anything from Earth?"

"Just an order to prepare to defend the system," Orwell said. "Admiral... there are twenty million people planetside. We're doing what we can, but... if the enemy bombards the planet, a lot of those people are going to die."

And not all of them are human, Adam thought. He felt a wash of self-hatred, even revulsion. It was fundamentally *wrong* to hope for a slaughter, to hope for an atrocity that would unite the galaxy against the Vulteks. And yet, he was honest enough to admit it might be their only hope. *If we can get some of the other interstellar powers on our side...*

He shook his head. The civilians weren't under alien jurisdiction. They'd settled on a world ruled—ultimately—by the Alphans. They'd chosen to stay when Coriander had been transferred to human jurisdiction. Their governments had all the excuse they needed to wash their hands of the civilians, if they wished. It might take more than a bloody slaughter to convince the Galactics to do something. Right now, the human race would be fighting alone.

"We'll just have to stop them short of the planet," Adam said. "And then see what we can do to teach them a lesson."

Contingency plans, half-formed contingency plans that were either genius or madness, danced through his head as he closed the channel. He hadn't lied, when he'd told the First Speaker that he *needed* to take command of the fleet. *Someone* would have to make the final call, someone with the authority to call the shots without constantly referring his decisions further up the chain. It was easier, he supposed, given he knew he would be retiring soon enough anyway. The new government might want to ensure the loyalists stayed loyal, but they couldn't keep him in his post forever. Not unless they wanted to stuff and mount him on the wall. The black humour made him smile. He'd dealt with bureaucrats who hadn't had the excuse of being *dead*.

"Admiral," Emily said. "The holochamber is ready."

Adam nodded as he stood. "Alert me if anything changes," he said. "Or if we get a message from Earth."

He smiled, tiredly, and walked into the holochamber. It never failed to terrify groundpounders. It looked as if he was walking amongst the stars, as if he'd accidentally gone through an open airlock and fallen into space. He felt his smile grow wider, remembering the first day he'd entered a holochamber. The instructors had considered it a learning experience. Anyone who panicked, instead of realising they were still breathing—or calmly looking around for life support equipment—was marked down.

Of course, if you were in vacuum and there was no life support equipment within reach, he reminded himself, *the only thing you could do was bend over and kiss your ass goodbye.*

The system glowed in front of him. A cluster of icons hung near the crossroads. Orwell had done well, given his limited resources. His defence wouldn't hold up for long, but it was better than nothing. He wondered, idly, if the attackers would try to take the planet or simply smash the orbital installations before proceeding to Earth. Coriander wasn't *that* important, not compared to the homeworld. But failing to take the planet would call their control over the system into question.

Assuming anyone cares, he thought, as the holoimages began to flicker into existence. The true beauty of holoconferences was that he could address hundreds, even thousands, of people without having to cram them into a tiny room. *The Galactics took their cue from the Alphans for so long, they're quite lost without them.*

His eyes narrowed. *And the ones that aren't lost without them are the ones that might decide to snatch power for themselves.*

He looked from face to face, wishing they'd had more time to train their crews and exercise their ships. Too many officers had been jumped forward, too many ships had been refitted in a tearing hurry...it was practically *certain* that someone had been promoted above their competence, that *something* hadn't been done properly, that a lone component was about to fail at the worst possible time. He dreaded to think how few of his ships would pass a competent command inspection. He'd worked the crews hard, he'd promoted and demoted whenever necessary, but he was all too aware of their weaknesses. And the Vulteks might be able to take full advantage of them.

Which is why we have to stay here, forcing them to either attack us or risk leaving a fleet in their rear, he mused. *And they know it too. They'll be looking for a way to beat us.*

"The war has begun," he said, curtly. They knew it as well as he did, but it set the scene nicely. "The Vulteks are on their way. They could punch their way into the system by Friday. We have that long to get ready for them."

He let out a long breath. He had seventy ships under his command, but only thirty of them were real warships. The remainder were a combination of armed freighters and logistics ships, the latter already preparing themselves to drop tools and flee if the coming engagement went badly. They could be trapped at Coriander if the Vulteks covered both crossroads before it was too late. And that would be disastrous.

"We'll make our stand on the crossroads," he said. "However, we cannot afford a prolonged battle. Therefore, we'll go with Alpha-III until we have enough defences in place to switch to Alpha-II. Does anyone have any objections?"

"Yes, sir," Captain Yasmin said. "We wouldn't be blocking the crossroads completely."

"We don't need a diplomatic incident," Adam reminded the younger man. "And besides, there's little point in emplacing mines *directly* on the crossroads."

Because any commander worthy of the name knows to send missiles or expendable decoys through first, he thought. The major powers might prefer to avoid a crossroads assault, if there were any other options, but they'd carried out enough such assaults to understand how the variables worked. *We'd lose the mines for nothing.*

"I'm going to deploy recon ships further up the threadline, in hopes of receiving some advance warning," he continued. "We must assume, however, that the enemy fleet will remain undetected until it comes through the crossroads. Accordingly, we will remain on tactical alert, one step down from battle stations. I want the alpha crews on full alert at all times, with the beta crews ready to take over if necessary. We cannot allow them to get the drop on us."

He sensed their unease. There was a limit to just how long a crew could remain on tactical alert. People would get anxious, then tired. They'd jump at so many false alarms they might not realise when a *real* fleet crossed the crossroads, not until it was too late. But there was no choice. They could *not* let the enemy fleet break into the system without a fight. Given time to deploy, the Vulteks might have an excellent chance of winning the coming fight.

"We'll also be laying mines, in accordance with the secondary plan," he said. "And yes, I am aware of the risks. Any questions?"

"Yes, sir," Captain Sark said. "Can I take my sick leave now?"

A chuckle ran around the chamber. "Because, you know, I feel an attack of knocking knees coming on," he joked. "And when I close my eyes I can't see."

"What a terrible condition," Adam said, dryly. The old joke had stopped being funny a long time ago. "I'm afraid all sick leave has been cancelled. And, more seriously, so has shore leave. We won't have time to rotate the crews through the facilities on Coriander for the foreseeable future."

"They'll understand," Captain Sark said. "It helps that we got rid of most of the loaners."

"Only to have to call them back into service," Adam said. He didn't pretend to grasp the economic arguments, but he understood the importance of trained manpower. The men on the repair and logistics ships were more important than anyone else. "The merchant marine is going to be gutted if we don't manage to end the war quickly."

"What do they want?" Captain Jackson sounded puzzled. "Have they sent us any demands?"

"Not yet, as far as I know," Adam said. It was never easy to transmit a declaration of war without sacrificing the advantage of surprise—and it was easy to get it wrong—but there was no suggestion the Vulteks had even tried. "And it looks as if they started the war without bothering to announce it."

"Bastards," someone said. "Just like the Lupines."

"And that worked out pretty well for them," Sark pointed out. "They would have won the war if we hadn't been involved."

"And the peacocks aren't bothering to help us in return," Captain Venice growled. "Fuck them, I say."

Adam held up a hand. "The diplomatic side of the war is out of our hands," he said, before the discussion could get any further out of hand. Had there been more discontent in the ranks than he'd realised? Or…or what? It wasn't as if any of them had expected to go from being part of the Empire to independence *and* the front lines of a whole new war. "Earth will handle such matters. Our priority is to stop the bad guys before they punch their way to Earth and dictate terms at gunpoint. Accordingly…"

He looked from face to face. "I know this isn't what any of us expected," he said, quietly. "I never expected to see independence in my lifetime. I wanted equality, not independence. But we're military officers. We cannot afford to delude ourselves. We cannot afford to cling to what might have been. The blunt truth, ladies and gentlemen, is that we have to stop them now…or independence will turn into slavery. And that will be the end."

His words hung in the air for a long chilling moment. How many of them understood? They were younger than him, the youngest young enough to *really* make him feel old. They'd resented the way things were, back before independence, yet…they weren't old enough to appreciate the good as well as resent the bad. And now the universe had changed. He wondered, grimly, if he was still flexible enough to cope.

"You know what you have to do," he said. They'd been over the plans time and time again, working out the weaknesses and compensating as best as they could. There was no point in going over it again. "Dismissed."

CHAPTER THIRTY-ONE

Star City, Earth

ABRAHAM DOUGLAS LIKED TO BELIEVE himself a cosmopolitan man, even if he dressed himself in the fashion of a bygone era and unashamedly put the interests of humanity first. He could hardly have been otherwise, given his family's long involvement in interstellar affairs and his own career in politics. Earth could not afford to offend, let alone alienate, races that had been travelling amongst the stars long before humanity had invented fire. Xenophobes—those incapable of hiding their dislike of aliens—were simply not permitted to hold office. The risk was too great.

And yet, as the Pashtali Ambassador was shown into his office, Abraham felt a chill run down his spine. He'd read many autobiographies from the post-invasion days, when some of the writers had talked about meeting aliens for the very first time, and he hadn't really understood. They'd talked about feeling uneasy, about feeling there was something truly *wrong* with the world. He'd thought they were silly. But now, staring at an alien that looked very much like a bizarre semi-humanoid spider, he thought he understood. There was something fundamentally *wrong* about the creature.

The vast majority of intelligent life forms, he'd been told, were humanoid. There were no shortages of explanations, from nature finding the same answer to the same problems to spores from a long-gone alien race, but it was undeniably true. And yet, the Pashtali weren't humanoid. Just looking at the creature was difficult. He tried not to count the legs, or meet the bulging eyes. It was hard to believe it was intelligent. And yet, the spider-like alien represented a third-stage race. He couldn't afford to offend it.

"Welcome to Earth," he said. He didn't mean it. The ambassador had requested a meeting shortly after the human race had learnt it was at war. If that was a coincidence, Abraham would eat his hat. "I understand the matter is urgent...?"

The Pashtali spoke through a voder. "We speak on behalf of our clients," it said, in a toneless voice that somehow conveyed a sense of threat. "They have requested we speak to you."

"The Vulteks, I presume," Abraham said. He wasn't blind to the significance. The Pashtali wouldn't have agreed to pass on the message unless they had an interest in the outcome. God knew they'd rejected all human attempts to talk to them before the war had openly begun. "What do they want you to say?"

"They have a claim to numerous stars held within your territory," the Pashtali said. "They demand you concede those stars at once or face war."

"They have already begun the war," Abraham said. His mind raced. A timing error? An attempt to convince the Galactics the Vulteks had *tried* to talk peace? Or a sign the Pashtali were going to support their clients? "We can hardly surrender any stars under threat of force."

"Those territories were taken from them by the Alphans," the Pashtali stated. "They are free to recover them."

Abraham frowned. "If that is the case..."

The Pashtali spoke over him. "Withdraw your ships. Concede the stars. Or face war."

It didn't turn. It didn't need to turn. It literally had eyes in the back of its head, insofar as it *had* a head. Abraham felt sick as the eerie creature walked through the door and ambled down the corridor, the door hissing closed in its wake. No wonder the Pashtali were so rare, outside their Empire. They were so alien that nearly every other race found them a little disconcerting. He wondered, idly, what their clients thought of them.

Not that it matters, he thought. *Client races are servants and subjects by definition.*

He leaned back in his chair and forced himself to think. What were the Pashtali *doing*? It made no sense. Or did it...? The Vulteks might have pushed the Pashtali into doing something they didn't want to do. The irony wasn't lost on him. Humanity had done the same thing to the Alphans. But...he found it hard to believe the Pashtali could be pushed around so easily. The Vulteks weren't *that* important.

His fingers touched the terminal. "Display starchart."

A cluster of stars materialised over the desk, a handful shaded in red. The Vulteks had taken Delaine and—probably—a number of other stars along the border. Delaine was the only one solidly within human jurisdiction, but there were millions of human settlers in the disputed region. And it was only a matter of time, he'd been warned, before the Vulteks pushed towards Coriander. Weeks, at best. The enemy only had a short window of opportunity to make their gains solid, before the Galactics got involved. If they *did* get involved. Abraham knew, better than anyone, that intelligent life was a rationalising animal. If the Galactics wanted to wash their hands of the whole affair, they'd find an excuse to do it.

The terminal bleeped. "Sir," Rachel said. "The Pashtali Ambassador has departed."

"Noted," Abraham said. "Has he made any noises about leaving the planet?"

"No, sir," Rachel said. "But it's only been a few hours since the news reached Earth."

Abraham nodded. In theory, the alien ambassadors in Spacetown would be safe if the enemy attacked Earth. They were ambassadors. Attacking them was an act of war. In practice, Spacetown was part of Star City. If the planet was bombarded, the ambassadors might be killed by accident. He would be surprised if some of them didn't start preparing to move before the war came home. They might not have any faith in Earth's ability to fend off the gathering storm.

He stood and paced over to the window. Star City was quiet, somewhat to his surprise. The state of emergency—announced only a few weeks after the end of the *last* state of emergency—had gone down better than he'd expected. It helped, he supposed, that both the mainstream and alternate media sources were singing the same tune. Humanity had been treacherously attacked, by an alien race that had barely mastered fire when it had been uplifted by its patrons. There was no time for debate. They had to stand together against the common foe.

And that will change, if we lose the coming battle, he thought. Admiral Glass had made it clear that the battle at Coriander, the battle everyone expected to happen, would be decisive. *There'll be panic and worse...*

He put the thought aside. "Rachel, ask Ambassador Yasuke if I can speak with him," he said, calmly. "And then call a cabinet meeting for 1500."

"Yes, sir," Rachel said. "You have a dozen urgent calls from corporate representatives and shipping concerns..."

"I'll deal with them after I speak to the ambassador," Abraham said. The war took priority now. Afterwards...he'd pay a price in the next election cycle, if there was a next election cycle. "Invite him to my office."

"You might be better meeting him downstairs," Rachel said. "It used to be *his* office."

And the Alphans are touchy about things like that, Abraham recalled. Yasuke had effectively been demoted, a crushing fall from grace. *That would have started the meeting off on the wrong foot.*

"Good thought," he said. "We'll meet in the Green Room. Let me know when he's on his way."

There was something galling, Yasuke had decided over the last few weeks, about being a mere ambassador. He no longer had the clout to do whatever he wanted to do, let alone override or simply ignore orders from his superiors. The council had promised him recognition, when he returned home, but so far they'd been slow to decide *when* he'd come home. There were too many loose ends to tie up, even now, for their peace of mind.

And they haven't named a replacement either, he thought, as the aircar drifted down to land in front of the skyscraper. It had once been *his* skyscraper. *That's a pretty big hint they don't want me home anytime soon.*

He ignored the striking lack of formality as he was escorted down the corridor and into the Green Room. Whoever had chosen the room had chosen well. If they'd met him in his office, in the chamber that had once *been* his office, it would have been an unmistakable sign of contempt, if not outright gloating. He'd trained the staff well, he recalled. He'd made sure they had opportunities to advance themselves in his service. He wondered, idly, how many of them had been allowed to keep their jobs.

Most of them, probably, he told himself. *The humans were not particularly vindictive.*

He took his seat, accepted the offer of a fresh drink and waited. *Humans liked making their guests wait*, he remembered, *if only to convince their guests that they weren't important.* It meant very little to an Alphan, particularly one who'd climbed quite some way up the ladder. Petty power games were a sign of immaturity, not of true power. A man with true power need never play games. His subordinates did not need to be reminded of his power.

"Mr. Ambassador." The First Speaker strode into the room. "Thank you for coming."

"It is my pleasure," Yasuke said. He waited for the human to sit, then leaned forward. "I assume we can speak informally?"

"If you would," Douglas said. He had the experience to know that being asked to speak informally was a great honour. "And I assume you know why I'm here."

Yasuke didn't bother to deny it. "The war."

"Yes." Douglas's face was as hard to read as any human. "The Vulteks have invaded our space, Mr. Ambassador, and the Pashtali have given us a vague message that...my xenospecialists are still arguing over the precise meaning. They may be threatening to support their clients."

"It's possible," Yasuke agreed. It was never easy to understand an alien race, but the Pashtali were weird even by Galactic standards. "Or they may feel forced into making a declaration of support."

"It's possible," Douglas echoed. "Mr. Ambassador, I'll come right to the point. Will your government provide assistance if the war gets out of hand?"

Yasuke fought down an insane urge to laugh. Douglas was *not* an Empire Loyalist. The Empire Loyalists themselves were having a genteel civil war over just where they stood in the post-independence era. The Humanity League had wanted independence...and now they had it, they wanted to go straight back to subordination? Or...or what?

"My government has not issued me with any instructions," he said. He'd had wide latitude when he'd been the Viceroy, but he'd also had a squadron of warcruisers under his direct command. Now, he was little more than his government's voice. "However—off the record, as you humans say—I think it's unlikely my government will intervene."

The human's face fell, just slightly. "Why not?"

"The war cost us badly, as you know." Yasuke swallowed another urge to laugh. "And we are still struggling with the aftermath. There is very little enthusiasm for going back to war, certainly not on your behalf. Too many of my people think of you as ungrateful clients."

"And what will you do," Douglas asked, "if the Pashtali come to dominate the sector?"

That, Yasuke admitted privately, was *the* question. He didn't fear the Vulteks. They might have access to GalTech, but they didn't know how to build, maintain or reproduce it. They could give the humans a beating, if they were lucky, yet...they couldn't threaten *his* people. A single warcruiser could slice their fleet to ribbons before it got into weapons range. And yet...the Pashtali were a potential threat. They *did* understand the technology at their disposal.

And they might prove a serious threat, if they gain control of Earth, Yasuke thought. The humans had shown a remarkable capability for devising newer and better ways to use GalTech. Who knew what they'd do for their new masters, if they lost the war? *And even without the humans, the Pashtali could do a lot of damage.*

"I shall raise the issue with my government," he said. "However, it is unlikely we can come to your aid in time."

Even if we wanted to, he added, silently. *Too many of us think poorly of you now.*

"We need help," the human said, bluntly. "And you may need our help in the future."

"Yes," Yasuke agreed. "But we don't want to get involved in another war."

He stood, bowing politely. Did the Pashtali *know* the Alphans were dangerously weak? Did they know there weren't many warcruisers left? Did they realise they might be able to win the war, if they launched it without warning? Did they realise they'd never have a better chance to win outright? Did they...he kept his mouth firmly closed as he made his way out of the building and back to his aircar. The crowds of humans on the street outside the gates looked at him curiously. He wondered, sourly, how many of them understood just how precarious their lives had become.

The aircar lifted off, heading directly for Spacetown. Yasuke leaned back in his chair, silently composing a message to his government. Douglas was right, unfortunately. They *couldn't* let the Pashtali dominate the sector. And yet...the Pashtali didn't know it—he hoped—but they might already dominate the sector. The Alphans were the only race that might manage to keep them under control and they didn't have the will. His people were sick of war. They really didn't want another one.

And that means leaving the humans to fight alone, he thought. Perhaps they could convince the Pashtali to back off, threatening intervention if the Pashtali joined the war openly. *When did we get so weak?*

He told himself not to brood as the aircar landed on top of the embassy. His aide was waiting for him, dropping into the posture of respect as soon as she saw him. Yasuke barely noticed. He was too busy trying to find the right words.

"Order a communications channel to Capital," he said, shortly. "I need to speak to the council as soon as possible."

"Yes, sir," his aide said.

...

"The real question," Douglas said as he addressed his inner cabinet, "is simple. What do the Pashtali want?"

"To cause trouble," Solomon growled, curtly. The industrialist scowled as he sipped his coffee. "They always were officious little bastards. They kept coming up with excuses to keep our traders out of their territory until the peacocks told them to knock it off."

"And yet, they could have won the war by now if they'd sided openly with their clients," Zoe Walker said. "Right?"

Abraham wished Admiral Glass had been able to attend. But he was on Coriander, too far for a realtime conversation. And too busy, too. His last report had warned there was little time before the Vulteks tested the defences, then launched an all-out invasion.

"Perhaps," he said. There was little doubt of it. "Which means…what? Are they using the Vulteks as a deniable force? Or are they feeling pressured to assist their clients?"

"It could be either," Richard Hawthorne said. "They've used the vultures as shock troops in the past. They may feel they need to support them now or else risk losing their services."

"I wish the Alphans felt the same way," Abraham said. "Ambassador Yasuke was non-committal. We can't expect anything from them."

"They did take quite a beating during the last war," Hawthorne said. "It may have been worse than we thought."

"It isn't as if any of their major worlds got bombarded," Solomon said, dismissively. "Right?"

"Their industrial base is second to none," Zoe said. She shot him a sharp look. "But you yourself pointed out they couldn't ramp it up in a hurry."

Abraham tapped the table. "That's not a problem right now," he said. "The Pashtali have told us that they expect us to surrender a number of worlds. They didn't give us a list of the systems they want us to give up, but I think we can reasonably assume they want everything on the far side of Coriander. And Coriander itself. The astrographics that make it a place we have to defend also make it a place they'll want. They'll be able to use it to block any counterattack while securing the remaining stars and systems."

"They may not have given us a list deliberately," Hawthorne observed. "They won't want to look greedy."

"Who cares?" Solomon waved a hand at the holographic starchart. The occupied stars were blinking red. "The Galactics are not going to get involved. Galactic Law is meaningless if no one's going to enforce it. How many laws do we have, on the books right now, that are never enforced? No one is going to tell them they're being greedy and they have to give back our worlds."

"Worlds to which they have no legal claim," Hawthorne snapped.

"If they can take them by force, they can take them," Solomon said. "If we don't fight now, we'll be fighting later."

"Admiral Glass believes he can hold them," Abraham said. The second part of Admiral Glass's plan was need-to-know only. "And if we can stop them, our position becomes stronger."

"Unless the spiders invade," Solomon said. He stood and started to pace. "They may react badly if their clients get a bloody nose. If we make the vultures look like fools, their masters will look stupid too."

"Or they might be secretly pleased," Zoe pointed out. "The Vulteks are dangerously unpredictable. They might turn on their masters as easily as they did on us."

"True," Abraham said. He suspected there was no point in holding out hope for an enemy civil war. "Are we agreed, then? We fight."

"Yes," Solomon said. "What else can we do?"

CHAPTER THIRTY-TWO

Multispace, Near Delaine

"YOU DO REALISE WE'RE BREAKING A NUMBER of interstellar laws?" Sarah didn't sound pleased. Her arms were crossed under her breasts, suggesting she wasn't going to be budged. "And that captain isn't going to go to bat for us if we get caught?"

Thomas shot her a sharp look, silently grateful she'd waited until they were in their cabin to raise her concern "Do you have any better ideas?"

"No," Sarah said. "But I wish we were somewhere else."

"We could be one of the unlucky bastards caught behind enemy lines," Thomas pointed out, dryly. He'd seen two freighters run down and forced to surrender by the invaders. He had no idea what lay in store for the captives, but he doubted they were having a good time. The Vulteks knew perfectly well no one was going to punish them for breaking interstellar law by mistreating prisoners. "Right now, at least we have a chance to hit back."

He glanced down at his terminal as Sarah snorted, loudly. She had a point. The family hadn't signed up to play spy, let alone minelayer. And if they were caught laying mines along the threadline—something that was very definitely against interstellar law—the Vulteks would be within their rights to shoot the entire crew out of hand. Or use the whole incident to turn interstellar opinion against Earth. Thomas had no doubt he'd be hung out to dry if the episode turned into a messy political crisis—it was what he'd do, if he was in charge—but there was no choice. The Vulteks *had* to be slowed down.

And if they don't actually see us laying the mines, they won't know for sure who did it, he mused. He doubted anyone would be fooled—there was no one else who benefited from laying the mines—but as long as there was no hard evidence no one would act. *And we should be far enough from Delaine to be completely out of sensor range.*

His wristcom bleeped. "Captain," Wesley said. "We have reached our destination."

"Reduce speed, but keep us on course," Thomas ordered. "Are the sensors clear?"

"Yes, Captain," Wesley said. "There's no hint of anything in transit."

"Which is meaningless, as you well know," Sarah snapped. "There could be an entire fleet breathing down our necks and we'd never know it."

Thomas nodded, curtly. "Go to the rear hatches and prepare to start laying the mines," he ordered. "I'll be on the bridge in a moment."

"Yes, sir," Sarah said, in a tone that promised trouble later. She caught up her helmet and attached it to her belt. "I'll start deploying the mines on command."

"Thanks," Thomas said.

He ignored the rude gesture she made as she hurried out the hatch and down the corridor. He didn't blame her for being concerned about the operation, even though it was their patriotic duty. It was never easy serving on a freighter, particularly when your husband was the captain and their children filled most of the billets. Sarah had no choice, but to stick with him. Normally, it wasn't a problem. In wartime...

And I'm putting the family in danger, he thought, as he scooped up his own helmet and headed to the bridge. *If we get caught, we get shot.*

He kept his face under tight control as he opened the hatch and strode onto the bridge. The main display was glowing with light, showing the narrowing threadline between Delaine and J-25. The Vulteks would *have* to pass through the threadline, following multispace's insane internal geography, if they wanted to reach J-25 in less than a fortnight. There was no point in taking the long way around when their entire operation depended on mounting a blitzkrieg and winning before the human race managed to establish a defensive line nearer to Earth and halted the advance. No, they'd *have* to pass through the threadline. And that would make them vulnerable to mines.

Thomas felt something clench in his stomach as he took his seat. They *were* taking a considerable risk. There was a chance, a very reasonable chance, that they'd accidentally destroy a human ship fleeing the war. Or an alien ship from a completely uninvolved alien race. Sweeping a minefield was difficult and time-consuming, made all the harder by the simple truth that no one would ever be sure they'd removed *all* the mines. Sure, they could be set to self-destruct after a certain time—and the gravity tides would eventually destroy them if they didn't destroy themselves—but no one could be *sure*. There were hundreds of legends about explorers discovering old and dangerous artefacts within multispace. Thomas had read them as a child.

And very few of them are real, he reminded himself, sternly. *The people who wrote them didn't understand how multispace really works.*

"Wesley, keep us on course," Thomas ordered. He keyed his console. "Sarah? Are you in position?"

"Yes, sir." Sarah's voice was crisp, professional. Whatever her doubts, she'd follow orders while they were in transit. "We can start deploying the mines at your command."

"Sandra, activate the recorders and copy everything into a secure datastore," Thomas ordered, calmly. "Sarah, begin deploying the mines."

"Aye, sir," Sarah said.

Thomas watched grimly as the first mine drifted away from the ship, barely visible to his sensors even though they knew precisely where to look. The mines were crude, compared to some of the devices the Lupines had used during the war—the Alphans had honoured interstellar conventions, to the despair of their human clients—but they'd be lethal if they struck a target. An impact that might be shrugged off in realspace would be fatal in multispace. If nothing else, even a *single* hit would force the enemy to slow their advance while they swept the threadline for mines. They'd certainly be a bit more careful about charging down a narrow threadline.

"Wesley, increase speed," he ordered. There was no point in allowing the mines to cluster, not when they could be scattered right down the threadline. "Sarah, how's it going?"

"Ten more minutes," Sarah said. She sounded distracted. "I've got twenty mines left."

"Keep deploying them," Thomas said. He wished they had a proper minelayer kit. It wouldn't have been hard to install one, if they'd had it in the first place. The EDF hadn't thought to include one when it had dispatched the freighters to Delaine. "Let me know as soon as they're all out."

"Aye, Captain," Sarah said.

Thomas forced himself to relax, even though he felt naked, exposed... and on the verge of being caught doing something he really shouldn't. He hadn't felt so vulnerable since he'd found a way to sneak through the tubes as a kid, something that would have earned him a thrashing if he'd been caught. And now...if a prowling alien ship happened to spot him, he and his family would be blown out of space. The hell of it was that being unceremoniously destroyed would be the *best* of a set of bad options.

His eyes drifted to the long-range sensor display. It was clear. Here, in the narrow threadline, it would be hard to *miss* an entire alien fleet. And yet, he was sure the aliens would resume their advance as quickly as possible. There was nothing to be gained by pounding Delaine to rubble when they needed to take Coriander and Earth itself if they wanted to win. Or, at the very least, secure Coriander and negotiate from a position of strength. The fleet he'd seen a few short days ago would have no trouble holding the bottleneck system. It had more than enough firepower to hold if it took up position on the wrong side of the crossroads.

"Captain," Sarah said, formally. "The last mine has been deployed."

"Close the hatches, then destroy the evidence and wipe the isolated datacores," Thomas ordered. "Sandra, have you finished copying the data to the secure datastore?"

"Yes, Captain," Sandra said.

"Then wipe the data from the remainder of the datacores," Thomas ordered. "Make absolutely sure the data does not exist, outside the secure store."

Sandra swallowed, audibly. "Aye, Captain."

Thomas felt a pang of guilt. Technically, it was illegal to order a junior officer to edit or erase data from a datacore. It wasn't even supposed to be *possible*, although spacers had been finding ways to evade the reporting requirements for centuries. The EDF had even rigged the datacore to allow him to rewrite the files at will, as a last resort. It wasn't easy—the slightest discrepancy would be noted and logged, if the files were ever reviewed—but it could be done. And, if he was caught, his licence would be suspended at the very least. There might even be jail time in his future.

His lips twitched, humourlessly. *If the war goes badly, jail time will be the least of my worries.*

"Wesley, take us to J-25, best possible speed," he ordered. There was no point in trying to observe the minefield from a safe distance. "We'll swing through the system and then head to Coriander."

"Aye, Captain," Wesley said.

The hatch opened. Sarah stepped onto the bridge. "The evidence has been destroyed, sir," she said, stiffly. "We're lucky they didn't find us a proper deployment rig."

"We're just lucky they had some mines," Wesley said. The EDF had intended to lay mines around the crossroads, although events had moved on too quickly for the freighters to put the plan into operation. "And we'd better hope they have some more at Coriander."

"If they even give them to us," Sarah said. "They won't be able to deny minelaying if they give us the mines or do it for themselves. I'd bet there's already a horde of reporters laying siege to the naval base."

"No bet," Thomas said. "But right now, that's the least of our worries."

He leaned back in his chair. The operation had been a success. There was no way to tell if their mines would actually *hit* anything, but…he shook his head. They'd had to try. It might just weaken the enemy fleet. And even if it didn't…if nothing else, the enemy would be a great deal more careful as they advanced towards their target. They'd have no way to know that only *one* threadline had been mined.

A shame we can't mine the others, he thought, grimly. *We could keep them back for months, if not years, if we had the mines on hand.*

...

Flockleader Trans paced the deck, impatience clearly visible in every flutter of his feathers as the fleet finally—*finally*—headed through the crossroads and into multispace. Delaine had been an easy target—the fleet had had no trouble securing the high orbitals—but the humans didn't seem to know when they were beaten. The army he'd landed had run into stubborn resistance, from heavily-armed human soldiers to civilians who didn't realise resistance was utterly futile. His subordinates had rapidly come to fear their human enemies, insisting they were terrifyingly ingenious when it came to converting civilian equipment into weapons of war. Trans had had to remind them, repeatedly, that the human world wasn't *that* important. The human population could be reduced—or eliminated—later, after the war was over. But the only way to win the war was to punch through to Earth before it was too late.

He snapped his beak with impatience as the fleet picked up speed. There was no sign of human resistance in space, save for a warship that had briefly engaged his ships before vanishing into the shadows, but reports from Earth suggested the humans intended to make their stand at Coriander. Trans had expected as much, when he'd reviewed the plans. It was hardly *honourable*, but it was practical. The humans had studied space warfare long enough to know it was their best bet, unless they wanted to make a stand at Earth itself. And *that* ran the risk of losing everything else.

We have to secure our gains before it's too late, he thought. The Nest had made it clear, time and time again. *And that means taking and securing Coriander before the humans can muster allies.*

The thought nagged at his mind. He feared nothing—indeed, he planned to take the war all the way to Earth if there was a reasonable chance of victory—but he knew his limits. It went against everything he'd been taught to accept that war was a matter of logistics, not tactics, skill and bravery, yet...he clacked his beak in disdain. To the fire with logistics! They *had* to secure a bottleneck before the Galactics intervened. If they didn't...he snorted. The Galactics weren't likely to do *anything*. They had to know his people would fight to the bitter end, rather than be slaves again. The Pashtali had been quite bad enough.

He forced himself to calm down. The fleet was on the way to its next target. There were no fixed defences short of Coriander itself. There were no human ships, unless the rogue cruiser had taken up position somewhere along the route. And if it had...who cared? The starship would be blown to atoms if it came within range and if it didn't...what did it matter, if the humans saw their doom crawling towards them? Let them see, let them fear. They might just offer their eggs in submission, if they realised resistance was pointless. Trans would be a gracious foe, in victory. He'd give them their rights, if they acknowledged his supremacy...

Alarms rang. He spun around. An icon was flashing red...a destroyed ship. He stared, shocked. No one, not even the Alphans, dared risk engagements in multispace. It was too hard to even *locate* the enemy ships, let alone coordinate one's forces in an attack. And yet...what had happened? There hadn't even been a hint of an attack!

"Report," he snapped. A red icon appeared on the display, drifting towards another ship. "What is that?"

"A mine," the operator said. He kept his eyes firmly fixed on the console, a sign—if any were needed—of how dangerous things had suddenly become. More icons sparkled to life, each one a potential threat. "Flockleader, we're in a minefield!"

Trans shivered. He was brave. He knew himself to be brave. But even he feared the unknown.

"Bring the fleet to full stop and activate the railguns," he snapped. They weren't *that* effective in realspace, but they were his best option in multispace. "Sweep the region for mines and clear them!"

He cursed out loud as another ship vanished from the display. A light cruiser and a destroyer, destroyed…not in honourable combat, but by foul and base treachery. It burned at him to know they'd been hurt by a sneaky trick, yet…it said something about how weak the humans truly *were* that they resorted to such tactics. The minefield wasn't very extensive either. The gods had not abandoned their children. If the humans had had more mines, they would have used them. They certainly hadn't the time to rig up makeshift antimatter containment chambers and deploy them as mines.

They used nukes, not antimatter bombs, he thought. It was a good sign. Nukes were fairly common, but useless unless they were deployed at very close range. Antimatter weapons would have been a great deal more dangerous. *They didn't have a chance to build anything more effective.*

He allowed himself a moment of relief as his smaller ships inched forward, sweeping for mines and firing their railguns at any prospective targets. Many of them would be nothing more than sensor glitches, he was sure, but it didn't matter. Better to waste thousands of tiny projectiles, which could be easily replaced, than lose an entire starship. He was all too aware the Nest couldn't produce capital ships itself. Their patrons were their suppliers…and if it looked like the Vulteks were losing the war, they'd back off or demand a price their clients would be reluctant to pay. He tapped an order into his console, instructing the logistics staff to make sure more projectiles were provided. The quartermasters might be regarded with disdain, but they'd come into their own during the war. The fleet could neither fly nor fight without fuel and weapons.

"Form up the fleet around the flagship," he ordered, coolly. It was unlikely the humans had managed to mine the entire threadline, but it was well to be careful. As long as his shipboard enemies didn't see it as a sign of weakness. It would be ironic if giving the right orders ensured someone would stick a knife in his back. "We'll advance slowly, targeting any mine before it can go active."

He fluttered his feathers as the remainder of the fleet started to move, all too aware of the shifting emotional tide around the bridge. Cold logic told him the humans couldn't have scattered mines *everywhere*, but there was no way he could convince his people of that. Their greatest strength—their willingness to risk everything on a single blow—was also their greatest weakness. If it looked like they'd run into someone tougher than themselves, if defeat appeared possible, they'd start to weaken. And then they might concede defeat without a fight.

And that means we have to get to Coriander quickly, he thought. The starchart glowed in front of him. There were a handful of systems on the near side that could be occupied, but none of them presented a real challenge. His crew needed a victory against real odds in order to rebuild their confidence. *Once we punch our way into the bottleneck, victory will be assured again.*

CHAPTER THIRTY-THREE

EDS *Washington*, J-25/Multispace, Near Coriander

"CAPTAIN," HAWKE SAID. "The enemy fleet is starting to come though the crossroads."

"Noted," Naomi said. "Inform me if they detect the recon platforms."

She leaned forward, watching with professional detachment as alien ships started to materialise on the crossroads. The crossroads was really too large for them to interpenetrate upon arrival, unfortunately; the odds of a collision were vanishingly small. The Vulteks didn't seem inclined to take chances. The moment their systems stabilised, they brought up their drives and headed towards the *next* crossroads. They didn't seem inclined to sweep the system and occupy the settlements. None of them were really worth the time.

"They're not going to pass within active sensor range of us," Roger muttered. "Do you want to slip closer?"

"No." Naomi shook her head. The recon platforms had already told her everything she wanted to know—and a lot of things she didn't—about the alien fleet. There was nothing to be gained by sneaking closer, not when so much firepower would reduce her ship to dust if the enemy realised she was there. "Just make sure the sensor records are transmitted to the crossroads."

"Aye, Captain," Walcott said. "The freighter will have plenty of time to escape before the enemy covers the crossroads."

Naomi nodded. *Washington* had made it back to Coriander, only to be ordered to turn around and head straight for J-25. The enemy fleet would practically *have* to cross the system if they wanted to reach Coriander sooner rather than later, giving her a chance to collect intelligence and—hopefully—hit their supply lines. The xenospecialists had predicted the enemy supply chain would be very weak, perhaps undefended. Naomi had her doubts, but she couldn't see any logistics ships accompanying the enemy fleet. The Pashtali had presumably handled all such matters for their clients.

Clever, she thought. *If they controlled the logistics, they'd be able to keep the Vulteks under their thumbs without resorting to naked force.*

She scowled as the enemy fleet glided past them and headed further into deep space. The intelligence staff hadn't told her what the Pashtali were doing. Were they backing the Vulteks openly? Or were they watching in hopes their protégés would take a pratfall? The Vulteks had not been ideal clients, if the reports were to be believed. Their masters might not be too displeased if the bird-like aliens got a bloody nose or two.

And yet, letting them lose would reflect badly on their patrons, she told herself. *What the hell are they doing?*

The enemy fleet reached the crossroads without incident and started to transit. Naomi shook her head slowly, knowing *Washington* was now cut off from Coriander. She *might* manage to slip past the enemy fleet, if she left now, but it would be one hell of a risk. A report flashed up in front of her, suggesting the hasty minelaying operation had claimed at least two enemy ships. Naomi wanted to believe the report, but she knew she couldn't take it for granted. The Vulteks could easily have detached ships to occupy other colonies or simply chase down freighters that might have tried to make a run for neutral space. There was no way to know.

And we're blind to whatever is happening closer to the border, she thought, sourly. *They could have scorched Delaine clean of life by now and we'd know nothing about it.*

She stood. "Mr. XO, you have the bridge," she said. "I'll be in my ready room."

"Aye, Captain," Roger said.

Naomi didn't let herself relax until she stepped into the compartment and the hatch hissed closed behind her. She hadn't been sleeping well, even though the war had finally started and the ambiguities of peacetime had been replaced by the cold calculation of war. There was no longer any doubt about the enemy's intentions, yet...she knew she had to be careful. The galaxy was watching, eager for the slightest excuse to wash its hands of the whole affair. A mistake on her part could lead to a diplomatic disaster or worse. And she was all too aware that a serious misstep couldn't be washed away by court-martial. Earth might pay a price for her mistakes.

Mining the threadline was a calculated risk, she told herself. *But one we had to take.*

She lay on the sofa and closed her eyes. She'd wanted command and now she had it, just in time to fight a war. The irony gnawed at her. She'd hoped for a year or two to settle into her post before she had to put her ship and crew to the test, but...it was not to be. She wondered, suddenly, how the would-be mutineers were coping. Some of them had gone home, only to be yanked back to the navy by the war. She hoped they were patriotic enough to keep their complaining to a dull roar.

The intercom bleeped. "Captain, a handful of enemy ships are making transit!"

Naomi blinked the sleep from her eyes. It felt like she hadn't slept at all, but the chronometer—the damned liar—insisted she'd been asleep for nearly two hours. She sat upright, tapping the terminal impatiently. The holographic display showed a small convoy of freighters gliding into open space. There were only two escorts, both destroyers. Her lips curved into a cold smile. They'd attached enough firepower to deter pirates, she thought, but not a light cruiser.

Unless one of those freighters is actually a Q-Ship, she reminded herself. *They won't need to worry about catching us if we have to come to them instead.*

"Plot an intercept course," she ordered. She tried to think of something clever, but nothing came to mind. They were going to have to engage at least *one* of the alien destroyers. "And prepare to deploy missiles on ballistic trajectories."

"Aye, Captain," Roger said. "Time to intercept, twenty minutes."

Naomi nodded. Roger would have been running intercept projections from the moment the enemy ships made their appearance. He was still rough around the edges—and Naomi was picking up far more of his formal duties than she should—but he was coming along nicely. She doubted Admiral Glass would have any hesitation in making his rank permanent, after the war. Wartime had a habit of speeding up promotion, in any case.

"I'll be on the bridge in five," she said. "Alert me if anything changes."

She poured herself a mug of coffee, drank it rapidly and splashed water on her face before heading for the hatch. Her body felt tired and worn, but the thought of action—even action against a supply convoy—galvanised her. She had no qualms about targeting and destroying the enemy freighters. They might be defenceless, but their mere existence posed a significant threat to her homeworld. Destroying them might be more effective, in the long run, than taking out one of the enemy battlecruisers.

Assuming we last long enough for the logistics situation to start to bite, she thought, as she stepped onto the bridge. Twelve red icons drifted in front of her. *They might just smash their way to Earth before they run out of supplies.*

"I have command," she said, formally. "Are we in position to attack?"

"Yes, Captain," Roger said. "Missiles are ready to deploy."

"Begin deployment," Naomi ordered. "And prepare to launch two ECM drones immediately afterwards."

"Aye, Captain," Janet said.

Naomi sucked in her breath as the enemy ships came closer. If she'd commanded a warcruiser, or a battlecruiser, she would have let them slip into point-blank range before opening fire and tearing them into ribbons. Simple, brutal and effective. But if she'd commanded a far more powerful ship, she wouldn't have been sent out on a commerce raiding mission in the first place. She smiled coldly, considering her options. In theory, she could afford to destroy the alien escorts and then hunt down and destroy the convoy. It would be a little harder to make it work in practice.

Particularly as I'm still under strict orders to refrain from risking my ship too much, she thought, sourly. Admiral Glass had been clear on that point. The navy couldn't afford to lose any ships, even now. *I'll only get one shot at the enemy convoy.*

"Helm, prepare to take us out of cloak and engage the enemy," she ordered. "Tactical, target the enemy convoy alone. Ignore the escorts."

"Aye, Captain," Janet said. Her fingers danced across her console. "Targeting pattern laid in, ready to fire."

"The missiles are ready to activate on your command," Roger added. "The ECM drones are in place."

"Good." Naomi took a breath. "Helm...*engage*."

Washington shivered as she disengaged her cloaking device and lunged forward. The lead enemy ship didn't react for a second, just long enough to make Naomi wonder if she'd barged into a trap, then hastily altered position to put itself between the convoy and the incoming ship. Red beams washed across the tactical display as the enemy ship locked active targeting sensors on *Washington*, a pointless exercise given that *Washington* was coming at the convoy like a bat out of hell. They didn't *need* active sensors, either to warn the cruiser off or target their weapons. She'd read the reports on the enemy very carefully. It looked as if she'd managed to startle them.

"Helm, don't let them get into ramming position," Naomi ordered, quietly. "Tactical, open fire as soon as we enter range."

She glanced at Roger. "Activate the missiles, then the drones."

"Aye, Captain," Roger said. "Missiles going active...now."

The enemy ship started to spit fire towards *Washington*, relying on the cruiser's speed to close the range. *Washington* altered course slightly, corkscrewing though space to minimise her exposure to enemy fire as her guns started to pound the convoy. Naomi braced herself as the convoy slipped into range, then relaxed as there was no returning fire. The Vulteks didn't seem to have thought of refitting their freighters with weapons, let alone designing a disguised warship from the keel up. It was frowned upon, by the Galactics, but the smaller powers could hardly afford to ignore something that might level the playing field. She allowed herself a tight smile as the first spacer exploded, followed rapidly by a second. The enemy ships simply didn't have a chance.

"The missiles are entering engagement range now," Roger said. "Enemy ECM support appears to be quite effective."

Naomi nodded, tightly. The missiles wouldn't pose *much* of a threat, not against even minimal point defence, but the ECM would make it harder for the Vultek destroyers to target their weapons before it was too late. And the cloud of sensor ghosts would suggest there were more ships coming towards them, under cloak. A canny commander would realise he was being duped, but...he'd still have to take the threat seriously. He couldn't afford to be caught with his pants down again.

And yet, if we really did have that sort of firepower, she thought, *would we bother being subtle in the first place?*

"Captain," Hawke said. "The second enemy ship is manoeuvring into engagement range."

Naomi nodded again. The rear escort didn't have a hope of keeping her from tearing the convoy to shreds, but they could try to avenge the death by damaging or destroying her ship. It was almost a shame she couldn't risk a duel. She could take out one of the escorts, if she was prepared to accept the risk of being rammed or forced to engage two ships at close range. It didn't matter, she decided as another pair of freighters vanished from the display and a third fell out of formation. The missiles were finishing the job. She could afford to break off and run.

"Helm, get us out of here," she ordered. "Best possible speed."

"Aye, Captain," Almont said.

Naomi nodded as the final freighters blinked and died. She tried not to feel guilty for smashing the ships and killing the crews, without even a word of warning before it was too late. The enemy ships might have been harmless, but the supplies in their holds might have made the difference between a successful invasion of Coriander and the enemy fleet getting a bloody nose. She told herself, tartly, she couldn't afford to be honourable. Humanity was massively outgunned. Cheating was their only hope.

"They're coming about, Captain," Hawke warned. "I think they intend to give chase."

Roger snorted. "Can't they read a plot?"

"I think they'll be more worried about what'll happen when they report back to their superiors," Naomi said. The EDF wouldn't be kind to an officer who'd watched helplessly as an entire convoy was smashed to rubble. "If they manage to run us down, at least they'll have *something* to show their superiors."

She shrugged. The enemy destroyers might have a higher acceleration curve than *Washington*, but they'd be hard pressed to keep up with *Washington* long enough to pound her into submission. Their missiles would be almost laughably ineffective. She studied the display, silently calculating the vectors for herself. There was a good chance they'd make it through the crossroads before the enemy ships could run her to ground.

They may intend to claim they drove us away, she mused. It wouldn't be very creditable, but she couldn't think of any better options. *Even if they destroyed us outright, they'd still be fucked when they got home.*

"Captain, the drives are holding steady," Almont reported. "We'll be through the crossroads in five hours."

"They'll be within missile range in four hours, if they hold their course and speed," Hawke added.

"They'll have problems hitting us," Naomi said. The missiles would be trying to catch a fleeing target, while *they* would be practically impaling themselves on her missiles. "Tactical, program a pair of drones to mimic our drive signature. We may as well confuse them as much as possible."

"Aye, Captain," Janet said.

Naomi settled back into her chair and watched as the alien ships slowly—very slowly—started to close the range. They *had* to know they were wasting their time, but what else *could* they do? She considered, briefly, launching a salvo of missiles on a ballistic trajectory, hoping one of them would strike an enemy ship at a sizable fraction of the speed of light. But there was enough sensor haze surrounding the ships to make it hard to be sure of their *precise* location.

It would be worth the risk, if we had supply ships waiting for us, she thought. *But Admiral Glass couldn't spare anything. Damn it!*

"Captain," Hawke said. "They're breaking off pursuit."

"Keep us on course," Naomi ordered. "And take us through the crossroads as planned."

Her thoughts raced. How long would it take for the enemy fleet command to be told the news? A couple of days? She keyed her console, working her way through the possible options. Assuming the enemy ships headed directly for Coriander, they'd need three days to pass the message to their superiors. And then...what? Would they stop the offensive? Or would they risk everything on one throw of the dice?

It doesn't matter, she thought. *Right now, we have to bank around and find a new target.*

• • •

Flockleader Trans watched the body crumple, purple blood staining the deck. The idiot deserved worse than a hasty beheading, but he simply hadn't had the time to make him suffer. There were too many other problems. The convoy might not have seemed important, not to his people, but it *was* important. Had *been* important. The enemy cruiser didn't know it—he hoped—but they had just put a serious crimp in his plans.

He motioned for the staff to dispose of the body—the other captain had committed suicide, rather than face his master's wrath—and glared at the display. There'd been no updates from Coriander, not since the human fleet had placed the system under martial law. The FTL transmitter had been shut down, ensuring no messages could get out. The Pashtali had lodged an official complaint, on the grounds they had trading interests on Coriander, but the humans—so far—had ignored the pressure. Trans wasn't expecting to have the transmitter reopened anytime soon. The Galactics were already making a fuss about the transmitter his forces had destroyed.

The humans have had time to prepare for us, he mused, coldly. *But have they had enough time to stop us?*

He clacked his beak in annoyance. It didn't matter. He could no more turn away from the unspoken challenge than he could crack his own eggs. They *had* to take the system or risk defeat—or outside intervention. And the humans knew it. He turned his gaze to the crossroads, gleaming on the display. So far, they'd faced nothing remotely capable of stopping his fleet. That might be about to change.

And if I don't order the attack, someone else will order it in my place, he thought. He understood, just for a moment, why the Pashtali found his people so frustrating. *They* would be happy spending years to prepare the attack, making sure the defenders had no hope even before the first shot was fired. *His* people couldn't tolerate delay. *Who'll be the first to stab a knife in my back?*

He raised his eyes, allowing his gaze to traverse the compartment. Who would it be? The ship's commander? His tactical staff? The ground troopers? Or…someone who saw assassinating his superior as the key to leaping *right* up the ranks? Who?

"Order the lead units to move into attack position," he said, quietly. He'd held his fleet back from the crossroads, although nothing had passed through for the last few days. It was basic common sense. He would have been surprised if the humans *didn't* have the crossroads under covert surveillance. "We will begin the attack in ten minutes."

CHAPTER THIRTY-FOUR

Coriander System

ADMIRAL ADAM GLASS had been half-asleep when the alarms began to howl, summoning the fleet to battle stations. It had been a long day, one consumed with everything from convincing the local manufactories to churn out what the fleet needed to arguing with the alien residents about the FTL transmitter. Thankfully, none of them had managed to get a complaint to or from Earth. *That* would have been tricky, given the need to avoid diplomatic incidents. And yet, he saw no choice. There were Pashtali on Coriander.

He rolled out of his bunk and stood. "Report!"

"The watchers just transited the crossroads," Emily said. "The enemy fleet is advancing on our position."

"Understood." Adam accepted a mug of coffee from his steward and drank it rapidly, then grabbed his jacket and headed for the hatch. "Signal the planet, order the system to go dark. And order the pickets to prepare to run if things go badly wrong."

His heart started to pound as he stepped into the CIC. It wasn't his first battle—he'd served in dozens of different engagements, during his long career—but it was the first one where the buck stopped with him. There'd always been someone else in charge, until now. He wondered, suddenly, if he was truly up to the challenge. He'd run a hundred simulations, and the good guys had won more often than they'd lost, but he knew better than anyone that simulations were not reality. Something unexpected always happened, something always threw his calculations into confusion. The Vulteks might have a *real* surprise up their sleeves.

He took his chair and watched as a state of organised chaos swept the room. He'd drilled his staff extensively, but most of them were as green as he was. They'd handled themselves well in the simulations, yet... how would they cope with reality? This time, the vanishing icons would represent destroyed ships and slaughtered men. Would they remain professional, when their friends were being killed...when there was a very real chance that *Thunderous* herself would be targeted? He glanced at the datanet, silently confirming the backups were in place. There would be no general collapse, if the heavy cruiser was destroyed. His second-in-command would take over at once.

"Admiral," Emily said. "The last report stated they'd be in position to make transit in two minutes."

"We'll have to see how they intend to force their way into the system," Adam mused. A bottleneck system was the kind of target most militaries would prefer to leave to wither on the vine, if there was a choice. The defenders would have a clear shot at the enemy hulls as they made transit. Worse, they'd have ample time to build up their fortifications until they were almost impregnable. "What is my opponent thinking?"

He wished, suddenly, that he *knew* his opponent. Who was it? What was he thinking? What were his favoured tactics? What did he prefer to avoid? But intelligence on the enemy's upper ranks was scanty. A handful of names, none connected to anything more than a handful of notations... neither the Alphans nor their human clients had really bothered to study the Vulteks. They'd been just another client race. That, in hindsight, had been a mistake.

"Activate Plan Theta," he ordered. "But prepare to bring the beta platforms online ahead of time if they decide to perform a mass transit."

He felt the seconds ticking away, a cold sweat forming on his brow. What would his enemies do? He felt, just for a moment, like an ensign standing watch for the first time, both hoping something might happen and dreading the prospect. If all hell broke loose...

The display sparkled with red icons. "Transit," Emily snapped, as a different set of alarms began to howl. "Forty-seven ships, all destroyers or smaller!"

"The alpha platforms are cleared to fire," Adam ordered, calmly. "Hold half of them in reserve until we see the first results."

His mind raced. *Forty*-seven ships? That seemed excessively high. He'd been taught, years ago, that one of the dangers of assaulting a bottleneck system was two or more of your ships trying to materialise in the same place. The odds of survival were still in your favour—it was funny how his instructors had never dared try it for themselves—but no one in his right mind would try it if there was any other option.

"Seventy-eight ships," Emily said. "One hundred and fifty ships..."

"Decoys," Adam said. He silently gave the enemy points for cleverness. They'd overdone it—they didn't *have* a hundred and fifty warships—but they'd won themselves time to start clearing the defences. And he'd just wasted a chunk of firepower blasting their decoys. "Order the remaining platforms to engage the active ships."

The enemy ships opened fire, blasting everything within range. His platforms returned fire, now they could separate the real targets from the decoys. The sensor ghosts proliferated with terrifying speed, projecting images of more ships than existed in the local sector. Adam scowled as a second wave of enemy warships materialised, shooting missiles in all directions as they steadied themselves and began to advance. They'd gotten lucky, very lucky. One of their ships must have jumped back through the crossroads, in all the confusion, and provided the attackers with updated targeting information. Their missiles were running into his point defence, thankfully, but there was an awful *lot* of missiles.

"Admiral, Commodore Hanson is requesting permission to activate the beta platforms," Emily said. "The alpha platforms have been expended."

"And they're targeting the beta platforms," Adam muttered. A third wave of enemy ships, including a cluster of heavy cruisers, appeared on the crossroads. He cleared his throat. "Clear the beta platforms to fire, if they come under threat."

"Aye, Admiral," Emily said. The display sparkled with red icons. "They're launching starfighters and gunboats."

"Hold our starfighters back until they commit theirs," Adam said. The human pilots had more experience, he thought, but they were outnumbered. "And then aim our starfighters at their ships."

"Aye, Admiral."

Adam nodded as the battle continued to evolve. The Vulteks had effectively claimed the crossroads, but as long as they stayed where they were his ships and starfighters could steadily wear them down. *He* might consider gritting his teeth and holding his ground, but would the enemy? They had most of their fleet committed to the invasion. They practically *had* to take advantage of the chance to crush *his* fleet. Unless they had a plan of their own...

"They're bringing the bigger ships through now," Emily said. "Two... no, *three*...battlecruisers, plus thirteen cruisers and destroyers."

"Understood," Adam said. The enemy starfighters lunged forward, ducking and weaving as they raced towards his ships. Their bigger brothers opened fire on the makeshift fixed defences, battering them to rubble as they orientated themselves. "Order the fleet to prepare to implement Plan Omega."

And hope to hell they read the same tactical manuals as we did, he added, silently. The sheer violence of the offensive had caught him by surprise. *This could go horribly wrong.*

• • •

"Incoming fire," an officer squawked. "I say again, incoming fire!"

Flockleader Trans tuned out the distraction—the battlecruiser's CO knew how to handle his ship—and studied the display with a profound feeling of dissatisfaction. It *looked* as though his forces were winning effortlessly, but—so far—all they'd done was shoot up automated weapons platforms and a handful of fixed defences. The humans hadn't had time to make the defences really formidable, but...he was lucky they hadn't massed their entire fleet on the crossroads. They'd still be outnumbered, yet they would have had the edge.

A low rumble ran through the battlecruiser as a missile slammed into the armoured hull. It looked as if the humans were firing so *many* missiles that *some* were bound to get through, even though his ship's hull was practically *covered* with point defence weapons and railguns. The humans seemed to have brought their entire stockpile of missiles to the front, although it was impossible to be sure. It was easy to count the number of warships under human command, but impossible to count the missiles they'd stockpiled. Or everything else, for that matter.

He clacked his beak as the crossroads was steadily cleared of human defences. The human ships were keeping their distance, holding position between his fleet and the *second* crossroads. They'd passed up on a chance to give his fleet a pounding, if they'd positioned themselves a *lot* closer to the crossroads; he reminded himself, sourly, that intelligence insisted the humans were afraid to die pointlessly. They might be right, too. But he knew better than to underestimate them.

"Bring in the remainder of the fleet," he ordered, firmly. The original plan called for a drive on the planet, forcing the humans to stand and die in defence of their settlers, but the humans had shown a marked reluctance to engage when the odds weren't firmly on their side. "And prepare to secure the second crossroads."

He allowed his beak to yaw open in a smile. The *true* target wasn't the planet or either of the crossroads. The Nest Lords might want to add to their domains, but Trans knew better. The true target was the human fleet. If it could be taken out, or driven out, victory would be certain. And, by the same logic, *not* destroying the human fleet meant that victory would never be final. There were hundreds of stories of a race losing a war, rebuilding in secret and then taking revenge. The humans wouldn't have the chance.

"The final ships are coming through now," the operator said. "They're taking up position in the fleet."

"Then prepare to advance," Trans ordered. "We move as soon as they're in position."

He studied the starfighter engagements for a long cold moment. His people had an advantage—they'd evolved from birds, after all—but not a decisive advantage. The humans had been blooded by combat, real combat. They knew how to get the best from their craft, they knew how to keep the bloodlust under control…he sighed, inwardly, as his pilots wasted themselves against their targets. The humans fought with a cold calculation that was ruthlessly practical, rather than testing themselves against their enemies. It chilled him more than he wanted to admit.

"The fleet is in position," the operator said. "Flockleader?"

"Begin the advance," Trans ordered.

...

"Dear God in Heaven," Wesley breathed. "And I wanted to join the navy!"

Thomas shot his son a sharp look. "You did?"

Wesley smiled, wanly. "I have to rebel against you somehow, don't I?"

"I think you're too old to rebel," Sarah said, primly. "And probably too old to join the navy too."

"I'm twenty," Wesley protested. "I'm not an old man."

"You won't live long enough to reach old age if you talk to a naval officer like you talk to me," Thomas said, dryly. "I give you plenty of latitude because you're my son."

"And because you'd have to pay someone else *more* if you had to replace me," Wesley added, equally dry. "Right?"

"Right," Thomas agreed. "But there *are* limits."

He smiled at the thought, then sobered as he watched the forces waging titanic conflict around the crossroads. It was hard to believe—Wesley would think he was lying, if he said as much—that it was a small engagement, compared to some of the contests waged during the Lupine Wars. There were hundreds of ships fighting and dying, thousands of starfighters and missiles flashing from place to place. He'd been given orders to watch the battle and, if necessary, retreat through the second crossroads if things went badly. Right now, it was hard to tell which side was ahead.

Not that it matters, he thought. *We have to kill all of their ships to win.*

Wesley looked up. "Is there anything we can do?"

Sarah eyed him, sharply. "Do you think we could make a difference?"

"We can't," Thomas said, before Wesley could say something they'd all regret. "Our popguns won't make any difference. All we can do is watch, record everything and pray."

And the minefield didn't really slow them down, he thought, darkly. The enemy fleet was starting to glide away from the crossroads, heading straight for their position. They'd have to power up the drives and sneak away before the back door was slammed closed. *Did we put our lives at risk for nothing?*

He shook his head. They'd never know.

• • •

"Admiral," Emily said. "They're heading straight for us."

"For the crossroads," Adam corrected. The fleet was in the way, but he'd bet his retirement pay—if there was anything left of it—that the enemy ships would remain focused on the crossroads. If they trapped the fleet within the system, they'd force him to either surrender or risk an engagement against overwhelming odds. "Order the fleet to put Plan Omega into action."

And let them think we're running, he thought. The enemy would have an excellent chance to overhaul them. They'd already built up speed. Battlecruisers were *made* for speed. They might be outmatched by warcruisers, or dreadnaughts, but they'd have no trouble catching and pounding *Thunderous* to scrap. *Let them think we're prey.*

"Deploy drones, then create an ECM haze," Adam added. "I don't want them getting any clear sensor images, not now."

"Aye, sir," Emily said.

Adam sat back in his chair, forcing himself to wait. The fleet itself had barely been scratched—the fixed defences and automated platforms had taken the brunt of the enemy assault—but that was about to change. They were about to be run to ground. The Vulteks had lost a dozen ships, assuming the count was accurate; enough to slow them, perhaps, but clearly not enough to stop them. And their heavy ships were untouched. He glanced at the latest report from the planet, silently cursing the speed-of-light delay under his breath. The planetary authorities had put the entire world into lockdown when the enemy fleet had been detected, but had it been enough to keep spies from signalling the fleet? He hoped so, but he couldn't be sure. The alien community on Coriander was large and diverse enough to be difficult to supervise.

"They're still tracking us," Emily reported. "Analyst deck suggests they're tracking our drive emissions."

"Good," Adam said. Let them think he'd made an amateurish mistake. "It'll lull them into a false sense of complacency."

And he hoped, as the seconds continued to tick down, that he was right.

• • •

A thrill of anticipation ran around the bridge, a desire that harked back to the days when his people had hunted with beak and claw rather than firearms and starships. Flockleader Trans was hardly immune to it, even though he knew he should keep the lust for the kill under tight control. The humans were running, showing their backs as they fled to the crossroads…the crossroads they were destined never to reach. They had to know they couldn't make it before they were run down and destroyed…

His beak fell open as the human fleet started to dissolve into a haze of sensor static. They were panicking. They *had* to be panicking. Their ships were wrapped within the haze, but it wasn't enough to conceal them. *His* ships already had solid locks on their drives. They'd have to put a great deal more room between the two fleets if they wanted to run and hide and they weren't going to get the chance. His missiles would weaken them, before his fleet closed for the kill. And then...he closed his beak as he studied the missile reports. His fleet needed resupply before it went any further. The idiot who'd lost a convoy hadn't suffered enough for what he'd done.

"Send a courier back to the Nest," he ordered, firmly. "Tell them we stand at the brink of victory—and that we need resupply."

The Nest Lords wouldn't be happy, but they'd understand. The victory would give them a chance to secure their gains, to establish themselves as masters of a great Empire. Earth itself would remain independent, perhaps, but the humans would no longer pose a threat. And if their masters came back...maybe they'd re-enslave themselves. He was almost disappointed in his opponents. Their fearsome reputation might have been more exaggerated than he'd thought.

"Entering missile range," an operator said. A rustle of laughter—almost a snicker—ran around the bridge. "They're deploying more decoys."

Clearly panicking, Trans thought. The human fleet was simply too close for their decoys to fool him. They were wasting expensive supplies, supplies they could use to bargain for better terms. *Or are they just trying something desperate in the hope it'll get them out of the trap?*

"Open fire," he ordered. "And continue firing until the targets are destroyed."

There was nothing wrong with the human point defence, he noted. They blasted hundreds of missiles out of space, allowing only a tiny handful to slip through the defences and slam into their hulls. But they were still running. Their starfighters were battling *his* starfighters, not making any attempt to slow his ships...not that they would have worked. His fleet was too strong, in too commanding a position. He could take a few losses, if they brought him a prize. The Nest Lords would forgive anything, if...

The display sparkled with red light. Alarms howled. Too late.

"Evasive action," Trans snapped. He saw his mistake, too late. They'd allowed the humans to lead them onto a minefield! The human ECM hadn't concealed their ships, but it sure as hell had concealed their *mines*. "Point defence…"

And then the mines started to explode.

CHAPTER THIRTY-FIVE

Coriander System

"IT WORKED, ADMIRAL," Emily said. "They ran right into the mines."

Adam nodded, watching as the enemy ships staggered under the impact. There'd been no time to deploy more than a handful of antimatter mines, but the nuclear and laser-tipped mines were doing a *lot* of damage. A dozen enemy starships, including one of the battlecruisers, were destroyed outright; only a handful of the remainder avoided taking at least *some* damage. He smiled, coldly, as the damage continued to mount. The invasion had been stopped in its tracks. No *sane* foe would continue the battle if there was a way out.

"Order the starfighters to shift to attack pattern," he ordered. The two remaining battlecruisers were still dangerous, but one was venting plasma so badly he suspected she was beyond immediate repair. "Target the enemy drives. Slow them down."

"Aye, sir," Emily said.

"And see if you can spot the command ship," Adam added. "Target her for destruction."

He felt his smile grow wider as the enemy formation started to come apart. It looked as if confusion had already infected their command structure, as if...he wondered, suddenly, if they'd already taken out the command ship. The enemy CO would have positioned himself on one of the battlecruisers, surely. If he was dead...it looked as if the chain of command had been shattered. Some subunits were continuing the advance, some were falling back in disarray and some were holding position. It would take time for whoever was in command to reassert himself, time Adam had no intention of giving him. The fleet had been bloodied. It had to be destroyed.

"Transmit a formal demand for their surrender," Adam said. He doubted they'd reply, but it was worth a try. "And then activate the drones."

"Aye, sir," Emily said.

Adam watched, coldly, as the human starfighters swept towards their targets. The enemy datanet had been shot to hell. They didn't seem to have bothered with contingency plans for what they'd do when the command ships and relay nodes were taken out. They clearly hadn't bothered to learn anything from the Lupine Wars. Their point defence was utterly uncoordinated, each ship thrown back on its own resources. He was tempted to try to seal off the crossroads, forcing the enemy to fight to the last or surrender. But it was too risky. The enemy ships were still dangerous. He had to let them *think* there was a chance to retreat until they were soundly beaten.

"Signal the fleet," he ordered, quietly. The starfighters were wearing down what remained of the enemy's point defence. They'd have problems coping with a new wave of missiles. "The battleline will advance to engage the enemy."

"Aye, sir."

...

"Reconfigure the command network," Trans snapped. "Get the point defence back online!"

Panic swept the bridge. He could *feel* it. He tried not to let himself be dragged into the maelstrom as his subordinates panicked, their fear threatening to lead the entire fleet to destruction. The display kept updating, an endless series of disasters that spelt doom flowing up in front of him...he twisted his claws until they were digging into his own flesh, centring him. The battle wasn't lost—yet—but it would be if the humans had a chance to take advantage of the panic. His formation was coming apart at the seams.

He clacked his beak in fury as the enemy starfighters swept down on his fleet. The human flyers were good. Very good. They would have posed a serious threat even if the point defence network had been up and running, ducking and weaving as they dropped below the horizon and strafed his hulls with plasma bolts, systematically taking out his defences. The display started to stutter as more and more sensor nodes were taken out. And the human fleet was starting to advance...

A new wave of panic swept through the compartment. "Sir! More human ships have arrived!"

Trans stared at the display. A cluster of red icons had appeared, gliding out of nowhere and heading straight towards the crossroads, towards his only line of retreat. They'd timed it badly, he noted, but his fleet was in disarray. They might *just* manage to make it work. And yet... suspicion flickered at the back of his mind. The new human squadron might not be *real*. He didn't think they'd have dared risk committing their entire fleet to the battle. But if it worked, if they won...they'd win the war. He knew, better than anyone else, how little his people *hadn't* committed to the war.

"Order the fleet to retreat," he said. It was a measure of how badly stunned his crew were that none of them challenged him, that none of them demanded he prove himself in a trial of strength. "The ships that can make flank speed are to proceed immediately to the crossroads. The remainder are to delay the enemy as long as possible."

A pang of guilt tore at him as the fleet slowly came about. Two-thirds of his force, of the entire navy, had been destroyed or battered beyond repair. There was no hope of extracting the cripples before the humans slammed the door firmly shut. The damaged ships would have to sell their lives dearly, if the humans gave them the chance. It was far more likely they'd be left to die alone. The humans had nothing to gain by wasting missiles on crippled ships.

Honourless creatures, he thought. Rage burnt at his gut, rage...and a grim awareness he'd seen what he wanted to see until it was too late. *May the fires take them and burn them forever.*

He controlled himself with an effort, watching as his fleet picked up speed. The damage was worse than he'd dared fear. Twenty-one ships *might* make it out, if the humans didn't push *too* hard. The remainder were doomed. There was nothing he could do to save them. The human fleet was picking up speed, curving around the cripples to ensure they stayed out of weapons range. Trans wanted to scream in fury. They were denying the cripples a chance to strike a final blow before it was too late! And yet...he told himself he should be grateful for small mercies. The curve would make it harder for the humans to bring their ships into weapons range before it was too late.

Not that it matters, he thought, as the human starfighters abandoned the cripples and streaked ahead of the capital ships. *They've already won the battle.*

His hand dropped to the dagger at his belt. His shame was so great that nothing less than ritual suicide could possibly expiate it. None of his subordinates would befoul their claws with his blood. He had nothing to look forward to, save a challenge that might never come...he clacked his beak in sudden amusement. Who'd challenge him, when they'd be taking his shame upon themselves? He should be removed—the code demanded it—but who'd want *his* place? He'd stay in command through an absurd perversion of the honour code!

"Continue the retreat," he ordered. He was doomed. The Nest Lords would remove him, when the fleet returned home. But he could see his duty through first. "And order the fleet to return to Delaine once we enter the crossroads."

He pulled up a starchart, trying to think as enemy starfighters came into engagement range. His people had made a fundamental error when they'd started to purchase and operate their own ships. They'd invested in starships, but not in logistics or heavy fortifications. It had seemed so unnecessary. The best defence was always a good *offense*. And yet, now... his heart started to beat faster as he realised how vulnerable they were. The humans had a reputation for being aggressive. If they knew how badly they'd crippled his fleet...

We can't make a stand at Delaine, he thought, grimly. There were too many threadlines crossing and re-crossing the sector, too many possible ways for the humans to advance across the border. *We might not be able to make a stand short of the Nest itself.*

. . .

"Ignore the cripples, unless they pose a threat," Adam ordered. The enemy ships hadn't bothered to reply to his demand for surrender. It looked as though their crews were struggling to repair their ships, although they didn't have a hope of getting out of the system before he returned to finish them off. A couple had tried to ram, only to be evaded with casual ease. "Focus on the active ships."

"Aye, sir," Emily said. "They're continuing to retreat."

Adam nodded. He'd positioned his drones with malice aforethought. It *looked* as if a second human fleet was racing to the crossroads, ready to sit on top of the position and force the enemy ships to engage at point-blank range while the first human fleet came up behind them. No *sane* commander could possibly take the risk, but the Vulteks were *alien*. They might decide that dying bravely was better than retreating and living to fight another day. A lost battle didn't mean a lost war. There was no shortage of places they could make their stand, if they wished. They might still come out ahead.

If we give them time to get organised, Adam told himself. The constant updates from the tactical deck suggested the aliens were rebuilding their command network. Their point defence fire was rapidly getting more coordinated. *We really dare not let them have the time.*

He silently calculated possible options as the fleet picked up speed. The hell of it was that he didn't *want* the enemy making a stand, not now. If the second fleet had been real, he'd be laughing...but if the enemy called his bluff, the battle might become a draw. Or a human defeat. Better to let them run than force them to fight, yet...the mere act of letting them go might tip off the enemy commander. Galactic tactical manuals called for the destruction of the enemy's fleet. Someone would suspect *something* if he declined to push his advantage as far as it would go.

Of course, we're not short of other enemies, he thought. *We might crush the Vulteks, only to be crushed ourselves by someone else.*

"Admiral," Emily said. "The first squadron of starfighters are requesting permission to rearm."

"Tell them to continue weakening the enemy point defence," Adam ordered. "We can't afford to give them time to breathe."

"Aye, sir."

...

Flying Officer Willard Smithton gritted his teeth as he hugged as close to the enemy battlecruiser as he dared, his guns snapping off shot after shot every time the targeting computers saw a possible target. He could coat the hull in plasma bolts without so much as leaving scorch marks on the alien ship, but every point defence weapon or sensor node taken out weakened the ship to the point human missiles could get through what remained of her defences and slam home. The battlecruiser was a deadly threat, but only if she could fly and fight.

His craft spun madly as an alien starfighter materialised above him, plasma bolts already stabbing down. Willard flipped his craft around and returned fire, watching grimly as the enemy pilot evaded his bolts with practiced ease. The briefers had claimed the Vulteks hadn't fought a real war in centuries, if at all, but they showed no lack of skill. Their training programs had to be excellent, he thought. His squadron had fought in the Lupine Wars and it would be hard-pressed to match the enemy pilots one-on-one.

But they fight as individuals, he thought, as another human pilot blew the alien starfighter into a ball of fire. A second alien craft flew into view, only to be crippled by Willard's fire. The starfighter pilot had no time to bail out before his craft crashed into the battlecruiser and exploded. *They don't fight as a team.*

He smiled, coldly, as the human starfighters formed up and allowed the alien craft to come to them. They showed skill, but no coordination. They charged at the humans one by one, as if they expected a genteel dogfight between gentlemen. Willard snorted at the conceit. If there was one thing he'd learnt, growing up in a rough district before he'd joined the navy, it was there was no such thing as genteel manners in war. The idea was to *win*, not have fun. There was nothing to be gained from giving the enemy a chance to fight on even terms, if it could be avoided. The Vulteks cared more about individual glory than victory.

Which makes sense, if one can only rise in the ranks by murdering one's superior, he mused, as he blasted another alien craft out of space. *How do they actually manage to get anything done?*

He put the thought aside as the HUD flashed up a warning. The enemy fleet was approaching the crossroads. He barked a command, ordering the squadron to fall back. They really *didn't* want to be caught in the battlecruiser's jump field when it passed through the crossroads. The starfighters were too small to carry jump generators of their own. They couldn't hope for more than a quick death if they found themselves stranded in multispace.

"The enemy fleet is jumping out," the CAG said. "All starfighters, return to base. I say again, return to base."

"I guess we won," Willard said. "Right?"

• • •

"Admiral," Emily said. "The enemy fleet is jumping out."

"Good." Adam relaxed slightly as the enemy ships vanished. They'd have time to repair and rearm, but—for the moment—the battle was effectively over. "Raise the enemy cripples. Inform them that they can surrender or be left to die."

"Aye, sir," Emily said.

And someone will complain about that, mark my words, Adam thought. *The eyes of the galaxy are upon us.*

He shook his head. The Convocations demanded the victors make every effort to take prisoners, yet they also expected the losers to cooperate once it was clear the battle was lost. The Vulteks would be within their legal rights to destroy their datacores, and ensure their ships were effectively beyond repair, but not much else. He had no intention of risking lives in an attempt to seize the ships. If the Vulteks refused to surrender, they could die when their life support failed.

"Order the fleet to start rearming," he said. They'd taken a beating, even if most of their ships had remained firmly out of missile range. "And get me a full damage report. I want the fleet ready for redeployment as soon as possible."

"Aye, sir." Emily sounded doubtful. "I don't have a preliminary report yet..."

"Pass it to me when you have it," Adam told her. He took a breath. He'd won a battle, but not the war. Not yet. "And establish a link to *James Bond*. I want to speak to her commander on a secure channel, once I'm in my office."

He stood. "And pass the word to all ships," he added. "Well done."

"Aye, sir," Emily said.

Adam smiled as he stepped through the hatch. It hadn't been the largest battle in recorded history. He'd fought in bigger engagements, back during the Lupine Wars. But it had been the first battle the EDF had fought as an independent formation, the first battle that had rested on his people and his people alone. And they'd won. The galaxy would have to start taking the human race seriously now. They were no longer a mere client race. They'd fought and won a battle on their own.

And we have yet to win completely, he reminded himself, sternly. His crews would be celebrating, even as they started to prepare for the next engagement. He couldn't allow himself to lose sight of the simple fact there would *be* a next engagement. *We have to win the war quickly, or we could still lose.*

• • •

The report did not make comforting reading.

Flockleader Trans scanned the damage control statements, feeling dead and cold inside. His subordinates hadn't killed him, but...part of him wished they had. The fleet had been shattered. Only twenty ships survived, all damaged so badly that there was no prospect of victory if they were forced to reengage before they managed to carry out some basic repairs. The once-proud fleet was gone. And it was only a matter of time before the humans pushed their advantage as far as it would go.

He tried to consider his options, but he couldn't convince himself there were many choices. The fleet was in no state for another battle. They'd been so confident of victory that they'd outrun their supply and repair chain, what little of it hadn't been shot up by prowling human starships. The humans didn't know it—he hoped—but they'd killed a bunch of experienced repair technicians. They'd done more than just cripple his fleet. They'd ensured he couldn't repair the damage in a hurry.

"The fleet is to cross the border," he ordered, finally. "We'll return to the Nest."

He sensed a wave of shock running around the bridge. Retreat was unthinkable. The mere thought of abandoning planets that had been taken with blood was practically treason. And yet, their confidence had been shattered along with their ships. The humans had given them one hell of a lesson. It was time to drop back, to take stock and plan their next step. If that meant giving up worthless systems...

The Nest Lords will have me killed, he thought. He felt the fleet glide into motion, a dull rumble running through the deck. *They won't have a choice. But at least some of the fleet will be preserved.*

He just hoped, as he prepared himself for death, that his people would be able to make use of it.

CHAPTER THIRTY-SIX

Coriander System

"CONGRATULATIONS ON YOUR VICTORY, ADMIRAL," Thomas said. He'd brought *James Bond* back to the fleet as soon as the enemy ships jumped out, to do what little they could to help in the aftermath of the battle. "I'm sure they'll never forget it."

"I certainly hope so," Admiral Glass said. "Is your ship in working order?"

Thomas felt his eyes narrow. "As good as she ever is, sir," he said. His ship hadn't actually taken part in the *fighting*. Admiral Glass knew it as well as he did. "What can we do for you?"

Admiral Glass smiled. "I have a specific task for you," he said. "At flank speed, how long would it take for you to reach the Nest?"

"At least two weeks," Thomas said. He keyed his terminal, bringing up the starchart. "It would be around seventeen days if we take the shortest route, thirty if we stay in multispace as much as possible."

"And probably quite a bit longer if you did the entire trip in multispace," Admiral Glass mused. "Very well. I want you to take your ship to the Nest, carry out a brief survey of the system and link up with me at the RV point. I'll send you precise orders in a moment."

Thomas blinked. "Sir?"

"We've given them a black eye," Admiral Glass said. "But we cannot afford to rest on our laurels. We have to finish this before someone intervenes in their favour or starts menacing the other side of our sector. I intend to take the fleet to the Nest and force them to surrender."

"I...I see," Thomas said. He felt a frisson of fear. Sneaking around the border stars was one thing, flying directly into the heart of enemy space was quite another. "And you think we can get in and out without being detected?"

"I believe so," Admiral Glass said. "I won't lie to you. We *need* up-to-date intelligence before we launch the offensive. And we don't have any other ships we can spare."

Thomas let out a breath. He didn't like the idea. His kids were on the ship. Sarah would *really* explode when she heard the news. And yet...he knew his duty. He'd agreed to serve the EIS when he'd accepted their cash. And it needed to be done. Admiral Glass was right. The fleet *would* need intelligence if it was to carry out the operation successfully.

"Yes, sir," he said. "One condition, if you don't mind. I'd like to transfer the girls off the ship before we leave. And I'll need replacement crew."

Admiral Glass didn't argue. "I can arrange that, if you send my staff the details," he said, curtly. "Good luck, Thomas."

"Thank you, sir," Thomas said. Sarah was *really* going to be annoyed, even if their daughters would be offloaded before the family went back into harm's way. "I won't let you down."

• • •

"Admiral," Emily said, over the intercom. "I have the latest set of updates for you."

Adam glanced at the terminal, then shrugged. "Do any of them require my immediate attention?"

"No, sir," Emily said. "The repair crews are getting to grips with the task in front of them. The starfighters are rearmed, ready to launch. The minelayers are scattering additional mines on the crossroads. The planetary authorities inform me that pressure to reopen the FTL transmitter is growing irresistible."

"How terrible," Adam said, dryly. He keyed his terminal and glanced at the report. "And the enemy ships?"

"Four have gone dead," Emily told him. "One apparently self-destructed. The remainder still have power, but otherwise remain crippled. We have them under observation."

She paused. "The marines are chafing at the bit, sir. They want to board those ships before it's too late."

"I'm not going to waste their lives for nothing," Adam said, flatly. The alien ships were beyond easy repair. They might be useful, if the EDF's repair crews had a chance to patch them up, but he wouldn't bet lives on it. It was far more likely the shipyards would find it easier and cheaper to build new ships from scratch. "Contact the FTL transmitter platform. Get me a direct realtime link to Earth. I want to speak to the First Speaker directly."

"Aye, sir," Emily said. "I'll get right on it."

Adam leaned back in his chair and waited. The Alphans had designed and built the first FTL transmitters—or so they claimed—but they'd never been able to improve the system. Adam had heard rumours that they'd kept more advanced technology to themselves, yet...he doubted it. The advantages of cheap and easy interstellar transmissions were so obvious that he found it hard to believe anyone would just sit on the technology. There would be evidence of its existence, even if the technology itself wasn't shared. It remained costly and difficult to hold a realtime transmission across interstellar distances. Adam wouldn't have ordered it if he hadn't needed to speak directly to Abraham Douglas.

And I have to be careful what I say, he reminded himself. The FTL transmitter had been built by the Alphans. There was a good chance their intelligence service received copies of everything that went through the transmitter. Even if it wasn't rigged, someone might be intercepting and decrypting his transmissions. *We're lucky we had a contingency plan for victory as well as defeat.*

He leaned forward as the First Speaker's face appeared on the terminal. It was curiously jerky, as if the communications link was constantly on the verge of dropping out. His lips and voice weren't quite synchronised. Adam reflected, sourly, that his distant ancestors must have found the telegraph—and early radio systems—to be just as inconvenient. It was difficult to hold a proper conversation with someone who might only hear half of what you said—and vice versa. The Alphans had worked hard to minimise the issues, but they hadn't succeeded completely. And there was always the risk that computer enhancement would make matters worse.

"First Speaker," he said. "The battle is won. The system is secure."

"That's very good news," the First Speaker said. His lips moved, soundlessly. "What is your status?"

"Macbeth, rather than Hamlet," Adam said. They'd agreed on a simple set of codewords, when they'd planned the operation. Hopefully, they'd mean nothing to listening ears. "I think we're looking at thirty to sixty grains of rice."

Or thirty to sixty days between launching the operation and our successful return, Adam thought. He hadn't dared discuss the concept with anyone other than the First Speaker. If an alien spy caught wind of it, the mission would become impossible. *Assuming we succeed at all.*

"Daddy-Long-Legs has not spoken since," the First Speaker said. "But we assume we'll get a letter shortly."

The Pashtali haven't tried to convince us to surrender, Adam translated, silently. *But that will change when they hear the news.*

He calculated it for a long moment. The Vulteks had destroyed the only other FTL transmitter on the near side of the border. They weren't going to be able to call home until they crossed the border, which meant it would be around ten to fifteen days before the Nest—and the Pashtali—caught wind of what had happened. News would leak out from Coriander, of course, but the Galactics might not take it seriously until they had confirmation.

He certainly intended to keep the FTL transmitter under tight control until the fleet was on its way.

"We will visit the opera in two days," Adam said. The fleet would be ready to depart in two days. They were pushing things, but he didn't want to give the Vulteks any time to calm down or beg their patrons for help. "Will the babysitters be here?"

"Yes," the First Speaker confirmed. "They'll be with you in a day."

Adam nodded, stiffly. "Then do we have your permission to watch the show?"

The First Speaker's image froze. Adam felt a stab of sympathy for the younger man. The provisional government had vast powers, particularly as the Empire Loyalists had yet to successfully rebrand themselves, but those powers required a certain degree of consensus. The First Speaker was pushing his authority to the limit by *planning* the offensive, let alone ordering it to go ahead. He might be booted out of office when word got out, even if the operation was a total success. And Adam might go with him.

Not that I'll keep my rank for much longer anyway, he thought, wryly. *I may as well go out with a bang.*

"You have my permission, as long as you caterwaul off the same song-sheet," the First Speaker said. "Don't go singing a different tune unless the words no longer fit."

Adam nodded, stiffly. They'd discussed possible terms for ending the war, but too much depended on what they found when they reached the Nest. Their contingency plans might flounder if they ran into a contingency they hadn't anticipated. Or...he shook his head. Telling people to expect the unexpected was all very well and good, but the problem was that the unexpected was unexpected *by definition.* They'd just have to improvise if they ran into something they hadn't expected.

"Yes, sir," he said. "I'll try not to break glass with my song."

The First Speaker nodded and raised one hand in salute. The image froze a second later, then snapped out. Adam nodded to the blank screen, then leaned back in his chair as his steward brought him a mug of coffee.

The plan had been nothing more than a series of bullet-points, a list of vague concepts he'd put together on his own. His staff hadn't been told—he hadn't even dared *hint*—that they might be going all the way to the Nest. They'd drawn up contingency plans that could, at a pinch, be stretched... but how well would they work in practice? He was about to find out.

And normally, there would be more time to cover the plan and work out the flaws, he thought, as he keyed his terminal. *Right now, we're dependent on my back-of-the-envelope calculations.*

"Emily, arrange a full holoconference for ten minutes from now," he ordered. "I want all my officers to attend."

"Yes, sir," Emily said. "The governor has sent you another message..."

"Tell him to wait." Adam said. There were going to be complaints, and questions asked in the assembly, when the FTL transmitter was finally unlocked, but...if he won, the matter would be allowed to rest. And if he lost, he'd be dead. "I'll talk to him later."

He finished his coffee and took a moment to splash water on his face before he strode into the holochamber. A handful of images had already arrived, blurred to indicate that the attendee had opened the channel, but wasn't directly linked to the conference. Adam wondered if it was a pointed reminder the fleet had work to do or simple common sense. There were too many other things to do for him to worry about etiquette now.

"We won the battle," he said, when the remainder of the attendees had arrived in holographic form. "But we have not—yet—won the war."

He paused. He didn't want to remind them that the battle they'd won only an hour or so ago was not the end of the war. They had wounded to treat, ships to repair, dead to bury...they didn't need to remember, not now, that they'd have to go back into battle sooner rather than later. And yet, they were all experienced now. They'd seen the elephant. They knew they had to win the war before the enemy rallied and retook the offensive.

"We've given them a bloody nose," he continued. "And that gives us a window of opportunity to take the war to them before they recover. We are going to take the fleet directly to the Nest and force the Nest Lords to surrender."

He pressed on before anyone could mount an objection. "They committed most of their fleet to the invasion," he said. "We gave their fleet a beating. They simply don't have time to repair their ships and rally before we hit them, if we leave now. And we can win the war completely, in a single shot.

"You have sealed orders in your safes, authorising the operation. Open them now."

There was a long pause. "Officially, we're going to retake Delaine and recover the border stars," he added. "I expect you to ensure that no one, even your XOs, gets a hint of the truth until we're well on our way. All official communications will insist that Delaine is the target, that we're merely going to carry out an offensive—in line with standard tactical manuals—with strictly limited objectives. We will act on the assumption our communications are being monitored and our operations are being watched by unseen eyes. I will personally *break* any officer who so much as *hints* we have a different objective until we reach Delaine. Is that clear?"

He smiled, grimly, at the chorus of agreement. "Good," he said. "Any questions?"

"Yes, sir," Captain Heather said. "When do we move?"

"I want to be on our way two days from now," Adam said. "Until then, the crossroads will remain sealed and the FTL transmitter will remain in lockdown. I don't think we can justify keeping it shut down past that point, which is why it is *vitally* important that no word of our true target leaks out. I didn't dare discuss it with anyone outside the very highest levels of our government."

He let the words linger in the air. The stakes were high, higher than they'd ever been. Either they won the war in one fell swoop, or they completely failed. The Galactics wouldn't see it coming—their tactics were more measured, more focused on limited objectives with limited risks, but would the Vulteks? Their patrons had tried to keep their aggression under control, unsuccessfully. They might reason out *precisely* what their enemies would do.

Particularly as they can't afford to trade space for time, Adam reminded himself. The Galactics *could*. The Vulteks simply didn't control enough space to make the risk tolerable...to any sane foe, at least. But they could be dangerously unpredictable. *What will they do now we've knocked them back on their heels?*

"If any of you have any objections, let me know and they will be noted in my log," he concluded. "If the operation fails...I'm sure they will be dragged out as evidence in my court-martial. Until then, I expect each and every one of you to do everything in your power to ensure the operation is both successful and secret. I do not want the enemy to get the slightest hint we're coming. Are we clear on that?"

He hated to belabour the point, but it had to be made. The Vulteks had very limited resources, particularly after the battle, yet...who knew which way their patrons would jump? Would they risk widening the war? Or would they let the Vulteks fall? There was no way to know until it was too late. And...he knew he couldn't let fear of outside intervention force him to keep second-guessing himself, but...the risk had to be acknowledged. And planned for, as best as possible.

We can't pick a fight with the Pashtali, he thought, grimly. He hated the idea of letting another race boss them around—the irony wasn't lost on him—but the balance of power was not in humanity's favour. *Not yet.*

"Dismissed," he said, quietly. "And good luck to us all."

He watched the images vanish, wondering why they'd accepted the news so calmly. He'd expected more of an argument. The First Speaker *had* prepared sealed orders, if they had a chance to turn the vague concept into a practical plan, but the officers hadn't had a chance to open and *read* the orders. Perhaps they didn't understand the risks. Or perhaps they understood that risks had to be run. The EDF was too small to cope with a long, drawn-out conflict. Ending the war as quickly as possible was their only logical option.

"Sir," Emily said as he stepped out of the holochamber, "the governor is calling. Again."

"Put him through to my office," Adam ordered. He wanted sleep, but there were too many things only he could handle. He didn't dare leave his staff to handle them without some supervision. They weren't practiced enough—yet—to know what was important and what could be left until a more opportune moment. "I'll speak to him in a moment."

"Yes, sir," Emily said. "*James Bond* just transited. She's on her way to Delaine."

She's going a little further than that, Adam thought. He made a mental note to ensure Captain Anderson's daughters were transferred to the planet before the fleet departed. *And we'll be going after her soon.*

"Good," he said. The modified freighters wouldn't be as powerful and dangerous as real warships, but they should be able to secure the system. The Vulteks wouldn't have time to launch a second invasion, if his calculations were correct. They'd be too busy worrying about their homeworld. "When the relief fleet arrives, inform the CO that he's to take possession of the crossroads and hold until relieved."

"Yes, sir," Emily said. She cleared her throat. "And I should remind you, sir, that you haven't slept for nearly a day."

"I'll sleep after I've spoken to the governor," Adam said. She was right. He knew she was right. It was her *duty* to remind him he needed to sleep. But he also knew he had too much to do to sleep comfortably. "Let me know the moment anything changes."

"Yes, sir."

CHAPTER THIRTY-SEVEN

EDS *Washington*, Delaine System

"CAPTAIN?"

Naomi started awake, wondering—blearily—why crises always seemed to pop up when she was in her bunk or trying to catch a nap on her sofa. It would have been far easier, she thought as she forced herself to sit upright, if problems appeared when she was on the bridge, surrounded by her crew. But then, many of the problems wouldn't really be *problems* if she was in a position to handle them immediately. She snorted at the thought—that really wasn't true—and keyed the terminal.

"Go ahead," she ordered.

"Captain, long-range sensors are picking up an enemy fleet transiting the crossroads," Hawke said. "They look to be in a pretty bad way."

Naomi's eyes narrowed. "Which crossroads?"

"Four, Captain," Hawke said. "They're not setting course for the planet. I'd say they were transiting the system."

"Really," Naomi said, slowly. She'd half-expected to run into a prowling enemy fleet, as she'd circled around to return to Delaine, but...she hadn't expected the enemy fleet to be in a bad state. "Do we *know* any of the ships?"

"We can't scan their IFF codes at this range, Captain," Hawke said. "But we do have a pretty solid lock on a battlecruiser. I think she's the ship that spearheaded the invasion of this system. And the other two battlecruisers are gone."

"Forward the sensor records to my console," Naomi ordered. If the enemy fleet was in full retreat...what did that mean? She cautioned herself, sharply, not to assume they *were* in retreat. They could be sending damaged ships home for repair. "How badly damaged *are* they?"

"Not that bad, but they've clearly been in the wars," Hawke said. "A skilled repair crew could patch up most of the damage...unless there's damage we can't see. They're right on the edge of sensor range."

Naomi studied the records, thoughtfully. Hawke was right. A skilled repair crew could fix most of the visible damage, without having to return the ship to the shipyard. She had no idea if the Vulteks had repair crews on their ships or not, but she found it hard to believe they didn't. The enemy could hardly afford to take ships out of the line of battle for the weeks it would take to send them home, repair them and dispatch them back to the front. Indeed, there were several ships that could have been *left* at the front. It looked, very much, as if the enemy was in full retreat.

Hawke cleared his throat. "Captain, the destroyers we noted orbiting Delaine are leaving orbit," he said. "They're heading directly for Crossroads One."

Naomi glanced at the timer. *There's been just enough time for them to order the destroyers to leave,* she thought. She'd been trying to think of a way to destroy the enemy ships without risking everything, but it seemed the enemy CO had solved that problem for her. *They must have lost their encounter with Admiral Glass.*

"Hold us here," she ordered. If it was a trap, she had no intention of springing it; if not, the planet could afford to wait a few hours longer. "Continue to monitor their fleet. I want to know the moment anything changes."

"Aye, Captain," Hawke said.

Naomi closed the channel, her eyes lingering on the display. She wanted to believe—she wanted very *much* to believe—that the Vulteks had been defeated. And yet, she didn't quite dare. The timing suggested the enemy had barely had time to enter Coriander before being shoved out again... unless they *had* taken the system and were merely repairing their ships before the next offensive. And yet...she'd expect the ships to be *more* damaged than they were. It was odd they weren't sending back near-cripples.

She put the thought aside as she stepped into the washroom, showered quickly and changed into a clean uniform before turning her attention back to the display. The enemy fleet hadn't altered course. If they knew they were being watched, they gave no sign. They just flew across the system and passed through the next crossroads without so much as bothering to signal the planet itself. Naomi felt a stab of pity for the enemy troops, invaders though they were. She'd downloaded a full brief from the recon platform. The enemy troops were barely holding their own, even with the advantage of fire support from orbit. Now...

They'll be desperate, she thought, as she walked onto the bridge. *And ready to do anything to hold their positions.*

"Captain," Roger said. "The system is now clear of enemy ships."

"As far as we can tell," Naomi warned, although the enemy had seemed more intent on abandoning the system than being sneaky. "Helm, take us back to the planet. Best possible speed."

"Aye, Captain," Almont said.

Naomi glanced at the communications officer. "Lieutenant Walcott, raise the planetary government through the stealthed platform," she ordered. "Inform them of our status and ask if they require fire support."

"Aye, Captain," Walcott said.

Roger caught her eye. "If the enemy fleet is only making a temporary departure, they may return to reclaim the high orbitals," he said. "We might be making things worse for the folks down there."

"I know," Naomi said. If the battlecruiser returned, with or without its escorts, she'd have to retreat without a fight. It was quite possible they *would* make things worse in the long run. But it wasn't her call to make. "We'll let them make that call."

She studied the display as the planet grew closer. The aliens had crushed most of the resistance, but—apparently—there were still some antishipping weapons on the planet's surface. It would be the height of irony if they were mistaken for a hostile ship and blown out of space by their own side. She gritted her teeth, wondering if she dared drop the cloaking device and display her colours openly. It might be dangerous. God knew *Washington* hadn't been designed by humanity. There were similar cruisers in the enemy fleet.

But none as capable, she thought. *We'd kick their ass in open combat.*

"Captain, they're requesting we provide fire support," Walcott reported. "They want us to hit every visible alien encampment."

Naomi winced. The planetary government had planned to evacuate the settled zone, as soon as the aliens began their landings, but she had no way to know if the area had been cleared completely. She didn't want to accidentally kill human civilians—or POWs. And it would be difficult to be sure they weren't targeting humans.

"Target their bases," she ordered. "But if you see a POW camp, leave it alone."

"Aye, Captain," Janet said. "KEWs firing...now."

•••

"Hug the ground," Tomas snapped, as the warning messages flashed over the makeshift communications network. "Hug the fucking..."

The ground shook, violently. He looked up, just in time to see a massive fireball rising from the alien base. From where the alien base had *been*, he corrected himself. A streak of light lanced down from high above, darting towards another alien base. The ground shook again, the rumbling thunder chilling him to the bone. They were far too close to the alien positions for comfort. If he'd known the navy was going to choose *this* time to return, he would have kept the little band of insurgents far back from the lines.

He forced himself to stand as the rumbling slowly died away. The aliens had established their base right next to a town, after they'd carefully searched the entire settlement for traps and then levelled the buildings to the ground. Tomas and his band of insurgents—he'd had to parcel out his squad, ensuring their training and experience was distributed amongst the resistance forces—had been on the verge of sniping at the base when the navy had returned to the system. It looked as though they might be able to recapture it instead.

"They're really pounding the bastards," Sergeant Ross said. He held a passive sensor in one hand. "They dropped a hundred KEWs in less than two minutes."

"Good," Tomas said. He glanced at his team. The seventeen men would never be featured on a recruiting poster—they looked as if they'd spent the last two weeks sleeping in a muddy field—but they knew how to fight. They lacked polish, he admitted privately, and the reserve of knowledge he'd come to take for granted, yet it didn't matter. They'd made the Vulteks pay a price for what they'd done. "Follow me."

He felt his heart sink as they left their cover and advanced towards what remained of the alien base. The Vulteks had done a good job, if the report from the survivors of the *last* team that had tried to penetrate the defences was accurate, but they hadn't expected the navy to return or they would have established a more formidable point defence grid. They certainly hadn't expected to be caught in the open, like a trooper who'd picked a really bad time to take a piss. Their base was nothing more than a smoking crater, their positions obliterated. He couldn't even see any bodies.

"Fuck," someone breathed. "I used to live over there."

"It's gone," Tomas said, sharply. He saw something move, within the crater. He had his rifle pointed at the moment before realising it was just rocks. "Keep your eyes open. They might not all be dead."

He led the team around the crater, towards where the vehicle park had once stood. A handful of flipped tanks and burning AFVs littered the ground, damaged beyond repair. He saw a body, caught within an open hatch and shuddered in horror. The alien's head and upper body were intact, but its lower chest had been mangled and its legs were missing. He heard someone being noisily sick behind him, despite the horror they'd seen over the past two weeks. The aliens no longer looked dangerous—or threatening. The war was over.

"They might come back," he said, grimly. The report hadn't been clear just how *much* of the navy had returned. "We have to watch our backs."

"Yes, sir," Ross said. He keyed his sensor one last time. "If there's anything left alive here, it's masked."

"It looks that way." Tomas didn't relax. "Who was it who said the only thing worse than a battle lost was a battle won?"

"You, just now," one of the locals commented. "And at least we won."

• • •

"Fuck," Governor Singh said. "Did we win?"

"Yes and no," General Tailor said. "The navy drove them away from the high orbitals, then smashed their positions from orbit, but did we win? They might come back."

"Fuck," Governor Singh repeated. "I don't know how much more of this we can take."

He forced himself to sit, uneasily aware it had been *weeks* since he'd had a proper bath, let alone a chance to stretch his legs. He'd never really understood—let alone believed—that house arrest could be an effective punishment until he'd found himself trapped in a cramped metal can. The handful of times he'd been allowed to leave hadn't been anything like enough. And the hell of it was that he'd been luckier than most of his people.

The reports had been clear. The abandoned towns and villages had been destroyed. The aliens hadn't tried to use them, they'd simply destroyed them. The handful of settlers who'd fallen into enemy hands had been shipped straight to detention camps, along with the military personnel who hadn't been simply shot out of hand. The aliens had shown no sign of wanting to negotiate with what remained of the human government; they'd not even shown any interest in trying to exploit or enslave the human settlers. And they'd been positioning their forces for a drive towards the hidden refugee camps. It boded ill for the future...

...Or it had, before the navy had arrived.

"We have to plan on the assumption they'll be coming back," Tailor said. "And we don't know how much time we have."

"I know." Governor Singh let out a long breath. "Do whatever you have to do, General."

And pray to God there's something left when peace finally returns, he added. *Please.*

"Yes, sir," Tailor said. "There's another problem. What do we do with the prisoners?"

Governor Singh hesitated. The resistance hadn't had the time or facilities to take prisoners, ever since the capital city had fallen. They'd rarely even tried. The Vulteks seemed to regard surrender as a fate worse than death, often fighting to the last rather than accepting the offer of surrender and captivity. But now...

"If there are prisoners, hold them for the moment," he ordered. He doubted the resistance would take many prisoners, even now. There were too many settlers who'd lost someone—or knew someone who'd lost someone—to the war. Or watched helplessly as towns and villages they'd helped to build had been razed to the ground. "And we'll let the navy decide how to deal with them."

"The order will be unpopular," Tailor warned. "And perhaps unenforceable."

"I know." Singh gave him a sharp look. He understood, but he couldn't condone. "Tell them to take prisoners, if the enemy soldiers are willing to surrender. The last thing we want is half the galaxy pissed at us."

"Admiral," Emily said. "The fleet is prepared to make transit."

Adam nodded. They'd seen no sign of the enemy ships, during their hasty advance through J-25 to Delaine, but that was meaningless. The enemy *could* have hidden themselves within multispace, if they'd guessed what he intended to do; they could have cloaked within J-25 and waited for him to press onwards before launching another assault on Coriander. Adam almost hoped they would. Their ships were in poor state, suggesting even the modified freighters would give them a very hard time. *And they'd be hundreds of light years from the Nest when the shit hit the fan.*

"Take us through," he ordered.

He braced himself as the heavy cruiser glided towards the crossroads. It was a huge crossroads, too large to be effectively mined...although that might not stop a foolish or desperate enemy. The Vulteks certainly had good reason to want to slow his fleet, if they even knew he was coming. Enough people on Coriander had heard the fleet was going to Delaine for him to be fairly sure the enemy homeworld had got the message. He smirked, humourlessly. The enemy leaders were probably wishing they hadn't authorised the destruction of Delaine's FTL transmitter *now*.

"Transit complete," Emily reported. The display started to fill with icons. "No enemy ships within detection range."

"Pike Squadron is to proceed to the planet, as planned, accompanied by the drone units," Adam ordered. "The remainder of the fleet is to cloak and proceed directly to Crossroads One."

"Aye, sir," Emily said. "Long-range sensors are not picking up any orbiting starships near Delaine."

"Hah," Adam said. They were operating at extreme range. There was no guarantee they'd see any starships orbiting the planet, even if they weren't trying to hide. "Deploy probes to sweep the system."

He settled back in his chair and waited. The plan was simple enough, on paper. Pike Squadron and its flock of surrounding drones would pretend to be the entire fleet, charging up and down the system in a futile search for watching eyes. The Vulteks—if they were spying on the system from a distance—would have no reason to think the main body of the fleet was elsewhere. They'd be reassured, he hoped, if they picked up copies of the orders he'd 'accidentally' sent to Coriander's governor. They insisted the fleet had clear orders not to cross the border. Hopefully, they'd be all the more surprised when the fleet arrived at their homeworld.

And yet, can we assume they'll take what they see for granted?

The thought nagged at him. The enemy were alien, with a very alien view of the universe, but they weren't stupid. They had to know humanity wouldn't stop at the border, particularly as there was nothing *stopping* them. The Pashtali hadn't intervened. Not yet, perhaps not ever. And the Alphans had no interest in intervening one way or the other.

"Admiral, I'm picking up a forwarded message from *Washington*," Emily reported. "She liberated the planet before we arrived."

Adam laughed. "Good thing we didn't start work on campaign medals," he said. The Alphans minted medals for each and every battle and campaign, but the EDF hadn't decided if it wanted to copy the practice. "That would have been embarrassing."

Emily looked faintly disapproving. "Sir, she's also reporting the enemy fleet buzzed through the system and jumped homewards, taking the orbiting guardships with her."

"I see," Adam said. Good news, of a sort. He wouldn't have to worry about his rear while he advanced on the Nest. "Order *Washington* to recover her marines, then join the fleet. We'll take her with us to the Nest. Pike Squadron's marines can take their place."

"Aye, sir," Emily said. "Sir...*Washington's* CO also reports the resistance captured a number of aliens. What should they do with them?"

"Hold them until the end of the war, like a civilised race," Adam said. "And when the fighting is over, we can send them home."

"If their homeworld is willing to take them," Emily warned. "They don't think highly of losers."

"That's their problem," Adam said. He shrugged. It was a valid point, but—right now—there were too many other things for him to worry about. They could worry about the POWs after the war was over. "First, we have to win the war. After that, we can decide what we want to do with our victory."

"Yes, sir," Emily said.

CHAPTER THIRTY-EIGHT

The Nest

"THERE'S LESS INDUSTRY HERE than I'd expected," Wesley whispered.

"You don't have to whisper," Thomas told him, lightly. "In space, no one can hear you…"

"Quote old movies no one has watched for a thousand years," Sarah said, flatly. "And somehow, I can hear you."

Thomas snorted, then turned his attention back to the display. The Nest looked fairly normal, for a planet that had given birth to alien monsters. There was nothing *different* about it, save for a surprising shortage of industrial nodes. He puzzled over it for a moment, then decided the Pashtali must have deliberately declined to provide more than the very basics. They probably saw it as a way to control their increasingly violent clients. The Vulteks would always be dependent on their masters if they couldn't purchase starships, spare parts and ammunition from anyone else.

"We'll keep our distance from the planet," Thomas said. "And keep a very sharp eye on the alien fleet."

His eyes narrowed as he studied the starships. It was clear the alien yard dogs were working overtime to fix the damage and get the ships back into service, but there was something oddly slapdash about their efforts. There was no way to be sure, yet...he wondered, suddenly, if they'd hired engineers from other races rather than training their own. It wasn't uncommon amongst barbaric races that had suddenly acquired starships and the keys to the stars. It was yet another way to keep them under subtle control.

Although it might be too subtle for these guys, he thought, darkly. *They might not be smart enough to realise their limits.*

"The planet isn't heavily defended either," Sarah commented. "What *were* they thinking?"

"I guess they put all their resources into their fleet," Thomas said. He could see their reasoning. Starships could be used for offensive as well as defensive purposes. And there were so many crossroads within the system that a crossroads defence was unthinkable. "And now it's come back to bite them on the bum."

Wesley looked up. "Do they *have* bums?"

"Shut up," Thomas said, not unkindly. "Some things are universal."

He snorted, then looked down at his console. "We'll make one final sweep, then turn and sneak back to the crossroads," he said. It wasn't clear if the aliens had any deep-space scansats or not, but they'd take every precaution to avoid being detected. "And then...our work here is done."

"It still seems boring," Wesley complained. "I want more excitement in my life..."

"And the moment a coolant pipe leaked, or an antimatter containment chamber threatened to fail, or *something*, you'd be wishing you were safely bored again," Sarah said, sharply. "Go join the navy if you want someone shooting at you for fun and profit."

Thomas chuckled as the ship continued its sweep through the system. Wesley was right. It definitely *was* quite empty, compared to Sol or a Galactic-level star system. There was one cloudscoop, a handful of mining colonies and a rocky world that seemed to be stubbornly resisting a long-term terraforming operation. He couldn't help thinking it actually worked in their favour, in the short term. The fleet had few targets to attack, short of the planet and its orbital facilities themselves. There was little point in laying siege to the system. They'd have to take their offensive to the planet and hope they won before outside forces intervened.

"Clever or stupid," he mused. "Who knows?"

Sarah glanced at him. "What?"

"Never mind," Thomas said. "Bring us about. It's time to report to Admiral Glass."

And hope the fleet made it, he added, silently. They'd been out of touch ever since they'd left Coriander. He was all too aware that the difficulties of coordinating operations on an interstellar scale were magnified when they had no access to FTL transmitters. *If something went wrong, in transit, they might be delayed...or they might never show up at all.*

...

"You lost the battle."

Flockleader Trans wondered, not for the first time, why he *hadn't* committed ritual suicide. It was his duty to wash his guilt away in blood; it would atone for his sin and spare his bloodline the taint of his failure. And yet, every time he'd reached for the knife, he'd found an excuse to spare himself for a few days longer. His crew needed him, his people needed him...they weren't *just* excuses. He couldn't let someone assassinate him if it meant they'd take the blame, along with his place.

"Yes," he said. There was no point in trying to deny it. "The humans beat us."

He wondered, morbidly, what they'd say. The Nest Lords could order him to commit suicide, if they wished, but it wouldn't be quite the same. He wouldn't have offered his own life to atone for his failure. Who knew what their people would make of it? Did they even have time to find out? The humans intended to reclaim the occupied worlds and then...and who knew what would happen? They might cross the border in force. He'd had more than enough time to think about it, during the long flight home. The humans might take the offensive themselves.

"You will attend upon us," the Nest Leader said. "And you will explain your failure."

Trans lowered his wings. He'd done everything right, he'd done everything according to the ancient codes...and he'd lost. He could point to his mistakes, yet...how could he have done otherwise? The humans had used the ancient codes against him. They'd lured him into a trap by offering him bait he couldn't refuse. And if he had...his subordinates would have killed him and fallen into the trap themselves. He understood, suddenly, why their patrons regarded his race with such contempt. They were slaves to their instincts. They didn't stop to *think* before they acted.

And now, we may have no choice but to ask our patrons for their support, he thought. *And their price will be high.*

He looked down at his claws. Perhaps it would have been better if he hadn't joined the trial of strength. Perhaps it would have been better if he'd flown apart from the flock. But he knew he couldn't have declined, when he'd hatched from the egg. Those who chose to fly alone were either isolated or slaves, the latter so pitiful that a dishonourable death would be preferable. He would sooner have died than flown alone. And...even in hindsight, he knew he couldn't have made any other choice. Better to struggle for power than to be powerless.

The alarms started to hoot. He spun around, looking at the display in horror. Icons—*red* icons—had appeared near the distant crossroads. Ships...*human* ships. His blood ran cold, his feathers flattening themselves against his chest. He'd assumed they had weeks, at least, before the humans overcame their fears—and their own supply problems—and mounted a cross-border invasion. And yet, here they were. The Nest itself was under attack!

"My Lord, the system is invaded," he said. "I go now to command the defence."

He closed the channel before the Nest Leader could respond. It didn't matter any longer. Either he won the coming battle, which would wash away his earlier failure, or he died. The Nest Lords would leave him to fight too, unless they'd forgotten everything they'd learnt about leadership. If he won, they'd share the credit; if he lost, they'd blame everything on him. They'd have no choice. They'd have to blame him even as they bowed their heads to their new masters, offering their feathers for plucking. He wondered, as he keyed his terminal and summoned his troops to war, if the humans would make good masters. And if they'd let his people wax strong again.

Not that it matters to me, he thought, as he bobbled to the CIC. A strange sense of fatalism overcame him. *Whatever happens, I won't survive the day.*

• • •

It was never easy to advance through a crossroads into enemy-held space, Adam knew from experience, even if the reports clearly stated the enemy hadn't had time to establish anything resembling proper defences. The Vulteks had to have been cursing their system's astrographics from the day they'd been taught how to enter multispace, even though having multiple crossroads within a system was normally the key to economic power. He wondered, idly, why the Pashtali had ever given the system up. It wasn't as if the Vulteks could have kept them from trashing their defences and reclaiming the high orbitals any time they liked.

Maybe they just signed a free transit agreement, he mused, as the display flickered and steadied. *The thing that makes this system so useful is the thing that also makes it terrifyingly vulnerable.*

His eyes narrowed as he studied the long-range sensor reports. *James Bond* had done an excellent job, even though the analysts had questioned the reports with a savagery that surprised him. But then, few of the analysts had ever left Sol. *Adam* had seen quite a few systems that had never been properly developed, for one reason or another. The Pashtali wouldn't have wanted to give the Vulteks any economic muscle, anything that might turn them into a long-term threat to their patrons themselves. His lips quirked into a cold smile as he spotted the alien fleet, holding station near the planet. One way or another, the war would end today.

The trick lies in not just winning the war, he reminded himself sternly, *but in preserving enough of our fleet to secure the remainder of our space.*

"Admiral," Emily reported. "The fleet has completed transit."

"Good." Adam studied the display for a long moment, although he already knew what he had to do. "Launch recon probes, then signal the fleet. We'll go with Plan Hammer."

"Aye, Admiral," Emily said. She tapped her console. The orders had already been programmed, during the transit from the RV point to the crossroads. "The fleet's ready to move on your command."

"Then take us into the fire," Adam ordered, grandly.

Sweat trickled down his back as the fleet left the crossroads, steadily picking up speed as it headed directly to the planet. There was nothing *subtle* about Plan Hammer, no room for cunning or cleverness or simple prudence. The fleet would make its way to the planet, engaging the enemy fleet along the way. He supposed he should be grateful the enemy hadn't bothered to invest in fixed defences, even though it had made them a much greater short-term threat. There was no point in falling back on the planet if the planet didn't have any defences it could pair with the enemy fleet. The only real danger was the risk of the attackers accidentally hitting the planet and committing genocide. Technically, *trying* to use the planet's population as human shields was against the Convocations, but he doubted anyone would bother to enforce them. The Vulteks might win the battle. They wouldn't win the war.

"Admiral," Emily said. "We'll be within starfighter engagement range in thirty minutes."

"Ready the squadrons for antishipping strikes, as planned, but do not launch without my direct order," Adam said, coolly. "We don't want to tip our hand too early."

He studied the enemy position as the recon probes passed through their formation. They weren't being very subtle either, although they had few tactical options beyond making a stand or fleeing to neutral space. A rational foe would start trying to discuss terms while they still had something to bargain with, but...he doubted the enemy was *that* rational. They stood to lose a hell of a lot, if they didn't surrender, yet...there were human opponents who'd kept fighting in worse positions, because surrender simply wasn't an option. The peace would be worse than the war.

"Transmit the surrender demand," he ordered. The terms he'd worked out, during the voyage, weren't harsh. Some would say they were overly generous. But they might just be accepted without a fight. "We'll give them a chance to stand down."

"Aye, sir," Emily said. "Message sent. Time to engagement range, fifteen minutes."

Adam waited, bracing himself. The ball was in their court now.

...

Trans studied the human message, unsure if the humans were mocking him or if they genuinely believed his people could accept their terms. Surrender their ships? Hand over anyone who'd brutalised the human settlers they'd enslaved? Concede defeat, once and for all? No one could accept such terms, not unless they'd been battered into submission. His people could *never* accept them. How could they? They hadn't been defeated yet.

"Ignore their message," he ordered. The human fleet hadn't altered course. They'd be within engagement range shortly. He'd taken a page from the human tactical manual and bolted missile pods onto his ships—and deployed free-floating missiles in space as a makeshift minefield—but they had the edge. He just hoped their weakness—they had to pass through his position if they wanted to threaten the Nest—would compensate for their advantages. "Fire on my command."

He waited, half-expecting to feel a knife in his back. If someone took his place now...

"The humans are repeating their message," the communications officer warned. "They're broadcasting it to the entire system."

"They're locking long-range targeting sensors on our hulls," the sensor officer added. "Their weapons are preparing to fire."

Trans snorted. The human ships weren't close enough to fire, not unless they'd somehow acquired Alphan-grade weapons. He doubted it. A lone warcruiser would have been more than enough to take out his entire fleet, if the humans had one under their command. No, they were trying to intimidate him. Didn't they know *anything* about his people? They'd feel challenged, not threatened. No one could bow his head to a threat without conceding total defeat. The instincts driving his people wouldn't allow them to surrender, not to a mere threat. The very idea was laughable.

"Launch starfighters," he said. The human ships were picking up speed, as if they were as impatient as he was. "And prepare to fire on my command."

• • •

"No response, Admiral," Emily said. "They're readying themselves to engage."

Adam nodded. He'd expected as much, but he'd had to *try* to convince the enemy ships to surrender. The Galactics were watching, damn them. It would be so much easier if he knew there was no prospect of intervention, friendly or not. There were just too many interstellar powers that had no interest in allowing humanity to join them as equals, even now. They wouldn't miss an opportunity to weaken the human race.

"Launch starfighters," he ordered. "And clear them to engage at will."

He frowned as a series of red icons appeared on the display. The enemy appeared to have deployed a minefield of their own. Good thinking on their part, he supposed, but...*he* had no intention of barging through the minefield when he could simply go around it. The enemy weren't trying to cut him off from the crossroads, not now. There was no way they could surround their entire planet with mines.

"Target the minefield with antimatter weapons," he added. It might demoralise the enemy if he swept the minefield without losses. "Clear as much of it as possible."

"Aye, Admiral," Emily said.

Adam watched, grimly, as the starfighters raced towards their targets. The enemy had clearly taken the opportunity to load more starfighters onto their ships, as they seemed to have replaced the craft they'd lost in the last engagement, but it wasn't enough to make a difference. They certainly hadn't learnt anything from the *last* engagement. Their pilots were good, but they still weren't working as a team. The data showed, all too clearly, that they were still fighting as individuals. His lips twitched. Starfighter pilots joked about mavericks, but any pilot who actually tried fighting as a lone wolf would be put in front of a court-martial and dishonourably discharged from the navy. Such characters made for good entertainment, he admitted frankly, but they were often worse than useless in the real world.

"They've improved their point defence," Emily warned. "Our starfighters are taking a beating."

"Noted," Adam said. There was nothing he could do about that, not now. The data would help, when the fleet started firing missiles, but little else. "Tell them to concentrate on the bigger ships."

"Aye, Admiral," Emily said. "Entering missile range in..."

She broke off. "They just swept us with tactical sensors, again. Warbook thinks they just locked missiles on us."

Adam blinked. The enemy didn't *need* active sensors to target his ships. Not now. Did they think he'd cloaked half the fleet, or hidden ships within his ECM haze? The fleet wasn't exactly trying to *widen* the range. There was no point in trying to hide ships that were making their presence obvious...

"Missile separation," Emily said. The display blazed with a solid wall of red icons. "I say again, missile separation!"

They put free-floating missiles in space and used them as mines, Adam thought, genuinely shocked. *That's right out of our tactical manuals.*

He silently tipped his hat to the enemy CO. He'd nothing to gain by holding whatever remained of his missile stockpiles in reserve, so...he'd turned them into makeshift mines. And he'd known Adam wouldn't look any further. He'd assumed the enemy was copying his tactics. It had given them a window of opportunity to mount a surprise or two of their own.

"Redeploy the fleet," he ordered. "And move the lighter ships into intercept position."

"Aye, sir," Emily said. "Enemy missiles entering engagement range in seventy seconds."

They let us impale ourselves on their weapons, Adam thought. *They really did learn something, didn't they?*

"Fire as soon as they come into range," he said. "And engage their ships with missiles as soon as they enter range."

"Aye, sir."

CHAPTER THIRTY-NINE

The Nest

"ENEMY MISSILES INCOMING," Hawke reported. "They're targeted on the larger ships."

"Tactical, update our link into the datanet and fire when they enter range," Naomi ordered, grimly. "Give priority to protecting the missile ships."

"Aye, Captain," Janet said.

Naomi braced herself as the solid wall of missiles roared towards her position. *Washington* was a small ship. Naomi was all too aware that a tiny fraction of the incoming missiles would be more than enough to turn her ship to dust. She shouldn't be anywhere near the line of battle, if only because she was too small to be effective and too big to be ignored by the enemy. And yet, there was no choice. *Washington's* point defence might make the difference between victory or defeat.

Good thing they had no time to wear us down, Naomi thought, as her point defence weapons opened fire. The alien missiles weren't *that* advanced, not compared to some of the systems she'd seen during the war. Their flight paths were predictable, even when they had room to manoeuvre and evade point defence fire. *If they'd weakened our point defence, they might have smashed the entire fleet.*

She gritted her teeth as a missile made it through the defence grid and slammed into her hull. The ship shook, the gravity field flickering as it struggled to compensate for the impact. Red icons blinked up on the display, only to fade as the datanet realised the ship hadn't *actually* been badly damaged. Roger barked orders, sealing off the damaged area and sending damage control teams to patch up the hull. Naomi allowed herself a moment of relief that the missile hadn't been antimatter-tipped—the blast would probably have vaporised her ship—then turned her attention to the rest of the fleet. Seven ships had been destroyed, badly weakening the fleet. They were lucky the losses hadn't been more severe.

"Engineering reports the hull breach is on the verge of being patched," Roger said, quietly. "We were lucky."

"The battle isn't over yet," Naomi said. "It could still go the other way."

She watched, grimly, as the last of the enemy missiles died. Enemy starfighters were swooping towards her ship, firing as they came. She felt a flicker of contempt. The pilots might *want* to paint a light cruiser on their hulls, or whatever they did instead, but they should be focusing on the bigger ships. She had every faith in her cruiser, yet she knew *Washington* wouldn't decide the battle. If the bigger ships were taken out, the battle was lost.

"They're targeting our point defence," Janet said. "Request permission to evade."

"Granted," Naomi said. If nothing else, sudden changes in position might cause an enemy pilot to crash into the hull. "But keep us linked into the datanet."

She glanced at the enemy fleet. It had lost a dozen ships, and two more were streaming plasma, but the remainder were still firing. They had to be desperate, she thought; they had to hope they could still win, somehow, by driving Admiral Glass back out of the system. But they'd shot their bolt. They had to be desperately short of supplies now. Who knew? Perhaps they were on the verge of running out...

A shudder ran through her ship. "Hull breach, deck four," Roger reported. "Damage control teams are on their way!"

Naomi nodded. The battle wasn't over yet.

• • •

"The human fleet is still intact," the sensor officer reported.

"I can see that," Trans snarled. "Focus on your work!"

His claws flexed in fury, his instincts demanding the idiot officer's immediate death for stupidity. He fought the impulse down as he studied the display. The massive missile attack had damaged the enemy fleet, but it hadn't been enough to *kill* it. The humans were still advancing and... and he had nowhere to go. Retreat wasn't an option. Surrender wasn't an option. And that left...what?

"Signal the fleet," he ordered, quietly. He'd massed everything he could, from damaged warships to armed freighters, but it wasn't enough. "The battleline will advance to engage the enemy."

He felt a frisson of excitement run around the bridge as the fleet started to move, picking up speed and converging rapidly with the human fleet. Either they won, buying time for the Nest Lords to rebuild, or they lost and lost gloriously. The shame of their defeat, and the submission their people would have to suffer, would be washed away by the blood of his crew. There was no way they could do anything else, not if they wished to remain true to themselves. They might win. And even if they lost, they won.

The Pashtali don't see the world that way, he thought, as a missile slammed into the battlecruiser's hull. *Nor do the humans.*

He clacked his beak in disgust. The strong ruled. The weak submitted to slavery. And if one could not be strong, better to die than live as a slave. And...he watched his crew readying themselves for death and glory. They could have killed him, if they disagreed. But instead they were ready to die by his side.

We die for the Nest, he told himself. *And to wash ourselves free of the stench of defeat.*

...

"Admiral, the enemy fleet is closing the range," Emily reported. "They're charging energy weapons."

Adam had expected the enemy to try to close the range sooner rather than later—the battlecruiser had formidable energy weapons, enough to do serious harm if the range narrowed significantly—but it was still a shock. There was no time to evade or retreat, not when the range was closing so rapidly. They'd have to close with the enemy themselves and hope they could take out the battlecruiser before it was too late.

"Order all ships to go to rapid fire," he said. There was no longer any point in trying to conserve missiles. If they won the battle, the war was over; if they lost, the missiles would be lost too. "And advance the lighter units to engage the battlecruiser."

"Aye, Admiral."

...

"Orders from the flag, Captain," Walcott said. "We're to engage the battlecruiser."

Naomi nodded. The battlecruiser was a deadly threat, but—hopefully—she'd be concentrating on the larger ships. *Washington* might just have a chance to do some damage before being swatted as the battlecruiser advanced on its real targets. And...she gritted her teeth. She disliked the idea of suicide, but ramming the battlecruiser would guarantee the destruction of both vessels. It was something to bear in mind.

"Take us into attack range," she ordered. "And go to rapid fire."

"Aye, Captain," Janet said.

The battlecruiser rapidly grew larger on the display, a monstrous brute of a ship firing missiles and energy weapons in all directions. It was hard to believe it wasn't the largest and most dangerous ship in the galaxy, that dreadnaughts and warcruisers were bigger and more powerful than anything the Vulteks had to offer. She had the feeling she was committing suicide as another light cruiser flew too close, only to be blown apart by enemy fire. The battlecruiser was just too powerful. She barely noticed another alien starship vanish from the display. It was no longer important. Only the battlecruiser mattered.

"Target their drives," she ordered, as Janet continued to pound the battlecruiser's hull. "And..."

Her ship rocked, again and again. "Direct hits," Roger snapped. "Multiple hull breaches, decks..."

"Rotate the ship," Naomi said. There were so many red icons on the display that she couldn't follow the damage. "Keep the undamaged hull..."

Another explosion shook the ship, followed by a dull *thump* that chilled her to the bone. The starship's spine had been broken. And that meant...

"Main power offline," Roger reported. "Emergency power cores online, but internal distribution nodes..."

Naomi hit her console. "All hands, abandon ship," she ordered. "Helm, point us towards the battlecruiser and give her everything you've got!"

A low vibration ran through the ship as the drives tried to steer *Washington* towards the battlecruiser. Naomi didn't wait to see the result as the bridge crew rushed for the escape hatches. The lights were already flickering and dying, bearing mute testament to just how badly the ship had been hurt. *Washington* was crippled, damaged beyond repair. Naomi took one last look at the bridge, *her* bridge, then hurried down to the escape pods. Half were already gone. She prayed silently that her crew made it out as she threw herself into the cramped pod and launched it into space. They were far too close to the battle for her peace of mind...

And all we can do now is pray, she thought. *And hope they don't mistake us for weapons and blow us out of space.*

• • •

"Incoming enemy ship," the sensor officer yowled. "She's on a ramming course!"

"Blow her away," Trans ordered. The enemy ship was a light cruiser... badly damaged, judging by how badly she was venting plasma and atmosphere, but still dangerous. His ship had no time to evade. "Blow her away and..."

The battlecruiser rocked. A series of explosions blasted though the hull. Trans felt the gravity fail, an instant before he heard the sound of air escaping into vacuum. Ice washed down his spine. They were so deep within the ship, so heavily protected by layer upon layer of armour, that they shouldn't have heard it at all unless the ship was damaged beyond all hope of repair. The lights failed a second later, plunging the compartment into darkness. But he could still hear the escaping air...

He reached for his knife, knowing—beyond all doubt—that he was a failure. He'd failed to win the war, he'd failed to keep his homeworld free...his entire race was doomed to slavery because of him. He could no longer lie to himself. Perhaps things would have been different, if someone else had commanded the battlecruiser. Or if he'd argued against the war...not that he *could* have argued against the war. It would have been a sign of weakness at the worst possible time. His beak lolled open as the sound of panic swept through the compartment. There was no point, not now. They were doomed.

Quite calmly, he put the knife against his chest and pushed as hard as he could.

...

"Admiral, the enemy battlecruiser has lost all power," Emily reported. "The remaining ships have been destroyed."

"Give her a wide berth," Adam ordered. *Washington's* sacrifice might have won the battle. "And order SAR teams to pick up the escape pods."

"Aye, sir," Emily said. "What about the enemy crews?"

Adam grimaced. "If they surrender, we'll take them into custody," he said. A handful of ships had eventually surrendered at Coriander, but the remainder had preferred suffocation to surrender. The prisoners had been odd, to say the least. They'd bowed and scraped and generally acted like slaves. The xenospecialists insisted it was perfectly understandable, but Adam had his doubts. "Order the remainder of the fleet to advance on the Nest."

He sat back in his chair as the alien homeworld appeared on the display. The Nest was practically defenceless now, save for a handful of automated platforms that would last as long as it took him to mount a kinetic strike. There was nothing standing between his ships and victory, yet... he knew he couldn't hope to land troops and take the planet by force. The fleet simply didn't have a sizable landing contingent. Earth hadn't sent him more than a few thousand marines. Even if he stripped his fleet of everyone who knew how to fire a gun, they'd still be outnumbered several hundred thousand to one.

"Transmit the surrender demand," he said. The Nest Lords would know they'd lost, right? They had to have watched helplessly as their fleet was destroyed. There was no shame in giving up before their planet was bombarded. Right? "And inform me the moment they respond."

"Aye, sir," Emily said. "I..."

She broke off as the display flooded with new contacts. Adam leaned forward, watching in horror as a mid-sized fleet decloaked near the planet. Small, compared to the forces that had fought and won the Lupine Wars, but still more than enough to tear his fleet to ribbons. He didn't need Emily to tell him who owned and operated the ships. There was only one interstellar power that might care enough to intervene.

"Admiral," Emily said. "I'm picking up thirty-seven Pashtali warships. Nine of them are dreadnaughts."

Adam cursed under his breath. A single dreadnaught would have given his battered fleet a very hard time. Nine dreadnaughts could wipe the floor with the human ships and never know they'd been in a fight. The display kept updating, telling him things he didn't want to know about their weapons and sensors. The Vulteks hadn't understood the technology they'd begged, borrowed or stolen. The Pashtali had invented *their* technology for themselves. They knew how to get the best from it...

"They appear to be deploying antimatter beamers," Emily said. "They might be bluffing…"

"They have good reason to try to duplicate Alphan weapons," Adam said. God knew the EDF was doing the same. "They might just have succeeded."

"Picking up a message," Emily said. "It's text-only."

"Forward it to me," Adam ordered. He'd been told the Pashtali preferred not to speak directly to other races—they were under no illusions how even their peers regarded them—but it was still a surprise. "And warn the fleet to stand ready."

His eyes narrowed as the message appeared in front of him. It was blunt, oddly direct for a message from a Galactic power. If the humans withdrew, they could have every system between the Nest and Delaine without a fight. If not…there was no 'or else' but one didn't have to be spelt out. The mere presence of a sizable enemy fleet was more than enough to make the threat clear, without ever quite crossing the line. The Vulteks had been saved by their patrons…

And they're offering to concede one hell of a lot of space if we don't push things any further, he thought. *Earth will definitely be pleased if we don't have to fight for those stars.*

He stared at his hands for a long moment. The hell of it was that the Pashtali were offering a pretty good deal. Humanity got a dozen star systems, the Pashtali got the credit for saving their clients…and the Vulteks were spared the shame of a final, inglorious defeat. And yet, he hated the thought of backing down. The war was over and humanity had won. It wasn't *fair* they should be denied the fruits of victory at the whim of a greater power. Cold logic told him he should concede; pure anger wanted him to fight.

And the decision is in my hands, he thought. There was no way to get a message to Earth before time ran out. He had full gubernatorial authority, but only within certain limits. He might be pushing them further than they should go. And yet, what choice did he have? *I have to make the call.*

He reached for his console, silently reminding himself he wouldn't have remained in the service much longer anyway. Earth could turn him into the scapegoat, if the government needed someone to blame. He wouldn't mind. Better to be dishonourably discharged than Earth plunged into a war it couldn't win. The Pashtali might just be hoping for an excuse to wage war on Earth, to deprive the Alphans of an ally and weaken them when—if—a general war broke out. And he could cut the ground from under their feet by conceding now.

"Inform the newcomers that we will recover our wounded, then depart," he said. It was a bitter pill to swallow, even if it did mean uncontested possession of a number of star systems. "And we will take possession of the star systems shortly."

"Aye, sir." Emily sounded as if she'd bitten into something foul. "They might intend to cheat us of our prize."

"Of more prizes," Adam corrected. It wasn't as if he'd wanted to *keep* the Nest. Earth had enough problems without adding a resentful alien population to the mix. He wasn't sure there were enough human soldiers to keep the alien homeworld under control. "But right now, we don't have those prizes anyway."

He leaned back in his chair, silently composing his report as the fleet prepared to depart. Earth wouldn't be happy, but...the war was over and they'd won. They'd proved humanity could stand on its own two feet, as an independent power. The galaxy would take note. Trade talks that had been put on hold, because of the war, would be reopened. Powers that had mocked humanity's claim to power, and laughed at requests for alliances, would have to take them seriously. And who knew? They might even wind up facing the Alphans as equals.

And our next opponents might be more dangerous, he thought. There were already races that regarded humanity as a potential threat. *We cannot afford to rest on our laurels.*

"Admiral," Emily said. "The last of the lifepods have been recovered."

Adam nodded, studying the display. The Pashtali fleet hadn't moved.

He felt a twinge of sympathy for the aliens, as irritating as they were. *They* would have to cope with a bitter client race. But...he shook his head. Hopefully, the Vulteks would keep the Pashtali busy enough to prepare for the next war. He was morbidly sure the peace would be nothing more than a period of cheating between bouts of fighting.

"Then order the fleet to retreat to the crossroads," he said, quietly. "It's time to go home."

CHAPTER FORTY

EDS *Thunderous*, Coriander System

"I WON'T SAY EVERYONE IS *PLEASED*, Admiral," Abraham Douglas said. His expression was unreadable. "But it has been agreed that you did the right thing, in accepting the Pashtali offer. The star systems ceded to us sweetened the deal."

"I'm glad to hear that," Adam said, sardonically. "However, I must caution you that *keeping* the systems may not be easy."

"So I've been briefed," Douglas said. "They might not have *quite* given us a poisoned chalice, but those systems won't be easy to defend."

"No." Adam nodded at the holographic starchart. "There are too many crossroads within the sector, including a number that have never been properly charted or surveyed, for us to be sure of keeping them. A couple of systems might become bottlenecks, but they'd be bottlenecks with nothing to protect. Not unless we *really* push to absorb our new possessions."

He leaned forward. "Have you heard anything more from the Pashtali?"

"Just the formal transfer of ownership," Douglas said. "They've disclaimed all responsibility for the war itself, of course, while somehow managing to keep their clients under control."

"Somehow," Adam said. "I think we're going to be fighting them in the very near future."

"I quite agree," Abraham said. "Given their willingness to apply both the carrot and the stick, and their general technological level, they pose a significantly greater threat than their clients ever did. The whole war might have been a dry run to test their clients before the masters showed their hand."

"It's possible," Adam agreed. He'd read the reports, although he thought some of them came too close to outright conspiracy theories for his peace of mind. In *his* experience, fantastically detailed plans that depended on everything going right were asking for trouble. But he had to admit that the Pashtali had been in position to come out ahead, no matter who won. "I think we'll just have to keep preparing."

"And working towards forging agreements with the other races, which you've helped do," Abraham said. "But we'll discuss those when you return to Earth."

"Yes, sir," Adam said. "I'll be ready to leave in a couple of days, once I tie up the loose ends here."

"No rush," Abraham said. "But it will be good to have you back."

"I look forward to it," Adam said. He was the victor, even if the media weren't sure if he was hero or villain. Or the coward who'd surrendered humanity's gains. He could make sure his experience didn't go to waste, even if he never commanded another fleet. "Commodore Tarn will take command here, with enough ships to ensure we can hold the system or harass anyone strong enough to take it from us."

"The Pashtali have little interest in rocking the boat right now," Abraham said. "But yes, there are other powers."

"And some of them have settlers along the border," Adam said. "But I don't think that will be a problem for a while."

He raised a hand in salute. "I'll see you later, Mr. Speaker."

"And you, Admiral," Abraham said. "Be seeing you."

Adam watched the image disappear, then allowed himself a sigh of relief. It could have been worse. It could have been a *lot* worse. The war had been immensely costly, not just in ships and lives. If the Empire Loyalists had managed to reassert themselves...there might not be an Empire worth mentioning any longer, but *someone* would have to serve as the opposition, if only to keep the government from becoming complacent. He considered, briefly, trying to run for office himself, then dismissed the thought. He was too used to the military life to give it up now. And besides, he'd make a terrible politician.

Every time I open my mouth, the truth comes out, he thought wryly. *I'd never get off the ground.*

The intercom beeped. "Admiral, Captain Anderson has arrived," Emily said. "Should I have him shown in?"

"Please," Adam said. "And bring coffee."

He stood and walked around the desk as Captain Anderson was shown into the compartment. "Captain," he said, extending a hand. "It's good to see you again."

"And you," Anderson said. "Although my wife has different ideas on the issue."

"I quite understand," Adam said. Captain Anderson had signed up to be a roving intelligence gatherer, not an outright spy. The difference was largely meaningless to him, although he'd been assured it meant a great deal to the EIS. "I'd like to promise we won't ask you to do that again, but I can't."

"I know," Captain Anderson said. He took the proffered seat and accepted a cup of coffee from Emily. "I take it you haven't called me here to discuss shore leave."

"I'm afraid not," Adam said. "The main body of the fleet will be returning to Earth, leaving a squadron here and another at Delaine. It may be some time before we can establish regular patrols throughout the sector. I'd like you to collect intelligence in preparation for that day."

"And to keep an eye on the Pashtali," Anderson guessed. "Just in case they have plans of their own."

"There's no doubt they *do* have plans of their own," Adam said. "And yes, we do want to keep an eye on them. They're preparing for something, Captain, and we don't know what."

"They've wanted to replace the Alphans for a long time," Anderson said. "I'd expect them to be planning to wage war."

"The Alphans had the luxury of establishing themselves before they ran into a peer power," Adam said. "The Pashtali will have a harder fight, if that's what they intend to do."

He shrugged. "Will you undertake the mission?"

"Unless my wife kills me first," Anderson said. "One thing: my son is adamant he wants to join the navy. Can you arrange for him to enter the academy?"

"If he meets the basic requirements, yes," Adam said. He had no doubt Captain Anderson's son *would*. He already had spacer experience, which was more than most prospective cadets had. "Let my staff know the details. We'll take him back with us."

"Thank you, sir," Anderson said. "We'll get back in touch as soon as possible."

"Watch yourself out there," Adam said. "It was lawless before the war. It's bound to be worse now."

"Yes, sir," Anderson said. "I'll make sure to cover my back."

• • •

Naomi felt oddly out of sorts as she followed the pretty young staff officer through a maze of corridors, through a CIC that seemed to be running a constant series of tactical exercises and into the admiral's office. Her ship was gone, ensuring she'd face a board of inquiry if not a court-martial and...she had no idea what she'd do with herself. The navy might give her a medal for helping to destroy the alien battlecruiser and then transfer her to an asteroid colony in the middle of nowhere. Or...

She straightened to attention and saluted as the admiral stood. "Captain Yagami, reporting as ordered."

"Captain," Admiral Glass said. "My condolences on the loss of your ship."

Naomi felt numb, numb and cold. Her ship had died well, but...she missed her first independent command. "Thank you, sir."

"I've discussed the matter with the authorities on Earth," Admiral Glass said. "Under the circumstances, they're in agreement that you and your crew did the right thing. Your ship took the enemy battlecruiser down with her. *And* you managed to get most of your crew off before it was too late."

"Most," Naomi echoed. Thirty-seven crewmen had been lost in the explosion, either trapped and unable to make it to the escape pods or killed before their lifepod could get out of the blast radius. She knew their names, but she couldn't recall their faces. She wasn't even sure what she'd said at the brief ceremony, held as *Thunderous* made her ponderous way back to Coriander. "I lost too many."

"It never gets easier," Admiral Glass said. "And I am sorry."

"I wanted command," Naomi said. She allowed herself a humourless laugh. "I never really saw the crew as mine, even when I was XO, until I assumed command for myself."

"It never gets easier," the Admiral repeated. "We'll be going back to Earth. As an experienced officer, and a naval hero, you'll be assigned to a new command. Before then"—his eyes focused on her—"you'll be assisting my staff in planning the next war. It's only a matter of time before we have to fight again."

"Yes, sir," Naomi said. She knew she should be relieved, but she was too numb. "The Pashtali?"

"And others," the Admiral told her. "There's a lot of work to go before we can truly consider ourselves safe."

"Yes, sir," Naomi said. "I won't let you down."

She felt conflicted as she saluted again, then left the office. She was getting a new command. It would have been good news, if she hadn't felt so guilty about the ship she'd lost and the lives she'd failed to save. And yet...she knew she should be pleased. It could have been worse. Her ship could have died for nothing.

And the next war will be a hell of a lot more challenging, she thought, as she made her way back to her cabin. *We have to be ready.*

• • •

"Governor Singh has recommended we promote you to Supreme General," Admiral Glass said, a hint of amusement in his tone. "As we don't have a Supreme General rank, and a plain *General* would be a jump too far, we're promoting you to captain instead."

"Thank you, sir," Tomas said, doubtfully. He'd lost a third of the squad in the fighting on Delaine, then two more during the desperate escape from the doomed cruiser. By any standard, that was a pretty poor record. Combined with his role in the massacre on Earth...he knew he was lucky not to be quietly shuffled off somewhere and forgotten. "I..."

Admiral Glass held up a hand. "General Siskin has requested you be assigned to his corps," he said. "We'll be establishing marine outposts and garrisons all along the border and you'll be joining them. I can't promise a return to Delaine, where you're a hero, but you probably will be assigned to one of the garrisons."

"Yes, sir," Tomas said. "I...what'll happen when they learn what I did?"

"It was clearly established you tried to stop the shooting on Earth." Admiral Glass did him the courtesy of not pretending he didn't know what Tomas was *really* asking. "And the blunt truth is that most of the colonials don't care. There may be problems if you go back to Earth, at least for the next few years, but...right now, no one outside the corps will know who you are."

"Not on the colonies, at least," Tomas said. "Thank you, sir."

"There will be another war, sooner or later," Admiral Glass warned. "We're going to do everything in our power to deter it—the garrisons are part of that, in hopes we'll look too hard a target—but I doubt we can put it off indefinitely. Keep your powder dry."

"Aye, sir," Tomas said. He saluted. "And thank you."

"Thank me by surviving," Admiral Glass said. "And good luck."

• • •

"Sir?" Emily peered into the compartment. "Shouldn't you be asleep?"

Adam glanced at her, thoughtfully. Emily was young, too young to understand the doubts that plagued him. She'd had no time to become set in her ways, to become so convinced that matters would remain constant that it was impossible to accept change. Adam knew, without false modesty, that he'd done well. He also knew he could do better.

"A year ago, we assumed we'd be a client race for at least another century," he said, more to himself than to her. "And now...look at us now."

"We won a war," Emily reminded him. "Sir."

"Yes." Adam stood, brushing down his uniform. His life was nearing its end, even though he might have a decade or two left. It was the younger officers who would bear the brunt of the next war. "But it's only the beginning."

EPILOGUE

Star City, Earth

YASUKE HAD EXPECTED, if he were forced to be honest, that the humans would win the war.

It was no great surprise. The Vulteks had the advantage of numbers and firepower, but they lacked the human instinct for war. Their tactics would have worked perfectly, against a smaller opponent, yet they simply hadn't been able to crush the humans before they rallied and struck back. Letting themselves be caught in a bottleneck had been stupid, to say the least. A more cunning commander—a *human* commander—might have struck *Coriander* first and then gone on to smash Earth before it was too late. But the Vulteks had missed their chance.

He paced the embassy chamber, frowning as he contemplated the results. The humans had been cheated of ultimate victory—and their prizes were scantier than the human media believed—but they'd done well. Very well. Yasuke admired their skill even as he feared for the future. The humans could easily pose a threat, if things went badly. He'd done everything in his power to convince his people to extend an offer of an alliance, or even a promise they would shield Earth against the other Galactics, but the council had had other problems. The economy was weak, the rebuilding program was faltering and the people were unhappy. And the aliens on his homeworld were demanding rights his people couldn't give them without conceding everything...

And the Pashtali are up to something, he thought. The council hadn't seen it yet, but Yasuke had seen enough to convince him that the enemy plans had been well underway before Earth had gained independence. *They want to replace us as the leading power and they may well succeed.*

He let out a long breath as he tried to look into the future, to reassure himself that his people still *had* a future. They still had their technology, they still had the finest ships in the known universe, they still had friends and allies...even amongst the human race. But, for the first time in what felt like eternity, he feared for the future. The universe was no longer his people's playground.

And, as he tried to look into the future, all he saw was darkness.

・・・

TO BE CONTINUED

AFTERWORD

All right...all right...but apart from better sanitation and medicine and education and irrigation and public health and roads and a freshwater system and baths and public order...what have the Romans done for us?
—MONTY PYTHON'S LIFE OF BRIAN

IF YOU READ THE ABOVE QUOTE, you might be forgiven for assuming that the plotters were a bunch of idiots. Why would anyone want to throw the Romans out? They brought so much *good* to Judea, right? The whole idea of tossing them out on their ear sounds like a plan to cut one's nose to spite one's face. And yet, if you look at the scene with any knowledge of history, it starts looking less stupid. Indeed, the question might really be phrased as "*what did the Romans do TO us?*"

Between the Third Punic War and the series of civil wars that ended with Augustus Caesar in firm control of the empire, the Romans conquered vast swathes of territory surrounding the Mediterranean. Some kingdoms were effectively annexed, ruled by governors appointed by Rome; others were granted limited internal independence, as long as they behaved themselves. The latter were luckier than the former, as the Romans were not *nice* imperialists. It was often said, in Rome, that a governor needed to make three fortunes: one to bribe the voters so he'd get his position, one to make himself wealthy and one to bribe the judges during the inevitable trial for misconduct during his term in office. They made themselves wealthy by extracting money from their provinces, which they did with extreme brutality. It should not have been a surprise, therefore, that so many of their subjects were happy to turn on them, when given half a chance. The Romans did make attempts to put their possessions in better order, but Roman internal politics often made that difficult. Rome was, in the view of its subjects, a demon that had to be placated. Cleopatra has been branded a whore—and other, less pleasant, things—for forming personal relationships with the two most powerful Romans of their era, but really…she had no choice. She *had* to keep the Romans sweet or risk losing everything, including her life.

I don't know how old Mary and Joseph were, when they were ordered to Bethlehem before Jesus was born, but they—and their grandparents—would be all too aware that Rome could turn nasty at the drop of a hat. Indeed, they were going to Bethlehem because the Romans had ordered them to register so they could be taxed. There would be good reason for them to resent and fear the Romans, even if the Romans *had* done a lot of good for their people. And the Jews—and everyone else in the region—would want to be free of the Romans, if it could be done safely. The Romans were, in short, people who'd been very nasty and simply couldn't be trusted not to turn nasty again.

As Tacitus (or Calgacus) commented, the Romans *"make a desert and call it peace."*

The desire for independence, to escape foreign domination, runs strong in the human mind. Indeed, we often turn against outsiders even when the outsiders genuinely *are* better than the natives. Events like BREXIT wouldn't have gotten so much traction, for better or worse, if the EU hadn't been seen as an outside power interfering in British politics…a view that may have little in common with reality, but one that caught on. The BREXIT referendum itself was merely the culmination of a series of problems that no one in office dared admit needed to be fixed. Put crudely, the EU fiddled while Rome burned (British public opinion turned against the EU) and discovered, too late, that it was seen as beyond reform. Indeed, this was not Britain's *first* BREXIT. Henry VIII's decision to cut ties with Rome in 1532 might have been spurred by his desire to sire a male heir, but it sprang from long-standing anti-papal sentiments that saw the Pope as a biased and therefore untrustworthy figure who could be—and was—far more easily influenced by France and Spain than England. The papacy's meddling in English—and Scottish—affairs was often seen as, at best, foolish; at worst, detrimental and greedy. There was no sense, by the time Henry VIII took the throne, that the Pope was a neutral arbiter. The more the ideal of the papacy got bogged down in real-world politics, the more it surrendered its claim to moral authority.

Point is, outside powers simply don't understand local matters. It is easy for outsiders to influence their politics, but harder for locals to influence distant overlords. This breeds resentment and eventual hatred, even with the best will in the world. Something that looks very reasonable to the outsiders, whatever it might happen to be, doesn't always look so reasonable to the locals. The various attempts to regulate the British America lead directly to the American Revolution!

And outsider politics can make it harder for the locals to seek justice. Brigadier General Reginald Dyer—often called the "man who killed the British Empire—presented his masters in Whitehall with a serious political headache after the Amritsar Massacre. On one hand, Dyer's actions were a political nightmare; they convinced countless Indians to turn against the Raj. On the other, it was hard to convict Dyer of anything without giving the impression Dyer was being railroaded, something that would (and did) turn his supporters against the government. Matters were not helped by confusion over who was legally in command, just how much authority had been devolved to Dyer, legal and military questions regarding what actions an officer could take to save his command and a somewhat odd set of excuses and justifications from Dyer himself. There was no good answer. It should not have surprised anyone, therefore, that India would seek self-determination and independence from that moment on. Faith in the Raj's justice died under Dyer's guns.

And all of *this* assumes a degree of goodwill. How do you think the East Europeans regarded Nazi and Soviet occupiers?

It is true, of course, that independence brings with it perils. British India separated into two pieces upon independence (and Pakistan would separate again, when East Pakistan became Bangladesh.) India did not fight a bloody war of independence, but it took time for matters to steady down and—of course—India and Pakistan would fight several wars over the coming decades. And yet, India was relatively lucky. Newly-independent African states devolved into tribal war and/or dictatorships as the glue holding them together. The social structures to keep the countries united weren't strong enough to survive independence. And if one separates during a war, as the Confederate States of America tried, it should be obvious that one's society (and attempt to build a new government) may not survive the war. The CSA lost, at least in part, because the government was *massively* dysfunctional.

These perils cannot go underestimated, despite the natural desire for freedom. Those who seek independence must think about what they'll do, the day after independence. Most independence activists, in my view, indulge in wishful thinking, believing—for better or worse—that things will both change and yet stay the same. The Scottish Nationalist Party is particularly guilty of wishful thinking, claiming to believe that oil revenue will remain high and there will be no economic hiccups (doubtful), that Scotland could remain in both the EU and NATO without any problems (really doubtful) and Scotland could continue to influence global affairs and—so to speak—punch above its weight (impossible.) Any cold-blooded and *rational* assessment of the situation would point out that oil prices (and Scottish production) have been falling, that England would feel no obligation to purchase goods from Scottish industries (particularly at the expense of *English* industries), that NATO would be understandably annoyed at having to rewrite a whole series of treaties to accommodate an independent Scotland (not to mention the problems caused by splitting Scottish units from the remainder of the British military) and many EU member states would be flatly opposed to *rewarding* Scotland for gaining independence. How many EU members have independence movements of one stripe or another? The answer is probably bigger than you think. Spain, for example, has quite serious movements. Why would they want to do something that would *encourage* those movements?

It is quite easy for intellectuals to dream up a political structure that works perfectly—on paper. God knows both liberals and conservatives have devised perfect states that work perfectly…on paper. The real world is rarely so obliging. Their political structures tend to come with massive downsides that make themselves apparent when they run into trouble, downsides that tend to make dealing with the problem harder. The structures demand a considerable amount of trust, yet the people promoting them act in ways that undermine trust and weaken society. And once trust is lost—as the Romans discovered, once they started to forget their scruples—it can never be regained.

The problems plaguing our world today have many causes, but one of them—in my view—is the belief that governments have long-since lost touch with their people. They mistake their preconceptions for reality, they listen to experts who are nothing of the sort (or are seen as being nothing of the sort), they let themselves be bullied by pressure groups, they let barmy bureaucrats run things…and, because of these failings, people want independence, to live their lives without interference. Nationalist and populist politicians were elected because, at base, people want to be free.

And this is not something we should take lightly.

And now I've written that, I have a favour to ask.

It's getting harder to make a living as an independent author. If you purchased this book and enjoyed it, please leave a review and share the title with your friends. Please join my mailing list, follow my blog and newsletter; believe me, every little helps. I've attached a list of ways to follow me on the next page, before the appendixes.

Thank you.
Christopher G. Nuttall
Edinburgh, 2021

HOW TO FOLLOW

Basic Mailing List—http://orion.crucis.net/mailman/listinfo/chrishanger-list
Nothing, but announcements of new books.

Newsletter—https://gmail.us1.list-manage.com/subscribe?u=c8f9f7391e5bfa369a9b1e76c&id=55fc83a213
New books releases, new audio releases, maybe a handful of other things of interest.

Blog—https://chrishanger.wordpress.com/
Everything from new books to reviews, commentary on things that interest me, etc.

Facebook Fan Page—https://www.facebook.com/ChristopherGNuttall
New books releases, new audio releases, maybe a handful of other things of interest.

Website—http://chrishanger.net/
New books releases, new audio releases, free samples (plus some older books free to anyone who wants a quick read)

Forums—https://authornuttall.com
Book discussions—new, but I hope to expand.

Amazon Author Page—https://www.amazon.com/Christopher-G-Nuttall/e/B008L9Q4ES
My books on Amazon.

Books2Read—https://books2read.com/author/christopher-g-nuttall/subscribe/19723/
Notifications of new books (normally on Amazon too, but not included in B2R notifications.

Twitter—@chrisgnuttall
New books releases, new audio releases—definitely nothing beyond (no politics or culture war stuff).

APPENDIX: THE ALPHANS

THE ALPHANS CLAIM TO BE THE OLDEST Galactic-level species in known space, a claim that few—if any—can openly challenge. It is certainly true that they are the oldest race currently active within the quadrant, with an Empire that—at their height—controlled thousands of star systems, multispace crossroad chokepoints and wealth beyond measure. Even now, even after the Second Lupine War, they remain a force that cannot be challenged lightly. Their influence on galactic affairs cannot be understated. Their claim to have been the original writers of the Convocations may actually be true (although it has never actually been confirmed, one way or the other).

Physically, the Alphans are orange-skinned hairless humans with giant bulging eyes and muscular frames. (Their human subjects nicknamed them *bemmies*, from Bug-Eyed Monsters.) Technically, they have two genders; practically, their bodies automatically transition from male to female and back again on a regular schedule between puberty and death. Unsurprisingly, gender dimorphism and sex-based oppression is almost unknown amongst them; they tend to be a little bemused by sexism and suchlike when they encounter it in other races. The idea of deliberately remaining one gender, without transitioning, is seen as a little weird.

Mentally, the Alphans are generally no more or less smart than the average human (or any other sentient race). They do, however, have an extreme superiority complex and tend to look down on other races, with the possible exception of their fellow Galactics. They might adapt themselves to handle other races, but they never truly convert. Nor do they let alien sensibilities stand in the way when they want something. They had no qualms about imposing their rules on Earth, after they overran the planet, and crushing anyone who dared resist. Lacking a religion themselves, for example, they saw human religions as nothing more than foolish superstition. They certainly didn't think about *converting*.

The Alphan Government is confusing, by Earthly standards. It is dominated by the Core, a council formed of the various clan leaders and their advisors, but each of them are elected by a complicated system that they rarely even *try* to explain to outsiders. Their government relies on a degree of cooperation and collaboration that would probably fail completely if humans tried to make it work. Outsiders speculate that, at least prior to the war, the Alphans were so satisfied, as a species, there was little to fight over. There was no need for conflict, at least amongst themselves, so they could collaborate in the certain knowledge that none of them would *really* lose.

It is probably best to think of their society as a cross between an aristocracy and a corporatocracy. Their society is dominated by giant organisations that serve as both clans and corporate interests, with the majority of youngsters either devoting themselves to climbing the ladder to the top or dedicating themselves to pure pleasure. The sheer wealth of their society allows them to create and maintain a social welfare state on a truly staggering scale. A young Alphan need never work, if he does not wish to. In a sense, the Alphans devised a system that allowed people to rise on merit without actually threatening the *status quo*. They claim their welfare system allows people to sow their wild oats, then take up their place within the clan. They may well be right.

An Alphan who does not want to climb the ladder or give himself wholly to pleasure has a number of other options. The military is always desperately short of manpower, particularly after the war. If that isn't exciting enough, an Alphan can take command of an alien-crewed vessel or military formation, serve as a trader or even go into deep-space exploration. The Alphan Government is always on the lookout for youths who can serve in such roles, particularly as it keeps them out of trouble.

The system only works because it rests on a base of (effectively) slave labour. The scutwork is done by alien immigrants, from Earth and a dozen other worlds, who are treated poorly by Alphan standards. They have no hope of climbing the ladder, something they've found increasingly onerous as the small colonies of immigrants became ghettos and small communities that are both part of the planetary system and apart from it. The ghettos are heavily policed, but the combination of manpower shortages and low-tech answers to advanced technology makes it harder for the Alphans to keep an eye on what's going on.

The Alphan military is divided into three subsections. The Capital Fleet—often called the Showboat Fleet by its human detractors—is a stately formation where spit and polish is more important than competence, dash or tactical skill. The Outer Fleet patrols the borders and is generally more competent and open to new ideas, not least because it is generally the Outer Fleet that meets enemies for the first (and often the last) time. The Elitists are ground-combat troops, intensely augmented and trained for meeting their enemies on even terms. They are regarded as extremely dangerous, unlike the Capital Fleet, but they are very few in number, a problem that worries their more thoughtful commanders. They get few volunteers, unlike the fleets, and most of the volunteers don't pass the training course.

It is not uncommon for outsiders to underestimate the Capital Fleet. It is true that the fleet's officers are trained more for formation flying than actual fighting. It is also true that their exercises are predictable, with the winners and losers determined well in advance. They would be in deep trouble if they had to fight an enemy on equal terms. However, their technical prowess gives them the edge against almost any foe. Their weapons, sensors, armour and starfighters are vastly superior to the vast majority of their potential enemies, their giant warcruisers almost untouchable...

This led to overconfidence. The belief they could not be challenged in open battle became a certainty they would *never* be challenged. The Alphans allowed their industrial base to atrophy, weakening their ability to fight a long and costly war. They turned their ships—their warcruisers, the mainstay of their fleet—into works of art, while cutting the number of support ships to the bone. It took five years, by the time war broke out, to build a new warcruiser from scratch. They didn't see the problem with this until it was far too late.

Unsurprisingly, the Alphans had a nasty shock when the Lupines proved capable of touching the giant warcruisers. The Lupines had planned the war carefully, deducing the weaknesses within the Alphans and calculating how best to take advantage of them. They traded hundreds of ships for each warcruiser they took down, but they had hundreds of ships to spare. If the human sepoys—and human-manned ships—hadn't held the line, the Alphan Empire might have been crushed. The shockwaves nearly brought the whole system crashing down. The simple act of building up their industry and rebuilding their fleet was almost too much to bear.

And even victory, when it came, brought its own challenges.

APPENDIX: A BRIEF OUTLINE OF ALPHAN EARTH

FROM THE POINT OF VIEW OF THE ALPHANS, the invasion and occupation of Earth was a relatively minor affair. Nothing larger than a frigate was required to put down the first—and pitiful—bout of resistance the human race could muster, while there was no need to deploy a truly massive army to garrison every city and village on the planet. The vast majority of the human race never saw an alien—outside information broadcasts—for decades after the invasion.

From the point of view of the human race, it was the greatest disaster since World War Two. Humanity's isolation from the universe—and conviction that it was effectively *alone* in the universe—ended in a single night of terror. The utter futility of resistance left a scar on the human mindset for generations to come. Some pre-invasion governments survived, in some shape and form, for nearly two centuries after everything changed, but they were subservient to alien Viceroys. The human race might have had new and seemingly boundless opportunities, as the invasion receded further and further into the past, yet they came at a price.

Humanity was nothing more than a subject race to alien masters.

Earth had been lucky, in a sense, that the Solar System rested within a previously-impassable region of multispace. It was not until two decades before the invasion that Alphan scoutships finally found a way to traverse the region, eventually emerging into realspace near Earth and surveying the planet. Noting that Earth's space program was too primitive to count as a *real* space program—which would have given the human race some rights, by galactic law—they spent twenty years quietly drawing up plans for the invasion. The combination of hyper-advanced surveillance technology and a simple lack of awareness of their mere existence gave them an unbeatable edge. By the time the invasion itself began, the Alphans knew the precise location of the vast majority of humanity's nuclear weapons. Microscopic bugs had been attached to humanity's submarines, serving as targeting beacons for KEW strikes. The invasion had been won well before the first shot was fired.

The invasion itself began at midnight, Washington time. The handful of Alphan warships decloaked and systematically destroyed humanity's network of orbital satellites. (The ISS was spared as a museum piece.) Even as the governments of the world screamed for information, the first KEW strikes were already inbound. Humanity's nuclear deterrent was effectively obliterated before missiles could be retargeted on orbital threats. The handful of missiles that *were* launched—with one exception—were useless. The orbiting warships were used to handling missiles that moved at a respectable percentage of the speed of light. The incoming missiles simply couldn't compete. Finally, clean fusion devices were used to destroy a number of capital cities around the globe. The Alphans intended to make it clear that humanity was effectively defenceless.

It worked. There was little effective resistance as alien troops landed in the remains of the destroyed cities and established fortifications. The handful of attacks mounted by human stragglers were rapidly and cheaply beaten off, sometimes smashed from orbit well before they reached their targets. The lone human success—it was later established—was an accident. A Pakistani submarine, operating on the assumption that Pakistan was fighting a nuclear war with India, launched its missiles at Delhi. The aliens were unprepared for the attack and their foothold was effectively destroyed. It was a tiny bright spot in a day of devastation and defeat. (The Pakistani Captain would later become a hero to the Humanity League, even though it was clear he hadn't known what he was doing.)

Despite this, it rapidly became clear to the surviving governments that further resistance was futile. There was no hope of winning any significant victories, let alone driving the aliens back into space. Chaos was already spreading as people fled the remaining cities, the economy collapsing into rubble. Reluctantly, a string of governments accepted the alien demand for surrender. The terms weren't *that* bad, they told themselves. They would still maintain a great deal of autonomy. But Earth itself belonged to the Alphans.

They wasted no time in exploiting the planet. Human tech couldn't reach orbit, but it *could* function in space. The Alphans funded settlements right across the Solar System—they started terraforming Mars and Venus—in hope of turning the system into an economic asset. Humans were recruited to work for their alien masters, both within the Solar System itself and outside. A surprising number of humans left the system entirely during the first century after the invasion. There was no shortage of steady employment—at high wages, by human standards—right across the Empire. If nothing else, it rapidly became clear that humans were good at war. Human sepoys started to appear on alien battlefields.

Earth itself was a mess during this period. The vast majority of governments had either been significantly weakened or effectively destroyed. Some parts of the planet did very well, particularly when they integrated alien technology into their societies. Others collapsed into chaos. The Alphans were largely unconcerned, unless it interfered with their goals. They didn't need to worry. There might be millions of humans who hated them, but they couldn't do much harm. The Vichy governments—the name stuck—took the brunt of their hatred.

There were, in fact, four major rebellions over the first two centuries. The first two—the Minuteman Rebellion in America and the Islamist Uprising in the Middle East and Central Asia—were driven by resentment at the changes the aliens brought in their wake. It didn't help that traditional societies were changing as the aliens insisted on modern education and other innovations. Both uprisings failed, at least in part because they didn't grasp just how advanced the alien surveillance technologies actually were. The third rebellion was a bid by sepoy troops to seize control of an alien warship and vanish into multispace. It remains unclear precisely what happened to them. (The Alphans claimed the ship was destroyed before it could escape.)

The fourth rebellion was a great deal more serious. Humanity's sepoy regiments were—technically—under alien command. Those officers ranged from very competent to grossly *incompetent*, mingled with outright speciesism against their human (and other) subordinates. The mutiny started as a spontaneous protest and rapidly grew into something nastier. It was eventually put down, through a combination of savage fighting and a handful of concessions, but it left scars on both sides. The Alphans were not prepared to give up Earth, but they had come to realise that humanity was more than just another client race.

They handled the situation by making a series of changes. The Vichy governments were swept away, to be replaced by local councils and a planet-wide assembly. Humanity *would* have a degree of say in its future, at least on Earth. (Naturally, they rigged the selection process to ensure their loyalists had *more* say.) The military was reformed, with sepoy regiments reorganised to ensure their officers were more aware of their subordinates. This was not wholly successful—the Alphan Empire was more ossified than anyone cared to admit—but it was so much better than anything they'd had before that everyone was delighted. Best of all, from humanity's point of view, Earth was permitted to develop a defence force. It was the dawn of a new age.

In some ways, it was. Humanity moved further into the galaxy. Human corporations flourished. A surprising amount of GalTech was reverse-engineered and installed in human ships, which were often cruder but more efficient than their alien counterparts. In others, it was deeply frustrating. The Alphans continued to hold the reins of power. Worse, there were technologies they were unprepared to share with their subordinates. The enigmatic 'black boxes'—advanced navigational systems that made it easier to enter and leave multispace—remained a mystery. Humanity, it seemed, would always be at a disadvantage. That didn't sit well with a growing number of humans.

Politically, things changed. The local councils were dominated by local issues, but the assembly rapidly became something *more*. Two political parties—the Empire Loyalists and the Humanity League—rose to power. They were led by men who'd studied Alphan Law and knew how to manipulate it, allowing them to steadily carve out more power for themselves. This didn't sit well with the Earthers—Alphans and other Galactics living on Earth—and eventually led to a crisis. Did humans have the right to serve as judges when Galactics were involved? There was no good answer and the outcome—the answer was *no*—led to a rise in support for the Humanity League. The Viceroy viewed this unwelcome development with alarm, but there was nothing he could do about it. Earth was growing far too important to the Alphan Empire. The Assembly kept growing—or mutating—into something new. The only thing keeping the reformers in check was fear of a violent reaction. The Alphans still had the legal right to intervene if they thought things were getting out of hand.

Unknown to most of the human race, the 'human problem' had already started a considerable amount of debate on the Alphan homeworld. Humans were just *too* important. They made up a sizable percentage of the Empire's groundpounders. Worse, there were millions of humans scattered across the Empire, many of them second- or third-generation immigrants. It was certain they would eventually start to chafe at the limited opportunities and start demanding more. And while they could—in theory—be deported, it wouldn't be easy. There were so many of them that trying to remove them all, or even a majority, would start a full-scale civil war.

The matter was put to one side when the First Lupin War broke out. It was, at least on the surface, nothing more than a series of tiny border skirmishes. The Alphans regarded the conflict as a minor headache, unaware that their opponents were testing them. Once they'd learnt what they wanted to learn—the weaknesses in Alphan warcruisers, the most powerful warships in the known galaxy—they pulled back and signed a peace treaty, then started to make their preparations for a more serious offensive. The Alphans, with too many other problems to worry about, let the matter lie. It was a deadly—near-fatal—mistake.

The peace lasted twenty years, long enough for the Lupines—as humans came to call them—to build up a new fleet and deploy more advanced weapons. There were no skirmishes *this* time. The war started with a sneak attack on an Alphan fleet base, followed by strikes deep into Alphan territory. The first counterattack ended in disaster, with no less than forty warcruisers destroyed. It looked as if the Alphans were going to lose a war for the first time in over a thousand years. In desperation, they threw their human sepoys—and the ever-growing Earth Defence Force—into combat. The humans held the line long enough to let the Alphans get back on their feet and prepare a final counter offensive. Five years of hard fighting followed, but the outcome was no longer in doubt. The Lupines lost. Their Empire was shattered beyond repair.

But the war *had* done immense damage to Alphan-Human relations. The humans knew their masters were no longer invincible. The hulks of destroyed warcruisers had proved *that* beyond all doubt. Worse, they knew that *they* had won the war. They wanted—they needed—to stand tall. The Alphans found themselves unsure how to react. They had authority, but not power. They could crack down, yet find themselves fighting another war. It slowly sank in—as they considered the situation—that they were in no state to fight even a *short* war. They'd lost too many ships. They didn't have the time to rebuild. And even if they fought and won, it could cost them everything. They didn't want to let go, yet—at the same time—they couldn't afford to hang on.

Three hundred years after the invasion, Earth is still something of a patchwork world. There are regions that have done very well out of the invasion, economic boom and so on. There are also regions that are poor, with very little hope of dragging themselves up. (A problem made worse by a brain-drain to space, deliberately encouraged by the government.) GalTech has made things better, at a price (for example, everyone knows that *every* message sent through the datanet is subject to examination). People have been studying the pre-invasion world, learning about history that is purely human. (This has been something of a mixed bag. The Alphans never carried out anything akin to the Holocaust, something they have never hesitated to point out.)

Ethnic tension remains a problem, although the Alphan willingness to crush ethnic and religious movements with extreme force has kept most of the tension underground. (It helped that the Alphans blatantly didn't *care* who was right or wrong. They applied the same rules to everyone.) Many pre-invasion societies have been disrupted beyond repair, at least in part to the education system teaching everyone the same set of rules. Others have been making a comeback, at least in the more isolated regions of the planet. No one is quite sure what to make of them—or what to do, if they become a serious problem.

The Assembly remains dominated by the Empire Loyalists and the Humanity League, although there are a handful of smaller parties that *might* shift the balance of power if the bigger parties find themselves in desperate need of votes. The Empire Loyalists want to remain part of the Alphan Empire (although many of them think humanity should have a bigger say in the Empire's government). The Humanity League wants independence, though it is prepared to compromise to some degree. The Empire Loyalists have a slight edge—their supporters fear the consequences if Earth leaves the Empire—but it isn't solid. There are too many people who want humanity to be rewarded for its services in the war.

The Solar System is densely populated, with massive settlements on just about every body of significant size. Humanity's industrial base may be crude, but huge. Outside the solar system, humans are the majority on seven worlds in a loose cluster surrounding Earth; there are also major human populations on numerous worlds in and out of the Empire. Human traders can be found everywhere within explored space, although they are not always welcome. There are persistent rumours of human mercenaries working for other alien races, even suggestions that there are human ships heading into unexplored space or setting up hidden colonies a long way from their masters. The truth of such rumours has never been established.

And now, three hundred years after the invasion, humanity sits on a knife edge…

Printed in Great Britain
by Amazon